RAVE REVIEWS FOR DEBRA DIER!

SCOUNDREL

"Debra Dier pens a delightfully original romance. *Scoundrel* is an enchanting book to treasure."

—*Romantic Times*

"This great romance has a cast of lively characters and fast-paced action that brings you right into the story. A thoroughly enjoyable book!"

—*Rendezvous*

"Another great read for Ms. Dier, *Scoundrel* sizzles with romance, intrigue, and memorable characters."

—*Paperback Forum*

BEYOND FOREVER

"Once again, Debra Dier gifts her numerous fans with another extraordinary tale of timeless love. *Beyond Forever* is a wonderful tale. . . . This is a great book to curl up with."

—*Affaire de Coeur*

"Debra Dier takes us on a journey that is peppered with tantalizing passion and spiced with intrigue. The exciting cast of characters is well defined, showing remarkable strength and sensitivities. The conclusion will delight you."

—*Rendezvous*

SAINT'S TEMPTATION

"Ms. Dier, with deft turn of phrase and insight into human nature, wrings an emotionally charged tale from her characters which engages both the interest and empathy of her readers!"

—*The Literary Times*

DEVIL'S HONOR

"Debra Dier will keep y entertaining, fast-paced tale with a little mystery, passio

D0827994

BELIEVE IN MAGIC

"There is no spell," she said, her voice a whisper.

He released his breath in a long sigh that brushed her cheek. Slowly, he eased away from her, as though he were tearing away a part of himself. A whimper escaped her tight control as he stepped back, releasing her from the exotic press of potent masculinity. For a long while they stood facing each other, her breath coming in the same ragged fashion as his.

"I will not succumb to your magic," he said, his dark voice strained, as if he were fighting against invisible bonds.

Magic. She felt as though he had cast a spell over her, as though he had conjured a need she had never known before. "There is no such thing as magic."

"No such thing as magic?" Twin lines formed between his black brows as he held her gaze. "Is that what you would have me believe? That I am this hated Englishman that you have married? That every thought and memory in my head is not my own?"

"I know it must be difficult to accept, under the circumstances, but you are Dominic Stanbridge."

"And you are a beautiful deceiver."

DEBRA DIER

MACKENZIE'S MAGIC

LEISURE BOOKS NEW YORK CITY

A LEISURE BOOK®

May 2001

Published by

Dorchester Publishing Co., Inc.
276 Fifth Avenue
New York, NY 10001

ISBN 0-8439-4866-3

The name "Leisure Books" and the stylized "L" with design are trademarks of Dorchester Publishing Co., Inc.

Printed in the United States of America.

In loving memory of Seamus, my dear friend.
I was blessed to have known his warm and loving spirit.
He left us too soon. Still, he left us with memories we shall
always cherish.

MacKenzie's Magic

Chapter One

What is life when wanting love?
Night without a morning!
Love's the cloudless summer sun,
Nature gay adorning.
                              —Robert Burns

"Of course there are many who believe Lancaster murdered Penelope and had her body delivered to a medical school in Edinburgh, to be used as a teaching specimen."

In spite of the din of conversation and laughter in the huge ballroom, Jane Eveleigh Stanbridge heard each word Eugenia spoke far too clearly. Apparently Eugenia felt it her duty to enlighten her brother's new bride as to each and every one of the scandals that littered Lancaster's past. "I cannot imagine Lancaster going to such bother to be rid of any woman."

Eugenia lifted her dark brows. "She did shoot him."

Jane had not needed Eugenia to inform her of this particular bit of mischief. Lady Penelope Clydestaff was a spurned lover who had not taken any pains to conceal her scorn. Last Season, Lady Penelope had made a complete fool of herself over Lancaster. For weeks after the affair had ended, she had haunted Park Lane in front of his mansion, made scenes at every party in town, and finally she had shot him in Hyde Park. "Apparently he has forgiven her. I saw her standing near the refreshment table a short time ago."

"Yes. I saw her arrive with Hargrove." Eugenia flicked her fan beneath her plump chin, fluttering the dark curls carefully arranged over her brow. "I never for a moment believed the rumors. If my brother were to murder every woman who became a nuisance to him, he would have precious little time to do anything else. Still, I do wonder if Lancaster knew Penelope was in London before tonight. He had her exiled to New York shortly after the incident in the park."

"He sent her away? Against her will?"

"He could have sent her to Newgate." Eugenia tilted her head, a sly smile curving her lips. "I am certain he gave her a choice. He certainly couldn't allow her to remain in London. Not when she was of a mind to put a bullet into him. One can only hope she has rid herself of her terrible jealousy. It would not do to have her go about shooting people."

Jane wondered what Lancaster had done to drive a woman to attempted murder. Although she had to admit, in her dreams she had pushed him off of London Bridge.

"I suppose I don't have to tell you how many of the women here have made fools of themselves trying to become the next Marchioness of Lancaster. Until this afternoon, Lancaster was one of the most sought-after bachelors on three continents."

Jane already knew the truth of Eugenia's words. Not only was Dominic Stanbridge obscenely wealthy, but he was also one of the most handsome men Jane had ever seen. And the most ruthless she had ever met.

"His marriage to you startled all of London."

"Yes. It did." No one was more startled than Jane.

Eugenia tilted her head and smiled at three young women who were standing nearby. They were staring at Jane as though she had just grown a second nose. When they noticed Eugenia's regard, they glanced in another direction. "I am afraid there are more than a few young ladies who would dearly love to push you in front of a speeding train."

Although she was wearing the elegant icy blue silk gown Lancaster had given to her for this occasion, Jane felt as though she were wearing nothing but a tattered petticoat. She could not help wishing Lancaster had not been so anxious to celebrate his victory. He had not been content with the simple wedding breakfast her parents had planned. Instead, Lancaster had filled his huge home with more than four hundred guests to enjoy a wedding feast followed by a party. And each guest was taking great pleasure in examining every aspect of the new Marchioness of Lancaster. Tomorrow she expected the *Times* to print a list of each and every one of her many flaws.

"Oh, my dear, I truly hate to tell you how many of the women here have at one time been his mistress."

From the glint of excitement in her companion's blue eyes, Jane suspected Eugenia in fact would relish introducing her to every former mistress in the room. Under other circumstances Jane would have dreaded any knowledge of her husband's mistresses. With Lancaster, she could only pray he intended to spend most of his time in another woman's company. "Is his current mistress here?"

Eugenia's lips formed a small *O*. She looked like a hound who had just grabbed the tail of a poor unsuspecting fox. "As far as I know, he hasn't taken another mistress. Not since the incident."

"Incident?"

Eugenia leaned toward her, spilling the heavy scent of

her spicy perfume around her. She lowered her voice as she said, "Lady Gretchan Winslowe. Viscount Newbridge's wife."

A splinter of ice shivered through Jane. "That was Lancaster?"

Eugenia nodded. "I suppose you never suspected. The article in the *Times* only mentioned her affair with a certain peer of the realm."

The statement was meant to shock Jane. It had. Still, she did not intend to give Eugenia the satisfaction of knowing just how deeply her barb had struck. "It was a tragedy."

Eugenia rolled her eyes toward the chandeliers. "Rather bad behavior on her part."

Jane swallowed the harsh words rising in her throat. "I saw her husband here."

"Yes. I was surprised to see Newbridge. And in his mourning. I would suppose he has to know it was Lancaster."

If he didn't, Jane supposed Eugenia would find a way to enlighten him. "I cannot imagine why he would be here tonight."

"It does make one wonder." Eugenia continued to flick her fan back and forth beneath her chin. "I certainly hope he does not intend to cause a commotion."

Jane could not tolerate another instant in Eugenia's company. "Excuse me, I see someone I really must speak with."

"Did I tell you about the opera dancer who performed on the lawn of Lancaster House one morning, trying to find her way back into Lancaster's good graces?" Eugenia grinned above the rim of her fan. "She wasn't wearing a stitch."

"I hope she didn't catch cold." Without another word, Jane left Eugenia. If she were forced to listen to more of the woman's gossip, she would run from the room screaming like a Bedlamite. Unfortunately she suspected most of what Eugenia said was true. She had no illusions about the nature of the man she had married.

She glanced to where Lancaster stood at the top of the three curving stairs leading from the hall down into the ballroom. Dressed entirely in black except for a bit of snowy white linen at his neck, his black hair swept back from his wide brow, he looked like a fallen angel, a creature created by a sinister hand for the purpose of ruining any woman who might cross his path. Her father stood beside him, the top of his head just reaching the tip of Lancaster's slender nose. She had never thought of her father as a small man. Yet beside Lancaster's tall, broad-shouldered physique, her father looked short and slight and so easily crushed.

From the look on her father's face, Jane could tell he was enjoying Lancaster's company. Lord Lancaster could be charming, when it suited him. She wondered what her father would think if he knew the truth behind her marriage. He did not know. He would not know. Jane had promised her mother and her sister she would never tell him the true circumstances that had brought about this marriage.

Lancaster looked in her direction, as though he sensed her gaze upon him. When his gaze met hers, the world narrowed. The sound of laughter and conversation dissolved into a low buzz in her ears. The people around her faded into a blur of color. Even though the width of the large room separated them, Jane felt it all the same—a prickle at the base of her neck, a chill that spread like frost across her skin. Images flickered in her mind—of Lancaster touching her in all the ways she imagined a husband would touch his wife. The images pounded like a hammer against her skull. Her skin grew cold beneath her gown. The mingled scents of perfume and overly warm human bodies stabbed her senses. Her stomach threatened to turn inside out.

"Really, Jane. You must take more care."

Jane flinched at the sound of her mother's voice. She turned and found her mother frowning at her. "What is it, Mama?"

"This is your wedding feast and you look as though you are about to be led to the gallows." Georgette glanced around, smiling as though it were the happiest day of her life. "You will have everyone thinking you are miserable. Including your poor sister. Hasn't Amelia suffered enough?"

In truth Jane hadn't given Amelia's feelings much thought today. She forced her lips into a smile. Yet she could not prevent her knees from shaking. "I am sorry, Mama. I didn't realize I was being so obvious."

Georgette waved aside her words with a delicate flick of her hand. "I realize this marriage is not precisely what you wanted. But that doesn't mean it cannot be a success."

Jane glanced across the room to Lancaster. If he were different, if he possessed the capability of affection, she might have a small chance of making a success of this travesty. As it was, her future with him would be cold and empty.

"A marchioness. I never expected you to marry. And here you are, a marchioness. Smile, child. You can do better than that wooden look."

Jane tried; she truly did. But her lips felt made of wood. "I am sorry. I just cannot stop thinking about . . . tonight."

"Yes, I suppose that is bothering you. When the time arrives, I suggest you close your eyes and think of something pleasant, such as gardening." Georgette patted Jane's arm. "You have always enjoyed digging about in the garden. Think of planting flowers, while he is going about his business. There will be a small amount of pain, but it will all be over before you know it."

Jane felt the blood drain from her limbs. "Mama, I've been thinking of something. I was wondering if I might try to find some way to persuade Lancaster to—"

"Oh, dear." Georgette frowned, her attention directed somewhere behind Jane. "I should have known."

Jane glanced over her shoulder. She could see nothing that would warrant the worried expression on her mother's face. "What is it?"

"Lord Farringdon is bothering Amelia. He is such a terrible bore. I really must rescue your sister."

"But Mama, I was hoping to speak with you about—"

"I have already given you my advice. Now you really must stop acting like a frightened mouse and start behaving like a marchioness. My goodness, my little Jane a marchioness." Georgette shook her head as though she could not quite believe it. "Now, dear, you know how upset Amelia has been about this entire affair. You don't mean to say you would want me to stay here chatting while she needs me?"

Jane withered beneath her mother's steady glare. "No. Of course not. Perhaps we shall have some time to speak later."

"Of course, dear." Her petticoats rustled softly as Georgette hurried to take care of Jane's younger sister.

Jane glanced around the room. Many of her friends were here, but she could not share this burden with any of them. The vow of secrecy she had made to her mother would not permit it. She hurried across the room and escaped through one of the open doors leading to the terrace.

A cool breeze scented with a trace of cut grass brushed her face as she escaped the crowded ballroom. She rested her hands on the stone balustrade and dragged deep breaths past her tight throat, like a swimmer who had stayed too long underwater. A woman's voice drifted to her on the soft breeze, the words hitting her as sharply as an open hand across her cheek.

"Of all the eligible ladies in London, Lancaster chose

that woman. What could he possibly have been thinking?"

Jane glanced in the direction of the voice and found two young women sitting on a stone bench in the garden beyond the terrace. In the dying sunlight, she recognized the women as Camilla Easterbrook and Lavinia Woodbridge, two of the young debutantes of the Season.

"I cannot imagine what possessed him," Camilla said, swatting her fan at a fly that buzzed about her head. "She may be called pretty at best. And she is old. Mama said she made her debut five years ago."

"I simply cannot imagine what attracted him to that woman. One would scarcely notice her in a crowd," Lavinia said. "I could understand it if he had chosen her sister Amelia. She may not be an heiress, but she is at least beautiful."

"I thought he was interested in Amelia," Camilla said. "And then he turns about and marries that spinster."

Jane stepped away from the balustrade and hurried toward the far end of the terrace. Several of the guests had also escaped the ballroom. They stood about in small groups on the terrace and in the gardens, conversing softly. How many were discussing the odd choice Lancaster had made for his bride?

The comments she had overheard had not shocked her as much as the truth behind them had embarrassed her. No one could quite believe the Marquess of Lancaster had actually married a woman like Jane. No one was more astonished or more perplexed than the bride.

Over the past two months she had often puzzled over the reason the Marquess of Lancaster had pursued her with such zeal. Every time she had demanded to know why he had set a trap for her, his only response had been: "You suit me." From what she knew of the man, she assumed she was like anything else in his life. Lancaster took what he wanted and he didn't care who he hurt or what damage he might cause in the taking. Still, why in the world had he pursued her?

She kept walking, following the terrace around the corner of the house, until she found a solitary sanctuary overlooking the topiary garden. She sat on the cushioned seat of a large white wicker chair positioned near the balustrade. It was one of several such chairs placed about this part of the terrace. Tall shrubs spread out from the terrace, taking the shape of various animals. It was only one of many gardens that graced the grounds of Lancaster House. Upon first glimpse of the house and gardens, Jane had thought this place straight out of the pages of a book of fairy tales. What had happened to her was also the stuff of a fairy tale—an ordinary woman winning the heart of a handsome prince. Unfortunately, something had gone awry in the telling of this tale. The prince did not have a heart to win. How in the world had she ever managed to capture his attention?

In her debut into society five years ago, she had noticed Dominic Stanbridge. She defied any woman not to notice him. He was the type of man who drew attention from any female in his vicinity. Although they had attended many of the same parties, she had never met Lord Lancaster during her Season. She had accompanied her family to London nearly every year since that first Season, occasionally attending a party with one of her sisters. Happily in all of those years she had never met Lord Lancaster. Until this year.

Two months ago she had been walking her dog near her family's house on Curzon Street when Arthur had suddenly dashed after a cat. Jane had careened into Lancaster in her pursuit of her suddenly maddened pet. That evening, a headache had prevented her mother from accompanying Jane's younger sister Amelia to the Maitland Ball. Jane had taken her mother's place. She had literally bumped into Lancaster again, this time in the Maitlands' crowded ballroom. Soon after their collision, he had asked her to dance. She had never dreamed her polite refusal would trigger a war.

Jane stiffened at the sound of footsteps upon the stone terrace. *Please don't turn the corner.* But like so many of her hopes these days, this one dissolved as Viscount Newbridge stepped around the corner.

He was tall and fair, and she had met him several times during her Season. Still, they certainly were not well acquainted. In fact, she doubted he even remembered her. She was merely one of the "gaggle," as she had overheard him say on several occasions. One of the many "ordinary females, without beauty, without connection, without wealth, who were without hope of snagging a husband." He had sounded so amused when he had quipped that witticism. At the time, she had been quite certain he knew she and two of her friends were standing close enough to hear the insult. She could imagine only one reason why he would approach her now.

"Lady Lancaster." Newbridge made a small bow. "Forgive me for approaching you in this manner. But I have something of importance to discuss with you."

They had only one connection, and that was of a scandalous nature. Any discussion he might wish to have with her would be entirely inappropriate. She had listened to more than enough scandal for one evening. "Lord Newbridge, I am sorry for your loss, but I—"

"Someone is coming." Newbridge glanced back the way he had come. A soft tap of footsteps upon stone heralded someone's approach. "Meet me tomorrow."

She had no intention of becoming embroiled in any illicit meeting with this man. "I do not believe—"

"I will be looking for you. Anytime you can break free for a few minutes, just take a walk on Park Lane. There is something urgent I need to discuss with you."

Before she could respond, Lancaster turned the corner and stepped into view. He looked from Newbridge to

Jane, a slow smile curving his lips. "I see you have been entertaining my lady."

Although she had no reason to feel guilty, she felt it just the same, a glimmer of embarrassment rooted in the sordid and tragic past these men shared.

Newbridge lifted his chin. "I sought only to return the compliment, Lancaster."

Lancaster rested his hand on Jane's shoulder, the heat of his palm smoldering against her skin. "I assure you, Newbridge, I shall not need any assistance in entertaining my wife."

Newbridge's lips pulled into a tight line. Jane held her breath, waiting for the next volley in this battle. Yet instead of crossing swords with Lancaster, Newbridge inclined his head toward Jane, then marched back the way he had come.

Lancaster flexed his fingers against Jane's shoulder while he held her captive with his gaze. Each time she saw him, she wished things were different. In so many ways he was everything she could hope for in a man. Aside from physical perfection of face and form, he possessed a keen intellect, a sharp wit, and a deeply masculine charm that could buckle a woman's knees. Yet in Lancaster these qualities were nothing more than weapons to be used to his own advantage.

"I wasn't aware that you were well acquainted with Newbridge," he said, his deep voice betraying nothing but mild amusement.

"I'm not." Jane pushed his hand from her shoulder and rose. She walked to the balustrade, then turned to face him. "But apparently you were well acquainted with his wife."

"Did he enlighten you?" Lancaster sat on the arm of the chair and stretched his legs. "Or did Eugenia fill your ear?"

The soft strains of a waltz drifted from the ballroom, a sharp contrast to the furious beating of her heart. "Is it

21

true? Did Newbridge's wife commit suicide because of you?"

He released his breath in a slow exhalation. "Gretchan Winslowe killed herself because she was a foolish woman. It is a common flaw in females. Still, she behaved very badly."

Jane studied him a moment, searching for some trace of sadness for the woman who had shared his bed. Yet ice was all that shimmered in his eyes. "You honestly don't care? You have no remorse? No sense of responsibility for what happened?"

"I simply ended a rather tiresome affair. I had no idea she would choose to make a spectacle of herself. In fact it was the first thing she ever did that truly surprised me. She seemed perfectly fine when I left her that night. I would never have suspected she was the type to take her own life, especially over a lover. I was not the first she had taken since her marriage." He rubbed the lobe of his right ear. "Still, I suppose I underestimated how devoted she was to me."

"While you felt nothing for the poor woman."

"You speak of her as though she were a saint. Gretchan was a spoiled woman who wanted a great deal more than her husband could provide, including a rousing good time in bed. If anything, I did the honorable thing." He smiled, as if pleased with himself. "I was, after all, about to be married."

"I do not believe it is honorable to become involved with a woman who is married."

"I am so glad to hear of your sense of honor, my dear wife. It is a novelty in your sex."

"If you have such a low opinion of my sex, why marry at all?"

"I have always found one place where women are of great use. And in one regard females are indispensable. You see, I have no intention of passing my fortune to the cadet branch of the family. They would only lose it. Again."

Jane's stomach clenched at the implication of his words. She didn't want to think of what would transpire between them this night.

He studied her a moment, his blue eyes narrowing slightly, as if he were trying to find a piece to an intriguing puzzle. "Your father has been telling me all of your secrets."

"My secrets? Strange, I didn't think I had any secrets."

"We all have secrets. And I must say, I never would have guessed that you were addicted to gothic romance novels. Your father said you haunt the circulating library."

"And why is it so difficult to believe that I enjoy reading about romance?"

"You appear far too practical. Too clever to read such nonsense."

She glared straight into his icy blue eyes. "I suppose it shows just how little you know about me."

He lifted his black brows, a glint of humor entering his eyes. "A woman of mystery."

"Nothing quite so intriguing."

"But you are." His thick lashes lowered slightly as his gaze swept the length of her figure. "Something tells me I shall enjoy getting to know you."

Her skin prickled at the intimacy of that look. "I cannot imagine why. There is nothing particularly intriguing about me."

"On the contrary." He rested his arm along the curved back of the chair. "I have found you intriguing since the first night you refused to dance with me."

"You found my refusal intriguing?"

"You are the first woman ever to say no to me."

A cool May breeze swept across the garden, rustling the leaves of a tall oak standing near the terrace. "You cannot be serious."

Long rays of the setting sun slanted across the terrace, painting gold upon his features, like an artist adding the final touches to his masterpiece. "Most women would have accepted my every word as fact. But you, dear Jane, you question everything about me."

"And you find that intriguing?"

"As you knew I would."

"As I knew I would? I don't understand what you could possibly . . ." Jane hesitated, a scraping sound snagging her attention. She glanced up in time to see a porcelain flowerpot tumble from the balcony, straight above Dominic. Instinct spurred her. She launched herself at her husband. She caught a glimpse of his surprised expression before she plowed into him.

Dominic careened off the arm of the chair. He grabbed her as they tumbled backward, as though she might prevent the fall. She couldn't. Her momentum carried them both toward the stone terrace. His teeth clicked together as the two of them hit the terrace. Though she was cradled against his wide chest, the impact still jolted the breath from her lungs. A heartbeat after they crashed to the stone floor, an explosion of porcelain smashing against stone cracked the air.

The sound vibrated through Jane. For several moments she lay paralyzed against Dominic's chest. Slowly, as the fear receded, her wits returned. A scent of sandalwood and spices smoldered through her senses. She became aware of one of the pearl studs lining his shirtfront poking her cheek. She lifted her head and looked down into his face. His eyes were closed, his lips parted, his breathing shallow.

"Lancaster." She sat back on her heels. When he didn't answer, she patted his cheek with her hand. "Lancaster, do wake up."

A soft moan slipped past his lips as he turned his head. He looked up at her, then blinked as though trying to bring her into focus.

"Are you all right?"

He frowned up at her. "Are you insane?"

She flinched at his brusque tone. "Perhaps I am."

He lifted his black brows. "Although I appreciate your enthusiasm, my dear, there was no need to throw yourself into my arms."

She stood and smoothed the rumpled silk of her gown, her hands trembling. "I cannot imagine what got into me."

He eased into a sitting position, then sucked in his breath as though in sudden pain. "I suppose you had a good reason for knocking me to the ground."

"Yes." Jane clasped her trembling hands at her waist. "I did."

The setting rays of the sun illuminated his expression, revealing his sarcasm. "I would love to hear it."

"A flowerpot."

He blinked. "A flowerpot?"

"Yes. It was falling." She gestured toward the shattered remains of the pot, where colorful spring blossoms lay scattered amid dirt and shards of blue-and-white porcelain. "Straight above you."

He struggled to his feet. When he stood, he swayed and grabbed Jane's shoulder to steady himself. He leaned against her and drew in his breath. "Bloody hell."

Jane had grown up in a house with three brothers. The oath did not shock her as much as the press of Lancaster's body close against her. Not nearly as close as what would come this night. It took all her will to remain steady and provide support. "You are dizzy."

"Little escapes you."

Jane set her teeth at his sarcasm. If she had expected gratitude for saving his life, she was mistaken.

Gingerly, he rubbed the back of his head, then stared down at his fingers. They were covered with blood. "You managed to crack open my head."

"I suppose a falling pot would have done less damage.

25

I really cannot imagine what I was thinking when I pushed you out of the way."

Lancaster looked down at the shattered pot, then up at the balcony. "You say it fell from the balcony?"

"Yes. Now you should sit." She slipped away from him and patted the back of the nearest wicker chair. "I will send for the surgeon."

"No." He leaned against the balustrade and rubbed his neck. "I will not be prodded and poked and bothered by a man who will in the end tell me I have a bump on my head."

"But you are bleeding."

He pulled a handkerchief from his pocket and pressed it to the back of his head. "A little ice should help. And a fresh shirt. I wouldn't want to shock our guests."

"You do not really intend to return to the party?"

He smiled at her. "I don't intend to allow a bump on the head to ruin my evening. It is, after all, our wedding night."

His meaning could not be missed. A weight pressed against her chest when she thought of the position in which she found herself. She would not die tonight. Jane knew her body would survive the loss of her virginity. There would be no outward signs of damage. Yet deep inside, her secret hopes and her dreams would not survive. Not unless she found some way to keep the beast at bay. The blackguard might have her in check, but she refused to allow him to win the game. Not without a fight.

Chapter Two

Or love me less, or love me more;
And play not with my liberty:
Either take all, or all restore;
Bind me at least, or set me free!
—Sidney Godolphin

An acrid scent stabbed her nostrils as Jane stirred the ashes in the fireplace, making certain nothing remained of the scraps of paper that had led her into this disaster. She had found the slips of paper on the bed when she had entered her bedchamber after the party. They had been placed beneath a gorgeous diamond necklace. She stiffened at the sound of the click of the door handle. Without turning she sensed her adversary approach. Her dog lay near her feet. He lifted his head and stared past her, a low growl emanating from deep in his chest.

When Jane had first seen him three years ago, Arthur had been a puppy of unknown origin haunting the kitchen of the family home in Leicester. Although the terrier characteristics in his face betrayed the impurities in his bloodline, his long tan-and-white fur and general physique made her suspect he was related to one of the collies on a nearby farm. Scrawny and frightened when she had given him a home, he had grown into a large, good-natured dog who usually liked everyone—except Lancaster. He had growled upon first sight of His Lordship. She had always known Arthur was an excellent judge of character. Now she also was hoping he might help her keep the beast she had married at bay.

"That is an interesting costume you have chosen for your wedding night, my lady. I suppose it has some significance."

The clang of brass against brass grated on her nerves when she slipped the poker back into the holder on the hearth. Jane took a breath before turning to face the scoundrel. Lancaster stood near the bed, eyeing her with a measure of humor in his stunning blue eyes. "I chose a gown that suited the circumstances."

Lancaster frowned, his eyes narrowing as his gaze lowered, taking in the black crepe of the mourning gown she had made for this occasion. "Mourning?"

"The loss of freedom."

Arthur stood and pressed against her leg, the hair on his back rising on end. He was growling as though he knew the danger this man represented to her. She stroked his neck.

"I thought I had exiled that mongrel to the kitchen." Lancaster rested his shoulder against one of the heavily carved posts at the foot of the large bed. "I suppose you liberated him to show me just how much you want to keep me at a distance."

Jane curled her fingers into Arthur's fur. "It would seem Arthur and I share the same opinion of you."

"There is no need to maintain this pretense, my dear. Your ploy worked beautifully."

"My ploy?" A cool breeze swept through the open

French doors leading to the balcony, rustling the heavy rose-colored silk brocade drapes. "Since I have no idea what you could possibly mean, it would seem you have me at a disadvantage."

He smiled, a slight curve of finely molded lips that held more than a whisper of cynicism. "And I thought I was the one at a disadvantage."

"I would find it immensely interesting to hear how I ever had you at a disadvantage."

"It was only a disadvantage until I recognized the strategy you were employing. It did not take long."

"You discovered my strategy early in the game?"

"It was clever, my dear. I will hand you that." Lancaster cast a dark glance at Arthur, who was growling at him again. "The animal is annoying me. I suggest you put him out of the chamber before I decide to put him out of the house."

Although she found Arthur's presence comforting, she would not take the risk of his being injured by her new husband. She took his collar and pulled him to the door. Arthur resisted her attempts to shove him into the hall, but finally she managed to put him out of the room. She closed the door and turned to face her adversary. "Feel safer now, Lord Lancaster?"

"You are a most interesting creature." Lancaster drew his fingers over the swag of rose-colored silk damask that flowed from the canopy of her bed, watching her with the cold, predatory look of a tiger. "In the past, I have found that members of your sex are usually easy to predict. Most women see a male with wealth and a title and immediately set out to trap him. Their ploys are usually far too obvious to be more than mildly amusing. Your tactics, on the other hand, have always been . . . intriguing."

Jane squeezed her hands into fists at her sides, her nails biting into her palms. "My tactics?"

"You are the first woman I have ever met who actually

pretended to disdain my regard. It was a marvelous ploy. I found myself intrigued with you from the first moment you plowed into me on the street."

Jane stared at him, reviewing his words in an attempt to make sense of them. "Do you mean to say you pursued me because I didn't like you? Is that what you meant by telling me I suited you?"

"I'm certain you are glaring at me, but you should know all of your theatrics are wasted. I can't see so much as one narrowed eye behind that veil."

She hesitated a moment before she snatched the hat from her head, sweeping aside the waist-length veil she had admittedly been hiding behind. She tossed the hat on the seat of a chair near the fireplace. "Now you shall see the disdain in my eyes."

Lancaster stared at her a moment, then shook his head. He sucked in his breath, as if the movement had pained him. "Confound it," he whispered, sliding his hand over the back of his head.

"You are obviously as stubborn as you are arrogant. You should be resting."

"And disappoint my bride?" He cast a glance at the bed. "I certainly have no intention of deserting you this evening."

He had removed his cravat and the first few studs of his shirt. The fine white silk had spilled open, revealing the hollow at the base of his neck and a dark wedge of golden skin covered with dark hair. Never had she been more aware of his blatant masculinity. Jane's stomach clenched. It was far too intimate standing here this way. Yet not as intimate as what he had in mind. "I assure you, I would not be disappointed. You could stay away from me the rest of our lives, and I would not complain of your desertion. In fact, I would be delighted."

Although he smiled, the expression in his eyes remained cold. "I keep getting the impression you aren't happy about something."

She folded her hands at her waist, the heels of her palms pressed tightly against the black crepe of her gown. "Is it possible you truly do not realize how very much I resent being forced into this marriage?"

He rubbed the tip of his forefinger over the arch of one black brow as he spoke. "You managed to capture my attention with your little game, Jane. It was clever."

"Life is a game to you, isn't it? A chess match. People are pawns to be used to your advantage. And through some twisted thread of fate, I somehow became your opponent in the game. My sister was the pawn you used to put me in check."

"I recognized a worthy opponent when I met you." Lancaster glanced toward the cheval mirror standing in one corner of the room, his attention centered on his reflection as he continued. "Your ploy worked beautifully. You succeeded where so many of your sex have failed. You have won the prize. And now—"

"The prize?"

"Obviously." He inclined his head, all the while watching his reflection in the mirror. "Still, it is time the game ended. I am getting bored with this 'damsel in disdain' role you have assumed. If you aren't careful, I shall lose interest in you very quickly. Let's say you are a clever girl and leave it at that."

The man was serious. She supposed his arrogance would not permit him to believe any female might genuinely disdain his regard. "I am not clever. Not at all. I wasn't playing some silly game with you. When I declined your offer of marriage, I meant it. I truly did not want to become your wife."

Lancaster looked at her, pinning her in a steady glare she imagined would weaken the knees of a less sturdy opponent. She might be trembling, but she had not and would not buckle. "Do you actually expect me to believe you had no desire to become the Marchioness of Lancaster?"

"None." She glared straight into his icy blue eyes as she continued. "The truth is, I think you are arrogant, overbearing, and ruthless. If it hadn't meant ruin for my family, I would never in this lifetime have consented to become your wife."

He crossed one arm over his chest, rested his elbow against his wrist, and propped his chin in his hand. "Do you have any idea how many women would sell their souls to be in your position, including your sister?"

"I can only say it is a great pity you did not marry one of those other women, my lord."

He rubbed his jaw, studying her in that way he had of making her feel as though he were contemplating a chess move—cool, dispassionate, pure intellect at work. "Well, I see only one way to solve this particular dilemma," she went on.

Jane's chest swelled with equal parts dread and excitement. She cringed at the thought of the scandal she would cause. Yet she felt certain her family could survive this particular scandal. "I believe an annulment would be best for all concerned."

"An annulment?" he repeated.

"I realize it might cause a bit of a stir, but you are somewhat accustomed to scandal. I feel certain my family would accept an annulment rather than see me unhappy." She spoke faster as she embraced an idea that had been teasing her since the marriage ceremony. "If you like, you can say I was insane at the time of our marriage. I believe that should be sufficient reason. And I suppose many people would believe it is insane to disdain your title and wealth. I am certain, with your influence, you could manage to have this marriage annulled without a problem."

Lancaster stared at her as though she had just spoken in a language he did not understand. The soft click of the clock on the mantel behind her marked each taut second until he said, "You shall have to forgive my disbelief,

32

but I am accustomed to being the target of every match-making mama in the vicinity. Including your mama."

Jane stiffened at the disparaging remark. "My mother did not realize the true nature of the beast."

He lifted his brows. "Your mama was anxious to have me for your sister. And your sister was anxious to have me."

"My sister is a girl in her first Season. She does not yet have the experience to recognize a scoundrel when she sees one."

"Scoundrel." He rested his hand upon his heart. "I fairly swoon over the pet names you have for me, wife."

"I must speak boldly, Lord Lancaster. Your actions have earned you my scorn. Only a scoundrel would lure a young, impressionable, far too naive girl into deep play, in your quest to force me into this marriage."

"Naive?" One corner of his lips twitched. "The truth is that your sister is an ambitious little chit, anxious to trade her beauty for wealth and a title. If she had not been so anxious to get me leg-shackled, I would not have found it so easy to find the means to blackmail you, my dear. All of which I assumed was merely part of the game you were playing. As you can see, I am truly the victim here."

Heat prickled her neck when she acknowledged some small measure of truth in his assessment of her sister. "Under the circumstances, I should think you might see how my family would accept an annulment. You should also know I burned Amelia's vowels. You no longer have a sword to dangle over my neck."

He rubbed the back of his neck, all the while watching her with that cold, predatory look. "I wouldn't think of annulling this marriage."

Jane's heart clenched. "But I thought you could see the mistake that has been made."

"Yes. I do see the mistake." He straightened and paused a moment, as though he wasn't quite certain of his balance. Still, each slow stride was filled with the peculiar grace of barely restrained power as he moved toward her. She took a step back, then halted, determined not to cower before this man. He paused in front of her, so close his legs brushed the black crepe of her skirt. A subtle aroma curled around her: the spicy scent of his expensive cologne. "You have obviously underestimated my charm."

"And you have obviously overestimated your—"

He whipped his arm around her waist and hauled her against him. Before she could draw a breath, he clamped his mouth over hers. Fear speared through her. She curled her hands into fists, then caught herself, crushing the urge to pound her fists against his broad shoulders. Her strength was no match for his. Survival depended on a different strategy. Instead of struggling, she remained rigid in his hold, her lips tightly pursed, her eyes squeezed shut, while she hoped he had too much pride to take a woman against her will. It was her best chance to keep the beast at bay. His pride would be her strongest weapon.

Lancaster held her tighter, his lips opening against hers, demanding a response. She had never been the object of a man's gallantry before. Her natural tendency to betray her intellect coupled with her complete lack of feminine wiles usually kept men at a distance. In a distant part of her brain, a place where intellect had not been drowned in a swift flood of fear, she recognized his tactic and acknowledged the miscalculation on his part. If there had been a shred of tenderness in this kiss, she might have responded.

Yet this kiss was not a tender kiss. Gentleness had no place in this embrace. This was a kiss meant to dominate, to subjugate, to impress his will upon her. He slanted his mouth over hers. Warm lips, but hard and demanding. This kiss served only as a confirmation of how terribly wrong this man was for her. Without respect and affection there could be no desire or passion. Where warmth should dwell, ice prevailed.

Panic surged through her with each quick contraction of her heart. The powerful press of his body against hers frightened her with the affirmation of how easily he could impose his will. She was his wife, his property, and no one would interfere with anything he chose to do to her. It took all her will to keep still in his hold.

He lifted his head and frowned down at her. "Have you ever been kissed before?"

Jane lifted her chin, hoping the gesture would not look as defensive as it felt. "No, I have not. But experience would not have made a difference in my response to you."

He grinned, a glint of humor filling his beautiful eyes. "You present an interesting challenge."

A challenge? She didn't like the sound of that. She pulled herself free of his embrace. "Do you often force unwilling women into your bed, Lancaster?"

"I have found it more necessary to throw them out of my bed."

"How very unfortunate for you. Still, you shall not have that problem with me, since I shall not be issuing you any invitations to my bed."

"Are you certain of that?"

"Quite." She turned away from him, staring down at the rose-and-ivory carpet as she put several feet between them. When she was certain her fear was hidden as well as possible, she turned to face him. "Now that you know the truth, do you really intend to remain married to a woman who does not love you? A woman who, in fact, does not even like you?"

"Love?" Lancaster strolled away from her and sat on the edge of her bed. He rubbed his temples as if his head ached. "You appear to be a sensible woman. Do you honestly put any faith in that fairy tale of undying love?"

"I have seen it. My parents have raised five daughters

and three sons together. And after that time, they are still deeply in love."

He considered this a moment. "I suppose it's a little like being struck by lightning. One hears of it happening, but the chances of it striking you are at best rare."

"I have never imagined marriage without it."

"And I have never imagined it existed."

Anxiety rose in her, threatening to buckle her composure. "Do you truly choose to live with a woman who does not have the least bit of affection for you?"

"I have found the most dishonest of your sex are those who profess a certain fondness for anything other than the coin in a man's purse or the title appended to his name. Your honesty is actually quite refreshing."

"Your arrogance is not."

Lancaster considered her a moment. "And is there some paragon who has caught your fancy, my dear? Some perfect knight in shining armor?"

"No, there is not." The smile he gave her made her wish she had not answered with such candor. "Still, I see no reason to settle for marriage with a man I shall never admire."

"Never? Hummm." He studied her as though calculating his next move, a glint of speculation entering his eyes. "Perhaps we did not enter into this union under the best of circumstances. That doesn't mean it should not be successful. Aside from your notions of romance, you are for the most part a practical young woman. You are also beautiful, in an understated way."

"There must be a hundred more beautiful women, eager to take my place."

"True. But beauty is not as significant as other attributes." He glanced down at the toe of his shoe, examining the high gloss of the black leather. "From the information I gathered about you when you first caught my attention, you have never in your life become entangled with a man. That, coupled with your other assets, recommends you. I am certain you shall make a suitable marchioness."

"You investigated me?"

"It is always wise to learn all one can about any opponent." He looked up, pinning her with a steady gaze. "With you, I find that I actually admire your honesty, which is startling. I seldom admire anything about a member of your sex. The truth is, I also like your intelligence and your candor. You suit me. I have every confidence you shall change your mind."

"I do not share your opinion."

He shrugged, broad shoulders stretching the white silk of his elegant shirt. "I shall have to change your mind."

"I shall not change my mind about you."

"Never underestimate your opponent. I seldom fail to get what I want."

"And what precisely is it you want?"

"Your regard. Your affection." He stretched his long legs out before him, folded his arms over his chest, and grinned at her. "And I shall have it."

"You have a very high opinion of yourself, my lord."

"It comes from experience."

Jane didn't know which was worse, his arrogance or the insidious doubts lurking within her. What if he succeeded? He was experienced with women, experienced in ways she didn't even want to imagine. Gretchan Winslowe and Penelope Clydestaff were only two of the women he had left trampled beneath his feet. According to rumors about him, his former mistresses could fill St. Paul's Cathedral. How many other sordid and tragic tales had this man inspired? Suicide, attempted murder, these things did not happen unless a man had the ability to dominate a woman's spirit.

What chance would she have if he truly launched an all-out attack upon her sensibilities? Her intellect told her he would do anything to gain an advantage. Manipulation was one of his specialties. Could he twist her emotions against her? When it came to war with this man, she was at a disadvantage. She actually had a heart that could be broken. Her best chance at survival was to convince him to annul this travesty of a marriage. "You expect a great deal from me. Yet what do you expect to give in return?"

"Anything money can buy, my dear. You shall never want for anything."

"Except a husband who loves me."

He studied her a moment, an opponent looking for an advantage. "Are you certain?"

"I'm not certain you are capable of loving anyone, except perhaps the man you see in your mirror."

He chuckled softly. "I think we are in for a tremendously enjoyable time."

"I have never regarded life in Hades as enjoyable."

"I might have been killed this evening if not for you." He glanced at her from beneath the thick fringe of his black lashes. "It looks as though you missed an excellent opportunity to be rid of me. Perhaps you don't dislike me as much as you think you do."

"Unfortunately my instincts betrayed me. If I had been thinking, I might have become a very wealthy widow."

Lancaster laughed, then sucked in his breath as though in pain. He smoothed the hair at the back of his head. "Confound it."

Jane frowned. "A wise man would rest. If you are not careful, you shall find yourself quite ill."

"Your concern is touching."

"It isn't any more than I would have for a dog I found injured in the road."

He lifted his brows in mock shock. "A dog?"

She molded her lips into what she hoped would appear a sarcastic smile. She had a feeling she would have to learn to wear a great many masks in the days to come. "Or a cat."

He cringed. "Now that hurt."

"You must forgive me, Lancaster. I can only hope you

will come to see the folly of this unfortunate union and petition for an annulment."

Lancaster's eyes narrowed, his lips tipping into a grin. "You really do not imagine I can change your mind?"

"I believe the only reason for marriage is true affection. Since you do not even believe in the existence of such a match, I do not see how you can change my mind."

"And you see little hope of changing my mind?"

It was another tactic, she reminded herself. Dominic Stanbridge had no intention of falling in love with anyone. "I have no such unrealistic aspiration."

A look of genuine surprise crossed his features. "If you are really serious about this, I shall make you a bargain."

Jane could not shake the feeling she had just moved her queen into danger. She held his steady gaze and hoped she did not betray her emotions. Lancaster would exploit her every weakness. She kept her voice level and controlled as she spoke. "What type of bargain?"

Lancaster drew his hand over the rose silk counterpane folded at the foot of her bed. The bedcovers had been turned down, revealing white silk sheets, the altar on which she was to sacrifice herself for the sake of her family. "If at the end of six months of marriage you still want an annulment, you shall have it."

A bubble of apprehension swelled in her chest, pressing against her lungs until it was difficult to draw a breath. "I see. You intend to assert your marital rights for six months. At which time you will discard me like a soiled piece of linen. From my perspective, it is not much of a bargain, sir."

"And if I said I would not make love to you unless you invited me to your bed, would you find it more acceptable?"

She nearly collapsed with relief. "Infinitely more acceptable."

He shook his head. "You obviously do not know what you are missing."

"What do you gain in this bargain?"

"Your company and a chance to change your mind about marriage to me. In exchange for a chance to be free of this distasteful marriage, all I ask is that you give everyone, including the servants, the impression you could not be more pleased with your choice of husband. I prefer to keep our differences between us. I will not tolerate gossip."

In that instant, as she looked into his eyes, she saw a glint of steel. She had wounded his pride. He intended to make a conquest of her, and he would use any means available to him. "I do not care to wear my feelings on my sleeve, Lord Lancaster. If I had, I would have worn this gown this afternoon."

"I am glad to hear it."

The back of her neck prickled as she held his icy stare. What would this man do if she should anger him? Suddenly the possibility of ending up as a teaching specimen at a medical college seemed entirely possible.

He held her gaze a long moment before he spoke. "Do you accept the bargain?"

"What choice do I have?"

He shrugged. "None."

She couldn't shake the feeling she was making a pact with the devil himself. "I trust you will keep your word, Lancaster."

He lifted his brows just enough to betray a flicker of annoyance. He stood and crossed the distance between them. He paused before her, blocking out the rest of the world. "I am a man of my word, Jane. If in six months this marriage has not been consummated, you shall have your annulment."

She didn't like that look in his eyes. It was far too confident. "You can save us both a great deal of annoyance. Petition tomorrow. I assure you, I shall not succumb to your masculine wiles."

"My dear lady, you have a great deal to learn about me."

He slid his hand down her arm, his palm warming her skin through her gown. Yet instead of the excitement he intended to evoke, all she felt was a horrible, prickling sense of dread. "And you have a great distance to fall, my lord."

"We shall see, my dear." He chucked her under the chin, a grin curving his lips before he strolled past her. At the door he turned and lifted his hand in a salute. "Let the contest begin."

With a soft thud, the door closed behind him. Never in her life had she been confronted with anyone so bold, so determined, so wickedly confident. This was war. One she could not afford to lose. Her defenses would have to remain strong against any tactic he might try. It was the only way to escape the disaster that had befallen her this morning, a disaster called Lancaster.

Until Lancaster had barged into her life, she had often wondered what it might be like to be swept off her feet by the man of her dreams. Deep in her heart she had always imagined there was one special man meant just for her. Unfortunately, Lancaster was not that man.

She walked onto the balcony, welcoming a cool breeze perfumed with the scent of crushed grass. A tall chestnut lifted branches nearby, the soft rustle of leaves a soothing sound in the darkness. High above, stars burned through the London haze, pinpoints of hope in the darkness. A full moon glowed on the far side of a cloud, casting silvery streaks along the filmy vapor. It was a night for magic.

Her father's mother was Irish and she had not lost her fondness for telling stories of the Sidhe, the magical people of Ireland. Although Jane had long ago abandoned any belief in magic, she still believed in something that

41

might actually prove more impractical than magic: she still believed in true affection. Until this morning she had actually believed the man of her destiny would find her. Standing at the altar in St. George's Hanover Square, she had prayed for deliverance. Now, even in the face of this disaster, she refused to abandon hope.

She chose one star, the brightest in the heavens, and spoke her heart. "I wish things were different. I wish Lancaster were different. I wish he were warm and caring, capable of love. I wish he were the man I was meant to love, the man who was meant to love me."

Still, she knew wishes did not come true. And since Lancaster was not the man of her hopes and dreams, she prayed for the strength to fight him. "Heaven knows I am going to need a great deal of help to get through this horrible nightmare."

Chapter Three

But man, proud man,
Drest in a little brief authority,
Most ignorant of what he's most assur'd,
His glass essence, like an angry ape,
Plays such fantastic tricks before high heaven,
As make the angels weep.
—William Shakespeare

Lancaster stood near the door of his balcony, safe in the shadows, while he watched his bride cast wishes upon a star high above her. She was actually determined to defy him. He turned away from the pathetic sight and prepared for bed. After tossing his clothes into a heap in the dressing room, he crawled into his bed, white silk sheets cool against his bare skin. Blood pounded in his temples. A dull ache throbbed behind his eyes. He eased his head onto the pillow and closed his eyes against a sudden wave of dizziness.

If not for Jane, he would have been killed this evening.

If what he suspected was true, it had not been an accident. At least he could be reasonably certain Jane had not been in league with the person who had tossed that flowerpot from the balcony.

He had a fairly good idea who had done it. He would have to think upon the proper strategy for getting the evidence he needed before another attempt was made.

He drew in his breath, his mind fighting the dizziness to grapple with the puzzle that was Jane Eveleigh. He had to admit, she had surprised him. More important, she had challenged him. Never in his life had a woman accomplished both of those feats. This war of wills should prove interesting for a while. He knew she would lose. It was inevitable. She might prove an intriguing opponent, but he would win this game. She lacked the proper measure of cunning to beat him.

It was simply a matter of time before he had her curled in the palm of his hand, as well as in his bed. He certainly wouldn't need six months to bend her to his will. Find an opponent's weaknesses, exploit them. It was the same strategy he applied to most things in life. She had already betrayed more than she ought to have revealed to her opponent. The lady believed in romance, and that all too ethereal of emotions: love. It was a weakness that should prove her downfall. He simply had to convince her he was not the man she believed him to be. He would transform himself, at least in appearance. He would be as Jupiter. Jane would be his Alcmaena, his Leda, his Io. He would become the man she wanted, until he had what he wanted—victory.

A breeze swept through the window, stirring the dark blue velvet drapes. The soft swishing sound did not soothe the pounding in his temples. He hoped his head was better in the morning. He had work to do, strategy to plan. A different man. How could he convince her he was the man of her dreams?

He wasn't certain of the reasons that had drawn him

to Jane Eveleigh. She was not his usual fare. The women he chose to share his bed were each and every one considered perfect by the standards of feminine beauty. Jane did not meet that ideal. The bones in her face were far too prominent, creating hollows beneath her high cheekbones. She was average in height, her nose a bit too thin, her lips too full. Her hair was neither light nor dark, but an unremarkable shade of brown. Still, from the first moment he had glimpsed that peculiar look of disdain in her large gray eyes, he had been captivated by her. It was almost as if she had bewitched him.

He had wanted her from the first moment she had softly told him she did not wish to dance with him. And he wanted her now. Wanted her in that very basic way a male wanted the female of the species. He had never been immune to lust. In the past he had suffered from the malady frequently. The cure was always the same: if the woman was a virginal debutante, he would find a suitable substitute, a widow or bored married woman, occasionally a prostitute. He had discovered at an early age that there really wasn't much difference between prostitutes and those women considered "respectable."

All women had a price. For some it was marriage—those women he had always avoided. For others it was jewels, clothes, carriages, expensive frippery. He had always paid the price the woman in question was asking, then enjoyed her until boredom took hold of him. The ennui was as inevitable as his appetite for the next beautiful female who crossed his path. And so he would leave one mistress and move on to the next. Until he had met Jane Eveleigh.

For some reason he couldn't understand, Jane intrigued him. He had tried finding a substitute for her, and had failed. He wanted her. And so he had set about acquiring her. He had thought marriage would be the price he must pay to have her. Now it seemed the woman wanted more. *Love.* If the emotion did exist, he was most certainly immune. Still, it would not prevent him from playing this game.

He would have Jane. He would strip away all those icy defenses and plunge into a fire of his making. All he need do was devise the proper strategy. He wasn't certain how long the attraction would last, but when he tired of her, he would send her to his home in Devonshire. By then he would have an heir to keep her occupied.

Sleep slowly stole through his body, easing the pain in his head. His body grew heavy, uncommonly so. He felt as though he could not lift his limbs. The injury had drained more of his strength than he cared to admit. As his breathing settled into a steady cadence, a voice whispered in his mind, a soft feminine voice.

The moon is high.

A shaft of moonlight slanted through the windows, capturing the woman standing beside his bed. The moonlight seemed to radiate from her. Tall and slender, her pale blond hair tumbled over the white silk of her gown, flowing in a silken cascade to her knees. The tiny gold stars embroidered in the gauzy overskirt of her gown glittered in the moonlight. It was an odd gown, certainly not the fashion, but it suited her. She was so beautiful it hurt to look at her. So very beautiful. Why did she seem so familiar?

He was dreaming, of course. He had to be dreaming. It didn't surprise him to find a beautiful female in his dreams. This was a goddess born from the split in his head, the way Minerva had emerged from Zeus. He expected her to slip out of that robe and into his bed, where she would properly deal with his lust. Instead she rested her hand on his arm, a soft touch barely felt. Yet her warmth penetrated his skin, a compelling heat that slid through his veins like heated brandy.

He tried to speak; this was not the way he intended this dream to proceed. Yet the heat glowing through his body distracted him. He couldn't gather his thoughts. He couldn't shape the words. A soft, comforting warmth suffused his every pore, filling soft tissue, sinking deep into his bones. Pain melted in that heat. He could feel it sliding away from him, washed away on the steady current of heat and light flowing from this woman into him. He felt as though he were growing lighter, as light as thistledown, and she was a warm summer breeze, whispering over him.

It is time to meet your destiny.

"Destiny?" The word swirled through his mind, his last coherent thought before he slipped away, carried far away from the realm of dreams and man, swept away on a compelling current of heat and light.

"May we speak with you, Your Ladyship?"

Jane froze at the question. It would seem the summons had at last arrived.

She had spent breakfast forcing her food past a throat tight with apprehension while she waited for the battle that would come when Lancaster descended upon her. Yet he had not chosen to join her. Grateful for the respite, but feeling as though she were walking on a narrow ledge in a gale, she had taken refuge in his library soon after breakfast. Still, it was too much to hope he would ignore her today.

She clutched a beautifully illustrated copy of Lewis Carroll's *Through the Looking Glass* to her chest and turned to face the men standing a few feet inside the room. Lancaster's butler, Hedley, was a tall, stout man who moved with the lumbering gate of a bear. Beside Hedley stood a short, slim man she had never before seen.

Hedley frowned as he spoke. "Beg pardon, Your Ladyship, we didn't mean to interrupt, but we have a problem."

Jane hugged the book close to her chest. What game was Lancaster playing? "Problem?"

Hedley nodded. "This is Pierson, Your Ladyship. His Lordship's valet."

"I fear there may be something amiss, Your Ladyship. I am truly concerned." Pierson folded his hands at his waist. He was about Jane's height, with dark hair and eyes, impeccable in a somber charcoal gray suit. "This isn't at all like His Lordship, is it, Hedley?"

Hedley shook his head, his thin lips drawn into a downward curve. His white hair was swept back from his high brow, drawing attention to his prominent Roman nose. "It is His Lordship's habit to be dressed by eleven, no matter how late the evening has been. It is nearly a quarter of twelve. I fear there may be something amiss."

"Yes. Yes, indeed." Pierson flicked his tongue over his thin lips. "His Lordship left instructions to awaken him by ten this morning. He is still abed. I fear he may be ill."

A chill whispered over her skin when Jane thought of the accident the day before. Still, she could not shake the feeling that this was all a ruse on Lancaster's part. "Have you tried shaking him a little?"

Pierson's dark eyes grew wide. "Shaking him, mi-lady?"

Jane nodded. "Perhaps he needs a little prodding this morning."

"Prodding?" Hedley stared at her as though she had just suggested shooting his master.

Jane frowned. "How did you try to awaken him?"

Pierson smoothed his forefinger between his neck and his starched white collar. "I rapped on his door. And called to him. As I do each morning at the prescribed time."

Jane frowned. "Do you mean you didn't enter his chamber?"

Pierson's thick dark brows lifted. "Definitely not."

Jane looked at Hedley. "Did you?"

Hedley shook his head. "We value our lives, Your Ladyship."

"No one dares enter His Lordship's chamber without permission." Pierson inclined his head. "Not even I."

"That is why we came to you, Your Ladyship. We fear His Lordship may be ill. Yet we would not dare send for the surgeon if it were not truly necessary," Hedley said.

Pierson nodded. "His Lordship would not like it."

Jane looked from Lancaster's butler to his valet. Both men were gazing at her like expectant puppies—a mastiff and a spaniel—each in hope of receiving a bone. If this was a ploy, she felt certain Pierson and Hedley were not part of the plot. Lancaster's servants were genuinely concerned for His Lordship's welfare. As much as she would like to tell them to allow the beast to rot in his lair, she could not. Even if it were not for the bargain she had made with the scoundrel, her conscience would not allow it. Lancaster might very well be ill. Or worse. She sent both servants away with the assurance that she would look into the matter.

Although the master's chambers were adjacent to her own, connected by a large withdrawing room, Jane approached Lancaster's chamber from the hall. It seemed far too intimate to approach from her bedchamber. Intimacy with the beast was the last thing she wanted on her mind, especially when she was about to venture into her enemy's lair.

She hesitated in the hall outside of Lancaster's bedchamber. If he hadn't cracked his head the day before, Jane would never have considered this course of action. Still, she felt compelled to make certain the scoundrel was not gravely ill.

She rapped on the solid oak, the sharp, staccato sound echoing down the long oak-paneled corridor. When she received no answer, she opened the door a crack and called his name. She held her breath and waited, hoping for a response.

Nothing broke the silence except the constant thud of her own heart.

Fine. If this was the first volley of the war, she would show him his tactic would fail. She drew in a deep breath, squared her shoulders, and marched into the beast's lair.

Sunlight spilled through the open windows, seeking every corner of the huge chamber. This room was similar in size to the one she had been given the day before. Both overlooked the extensive gardens that surrounded the mansion. That was where the similarities ended. Her chamber had been furnished to please a feminine eye, with rose and ivory upholstery and delicate gilt-trimmed furniture. There was nothing at all feminine in this chamber. Even the scent that lingered here, a smoldering mix of sandalwood and spices, was distinctly masculine.

Sunlight glimmered on mahogany wainscoting. A large armoire stood near a dressing table across from her, the pieces shaped from intricately carved mahogany. Dark blue velvet framed the long windows and covered the large wing-back chairs near the fireplace. The same dark blue velvet fell in heavy swags from the canopy above the massive bed. There her gaze fastened on the man lying upon the white sheets.

She remained standing just inside the door, twenty feet from the bed, and still she could see very clearly. A white sheet lay across his waist. Since Lancaster was nude from the waist up, she suspected the sheet was the only covering he wore in bed. Her stomach tightened.

"Lancaster," she said, her voice sounding abnormally loud in the quiet room. A soft rustle of leaves rippled through the open windows with a whisper of cool air. Lancaster didn't stir.

She crossed the room, apprehension pressing like lead against her heart. She paused beside the bed. Lancaster lay facing the windows, very still, much too still. Could he have died in the night?

His skin looked pale in the sunlight. His left hand

rested upon his waist; his right arm was flung toward the windows, his hand outstretched, as though reaching for the sunlight streaming through the windows. The lemon yellow light spilled over him, lovingly stroking the hard curves of his shoulders, sprinkling gold upon the black hair that covered his chest.

She stared at the wide plane of his chest, trying to ascertain whether he was breathing. His chest rose, then fell with an exhale she could scarcely hear. Still, that soft exhale pierced the apprehension in her chest, releasing the tension.

"Thank goodness," she whispered. Once she noticed the soft rise and fall marking each breath, she caught herself staring for a completely different reason—one she didn't care to admit, but could not deny.

The sheer male beauty of the man could not be ignored, even by the most practical of women. His was a beauty shaped with finely etched muscle and bone, a beauty born of power and strength. Even in slumber he seemed bold and reckless, a danger to any unsuspecting female who might stumble into his path. And no one was more certain of his beauty or his potent masculinity than he was.

Lancaster would employ his masculine charms to bend her to his will. If she permitted it. If she forgot to look beyond the appealing wrapper to the empty package inside, the man would win. Fortunately she found little trouble overcoming the mere physical appeal of the scoundrel. The man would lose this wager.

She raised her voice as she said, "Lancaster, it's time to awaken."

A sound slipped past his lips, a soft moan.

Was he ill? She leaned over him and touched his arm. "Are you all right?"

He opened his eyes, then blinked against the sunlight. She saw the moment he focused on her face, the instant of recognition before he spoke. In that instant the expression in those beautiful blue eyes softened.

"Angel," he whispered.

The endearment caught her off guard. Yet not as much as what happened next. He gripped her thigh and pulled her down upon him. In the span of one quick heartbeat, he turned, pinning her beneath his powerful body. In the next instant his mouth closed over hers.

Last night had been the first time she had been kissed. Yet that kiss had not prepared her for this. This kiss was something entirely different. His lips moved against hers, firm, soft, warm, and tempting. He kissed her as though he had been waiting a lifetime to hold her in his arms, kissed her as though she were the only woman he wanted, the only woman he had ever desired. He held her as though she were rare and precious, a gift sent to him from heaven itself.

Last night he had failed to raise a single tingle. This morning an entire legion of tingles rippled through her limbs. The heat of his body soaked through her gown, sinking into her blood. Emotion swept over her, but her mind clutched for logic.

This kiss and the emotion behind it must be a ploy. It seemed genuine, but nothing about Lancaster could be trusted. This kiss was new strategy. She pressed her palms against his shoulders, intending to push him away. Her fingers slid against smooth skin, so warm, so vital. Her fingers curled upon his skin, ignoring logic and sense.

In her mind, a sane voice screamed the reason she should not respond to this kiss: He was a blackguard. He slid the tip of his tongue over her lips. She shivered deep inside.

Scoundrel!

In spite of every dire warning pealing in her brain, her body responded, drawn to him as though he were the lover she had been waiting for all her life. Instincts normally dependable as the rising sun betrayed her. Desire swelled within her, like a spring fed by a torrential rain. It rose inside her, threatening to drown her in its fury.

Without warning he pulled away, just far enough to look down at her, his gaze stroking her face. He gazed upon her as though he could go on looking at her until the last stars burned themselves into cinders in the heavens. The look in his eyes was something she had never before seen. Instead of the icy glint of intellect she had come to expect in Lancaster's eyes, she found warmth glowing in those incredible blue depths, a warmth that slipped past her defenses. Beneath that warmth, emotion unfurled inside her, like the delicate petals of a flower opening to the first rays of the sun.

She felt it then, a compelling attraction she had never in her life experienced. In defiance of all logic, she could not shake the feeling she was looking at him for the very first time.

He touched her cheek, a gentle slide of long fingers that traced warmth upon her skin. His fingers stilled upon her cheek, a curious expression filling his eyes. "You are real."

She lay against the sheet, her breath tangled in her throat, her wits as scattered as dandelion seeds caught in a storm. She wasn't certain what she had expected him to say, but she knew it wasn't this. "Real?"

"How can this be?" He ran his hand through his hair, grimacing as his fingers connected with the lump at the back of his head. "What the devil is happening here?"

Chapter Four

Did not Jupiter transform himself into the shape of
Amphitrio to embrace Alcmaena; into the form of a
swan to enjoy Leda; into a bull to beguile Io; into
a shower of gold to win Danaë?

—John Lyly

If he expected discourse, he would have to wait until she
could gather some measure of control. Yet he didn't wait
for her response. Instead he tossed aside the sheet and
climbed from bed. She knew she should not look at him.
It would be a dangerous breach of strategy to look at
him. Yet she couldn't help herself. A physique such as
his demanded attention.

He stood beside the bed, naked as the Almighty had
made him, looking around the room as though he wasn't
pleased with what he saw. She only wished she could
manage a fraction of the same disdain she saw on his
face. Unfortunately all she could manage was to stare
while her mind made comparisons to classic Italian sculp-
tures.

What was she doing? She shook her head, trying to break the spell softly stealing over her, the insanity she could scarcely control. To her horror she wanted to touch him, to explore the intriguing expanse of masculinity presented so temptingly before her. She wanted to touch Dominic Stanbridge? A shiver of revulsion gripped her. He had taken her unawares, shocked her into these odd sensations.

He glared at her. "This is not Kintair."

"Kintair?" Despite the muddle he had made of her brain, she recognized a difference in his speech. A soft Scottish burr colored the dark notes of his voice.

"What manner of mischief is afoot here?"

The question swirled in her brain. It occurred to her then that she hadn't moved. She was sprawled across his bed, staring at him like a demented spinster taking her first glimpse of a male in all his glory. If this was war, she was in danger of suffering major casualties. She sat up and straightened her gown. "I think it is quite obvious what mischief is going on here."

"Aye, 'tis." He marched to the French doors standing open to the balcony. Without a moment's hesitation he left the room, striding naked into the sunlight.

"What in the world . . ." Jane climbed from his bed, stunned by his behavior. Apparently the man did not have a shred of modesty. Of course he didn't. A man like Lancaster would laugh at the thought of modesty. She headed for the door. Since he was obviously fine, there was no need for her to stay. It was far wiser to retreat to fortify her defenses for the next battle. As she hurried toward the door, a soft cry from the gardens caught her attention. Ignore it, she told herself. Yet even as the sage advice sounded in her brain, she was hurrying onto the balcony.

Lancaster stood with his hands braced on the wrought-iron balustrade, frowning down into the gardens. Below, one of the housemaids was staring up at His Lordship, a basket of strawberries clutched in her hands, her mouth open, her eyes wide as she took in the glorious sight displayed above her.

Jane's cheeks warmed. She told herself it was merely embarrassment. The behavior of a husband inevitably reflected on his wife. It was one thing to humiliate himself; it was another to humiliate her with his outrageous behavior.

Yet as much as she wanted to file all of these feelings under the heading of outrage, she could not shove one insidious emotion into that nice, acceptable designation. Certainly what she was feeling could not be jealousy. Not in regard to Lancaster. Still, it was there, like a huge, hungry hawk with its talons firmly attached to her soft insides. No matter how hard she fought it, she wanted to pull the white cap over that maid's bulging eyes and kick her square in her plump backside.

Jane cleared her throat. The maid flinched as though Jane had slapped her. Jane simply looked at her, her meaning clear in that silent glare.

"Beg pardon, Your Ladyship." The maid bobbed a curtsy, then scurried away, casting one more startled look toward Lancaster before disappearing around the side of the house.

Jane silently cursed her own stupidity. She would rather hang by her thumbs above boiling oil than to admit to this arrogant buffoon how easily he had damaged her defenses. Jealousy? Possessiveness? Over a man she despised. She really had to get hold of her wits.

"Do you always entertain your servants in this manner? I must say it is most undignified of you." Although she tried for a calm tone, her voice sounded brittle.

He merely stared at her as though he hadn't understood a word she had spoken.

She pivoted and marched into the bedchamber. If the man wanted to exhibit himself, there was little she could do to prevent it. Let him roast in the sun. She smiled, contemplating the complications that would arise from exposing certain parts of his anatomy to the sun. Yes, it would certainly serve him well if—

Lancaster grabbed her arm and spun her around to face him. "Where is this place?"

A chill scampered down her back at the icy fury in his eyes. "What are you talking about?"

"Tell me, wench." He leaned toward her, so close the tip of his nose nearly touched hers. The damp heat of his breath brushed her lips as he spoke. "Where is this place?"

"I don't know what your game is, but I'm not at all interested in playing." She tried to twist free of his grasp. He squeezed harder, his long fingers biting into her flesh beneath the dark blue cotton of her gown. Pain splintered along her nerves. "You're hurting me."

He released her arm as though it were a hot coal, but he remained close, his legs pressed against the skirt of her gown. She kept her gaze fixed on his face, determined not to notice his nudity. Yet she could not block out the sight of those wide bare shoulders any more than she could completely shut out the dark expanse of his chest. "If you think parading about without wearing a stitch of clothing and behaving like a barbarian will change my mind about your character, you have chosen the wrong strategy."

He frowned, twin furrows digging into the skin between his black brows. "You are speaking in circles. As for not wearing a stitch, where did you put my clothes?"

"Where did I put your clothes?" The man was acting like a Bedlamite. She noticed a dressing gown tossed over the back of a chair near the bed. She pushed past the scoundrel, snatched the black silk robe, and tossed it at him. "If you insist on conducting a conversation, I insist you dress. I find this most offensive."

Lancaster stared at the dressing gown a moment before he shrugged into it. As he tied the sash he glared at her.

"I have a lump on the back of my head where someone hit me."

Jane stared at him. Why was he pretending not to remember the accident? "You hit your head in a fall yesterday. And why on earth are you using that peculiar accent?"

He frowned, as though he couldn't decipher her words. "Someone brought me here. Name my enemy."

"I have no idea what nonsense you are talking about. As far as naming your enemy, I suspect there are many."

" 'Twas my uncle; he did this to me. Did he not?"

"Pembury? I would have to agree the man is not very trustworthy. What is it exactly that you imagine he did to you?"

"Pembury? It would seem I will have no answers from you." He turned away from her and marched across the room, headed for the door she had left open upon entering the chamber. "You will not hold me here with your English tricks."

"English tricks?" Jane hesitated a moment before following him out of the room. She realized she should not allow him to pull her into this game, but her curiosity already had the better of her.

She caught up with him near the top of the stairs. He had stopped to examine a suit of armor that stood against one of the paneled walls. "Do you mind telling me precisely what game you are—"

Metal clanged against metal as he pried the sword from the steel glove of the display. He turned to face her, holding the sword, the tip pointed toward the plastered ceiling. "Your master was a fool to leave such weapons unguarded."

"My master? What in the world are you talking about?"

He kissed the blade, then swept it out to his side. "Such innocence. I could almost believe you are truly my angel."

"Angel?" She stared at him. "I realize this must be some—"

Without warning he grabbed her, cinching one powerful arm around her waist. The breath jolted from her lungs as he hauled her up against his chest, until her feet left the floor. In the next heartbeat he kissed her, clamping his lips over hers. The kiss ended as quickly as it had begun. She hardly had time to register a protest before he released her. She staggered back a step and bumped into the wall. She stayed there, thankful for the support of solid oak, because her knees were far from steady.

He swept her a bow, wide and courtly. "Until we meet again, my beautiful deceiver."

Jane just stared, too stunned by the heat coiling through her veins to do anything more. Lancaster didn't seem to notice or care that he had set her on her ear with that one brazen kiss, for which she was very grateful. If he had noticed, she suspected he would close in for the kill.

She watched him as he dashed down the stairs, the black silk of his dressing gown rippling around his long bare legs, his sword capturing the light spilling from the windows in the domed ceiling high above the staircase. This could not be happening, she assured herself. She was not succumbing to the blackguard's masculine wiles. Yet the heat rushing through her veins mocked her every attempt to deny the attraction. It was the surprise of it all, she assured herself. His ploy had taken her unaware. She most certainly was not attracted to that conceited, arrogant blackguard.

He was up to something. He must be up to something. The Marquess of Lancaster did nothing without purpose. This was all part of a strategy. Still, what in the world could he be doing by acting as though he had lost his senses?

"Stand aside!"

Lancaster's dark bellow rose like thunder from below.

She pulled away from the wall and looked over the gilt railing of the gallery. Lancaster stood at the base of the double staircase, sword raised, ready for battle. Pierson and Hedley stood a few feet away, turned to stone by their master's words.

"Not a move," Lancaster said, backing away from the servants.

He certainly didn't intend to leave the house dressed that way, Jane thought. He might be a scoundrel, but his attire was always impeccable. Men young and old tried desperately to copy his style. No, Dominic Stanbridge would never set foot outside his house dressed in . . . The thud of the front door closing echoed through the hall.

What on earth was he doing? Jane lifted her skirts and rushed down the stairs. She found Hedley and Pierson near the foot of the stairs, staring across the wide expanse of the entry hall toward the double front doors.

"I told you we shouldn't try to awaken him before he was ready," Hedley said.

"He isn't wearing any . . . shoes." The valet stared at the front door, as though in shock. "If anyone notices, I shall be ruined. You will stop him. Won't you, my lady?"

Jane didn't take time to respond. She hurried across the polished white marble entrance hall and pulled open the door. She didn't know precisely what game her husband was playing. She did know she had no intention of being humiliated by his actions. Strolling about London without shoes was bound to attract notice. Not to mention the fact that he was half-naked.

Lancaster House was set back from Park Lane. A wide expanse of lawn rolled from a wrought-iron fence upward to the house. Jane started down the stairs just as Lancaster strode through the gate leading to the sidewalk, holding his sword at the ready. He was actually going out into public in his dressing gown. Carrying a sword. A sword? She didn't want to contemplate the reasons a man in a dressing gown might want a sword.

Thank goodness the street was quiet at this hour. In a few hours from now the fashionable horde would begin to descend upon the park. If fortune smiled upon her she might reach him and drag him back to the house before anyone saw him.

Crouched stone lions atop brick pillars flanked the wrought-iron gate leading to the front walk of the house. The gate swung on well-oiled hinges. Everything at Lancaster House was always as it should be. Except perhaps the master, who had taken a sudden urge to stroll about London in his dressing gown. As she hurried past the lions, a high-pitched scream ripped through the warm air.

Jane froze on the sidewalk. Lancaster stood a few yards away, sword at his side, staring at a pair of dragons who stood a few feet away from him. Jane's chest tightened when she recognized Harriet Gladthorne and Sylvia Wadswyck, two of the ton's most notable hostesses. In her first Season she had dubbed them "the dragons" for their ability to breathe fire upon any debutante who did not meet their stringent code of decorum.

Harriet held a bony hand before her eyes, her horrified stance spoiled by the fact that she was peeking at Lancaster from between her splayed fingers. Sylvia, on the other hand, was staring openly, the way the plump matron might stare at a piece of chocolate cake. At least he wasn't brandishing the sword at them, Jane thought.

Lancaster turned away from both women as a curricle drawn by a pair of matched grays drove past him. He seemed as fascinated with the carriage as the man driving the conveyance was with seeing the elegant Marquess of Lancaster in his dressing gown, carrying a sword.

Wonderful.

Her first thought was to run back to the house and hide. But she could not hide from the fact that he was her husband. She had her own reputation to maintain. Jane walked toward Lancaster, ignoring the urge to run. She strolled along the sidewalk as if she hadn't noticed her husband standing on the sidewalk in his dressing gown carrying a three-foot-long sword. When she reached him, she took a deep breath and slipped her arm through his. If he pulled away from her, she would wrench the sword from his hand and hit him over the head with it. Yet he didn't pull away from her. Instead he just looked down at her, his expression somewhat dazed.

With a smile, Jane greeted both ladies as though she were not standing beside a half-naked man who happened to be carrying a lethal weapon. As she had hoped, years of strict social training prompted both women to reply with polite civility.

Jane squeezed Lancaster's arm, praying he wouldn't start spouting some nonsense. "Lovely morning, isn't it?"

Sylvia lowered her gaze to Lancaster's feet. She blinked as though the sight of those long bare feet was somehow more shocking than everything else. "Quite extraordinary."

Harriet lowered her hand to her neck. Her voice dripped with indignation as she spoke. "Lovely morning?"

"Yes, it is." Without another word, Jane turned and headed back toward the gate, applying subtle pressure to Lancaster's arm. Since nothing could possibly explain his appearance, she did not try. "Please don't fight me," she whispered.

Although she could feel the tension in the thick muscles beneath her hand, he didn't fight. Instead he came as docilely as a child who had been found wandering the woods.

"The chariot," Lancaster whispered as they reached the gate. "I have never seen anything such as it."

"The chariot?"

"Aye. What manner of chariot was that?"

Jane didn't pause to respond to his odd comment. She had no intention of conducting a heated discussion in the street. As they passed through the gate, she saw Hedley and Pierson standing on the landing outside the front doors. When they saw their master, they both turned and bumped into each other in their haste to retreat inside the house. They were nowhere to be seen when Jane entered the house, which suited her. She and His Lordship had a great deal to discuss. In private.

Lancaster was not in the same rush as she was. In fact he seemed to be moving in a daze. He paused by a table in the hall, his gaze fixed on a copy of the *Times* lying folded beside a stack of correspondence. He lifted the paper and stared at it, an odd look on his face. "The printing. 'Tis wondrous strange." He ran his fingertip over the paper, his gaze fixed on the front page. "Why is this date printed here?"

"As I recall, the date is generally printed on the paper."

He gazed at her, a puzzled look in his eyes. "Why this date?"

"What an odd question. But then, why wouldn't your questions be odd, considering your behavior." She tugged on his arm. He stood rooted to the floor, staring at the paper. "Do come along."

He obeyed, allowing the paper to tumble from his fingers. It fell with a thud against the marble floor as he followed her. He looked around the grand entrance hall, staring at the marble-lined double staircase curving gracefully to the gallery as if he had never seen it before. He ran his fingers over a gilt-trimmed balustrade. " 'Tis strange."

"Not nearly as strange as your behavior." She tugged on his arm and he followed, his gaze darting from the marble statue of a mother cradling a babe on the landing to the paintings hanging on the wall above it, the largest depicting Wellington's victory at Waterloo. He looked as though he were seeing everything for the first time, and the sights amazed him.

She ushered him back to his chamber, closed the door, and glared at him. "What do you mean by parading about the streets of London in your dressing gown?"

He looked stunned, as though she had slapped him hard across the cheek. "The streets of London?"

"It's a wonder you did not give the dragons apoplexy, coming at them dressed like that, and carrying a sword. A sword, for heaven's sake."

"Dragons?"

"Harriet Gladthorne and Sylvia Wadswyck. I don't want to imagine what stories they shall spread about this." She glanced at the sword he still clutched at his side. "What are you doing running about with that thing? You could trip and kill yourself, for heaven's sake."

"Trip over a sword? What think you? I am not a stripling lad, woman."

"You make it sound as though it is an everyday occurrence to go strolling about with a five-hundred-year-old sword in your hand."

"Five hundred years?" He looked uneasy suddenly. "Why are you dressed in such a strange manner?"

Jane glanced down at her blue cotton gown. There was nothing at all strange about the garment, except that it was three years old. Given her family's situation, it was far more practical to refurbish her gowns rather than buy new ones each year. "I suppose my clothes do not suit your sense of fashion."

"Nothing here is as it should be." He ran his hand over the back of his head. "Something is amiss."

"Yes, something is very wrong." She folded her hands at her waist and fixed him with a steady glare. "If this is some kind of ploy to gain my sympathy, I must tell you I do not like it. Not at all."

He ignored her, his gaze fixed on a photograph in a rosewood frame sitting on a table near the hearth. He lifted the frame, stared at the photograph a long moment, then showed it to her. It was a photograph of him, as were most photographs in the house. In this one he knelt beside a deer he had killed, while holding up the antlers in one hand. "What sorcery is this?"

He really was acting very strangely. "Do you mean the photograph?"

"This image. Everything here. I would try to deny all that has been set before me. Yet I cannot." Lancaster looked at her, a wild look in his eyes. "What year is this?"

She blinked. "The year?"

"Aye, what year is this?"

"The same year as it was yesterday. 1889."

" 'Twas the year printed on that odd manuscript." A muscle bunched in his cheek at the clenching of his jaw. "Why did you bring me here?"

"You really must stop playing this game, if it is a game. Because I warn you, if this is a game, you shall manage only to make me dislike you more than I do now, Lancaster."

"Who is this Lancaster?"

Just how far did he plan to take this little farce? "You are Dominic Stanbridge, the Marquess of Lancaster. And at the moment you are playing a vile game with me. At least I believe you are. With your propensity for playing games it is difficult to know when you are telling the truth."

"You are speaking in circles again." He turned toward the balcony, then to the door leading to the hall, as if he were looking for a means to escape. Finally he faced her, a frown marring his features. "I do not know your reasons for abducting this man you speak of, but you have caught the wrong man in your snare. I am not this Dominic Stanbridge."

"You aren't Dominic Stanbridge?"

"No. I am Colin MacKenzie, third Earl of Kintair." He moved toward her, his blue eyes narrowed, a look of fury chiseled into his features. "Send me back, witch."

The back of her neck prickled as she held his furious

glare. "I do not appreciate being called a witch."

He lifted the sword. Sunlight glinted red-gold upon the blade. "Send me back to my family."

If this wasn't a game, then he was very ill. And if he was as ill as he appeared, he could very well slice her head off with that blade. *Oh, for heaven's sake.* It had to be one of his tactics. "It's an interesting ploy; I will give you that. Accusing me of witchcraft. Pretending to be a different man. But it isn't going to work. I am not as gullible as you imagine."

"Pretending to be a different man? I am not pretending anything."

Jane searched his eyes, looking for the lies that must lurk behind these words. Sincerity, anger, and a trace of fear—she saw all of these in the blue depths, but not a flicker of deceit. Could he possibly lie with such sincerity? With any other man she would believe him, attribute his eccentric behavior to the blow he'd received. But this was Dominic Stanbridge, which gave her enough reason to doubt his sincerity. "I have never known anyone who could lie with such sincerity. It certainly reveals a great deal about your character."

He grabbed her arm when she turned to leave and forced her to face him. He leaned toward her, so close the damp heat of his breath hit her face in soft puffs as he spoke. "I am Colin MacKenzie. When last I took breath at Kintair, it was the year of our Lord, fifteen hundred and sixty-two. You brought me to this place and time. And you must send me back, witch."

It was an inventive tale; that she had to admit. "I am certainly not a witch. If I were, I would have turned you into the toad you are a long time ago."

Chapter Five

In blissful dream, in silent night,
There came to me, with magic might,
With magic might, my own sweet
　　love. . . .

　　　　　　　　—Heinrich Heine

"A toad?" Colin recoiled at the thought. Yet even though he felt dizzy and ill, he managed to stand steady and face the witch who held his future in her delicate hands. "I will not buckle beneath your threats, witch."

"And I will not believe your lies, Lancaster."

"Who is this man Lancaster? Why do you keep addressing me by his name?"

"Perhaps because it is your name."

"If you know this man, you must know I am not he."

"I am not certain what you are trying to imply, but I am certain of your identity. I could scarcely forget the man who coerced me into this travesty of a marriage."

"Marriage? You are married to this man Lancaster?"

She smiled, an icy look in her eyes. "Do you gain some twisted satisfaction by hearing me say it?"

"Married." She was married to another. It should not matter. Yet the knowledge pierced him like a dirk. It was the spell, he assured himself. The magic that had bound him to her was the cause of all of his troubles. And she was at the core of his trouble. "You are married to this man?"

"Yes. And a Scottish accent is not enough to alter your appearance. By the way, it is the strangest Scottish accent I have ever heard."

"Your speech is difficult to understand. 'Tis English. Yet 'tis different from any English I have ever heard before."

"That is an odd thing to say."

"If you know this man, then you must know I am not he," he repeated. "Why is it you cannot see I am not this man?"

Her eyes narrowed as she studied him, looking at him as though she would pierce his soul with her gaze. He held his ground, refusing to buckle beneath the silent threat of her power. If she intended to turn him into a toad, his last breath as a man would not be as a coward.

"Come with me," she said, taking his arm.

Blood swam before his eyes as he followed her, allowing her to usher him to the far side of the room. She gestured toward a large framed mirror above a long mahogany chest. He had never seen any mirror this size. He had never seen any that would reflect an image so clearly. Yet the image staring back at him was not his own.

"Recognize the man in the mirror?" she asked. "You usually like to look at him."

He touched the surface, feeling the smooth texture of glass beneath his fingers. "What have you done to me?"

"Now what are you accusing me of doing?"

He stared at the image looking back at him. The eyes were the same, as was the color of the hair. The cast of

the features was similar. But there were differences. His
beard was gone. His hair shorn. The scar above his right
eye had vanished. And there were other subtle changes,
like lines at the corners of his mouth and eyes. He looked
older than his four and twenty years. "This is not my
reflection."

She touched his arm, a soft brush of her fingers against
the silk sleeve. Although he could scarcely feel the pressure of her hand, her warmth seeped through the fabric
and bathed his skin. "I swear, if you are playing a game
with me, I shall make you regret the day you were born."

Colin's heart thumped against the wall of his chest. "If
you turn me into a toad, I shall curse you with my last
breath."

"A toad?" She lifted her brows, a curious expression
entering her eyes. "All right, let's say you are suffering
some confusion due to that bump on the head. In which
case, you should lie down. If you are serious about all
of this, then you need a great deal of rest. And perhaps
a surgeon or a physician, or—"

"This is not my face. Not my body. When I look in
this mirror I see a stranger. Yet inside I know who I am."
He turned and looked down into her face, fighting against
the panic rising like a tide inside him. "Why have you
done this thing? Why have you placed my soul in this
body?"

"Placed your soul . . ." She stared at him a moment, a
puzzled look on her face. "You cannot truly expect me
to believe this."

"Why have you done this to me?"

"I didn't do anything to you. I am not a witch. The
simple fact that you are still walking around on two legs
rather than hopping about lurching after flies is a testa-
ment to that fact."

"What kind of man is this Lancaster? If this man is
truly your husband, then how can you imagine he would

lie to you in this way? How can it be that you doubt his words?"

She folded her hands at her waist, her chin tipping at a defiant angle as she glared at him. "Lord Lancaster is a scoundrel."

"A scoundrel? And by this you mean he is some type of ruffian?"

"He is indeed a ruffian. A blackguard who will say or do anything to get what he wants."

Scoundrel. Blackguard. Although the words were strange to him, he could gather their meaning from her. "I see yours was not a love match."

She lifted her brows. "Impossible. Since you do not believe in love."

"Perhaps this Lancaster does not. But I am not this man." He gripped her arm. "The spell you meant to cast against him . . . whatever your mischief might have been, your magic brought me here."

"I did not cast a spell. If I had I would have sent you to the far side of the moon."

She stepped away from him, breaking the physical connection. Yet distance could not sever the invisible tether that connected him to this woman. He felt it as keenly as the sash cinched about his waist. From the first moment she had appeared in his dreams the night before, he had wanted her in a way he had never wanted another woman. He wanted to hold her, to protect her, to chase away the sadness in her eyes. The need had hit him with the force of a charging horse. Now he realized it was sorcery at work. Her spell had wrapped around him, drawing him to her, binding one to the other. "I would have the name of the witch who has played her mischief with me."

"I am not a witch."

"What is your name?"

She pursed her lips, and for a moment he wondered if she would reply. "It is Jane. And I must say it's very convenient that you have suddenly misplaced your memory. It wouldn't have anything to do with putting me off guard, would it?"

"I know not the reasons for your distrust of this man you have married. And I do not know why you have brought me here in his place, but I do know I am not Lancaster. I am Colin MacKenzie, Earl of Kintair, chief of the MacKenzies. And none of your wicked sorcery will alter what I know is truth."

"Do you actually expect me to believe you awakened this morning an entirely different man?"

" 'Tis sorcery. You appeared in my dream and next I awakened to find you leaning over me." Heat pumped slowly into his veins at the memory of holding this woman in his arms. She was so close he could catch the scent of her—not a heavy perfume as was common in the women he knew, but a light, lemony scent that made him want to press his lips against her neck and breathe her fragrance deep into his lungs. The power of the attraction stunned him. What manner of spell had she cast upon him? "I thought I was dreaming still. Yet dreams have never felt so real."

And not even in dreams had it ever felt so right to hold a woman. It felt as if she were made for him alone. It must be sorcery, the magic that still gripped him, a spell that made him want to sweep this woman into his arms and make love to her until he took his last breath. It must be enchantment.

She backed away from him, her eyes wide, filled with suspicion. "You expect me to believe you are a Scottish earl, transported here by witchcraft. Your soul was just plucked out of your body and dropped into the body of Dominic Stanbridge. And what would be the reason for your sudden appearance?"

"I know not what sorcery brought me here. And I cannot say the reasons behind it. But I know I cannot stay." He closed his hands into fists at his sides when he thought of all that remained unfinished in his life. "There is great trouble brewing in my family. My uncle means to march against the MacDonnells. And if that happens the queen will intervene. All will be lost. I have to stop my uncle. I must return to my home."

"All right." She crossed her arms at her waist. "I assure you, I will not try to prevent you. If you must return to 1562, then do so."

"You must hold the key to sending me back."

She released her breath in a long sigh. "I hold no key to anything about you."

"You have made a grave mistake in bringing me here. I will not bend to your sorcery, no matter what purpose you have. My will is stronger than you imagine. You might as well send me back now, and save yourself the torment of battling wills with me."

She studied him a moment in that soul-searching way she had of looking straight through him. "I'm going to send for a surgeon. He will no doubt prod and poke and make you quite uncomfortable. So if you are just playing a game with me, I suggest you admit it now."

"I am not ill. I am not playing a game. And I have not succumbed to your sorcery. I know who I am."

"Fine. We'll see what a surgeon has to say about this."

"Your surgeon will see only what is before him. He will know not what to do to send me back to my home. Only the witch who brought me here can help me." He leaned toward her, tempting fate. If she intended to turn him into a toad, she would have done it by now. "Last night I saw you in a dream, standing in the moonlight, wearing a gown as black as night. What were you wishing for, beautiful enchantress? A man to take the place of the one you married? One you might find more to your liking?"

"In your dream?" A wary look entered her eyes. She stared at him as though she expected him to draw a dagger any moment. "What did you hear last night, Lancaster? How long did you stand in the shadows of your balcony and spy on me?"

"I am not Lancaster. If you meant to cast a spell upon this man, your magic has gone awry. You have captured the wrong man in your web."

She shook her head. "I am having a very difficult time believing you are actually ill. Not when I know you were spying on me last night."

"Last night, in my bed, a woman's voice whispered, ' 'Tis time to meet your destiny.' 'Twas then I saw your face." He held her gaze in spite of the fury raging there, fighting to keep his own anger under close rein. "You brought me here. And now you must send me back."

She lifted her brows. "I suppose I am to believe you are the man destiny meant for me. Is that it?"

"It cannot be."

"No. It cannot. The man of my dreams does not go running about brandishing a sword and accusing me of witchcraft."

He rubbed the back of his neck, the muscles tight beneath his fingers. "I will accept that you have reasons for wanting to rid yourself of the man you married. But I cannot stay and take his place. I must return to my family. 'Tis my duty to protect them."

She clasped her hands at her waist as if she needed to contain the emotion raging inside of her. Yet her fury escaped, revealing itself in the color rising high in her cheeks and the sparks of fire in her eyes. He had thought her lovely upon first sight of her. Now he realized he had underestimated her charm. He could not shake the feeling that she was the most desirable woman he had ever seen. It must be magic.

"I shall wait to see what the surgeon says." Her voice trembled with barely contained anger. "Perhaps he can tell me whether you are a tremendously clever liar or a madman."

He held her gaze, unflinching beneath the heat of her

fury. His own anger was roused by the insult. "My word is my bond, Lady Jane. A man of honor would never lie to you. And I would die before I lost my honor."

She backed away from him, as though she were afraid to turn her back to him. "You are Dominic Stanbridge, Marquess of Lancaster. And you would do anything to put me at a disadvantage."

He stalked her. She took a step back, then froze, lifting her chin at a defiant angle. He leaned toward her until his nose nearly touched hers. "I am Colin MacKenzie, Earl of Kintair. And I will have the truth. Never doubt it."

"When the surgeon arrives, you can tell him all about your suspicions of witchcraft and switched souls. I am certain he will find it amusing."

He curled his hands into tight balls at his sides, resisting the urge to grab her slender shoulders and shake her until all the pins fell from her hair. An image flickered in his mind: this woman with her hair unbound, all that glorious, shining mass tumbling over pale skin. Against his will, heat flooded his loins.

Without conscious thought he touched her, brushed the backs of his fingers over her cheek. Her skin felt like satin in sunlight, so smooth and warm. He could not prevent the thoughts flooding his mind—of all those places hidden beneath the cloth of her gown. The soft swells of her breasts, her belly, her thighs. His chest tightened with a need he could not crush.

Her expression altered, anger dissolving into surprise. Her lips parted on a startled sigh, drawing his gaze and his thoughts. He knew the softness of those lips, the taste of her sigh. Yet one taste was not enough. The fresh lemony scent of her swirled through his senses. He felt drawn to her, as though bound by silken threads, growing tight and tighter, drawing him closer and closer.

He lowered his head until each quick pant of her breath brushed his lips. He wanted her with a hunger that sank like a hawk's talons into his belly. He wanted to strip away all of the layers keeping him from the warm satin of her skin, to lay her back upon that big soft bed, to wrap himself in her fire. He wondered when lust had ever gripped him in such a powerful fist. Yet the answer rang like a bell inside of him—never. Never in his life had he wanted with such an intensity that he felt he might splinter into pieces if he did not have her.

He pulled his hand away from her cheek, fighting the sorcery gripping his vitals. It took every ounce of will-power to step away from her. He held her gaze, his breath tangled into a tight knot in his chest. She was staring at him as though he were the first man she had ever seen, and the sight filled her with awe and fear. Lord in heaven, how could she look at him with such innocence? Yet he knew. The truth had been revealed to him in a dream. He had seen her standing in her witch's robes, casting her spell beneath a full moon. Such sincerity could be summoned only by a woman of great skill and cunning.

"I will not be fooled by your sorcery," he said, his voice harsh.

She flinched as though he had slapped her. "And I will not be fooled by a scoundrel's tricks."

"There is something else you should know, my beautiful enchantress."

"What?"

"Any woman who plays foul tricks such as yours deserves as good as she gives." He smiled, making that smile as threatening as he could manage with his blood still burning. "I will fight you with every means available to me. Recant your spell now and save yourself a war."

"I didn't choose to fight this war, Lancaster. But I have no intention of losing it. Never imagine I do not know precisely who and what you are." She pivoted and marched toward the door. "We shall see what the surgeon says of your little game."

Colin watched her march from the room, fighting the

urge to run after her. She must hold the key to his coming here. Yet he knew trying to pry it from her now would prove futile. What if she never recanted her spell? What if he could not break through her defenses? The weight of those doubts pressed against his chest until he could scarcely draw a breath.

The room grew warm. Blood swam before his eyes as his skin turned damp and cold. He sank to the edge of the bed and lowered his head. Slowly he forced air past his tight throat, steeling his body against the sickness. Finally the dizziness passed. All that remained was a sour taste on the back of his tongue—and a horrible realization that he might be lost forever. His family, every friend he ever knew, they were all gone. What had happened to his family? What had they suffered because he had not been there to protect them?

He had to find a way back to his family. He could not abandon them, not with the threat of a clan war. He had to prevent it. And he would find his way home. He would have the truth from the witch called Jane, no matter what he had to do to get it.

What was her plan? It was tied together with her husband. He was certain of it. He rubbed his aching temples. Lady Jane had cast this spell upon him. It was magic; of that he was certain. For each time he gazed upon her, she was more beautiful to him than the last. Each time she was near, he wanted more and more to hold her in his arms. She had bewitched him.

He did not doubt her power. He had lived his entire life in the Highlands, where people knew of fairies and sorcery and magic. The reason was not clear, yet he knew she had trapped him in her enchanted web.

She might have the power of magic, but he would not succumb to her enchantment. No matter what her machinations, he would find a way back home. There was too much at stake to remain here. He must find a way to reveal her secrets, discover the reasons she had brought him here. And he must resist the spell that had taken hold of him. He could not allow the woman to own his heart. No matter what he must face, no matter what sorcery she employed to bind him to her, he would resist her and the lust she had ignited within him. The beautiful enchantress would soon learn she had met her match.

Jane closed the door to Lancaster's chamber and leaned back against the solid oak. Her heart was pounding as though she had just run to Kensington and back. She had known he would devise a strategy against her, but this was far beyond anything she had imagined. Yet even as she contemplated the absurdity of his tactic, deep inside she acknowledged the cunning beneath this ploy. He knew his opponent well enough to calculate the doubts she could not completely suppress.

Was it possible? Had that blow to his head addled his wits? If it had, why had it taken a day for the illness to appear? With anyone else of her acquaintance, she would not hesitate to believe him. But this was the most treacherous soul she had ever had the misfortune to know.

If the dragons were true to form, most of London would soon think of Lancaster as an eccentric. Would Lancaster actually choose a strategy that made him appear to be insane? Somehow she could not imagine Lancaster allowing himself to be thought of as anything but impeccable. She could not imagine he would present himself as a Bedlamite in this outrageous manner, unless he was truly ill. He had far too much pride. Still, this was Lancaster, a clever scoundrel who knew no bounds when it came to getting what he wanted. She only hoped the surgeon could provide some answers.

If he was ill, then as his wife it was her duty to tend to him. She glanced at the door to Lancaster's bedchamber, wondering if she should stay with him until the surgeon arrived. An unexpected sensation quivered through her when she thought of seeing Lancaster again. Heat slithered through her veins, radiating in all directions until even her skin tingled.

It could not possibly be excitement, she assured herself. She did not have any tender feelings for Lancaster; therefore the sensations coursing through her at the mere thought of the man must be something altogether different. And the sensations that had ripped through her when he had held her? She crossed her arms at her waist.

He had taken her by surprise, that was all. He had altered his tactics. Somehow he had managed to infuse that kiss with gentleness and passion, and in the process had managed to tip her upside down. It was an aberration, certainly not a sign that she was in danger of succumbing to the scoundrel. There was nothing at all to fear by entering his room. She was made of stronger stuff than he suspected. Still, she had to send someone for a surgeon. She backed away from his door, grateful for a reason to avoid another confrontation with the scoundrel. She needed time to fortify her defenses—at least a decade or so. Still, she had never in her life turned her back on responsibility. She would not do it now.

Less than an hour later, Jane stood in the hall outside of Lancaster's chamber, debating the wisdom of once more bearding the lion in his den. By all rights, she should let the scoundrel starve to death. Yet her conscience would not allow it. She glanced down at the heavily laden tea cart. Lancaster hadn't eaten since the day before. If he was ill—and she was willing to admit there was a small possibility he was ill—perhaps his head would be clearer if he had a full belly. She knocked on his door.

No answer came from within. She pulled open the door and peered inside. He was lying upon his bed, apparently sleeping. She crossed the room, pushing the tea cart slowly over the thick carpet. Since he was asleep, she would leave the cart and escape the room before he awakened. When she drew near the bed, he opened his eyes and looked at her.

His gaze slid from the hair twisted on top of her head to the shoes peeking out from beneath her gown. It was not the leering gaze of a libertine, but a frank, open exploration, as though he wanted to know every detail of her face and figure, as though simply gazing upon her pleased him in some profound way.

In that instant, she felt something she had never truly felt before: she felt beautiful. The look lasted only an instant before his expression hardened. She could almost see him lift a shield between them, a man prepared to do battle. She only wished she didn't feel as though she were stepping into a cage with a hungry lion.

Chapter Six

Who ever lov'd that lov'd not at first sight?
—Christopher Marlowe

Lancaster sat up and gripped the edge of the bed. He had discarded his dressing gown in favor of a shirt and breeches. Yet his choice of garments would have sent Pierson into a fit of apoplexy. The white silk of his dress shirt fell over close-fitting, buff-colored riding breeches. Apparently he had not found any studs, since the shirt gaped open down the length of his chest. His legs were bare below the knee-length breeches. "Interesting choice of clothing."

He glanced down at his shirt. "For a wealthy English lord, the clothes of this man Lancaster are very plain."

"I suppose your choice is meant to show me how little you know of how men dress in this century."

"I know not the fashion of this time." He pinned her with a steady gaze. "As well you know."

She didn't know what to believe with this man. "I

thought you might feel better if you ate something," she said, wheeling the tea cart toward him.

He eyed her warily, as though he was debating the wisdom of consuming anything she brought him. "Has not this Lancaster any servants?"

She paused beside him. "Strange thing about servants: once they know the master of the house is running about with a sword and an ugly temper, they tend to shy away from him. Since I cannot be certain if you are playing a game or if you are truly ill, I thought it best if I was the one who dealt with you."

He held her gaze, a glint of steel in his blue eyes. " 'Twould seem you are not so frightened of me?"

Luckily he could not see how dreadfully her legs were trembling. She grabbed a napkin and tossed it at him. "I am hoping you will feel more yourself once you have eaten something."

"Aye. I am fair to famished, I am." He lowered his gaze and surveyed the dishes crowded on the cart. "Still, I wonder what you may have put in this food."

"What I may have . . ." She twisted a piece of roast beef from the stack Cook had placed on a plate and popped the morsel into her mouth. "There. You see. No poison. No magic potions. Just slices of roast beef, cheddar cheese, hot bread, butter, and tea. If you don't want it, I will take it back."

He gripped the edge of the cart when she started to wheel it away. "I think I will take my chances."

"Fine."

After a cautious bite of beef and cheese, he seemed satisfied with the flavor of the food. She sat on a chair near the bed while Lancaster devoured everything she had brought, including an entire pot of tea, which—after downing the first cup—he declared was a most delicious drink. And through the entire meal, she noticed something peculiar about him.

When he was finished he rubbed the napkin between

his hands and grinned at her. "You are looking upon me as though you have discovered a brownie in the woods."

Jane tapped her fingers on the arm of her chair, still not completely certain he was not attempting to make a complete fool of her. "You didn't use your fork."

He glanced down at the tea cart. "And what would you be speaking of?"

She stood and lifted the silver fork from beside his plate. "This is a fork. We use it to eat."

He looked up at her, his black brows tugging into a frown. "And why would I be using such a thing as that, when a knife and spoon do the job?"

She studied him, hoping to find some break in his facade. "It would seem you have a particular interest in medieval and Renaissance studies. Did it start when you were at Cambridge?"

He leaned forward, resting his forearms on his thighs. "I have never been to Cambridge."

"Aha! That's true; you haven't been to Cambridge. You attended Oxford."

He tilted his head and regarded her with the cool appraisal of a soldier eyeing an opponent. "And what is it you are about, my beautiful witch? What game are you playing with me now?"

"I think it is you who are playing the game, my Lord Scoundrel. There is something just a little too perfect about your performance. Not one little slip. If you were truly ill, I should imagine you would make mistakes, forget yourself and use a fork perhaps."

"I have told you before, I am not ill." He stood and closed the distance between them, standing so close she could feel the brush of his leg upon her skirt. "I am thinking 'twould be hard to explain if your husband suddenly vanished. Perhaps 'tis the reason you are careful with your magic. The reason 'tis important I believe I am Lancaster."

"Of course one must be careful about whom one turns

into toads these days. I certainly would not wish to end
up burned at the stake, or hanged, or drowned. Hummm,
I can never remember what the punishment is for witchcraft nowadays." She held his steady look, hoping he
would not see the way his nearness had set her pulse
racing. "The truth is, it is important for you to believe
you are Lancaster because you *are* Lancaster."

"Why is it you brought me here? What purpose do you
have in mind for me?"

"Purpose? And I thought your main purpose in life was
to make mine miserable."

"I wonder why it is you wish me to believe I am ill.
Is it part of your plan? Do you think to make me believe
I am your husband, ill in my mind? Is that what you
want?"

She tried not to acknowledge the excitement sizzling
through her at his nearness. Yet it was there all the same,
swirling and coiling, threatening to melt her brain and
make a complete fool of her. Her voice sounded far too
breathy to her own ears when she replied. "I want the
truth from you."

A muscle in his cheek flickered with the clenching of
his jaw. "I wish to heaven the truth was all I wanted from
you."

Jane stared into his eyes, stunned by the hunger burning there. She was not a woman accustomed to gallantry
or compliments or flattery. She had never in her life inspired a man to poetry. Yet the look in his eyes went far
beyond poetry. That look whispered of a longing so intense it touched the soul. Fires burned deep in this man.
Hidden depths she had never even expected existed
within the icy hulk of Lancaster.

"Recant your spell, witch. You will not win this
game."

She thought of all the women he had trodden under
his feet. Could any woman melt the ice that surrounded
his heart? Until this moment she had never even imag-

ined the possibility. She had no doubt he disliked women, even though he was never without a mistress. He used women. She could not be certain if any woman could cure Lancaster of his misogyny. However, she was certain of one thing: she was not the woman to tame Dominic Stanbridge. "I do not play games, Lancaster. That is your specialty."

His eyes narrowed. "I am not your Lancaster. You have trapped a much more dangerous beast than your Englishman."

Before he had dragged her into this horrible tangle, she might have cowered under his ferocious look. Yet she did not have the luxury of cowardice. She was fighting for her life. "I am not frightened by your—" He wrapped his hands around her upper arms and dragged her against him, until her toes brushed the floor and her breasts collided with his chest. Sensation splintered through her, white-hot sparks that darted in all directions. She stared up into his furious eyes. Even on her toes she barely reached his chin.

In the back of her mind, in a place panic had not reached, she realized this was a tactic meant to demonstrate his power. He intended to show her precisely how easily he could toss her out one of the windows. Still, he did not look like a man who intended to toss her to her death. No, he looked like a man who intended to toss her to the bed. "Don't you dare."

He lifted one black brow. "A challenge?"

"Put me—"

He clamped his mouth over hers, so hard he forced her head back. For an instant she thought he must have killed her, for she could not feel the beating of her own heart. The horrible stunned sensation lasted only an instant before her heart beat once more, pounding so hard her chest ached.

He slanted his mouth over hers in a brazen kiss designed to bring her to her knees. She pushed against his shoulders, anger sluicing through her. If he thought he could defeat her with a kiss, he was mistaken. He was her enemy. No matter what disguise he might don, she would not be deceived into surrender.

He had kissed her once before in an attempt to intimidate her. Yet through her anger she recognized a difference in this kiss, a difference in this man. Where icy intellect had dwelled before, now fire and passion burned. And her response reflected that change. Before fear and panic had collided inside her; now desire surged, crackling through her like a streak of lightning slicing the midnight sky.

A growl emanated from low in his chest, a deep rumble that vibrated through her, whispering to a secret place deep within her. He shifted her in his grasp, sliding one powerful arm around her, slowly lowering her until she stood once more before him. Yet he did not release her. Instead he opened his lips over hers, all the fury in his kiss melting beneath something far more heated, something her innocence could not prevent her from recognizing as the pure heat of desire.

He kissed her as though he had been waiting all his life for this kiss. She opened her hands upon his broad shoulders, the heat of his skin searing her through the silk of his shirt. He was her enemy. She could not surrender to this kiss. Yet her body responded as though she were a rare instrument and he the only man in the world who could coax her music to flow. She tasted the hunger in his kiss, recognized the same echoing emptiness that dwelled deep within her.

She twisted in his grasp, turning her face from his, breaking the kiss. She stumbled back and bumped into the side of a chair. He took a step toward her, then froze as if he had bumped into an unseen barrier. She pressed her hand to her throat. She had no idea how long they stood facing each other, short, choppy breaths filling the silence, like a thousand questions seeking a single answer.

"Recant your spell," he said, his voice husky and lower than usual.

It took a moment to corral enough breath to respond. "I am not a witch."

She started at a soft knock on the door. A moment later, Hedley's voice vibrated through the closed door, announcing the arrival of the surgeon. Jane backed away from her opponent, grateful for the diversion. She needed time to gather her defenses. "I think it is time we had some answers."

A muscle flickered in his cheek with the clenching of his jaw. "Aye. And I shall have answers, my beautiful enchantress. Never doubt it."

An hour later, Jane sat in the withdrawing room between her chamber and Lancaster's, waiting for the surgeon to complete his examination. She stared at the lace trim of the handkerchief she held, trying to understand her foolish attraction to Lancaster. She had not realized the depth of his ability to manipulate a woman until he had engaged her in this battle. Last night she had been repulsed by the man; his touch had left her chilled and frightened. This morning he had awakened a much more dangerous opponent, a man who could make her tingle with a single glance.

What were you wishing for, beautiful enchantress? A man to take the place of the one you married?

Lancaster must have heard her last night. Was it then he had decided to play this clever game? He must be playing a game with her. It was the only reasonable explanation.

Yet somehow she could not shake the feeling that he actually believed in his fairy tale of traveling across the ages. Still, in direct opposition to her belief in his illness was the simple fact that he knew too much about her.

How would he have known of her foolish romantic wishes if he was not playing a game with her? The more she thought about him, the more anxious she felt. She only hoped the surgeon could supply a few answers.

Time to meet your destiny.

It was a lovely thought, incredibly romantic to imagine she had somehow conjured up the soul of her one and only love. Lovers separated by more than three hundred years, destined to meet through a twist of magic. She shook her head. Even she was not romantic enough to believe in that fairy tale. It was much easier to accept the possibility that Dominic Stanbridge had lost his wits.

"Your Ladyship?"

Jane flinched at the sound of the surgeon's voice. She rose as he entered the room. The soft click of the door closing behind him cracked like a gunshot on her frayed nerves. "You are finished with your examination?"

"Yes." Anderson slipped off his glasses and pulled a white handkerchief from his coat pocket. "And I must say I never expected this."

Jane twisted her handkerchief between her fingers. "Did he tell you his name?"

"He said he was a Scottish earl by the name of Colin MacKenzie. A man who was born in 1538." Anderson rubbed the lenses of his glasses with his handkerchief as he spoke. "A Scottish earl. I should think His Lordship will be quite astonished to discover his choice of identities when he regains his memory."

Jane forced air into her constricted lungs. "He seemed sincere in his belief of being this man named MacKenzie?"

"Oh, yes." Anderson released his breath in a quick sigh. "He became quite agitated when I implied he was not this man."

"Do you imagine then that he is ill?"

Anderson looked at her. "He did mention to you that

he thought his soul had been transported here from 1562?"

Jane gathered her handkerchief into a tight ball in her hand. "Yes. He did mention it."

"And you are wondering if he is ill?"

Jane did not care to expose her reasons for doubting her husband. "I have never heard of someone awakening one morning certain he was another man."

"I have heard of cases of amnesia being brought about by head injuries." Anderson held his glasses up and looked through the lenses. "Still, it is true I have never seen anything quite like this. His Lordship actually believes he is a man from the sixteenth century. He answered questions about his home and family as though he had truly lived in 1562. It is remarkable."

Would Lancaster lie to a surgeon? Would he dare take the risk of appearing insane? She could not imagine even Dominic Stanbridge doing anything so reckless. "You say it is some type of memory loss. Yet he remembers things from yesterday, before he became ill."

Anderson shrugged. "His mind is obviously in turmoil. He may remember bits and pieces of things that happened in his past, but they may not come out quite right. He may look at them through the eyes of this man he imagines he is."

"How do you mean?"

"Well, he may try to twist them to suit his delusion of being this man MacKenzie. For example, he may say you look and sound just like his wife, meaning you look and sound like the wife he left behind in 1562."

"What can be done for him?"

Anderson slipped the wire frames over his ears. "As I told His Lordship, rest is the only remedy I can prescribe."

"But he will get better. He will remember who he is."

"Well, now, that is the question." Although he was several inches taller than Jane, his habit of stooping brought them eye-to-eye. Anderson looked at her, his brown eyes distorted by the thick lenses. "I cannot say for certain. He may recover in a matter of days, or weeks, or perhaps even years. Or he may never regain his memory."

Jane glanced at the door to Lancaster's chamber. "Do you mean to say he may always believe he is this Scottish earl?"

Anderson shrugged, his bony shoulders barely lifting the black cloth of his coat. "I cannot say for certain. Perhaps. And then perhaps he will be back to himself tomorrow."

Jane looked the surgeon straight in the eye. "I trust you shall keep this in the strictest confidence."

Anderson's brows lifted above the small lenses. "Of course, Your Ladyship."

She folded her hands at her waist. "Is there anything I can do to help him regain his memory?"

"I cannot say for certain."

"There seems to be a great deal you cannot say for certain."

"I am afraid that is true." Anderson rubbed his chin. "I once heard of a case of amnesia that was cured by a second blow to the head."

"Do you mean I should hit him over the head?"

"Perhaps."

The possibility had a certain appeal, Jane thought. More than once today she had wanted to strike him with a blunt object.

"Although you may simply cause more damage. And if you struck him too hard, you could actually end up in Newgate." Anderson glanced down at the floor, then met her eyes. "You might try reminding him of the circumstances of his life. The more you remind him of his life, the more he may remember."

"I should try telling him about his life, showing him things and people from his life?"

"Yes. Perhaps you can awaken his memory. It could help. And then again it might make him angry."

"Angry?"

"He is quite adamant about his delusion. It will not be easy to convince him he is not a Scottish earl. One thing for certain: he must rest." Anderson stuffed his handkerchief into his coat pocket. "I have given him something to help him sleep. I suspect he will sleep the rest of the day. We shall see how he is doing in the morning."

Jane remained in the room as the surgeon left. She stared at the door leading to Lancaster's chamber. Anderson's words swirled around and around in her brain. Lancaster might never regain his memory. And then again, he could regain his memory at any moment.

All the horrible implications of that possibility struck her. She leaned against a wing-back chair near the fireplace. As his wife, she was honor-bound to look after him until he was well.

She might be eighty when he regained his memory. She might spend years with a man who thought he was someone other than who he truly was, a man who had the unfortunate ability to turn her legs into quivering aspic. He might go to bed in the evening as Colin and awaken the next morning as Dominic. She rubbed her throbbing temples.

"What a tangle," she whispered.

She needed to think. Perhaps a nice long walk might help clear the muddle in her brain. She turned to leave, and then jumped, a soft gasp escaping her lips. Lancaster stood in the doorway leading to his chamber, frowning at her. "What are you doing out of bed?" she demanded.

Chapter Seven

And when the stream
Which overflowed the soul was passed away,
A consciousness remained that it had left,
Of memory, images and precious thoughts,
that shall not die, and cannot be destroyed.
                    —William Wordsworth

Lancaster smiled, but the look in his eyes remained cold. "I did not take the drug your surgeon left for me."

He was half out of his head, she reminded herself, forcing down her quickly rising anger. "You make it sound as though he intended to poison you."

He rested one broad shoulder against the doorjamb. "Your surgeon has no doubt told you I have a confusion in my mind, some illness that makes me imagine I am a man who has traveled here from the sixteenth century."

She tried not to notice the way his shirt gaped, revealing the dark expanse of his chest. Yet heat simmered through her, a shimmering warmth that filtered through her every vein. She would definitely have to examine these odd sensations when she had a clear head. She glanced down at his feet and discovered he had shoved his bare feet into a pair of polished black dress shoes. His ankles looked incredibly smooth compared to the rough-looking hair that covered his legs. "He said you needed rest."

"Aye. So the fine quack did say. But at the moment I find I am in need of a privy. Or a chamber pot. I did not find one in this huge chamber of Lancaster's. And I am thinking you would not like for me to be relieving myself into the flowers below the balcony."

An image quickly rose in her mind, a terrifying image of the Marquess of Lancaster standing on his balcony. *Good heavens!* "You have a bathroom, as do all of the larger bedchambers in the house."

"A bath room? This is a place to bathe?"

"Yes. And it also has a water closet."

"You have a room to keep water?"

Heat prickled her neck. "The water closet is an indoor privy. I suppose I should show you how it works."

He inclined his head. "Unless you prefer I water the flowers."

"No. I would not." She marched past him, keeping as close to one side of the door as possible. Still, her shoulder brushed his chest, the accidental contact sizzling along her nerves. She clenched her teeth. She could not allow him to see this weakness or he would pounce like a hound on a wounded fox.

He followed her as she crossed the room. Since she had never explored his chamber, she was somewhat at a loss. The first door she tried opened to the dressing room.

"You are not very familiar with your husband's bedchamber," he said, a soft note of curiosity in his dark voice.

"No. I am not." She ignored the questions in his eyes and turned away from him.

He grabbed her arm when she started for the next door, meeting her glare with a smile. "And would that mean he pays his nightly visits to your chamber?"

The implication of sexual intimacy was in the soft, dark tone of his voice and the speculation in his eyes. The intimacy she must avoid to gain her freedom. Yesterday it had seemed a great deal easier than it did today. "It really isn't any of your concern."

A glint of mischief lit his eyes. " 'Tis not?"

"No. *'Tis* not." She pulled away from him and marched to the next door.

"But 'twould seem I am your husband," he said, following her. "At least if I am to listen to the surgeon. And as your husband, 'tis my duty to see that you are well pleasured."

His words teased the doubt that still dwelled deep within her. She paused with her hand on the brass handle and glanced up at him, searching for the truth behind the facade. Was he truly ill? Or was this the way he intended to lure her into his bed? "You have been telling me all morning that you are not my husband. Or at least that is what you would have me believe. Certainly you do not expect me to allow another man into my bed."

He leaned toward her, his unfastened shirt spilling open, exposing the dark expanse of his chest. "And here I was thinking that was the reason you brought me to you. Was that the reason, my beautiful enchantress? Is this your way of replacing a man who did not suit you with another? Did you bring me here to warm your bed?"

She curled her hands into tight balls at her sides; she would dearly love to slap him. "I did not bring you here. And I certainly do not want you in my bed."

He held her gaze, his lips slowly tipping into a grin. "Then perhaps you should tell me why you did bring me to you."

"Your illness has apparently rendered you incredibly stubborn."

He winked at her. "I see you suffer from the same ailment."

Impossible buffoon! She threw open the door and found a large mahogany-paneled bathroom even more elaborate than the one in her bedchamber. "The bathroom."

Lancaster strolled past her, his footsteps silent on the white marble floor. He paused in the center of the room, his gaze drawn to the large mirror above the pedestal sink. Golden sunlight poured through the long sash windows at one end of the room, wrapping around the figures captured in the mirror, trapping them, like creatures locked in a drop of amber. She met his gaze in the mirror.

In that instant time itself seemed to catch its breath. She felt drawn to him in a way she had never in her life been drawn to another being. Drawn in a way that defied logic. Drawn as though on a tether that was slowly growing more taut, dragging her toward him. Even more amazing than the sensation he evoked within her was the turmoil in the depths of his eyes. Did he feel it too?

He turned and looked at her, as though he needed affirmation that she was truly standing there a few feet away from him. She had the uncanny feeling that if she moved toward him, he would sweep her up into his arms and make love to her, right here, on the elegant chaise longue sitting a few feet away from him. Images rose in her brain of this man standing naked in the sunlight. What might it be like to touch him? Her quick heartbeats stretched into an eternity as she stood captured by his gaze, poised on the brink of disaster.

He glanced away from her and muttered something about magic under his breath.

Good heavens, what was wrong with her? She was the one who should have turned away from him. If she maintained this course, she would soon find herself on her back with this man in her arms, trapped in this marriage for the rest of her life. It was all she could do to keep from running out of the room.

He glanced at the Grecian chaise longue covered in rich dark blue silk velvet near the large marble bathtub, then at her, a hard glint in his eyes. "You said this is a place to bathe?"

"Yes," she said, appalled at the breathless sound of her voice.

One black brow lifted just a bit. "It would seem a place to entertain as well."

She glanced at the thick velvet-covered pillows on the large chaise longue. There was little doubt in her mind that Lancaster had enjoyed his mistresses in this room. She tried not to imagine him lying there as naked as God had made him. Yet the images were there, seared across her brain. And worse, much worse, were the other images that came. This man lying there, his long limbs entwined with her own. She shut her eyes and drew in her breath. She would not follow that line of thinking. No, she certainly would not.

She crossed the room in search of the water closet, her footsteps sharp staccato notes mimicking each quick thud of her heart against her ribs. She opened a door that led to the dressing room. Another opened to a large linen closet. Finally, in the far corner of the room, behind a paneled door stood a mahogany-encased toilet.

"This is your privy," she said, glancing over her shoulder.

Lancaster had paused at the large white marble bathtub, where he was running his fingertips over the gold fixtures. As she watched, he turned one of the handles. A moment later, water tumbled from the curved gold spout and splashed into the tub. He laughed, a soft rumble that rose from his chest and swept across the room to embrace her. "Will you look at that."

She was looking. In fact she could not drag her gaze from him. There was something about his smile, something in his laughter, something almost innocent. It was a smile and a sound she had never expected to hear from the worldly Lord Lancaster. "The tub is for bathing."

A glint of mischief entered his stunning eyes. "I see it is big enough for two."

She glanced at the big square tub. It was indeed big enough for two. What might it be like to feel the slide of his wet skin against hers? *Heaven above!* She glared at Lancaster, silently cursing the man for evoking images that made her want to run screaming to her chamber. "When you . . ." She cleared her throat, appalled at the raspy sound of her voice. "When you have taken care of your needs, pull this chain."

She pulled the gold chain attached to the mahogany box above the seat. Water rushed into the basin below the seat, swirling, gurgling, drawing the attention of the man at the far end of the room. He headed for her. She headed for the door.

"Afterward, you can wash your hands in the sink," she said, edging toward the door, "which is that basin below the mirror."

He turned to look at the sink. She hurried out of the bathroom and closed the door behind her. Although she wanted to keep running, she could not. He was in a very real sense her responsibility. He needed help to get well, and she intended to give it to him. She pressed her hand to her chest, feeling the quick beat of her heart beneath her shaky palm. He needed to regain his memory. Soon. She had no trouble at all resisting Dominic Stanbridge, but Colin MacKenzie . . . Now, he was an entirely different opponent.

She waited in his bedchamber for him. When she heard the flush of the toilet, she thought he would join her soon. When it flushed a third time, she suspected he was simply fascinated by the mechanism. By the time it had flushed a fifth time, she was certain he was simply playing in the water closet. When he walked out a moment later, the grin on his face confirmed it. "You seem to be enjoying yourself."

"This place is filled with marvels. I would greatly like to have one of those bathing chambers at Kintair."

"I suppose you still don't remember anything of your life as Dominic Stanbridge?"

"Since I have not lived his life, I cannot remember any of it."

"Anderson said it might be helpful if I reminded you of things in your life before the accident."

He fixed her with a direct look, his gaze clear and certain. "I know who I am. The spell you cast upon me has not dimmed my mind."

She folded her hands at her waist and reminded herself of the need for patience. "I have not cast a spell upon you."

"If you did not cast a spell, then what were you doing dressed in robes as black as Lucifer's heart, whispering beneath the full moon?"

She glared at him. "A better question is, What were you doing spying on me?"

"It was you who invaded my dreams, my beautiful deceiver. You who called me across the ages. Why do you deny your magic?"

"There is no such thing as magic."

He lifted his brows. "If you wish me to believe that, you are speaking to the wrong man. In the Highlands we know that magic can be found in all things great and small. It can hide in the heart of a pretty lass and escape in a simple wish."

Chills whispered across her skin when she thought of the words she had spoken last night. It was absurd to imagine that a simple wish could work a miracle. It was far more logical, infinitely more realistic, to believe Lancaster had heard her pitiful words and was now using them against her. Apparently part of his memory was still working enough to remember seeing her on the balcony last night. "To imagine I would wish for you to come to me goes far beyond conceit. You might not remember who you are, but you certainly are every bit as arrogant as you have ever been."

"A wish?" His eyes narrowed as he studied her in that soul-piercing way that made her want to hide. "Is that what you were doing last night? Making a wish?"

She shook her head, trying to deny the uneasy feeling twisting deep inside her. "I can think of many things I might wish for, Lancaster. You are not one of them."

"I am not Lancaster." He grinned, then strolled across the room. He paused near the fireplace and lifted his gaze to a portrait of Lancaster that hung in an ornately carved rosewood frame above the mantel. "This is a fashion of your time?"

Jane had noticed nine other paintings of the marquess in the house. In this one, Lancaster had posed in a garden, standing beside a white marble pillar. He was dressed in a Roman tunic, one brawny shoulder bare, a laurel wreath about his head. "I believe you were posing as a Greek god in this particular painting."

Lancaster lifted his black brows. "A Greek god?"

"Yes. There is also a portrait of you dressed as Napoléon in the library and one of you dressed as an American cowboy in the conservatory. Since the background is a stage, I believe the one of you standing beside a piano in the music room might be you about to give a concert. Probably for the queen." She shrugged in the face of his surprise. "Pretending to be someone else seems to be a pastime of yours."

"I have never heard of these things, a Napoléon or American cowboy or a piano." He glanced up at the portrait, then at her. " 'Tis clear this man you married has a great affection for his own likeness."

"Yes. Your countenance is one of your favorite works of art."

He held her gaze a long time in that way he had of

making her feel he could look straight into her soul. "What did you do with him? Did you slip his soul into the body of a boar?"

She shook her head. "Must you continue with this notion that I am a witch?"

"From my perspective, it is the logical conclusion."

She supposed from his point of view, in the confusion of his mind, it would seem logical. "Strange, I have never before thought there was anything logical about magic."

"Of course there is. If my soul is now in this body, then your poor husband must be . . ." He paused, his lips parted, a look of horror crossing his features. "By my faith, you switched us, that is what you have done. That English jackanapes is now in my body, living my life."

She considered this a moment. "I suppose there is some logic in your words—that is, if I were a witch. Which I am not."

He glared at her. "Why have you done this to me?"

The anger in his gaze sent shivers rippling over her skin. "If I had the power to go about switching souls, why would I not choose a perfectly glorious body for myself? Young, fair haired, beautiful, wealthy."

"A look in your mirror will prove your magic." He stalked her, his eyes narrowed to blue slits, fury etched upon his handsome face. "Beautiful, deceiving witch."

"I am not a witch." She stepped back, her heart thumping as he drew near. He wouldn't actually harm her, would he? Yet this was a man who had brandished a sword not more than a few hours ago. "You are not thinking clearly right now."

He moved toward her, an angry tiger with his sights on a tender antelope. "I am thinking of my family and the devil you have unleashed upon them."

She bumped into a paneled wall, a soft gasp escaping her lips. "I have not unleashed anything."

He planted his hands against the wall on either side of her shoulders, imprisoning her between the solid mahogany at her back and the solid bulk of masculinity at her front. "Three hundred years. My family, all of my friends, their lives lived without me. And now to know you have unleashed this English dog in my place."

"I haven't done—"

"Reverse your spell," he said, his dark voice low and deceptively soft.

She held his furious gaze, determined not to show her fear. "I did not cast a spell."

He leaned closer, pressing the strength and heat of his body against her. His long legs brushed her limbs through the layers of her gown and petticoat. His hard chest grazed her breasts. Without warning, a spark of excitement sliced through her. It burned through the fear gripping her, sizzling along her every nerve, heating her blood. She sucked in her breath, drawing the subtle spicy scent of his skin deep into her lungs. The scent enticed her, tempted her, until it took every shred of her will to keep from pressing her lips against his neck, where the white silk of his shirt fell away from his skin.

She glanced up into his eyes and instantly wished she had not. The anger was still there in the blue depths, but there was something even more heated, something primal and raw. A hunger that whispered to a part of her she had never known existed.

"Oh, my goodness." She pressed her hands against his chest, intending to push him away from her. Yet her fingers slipped inside the open edges of his shirt, meeting the heat of his bare skin. "Do step away from me."

He did not obey. Instead he slipped his hand around her neck, his long fingers sliding into her hair, cradling her scalp. "What have you done to me, witch?"

"Nothing." She curled her fingers against his chest, captivated by the feel of silky hair and sleek muscles. "I have done nothing to you."

"It cannot be true." He lowered his head and brushed his lips over the curve of her jaw. "This spell, I feel it."

"It's the bump on your head."

He nipped her earlobe, scattering shivers along her shoulder. "You have bewitched me."

"No. I . . ." Her words faded as he touched the sensitive skin beneath her ear with the tip of his tongue. The sleek slide of his tongue seemed to echo low in her belly, tugging on her in the most beguiling fashion. "It's the illness. Only the illness."

" 'Tis magic." He lifted his head and looked at her, turmoil naked in his eyes. "Remove your spell. Set me free of this enchantment."

She stared up into his eyes, mesmerized by the desire flaming there. She had never imagined Lancaster capable of such desire. Still, this was a man who had caused a woman to commit suicide. And if she was not careful, she would succumb to him, too, killing her chance for freedom. "There is no spell," she said, her voice a whisper.

He released his breath in a long sigh that brushed her cheek. Slowly he eased away from her, as though he were tearing away a part of himself. A whimper escaped her tight control as he stepped back, releasing her from the exotic press of potent masculinity. For a long while they stood facing each other, her breath coming in the same ragged fashion as his.

"I will not succumb to your magic," he said, his dark voice strained, as if he were fighting against invisible bonds.

Magic. She felt as though he had cast a spell over her, as though he had conjured a need she had never known before. "There is no such thing as magic."

"No such thing as magic?" Twin lines formed between his black brows as he held her gaze. "Is that what you would have me believe? That I am this hated Englishman that you have married? That every thought and memory in my head is not my own?"

"I know it must be difficult to accept, under the circumstances, but you are Dominic Stanbridge."

"And you are a beautiful deceiver." He turned and marched across the room, his shirttails flapping at his hips.

She did not wish to follow him. In truth, she wanted to run as far away from this confusing man as possible. Yet she had a duty to uphold. "Where are you going?"

He turned at the door and shot her an icy glare. "I am going to find a horse."

She stared at him. "A horse?"

"Aye." He pivoted and marched from the room.

She ran after him, and nearly collided with Hedley in the hall. "Beg pardon, Your Ladyship. Lord—"

"Not now, Hedley." Jane ran past the butler, hurrying after Lancaster. She caught up with him at the staircase. "What do you intend to do with a horse?"

He didn't so much as glance at her as he started down the stairs. "Return to Kintair."

She lifted her skirts and chased him down the stairs. "You don't seriously intend to ride a horse all the way to Scotland?"

"Aye. I do."

She had to stop him. If he left, who knew what kind of trouble he might tumble into? He paused at the base of the stairs, gripping the banister, his head bowed, as if fighting a bout of dizziness.

"You should not be running about like a perfect henwit." She gripped his arm. "You need rest."

He opened his eyes and fixed her with an icy look. "I will find a way back to my family."

"Your family is here, in London."

He looked past her, his eyes growing narrow. "You there."

She followed the direction of his glare and found Pierson standing in the hall. The short valet was staring at his master as though Lancaster had just sprouted antlers and a tail.

"Me, Your Lordship?" Pierson asked, his voice breaking shrilly.

"Aye. Fetch me a horse."

Pierson stared, his mouth open. "A horse, Your Lordship?"

Jane shook her head. "Pierson, His Lordship is not—"

"Now." Lancaster's voice lowered as he issued the command.

Pierson bobbed his head, turned, and scampered down the hall. Jane looked up at the man standing beside her. For the first time in her life she truly understood the meaning of the word *commanding*. From what she had witnessed, Lancaster had managed his servants efficiently, but never as a general might manage his troops. "You shall be fortunate if Pierson does not leave you after this. I can only imagine the gentlemen who would dearly love to employ him."

Lancaster turned his glacial glare upon her. "Take your hand from my arm, witch."

She gripped his arm tighter. "You are ill. You must rest."

He frowned, the muscles beneath her hand growing taut. "You will not keep me here."

"What do you think to accomplish in Scotland?"

One corner of his mouth tightened. "I will learn what damage your husband has wrought upon my family."

She saw it then, the fear behind the anger burning in his eyes. He honestly believed in this fable, this switching of bodies and souls. And he was afraid for the family he imagined he had left behind. "I am not even certain there ever really was a Colin MacKenzie," she said, keeping her voice soft. "He may be only a creation of your imagination."

He ran his hand over the back of his head, an expression of pain crossing his features. "I exist. As well you know. My family exists, or at least they did. And I must know what happened to them. I must return to Kintair."

Would it help if he faced this fantasy? "If Colin MacKenzie did exist, there might not be any record of him. It was three hundred years ago."

"The *Chronicles of Kintair* began with my grandfather, each important event of the family noted and stored in a safe place. The books are passed along to those who inherit the title. If your devil of a husband did not destroy my family, there will be a chronicle of them at Kintair." A glint of determination filled his eyes. "I need a horse."

She stared at him. He needed many things, not one of which was a horse. "You truly expect to ride there on a horse?"

"Aye." He frowned, momentarily puzzled by her question. "And how else would I travel to Kintair?"

If he discovered the truth about this man he imagined himself to be, would it help him regain his memory? "I am not certain it is wise to travel until you are better."

He gripped her wrist and pulled her hand from his arm. "I will return to Kintair."

Determination glinted like polished steel in his eyes. He would do it. He would mount a horse dressed as he was and head off out of London. "All right."

His black brows lifted. "You will remove your spell?"

She frowned. "No."

He smiled. "Then you admit you did cast this spell."

"No." She released her breath in a sigh that sounded every bit as frustrated as she felt. "I did not cast a spell. I simply meant I cannot have you riding about the countryside. If you intend to travel to Scotland, then I shall make all the necessary arrangements."

His eyes narrowed with suspicion. "What arrangements do you have in mind?"

"Nothing at all to do with a broom, I assure you."

"A broom? And what would a broom have to do with it?"

She shook her head. "I will arrange to have your private train made ready for the trip."

"A private train?" He considered this a moment. "Is this a type of chariot?"

"Yes. A chariot run by the power of steam. Much faster and able to travel much farther in a day than a horse."

He looked intrigued. "Steam, you say?"

"The trip will take less than a day." She shook her head. "I feel rather foolish standing here explaining something you know perfectly well."

"Lancaster may know. But I am—"

"I know. You think you are Colin MacKenzie."

He fixed her in a steady glare. "I *am* Colin MacKenzie. No spell will make me forget who I am."

It was so strange talking to him this way. Although his features had not been altered, his expression was now so different, he actually appeared to be a different man. It would be difficult to keep in mind just who and what she was dealing with in this man. Yet she must. It was far too dangerous to forget this was indeed Dominic Stanbridge. "I will see to all the arrangements for our trip."

"Our trip? And are you thinking you will be coming along with me?"

"In your condition you certainly cannot travel to Scotland without someone to watch over you. And as much as I wish it were otherwise, it is my duty to see you do not hurt yourself. Now, please go back to your chamber and rest. And try not to terrify any of the servants."

He gripped her arm and drew her toward him until her breasts brushed the hard plane of his chest. "If you deceive me, I will find a way to make you regret it."

She looked him straight in the eyes and thought of all the many things she regretted. Never meeting a real man who could make her tingle the way this man could was at the top of that list. "I want you to regain your memory, Lancaster. And if it takes a trip to Scotland to help accomplish that feat, I will do it."

*   *   *

Colin stared into her eyes, searching for a trace of deceit. The pure light of sincerity shone in her eyes. Yet how could he believe her? If she had not cast a spell upon him, if she had not brought him here, then what had befallen him?

With injuries such as yours, it is not unusual to suffer some confusion. The surgeon's words echoed in his memory. He ran his hand over the bump at the back of his head. Was it possible? Had the injury destroyed his mind? Could he trust his own thoughts and memories? The air felt heavy, hot, and thick. Despite the heat, his skin turned cold and damp, a fine chill gripping him as the possibility swept over him like an icy wind. Had he lost his mind?

"Go back to your chamber. You need rest."

She touched his arm, the soft gesture of a nurse to her charge. Still the gentle touch triggered a rush of heat through his veins, a cascading wave of fire. He pulled away from her and grabbed the newel post, fighting the dizziness that washed over him. Yet the physical malady was far less potent than the spell she had cast upon his soul.

As ill as he felt, he still wanted her. He wanted to bury his face against her neck, lift her into his arms, hold her close and hard against his body. He closed his hands into fists at his sides. It must be magic. Nothing had ever gripped him with such intensity as the attraction he had for this woman.

"I know who I am. I remember my family. I know every detail of my life and nothing about this man you call Lancaster. No manner of spell shall dim the truth that shines within me. I am Colin MacKenzie, Earl of Kintair," he said, forcing the words past a throat tightened by uncertainty. "I know who I am."

"Rest," she said, her voice a soft caress. "And perhaps things will be clearer when you awaken."

Colin allowed her to usher him back up the stairs and

to his chamber. He watched her cross the room and leave him. Although Jane vanished from his sight, she did not leave his thoughts. If she was not a witch, then he was a madman. The life he remembered was either real, or a creation of his imagination.

Was this what she had planned for him, this moment of doubt? Did she wish him to believe he was ill so he would be completely at her mercy?

Colin closed his eyes and leaned back against the bedpost. Lord Almighty, what was real? What could he believe? What was truth and what was merely an illusion?

Chapter Eight

Forward, each gentleman and knight!
Let gentle blood show generous might,
And chivalry redeem the fight!
　　　　　　　—Sir Walter Scott

Jane closed the door to Lancaster's chamber and started down the hall. She found Hedley waiting for her near the stairs. "What is it?"

Hedley cleared his throat. "Lord Pembury is awaiting His Lordship in the gold drawing room."

Jane's muscles tensed at the mention of Lancaster's uncle. He was one of the last people on the face of the earth who should be here at the moment. His dislike for Lancaster was, according to Eugenia, hardly a secret in the family. Apparently Pembury had never forgiven his nephew for attaining his majority and assuming the title and the estate. Eugenia was certain Pembury had held hopes the young man would break his neck in some way. Afterward, Lancaster had committed the unpardonable sin of dragging the family from the brink of financial disaster and earning a fortune in his own right, making Pembury look all the more foolish for nearly sinking the family in the first place. Jane did not want to contemplate the disaster that might occur should Pembury learn of Lancaster's illness. "Tell Lord Pembury his nephew is not receiving guests this afternoon."

Hedley's white brows lifted. "With pleasure, Your Ladyship."

Jane remained in the hall while Hedley descended the stairs. She just stood there, staring blindly at the floor, trying to pry some sense out of the muddle Lancaster had made of her mind. Two months ago if anyone had told her she would be married to the Marquess of Lancaster, she would have dismissed the notion out of hand. She was not equipped for this. She was a quiet, practical female who belonged in the country, not in this huge mansion. Certainly not with a cunning rogue. Still, she was in this mess. And somehow she would find her way out of it.

"A list," she whispered, turning away from the stairs. She started down the hall toward her chamber. Silently she commenced a list in her head of all the things that must be done before they could leave for Scotland tonight. She had gone no more than a few steps when a voice echoed in the hall behind her.

"Is that you, Miss Eveleigh?"

Jane froze, a chill etching down her back like frost upon a windowpane. She drew in her breath and turned to find Pembury strolling toward her down the hall. "Lord Pembury."

He was nearly as tall as Lancaster. Yet instead of the lean, athletic look of the nephew, the uncle looked soft. Although he wasn't rotund, he looked as though he spent more time in an armchair than he did in a saddle. He lifted his hand and wagged his finger at her. "You really should not wear such a dowd of a gown. It is difficult enough to distinguish you from the chambermaids as it is."

Although she hadn't thought it possible, she had come to realize Edwin Stanbridge was even more arrogant than his nephew. "Apparently you did not believe Hedley when he told you Lancaster was not receiving visitors."

He paused a few feet before her, his lips curving into a cool, condescending mockery of a smile. Beneath thick, dark brows, he regarded her with a look of disdain in his blue eyes. "I heard an interesting rumor this morning."

Jane's chest tightened. "Funny thing, rumors. People seldom fabricate ones that are not interesting."

He tilted his head and studied her a moment, trying to make her feel inferior. In Edwin she had met a man she loathed more than the scoundrel who had forced her into marriage. At least Lancaster believed she was good enough to bear the Stanbridge name. Edwin had actually come to her after the engagement had been announced and tried to bully her into ending the betrothal. He had made it clear he and other members of his family did not believe her pedigree was pure enough to suit them. "Do you mean to say my nephew was not running about the streets of London naked and carrying a sword?"

She bristled at the condescending tone of his voice. "He was certainly not naked."

"Perhaps not." Edwin lifted his brows, a glint of triumph entering his eyes. "But he was wearing a dressing gown and threatening unsuspecting ladies with a sword. Was he not?"

An unexpected wave of protectiveness washed over her. Lancaster might be her enemy, but this man was far worse. "Lancaster is not feeling quite himself today."

"From what I have heard, he is acting like a Bedlamite." He lifted one thick brow. "Of course, I have suspected he was on the verge of insanity for the past two months. He certainly has not demonstrated much sense lately."

Jane closed her hands into fists at her sides. Heat crept upward along her neck. "Since Lancaster is not receiving visitors, there is really no reason for you to stay."

"I think there is."

"You are mistaken." She started down the hall, hoping he would take the hint and leave.

"I think not." He followed her a short distance, then grabbed her arm, bringing her to a halt. "It is my duty to see how my nephew is faring after his *accident* yesterday."

She twisted free of his grasp and faced him, her heart hammering. "I think you should leave."

He stepped closer. It was an intimidation tactic he had employed with her before. He leaned toward her, his sickly sweet cologne stabbing her senses. "Tell me something, *Miss Eveleigh*. Did you actually try to murder my nephew yesterday afternoon?"

She stepped back; she couldn't prevent it. His words hit her with the force of an open palm. "What nonsense is this?"

"It is no secret you married my nephew for his fortune." He smiled, his eyes narrowing. "There are those who believe you might be interested in becoming a wealthy widow."

"Only someone with a twisted mind would believe such a horrible thing." He moved forward. She stepped back and hit the wall. She pushed against his chest when he leaned toward her. "Stand back."

He made no move. "I wonder what it is about you, Miss Eveleigh? What could have driven my nephew to marry you? Did you use some kind of blackmail?"

She swallowed hard. "I do not intend to—"

"Let me warn you, Miss Eveleigh. I do not intend to allow the family fortune to be—"

His words ended in a sharp gasp. One moment he was leaning over her; the next he was sailing across the hall. He whacked the oak paneling across from Jane, his breath escaping in a loud whoosh. It was then Jane saw the reason for her sudden deliverance. Lancaster stood before her, sword drawn, the point against Pembury's neck. "What would you have me do with this ruffian, Lady Jane? Should I slit him from ear to ear?"

Jane looked from Lancaster to Pembury, too shocked to utter a word. The older man stood staring at his nephew, his eyes wide, his features revealing stark disbelief. Lancaster stood before her, tall, broad-shouldered, the sheer male power of the man filling the space around her, as tangible as the solid oak at her back. He had come to her defense like a knight charging to his lady's side. A knight complete with drawn sword.

It was shocking. It was primitive. It was a display straight out of a medieval play. Any proper lady would be horrified at such an action. Yet, in spite of her natural abhorrence of violence, she could not dismiss the excitement tingling through her. It was the most romantic thing that had ever happened to her in her entire life.

"What the devil are you doing?" Pembury asked, his voice several notes higher than usual.

"Waiting to hear what Lady Jane would have me do with you."

Jane could not drag her gaze from Lancaster. How easy it would be to imagine this man a prince from her very own fairy tale.

With the tip of his sword Lancaster tipped Pembury's chin up, exposing the vulnerable column of his neck. "Tell me, my lady. Would you have me slit him open?"

He wouldn't actually slit Pembury's throat, would he? As the thought formed, Lancaster glanced at her and winked. In that one look, Jane realized this was a game, a lesson delivered to the arrogant viscount. Apparently a bump on the head had not altered her husband's sense of humor. It took all of her will to keep from smiling.

Pembury stared at Lancaster. "What nonsense is—"

"Not a word from you." Lancaster pressed the tip into

the soft skin beneath Pembury's chin. "Tell me, Lady Jane. What would you like me to do with this ruffian?"

Jane was naturally softhearted. Still, looking at Pembury's arrogant face, she had an unexpected measure of satisfaction at seeing his fear. She allowed the moment to stretch just a little longer before she replied. "I'm afraid you would make a dreadful mess in the hall should you slit his throat."

"My lady has seen fit to spare your worthless life." Lancaster swept the sword away from Pembury's neck and brought it to his side. "Now apologize for your behavior."

"Confound it, Dominic." Pembury rubbed his chin, then examined his fingers. "You might have drawn blood."

"I might have slit you from ear to ear." Lancaster lifted the sword in front of Pembury. "You will apologize to Lady Jane."

Pembury's eyes narrowed. "What the devil kind of game are you playing now, nephew?"

"Nephew?" Lancaster glanced at Jane. "It would seem your husband is not the only scoundrel in his family."

Jane stared at him. What would Pembury make of Lancaster's bizarre behavior?

"What nonsense is this?" Pembury pulled a handkerchief from the pocket of his dark green coat and rubbed first his left then his right palm as he continued. "And what the devil are you doing dressed like that?"

Lancaster shrugged. "I do not pretend to know the fashion of this day."

Pembury swiped his handkerchief over his brow, mopping the beads of moisture that had risen there. "Fashion of this day?"

"Aye. This man Lancaster has a great many garments. All of costly fabric. Yet crafted in a most odd manner."

Pembury frowned. "This man Lancaster?"

Jane had to stop this. "Pembury, we really are not—"

"This man Lancaster?" Pembury repeated, his voice growing more shrill. "First I hear you are running about the streets of London in your dressing gown. Then you attack me. Now you are speaking of yourself as though you were a stranger. And why the devil are you speaking in that deplorable Scottish accent? I don't mind saying, nephew, you are acting very strangely this afternoon."

Lancaster rested the tip of his sword on the carpet. "And I do not mind saying that I am not your nephew."

Pembury froze, his gaze fixed on Lancaster. "Not my nephew?"

Jane rested her hand on Lancaster's arm, hoping to quell any more discourse. She didn't question the protective instincts swelling inside her. Upon more than one occasion she had rescued stray dogs from the streets. If Lancaster was ill, he needed her help. Her feelings for Lancaster were akin to those she might have for a lost mongrel, she assured herself. "Pembury, I think it might be wise if you left. Now."

"Not my nephew?"

"Aye."

Pembury did not so much as blink. He continued staring at Lancaster as though his nephew had just stated he had traveled here by witchcraft. Which was what Jane was afraid he might say next. "Pembury, I really think—"

"Not my nephew?" Pembury repeated like a demented parrot.

"Lancaster is not feeling altogether well. Since he needs rest, I really must insist you take your leave."

Color rose in Pembury's cheeks. Jane might not have been standing there, for all the man noticed her. His gaze never left Lancaster as he spoke. "What the devil do you mean by saying you are not my nephew?"

Jane squeezed Lancaster's arm, a silent plea for him to remain quiet. "This really isn't a good time. . . ."

"I mean to say I am not this Lord Lancaster that everyone keeps saying I am."

Jane clenched her teeth. If Lancaster continued in this manner, he would soon have Pembury believing he was insane. "Pembury, I really must insist you leave and allow Lancaster to—"

"What kind of nonsense is this?" Pembury shoved his handkerchief into his pocket. "Are you trying to tell me you don't know who the devil you are?"

"I know exactly who I am. I am Col—"

Jane stomped her heel down on Lancaster's toes. It was the only way she could think to stop him. He gasped at the sudden pain, then shot her a questioning glance. "Oh, dear, I am afraid his head is aching again. Lancaster really must rest for a while."

Lancaster frowned down at her. "My head, is it?"

"Yes." Jane smiled at him, silently warning him to remain quiet. One corner of his lips tipped upward in a smile, his eyes reflecting his understanding. Caught in the steady regard of those blue eyes, she felt something flutter in her chest, something that could not possibly be excitement, she assured herself. She turned her attention to Pembury, giving him a look she could only hope was filled with enough hauteur to make him go away. "I am certain Lancaster will not need to convince you to take your leave. Will he?"

Pembury glanced down at the sword Lancaster held before him, then flicked his tongue over his lips. "No. No, he need not convince me of anything more than he already has."

An uneasy feeling uncoiled in her stomach as she watched Pembury march down the hall. She had a feeling the man could be trusted to cause trouble. She only hoped he had enough pride in his family to keep Lancaster's eccentric behavior to himself.

Chapter Nine

You have ravish'd me away by a Power I cannot
resist; and yet I could resist till I saw you; and even
since I have seen you I have endeavored often "to
reason against the reason of my Love."

—John Keats

"You stepped on my toes," Lancaster said, his deep voice
colored by a hint of humor.

She looked up at the man standing beside her. He was
regarding her with a smile, a curious look in his eyes.
"You were about to tell him you were Colin MacKenzie."

"Aye. I was."

"And if you had told him, he would have assumed you
were insane. And if he assumed you were insane, it
would be difficult to say what nasty things he might do."

"I was thinking you did not like your husband."

"I loathe him. I mean you."

"And yet you are trying to protect him." Suspicion
tinged the deep notes of his voice. "And why is this?"

116

"If you truly believe you are Colin MacKenzie, then you are ill. I am your wife, even if I don't wish to be your wife. I feel it is my duty to protect you while you are unable to protect yourself." It was a simple explanation, she thought. Far too simple to explain the feelings this man evoked within her. Still, there was no reason to allow him to know just how easily he muddled her senses.

"Do you honestly imagine I am not able to protect myself?"

"I do not mean with a sword. Which, by the way, you really must stop brandishing. Men do not go about threatening people with swords these days."

He glanced down at the sword, then back at her, a frown tugging his brow. "From what I could see that ruffian was annoying you. I thought he needed a lesson in how to address a lady."

"A lady? Does this mean you have given up this ridiculous notion that I am a witch?"

He smiled, if that chilling curve of his lips could actually be labeled a smile. "You are a witch."

"If you truly believe I am a witch, why did you come to my rescue?"

He held her gaze his expression fierce. "I would fight any man who tried to hurt you."

Jane stared at him, all the air evaporating from her lungs. "You would?"

"As well you know. This spell you have cast is powerful, my Lady Jane. It has bound me to you. You have set my heart and my mind at odds with one another. I know you are my enemy, that I should not trust you. And yet, I know I would risk my life to save you from harm."

"It is the illness," she said, more for her own sake than for his. She could not succumb to the romance of this man.

He regarded her with eyes slightly narrowed, looking at her as though he were evaluating a strange creature he had come upon in the woods. A creature that might possibly be dangerous. " 'Tis sorcery."

"I wish I did have magical powers. If I did, I certainly would never find myself in this situation."

He lowered his eyes, his gaze brushing her breasts. Heat shimmered and spread beneath his gaze, as though he had stroked her with his fingers. "And yet you brought me here."

She clamped down hard on the stirring of emotion within her. "I did not bring you here."

"If that be true—"

"I do not twist the truth."

He rubbed his hand slowly over the back of his head, grimacing as though in pain. "If what you say is true, and you did not cast this spell, then you must know who did."

"I'm afraid I have never met a witch in my life. Of course my great-aunt Deirdre did claim she saw a fairy once, but we suspect it was after she had imbibed a few glasses of whiskey."

He studied her a long moment, as if taking her measure. She saw suspicion in his eyes and the wariness of a man who had an intimate acquaintance with betrayal. "This man who was bothering you, he is your husband's uncle. Yet he treats you with such contempt in your husband's house? I wonder what grievance he has against you."

"He doesn't believe I am worthy of his nephew. He actually implied I had blackmailed the man into marrying me. When it was Lancaster who blackmailed me."

"He blackmailed you?"

"Yes." Jane rubbed her hands together, remembering how helpless she had felt at this man's hands.

"And what would you mean by this *blackmailed*?"

The question caught her off guard. For a moment she just looked at him. "You seem to be having trouble with your grasp of language."

He shrugged as though his sudden lack of vocabulary was to be expected. "You use many words I have never before heard."

Could his illness be so precise as to exclude words that had not come into usage before 1562? "Lancaster lured my sister into deep play at faro, which is a card game. They were gambling. Then he used her debts to force me to marry him."

"If what you say is true, then this man is a *scoundrel*."

"Yes, he is."

Lancaster lifted one black brow, a look of triumph crossing his features. "Do you realize you have been addressing me as though you realize I am not this Lancaster?"

She frowned, annoyed with her own foolish slip. The truth was, she had begun to think of him as another man. "It would seem your illness is contagious."

" 'Twould seem you know I am not he."

"You are ill. At least you appear to be ill. I am only trying to help you."

"And it appears you are an unusual woman, Lady Jane. To protect a man who has served you such an injustice. 'Tis rare, I believe. Most women would deliver him into the hands of his enemies if given the chance."

"It is nothing more than duty, I assure you." She did not miss the suspicion that colored the praise. It was obvious he did not trust her. With his illness she did not truly know what to expect from him. Jane felt as though she were creeping through a darkened room in which she had never been before, searching for a doorway that would lead her to the light. "If you truly believe you are a Scottish earl named Colin MacKenzie, it is because the injury you sustained yesterday has caused some type of confusion."

His eyes narrowed as he searched her expression. "Someone cast a spell and brought me to this place and time."

"Maybe someone you know wished to be rid of you."

"Would you have me believe my uncle enlisted the services of a sorceress?"

Although she had meant it as a jest, he clearly thought she was serious. "Your uncle wishes to be rid of you?"

"Aye." He ran his hand over the back of his head. "With me gone, 'twould be only my brother to bar his way, a lad of fourteen summers."

It appeared he was once again twisting things to match his delusion. Lancaster knew very well the way Pembury felt about him, the fact that his uncle wished him gone. She wondered if there was a way of making him see the flaws in his logic. "Wouldn't hiring a sorceress be going to a great deal of trouble? Why wouldn't he simply murder you? I understand murder was quite common in the sixteenth century. Especially in Scotland. All one need do is read Shakespeare."

"Shakespeare?"

"Yes. William Shakespeare."

"I have never met him."

"Never met him." Jane studied him a moment. If he was playing a game, he was very good at it. "Wouldn't your uncle simply stab you, rather than go through all the trouble of finding three witches to cast a spell?"

"He would need only one witch."

"I was thinking of *Macbeth*."

"I have no quarrel with MacBeth. Why would you imagine he has anything to do with this?"

"I don't. *Macbeth* is a play." She raised her hand when it appeared he would question her. "I simply think murder would be easier than finding a witch who would cast a spell to send you here."

"Aye. 'Twould be easier and more like my uncle to have me murdered. Aside from my uncle, I do not know of anyone who would want to . . ." He hesitated, his words dissolving in a long sigh. A surprised expression crossed his features. He wobbled on his feet.

She gripped his arm and pressed her other hand against his chest, trying to steady him. "Are you all right?"

"Aye." He rested his hand on the wall, lowered his head, and drew in a deep breath. He swallowed hard before he spoke. "And I will be even better when I am back in my own body. This Lancaster has one devil of a bump on the back of his head."

"You should rest." She slipped her arm around his waist. "Come back to your chamber. Lie down and I will take care of everything for our trip."

He slipped his arm around her shoulders and leaned against her, wrapping the warmth of his big body around her. Her body commenced the same slow simmer that had assaulted her earlier that day, when he had held her in his arms. She tried to ignore it as the heat darted and tingled along her limbs, just as she tried to ignore the powerful arm resting over her shoulders, the sleek, muscular frame pressed against her side, the spicy scent of cologne mixed with a surprisingly appealing musk that was his own. She had to ignore it all, or be lost.

She knew this, just as she knew she had to keep drawing breath into her lungs. Yet drawing breath while this man was near ceased to be the easy, natural thing it was when he was not. She was discovering, much to her chagrin, that her entire body behaved in a most unpredictable, highly agitated, extremely dangerous manner when this man was near.

He was Dominic Stanbridge, she reminded herself. He was not—no matter how much he declared himself to be—a Scottish earl by the name of Colin MacKenzie. And by any name, the man was dangerous. She helped him back to his chamber. When she turned to leave, he stopped her.

He touched her cheek. "I will have the truth from you. One way or another."

His voice remained soft, as gentle as the touch of his fingers upon her skin. Yet there was nothing soft in his

121

eyes. He regarded her as his enemy. She had little doubt he would try any tactic to win this war. "You do have the truth. You just aren't willing to accept it."

"We shall see, my lady."

She saw the glint of challenge in his eyes and wondered how on earth she was going to make him see reason. She wasn't certain what horrible thing she had ever done to end up in this mess. She did know it would take all of her wits to escape in one piece.

After making the arrangements for their trip to Scotland, Jane liberated Arthur from the kitchen and left the house, intending to visit her mother. She needed to talk about what had happened in the past few hours. Perhaps her mother could help her make some sense of it all.

Jane had gone only a short distance down Park Lane when a man approached her. She had completely forgotten about Newbridge.

"Lady Lancaster." Newbridge made a small bow. "I had almost given up hope that you might meet me."

Jane drew Arthur's tether short. The large dog sat by her side and leaned against her leg. He growled at Newbridge, apparently as annoyed with the man as she was. "I'm afraid I did not come here to meet you, Newbridge. In truth I am on my way to visit my family."

His brows lifted, a look of annoyance crossing his features. "I shall take only a few moments of your time. I wonder if you might sit with me in the park?"

A town coach rattled past, drawn by four matched chestnuts. She did not wish to imagine who might see her talking to the viscount. She had no intention of flouting propriety; nor did she wish to wallow in any of the sordid details of her husband's affair with this man's wife. "If there is something you feel I must hear, I would suggest you speak your mind here and now. I assure you, I will not swoon or collapse in a fit of vapors."

"There is no easy way to say this." He glanced past

her to where Lancaster House could still be seen on the corner of the street. "Perhaps I should not broach this subject at all. Yet my conscience will not allow me to remain mute."

Jane squeezed the leather tether in her hand. A warm breeze fluttered the ribbons of her hat, flicking the blue satin against her cheek. Tension coiled in her chest as she stood quietly waiting for him to continue with something she did not wish to hear.

He kept his gaze focused behind her as he said, "I assume you are aware of a certain relationship my wife—my late wife—had with Lancaster."

Jane squeezed Arthur's tether harder. "I have heard the rumors."

"Most people know she had an affair with Lancaster. All of London is aware of the fact she died in a fall from the balcony of her bedchamber." He looked at her then, his hazel eyes fierce with emotion. "But I doubt many know she was murdered."

Jane's stomach clenched. "Murdered?"

"Yes. Her maid overheard her arguing with a man the night she died. The man was your husband."

"I know he was there that night. I know they argued. But that does not mean he murdered her."

"Gretchan had come to me that morning and confessed everything. She told me she was going to send Lancaster packing that night."

"She told you she intended to end the affair?"

"Yes. She had grown tired of him."

Someone was not telling the truth. She supposed it was possible that Lancaster had twisted the truth to suit his pride. Then again, this man might have altered it to suit his own purpose.

"Her maid said Lancaster sounded furious. He must have gone into a rage and . . ." His Adam's apple bobbed as Newbridge swallowed hard. "He pushed her from the balcony."

A single chill skittered down her back. When she had heard the rumors that Lancaster had murdered Penelope Clydestaff, she had not completely dismissed them. The idea of delivering the body to a medical school would have suited him. Yet to throw a woman from a balcony in a fit of rage, that did not at all fit the image she had of Lancaster. "I appreciate your concern. I understand the terrible ordeal you have been through. But I must say I believe you are mistaken in this. Lancaster prides himself on his icy demeanor. I cannot imagine he would do anything so hot-headed."

Newbridge nodded. "That is why I thought you should know what he is capable of when he is angered."

How much of this was for the sake of vengeance? She had never known Newbridge to do anything to help anyone. "Do you have any proof of this crime?"

Newbridge lifted his chin. "If I had proof, your husband would be facing the gallows."

"In that case, I trust you will keep your suspicions private. I hope you agree there has been enough scandal already."

He inclined his head. "I sought only to warn you."

"And you have. Good day, Lord Newbridge."

A muscle flashed in his cheek. "I hope you do not have cause to regret your trust in the monster you married, Lady Lancaster." He pivoted and marched away from her.

Jane looked down at her dog. "I don't suppose we could just keep walking straight back to Leicester."

Arthur tilted his head, regarding her in that odd way canines had of seeming to sympathize with everything their humans might say.

"I know, I am being a coward. Yet at the moment I would like very much to run back to Leicester and hide in my bedchamber, where I would try very hard to pretend the last few days had not happened."

Arthur planted his paws on the front of her gown. Jane stroked his head. "I know, running away will not solve anything. Just as wallowing in self-pity will gain us nothing. Still, I cannot keep from thinking I am out of my depth."

Jane tried not to think of what Newbridge had said while she continued on her way. To murder someone in a fit of passion one must first have a fiery nature. Lancaster did not. Still, a murderous rage would certainly not be beyond the capability of the man she had seen brandish a sword this morning. Could Lancaster be hiding a violent temper behind an icy facade?

Newbridge was angry and distraught for more than one reason. All of London knew his wife had taken another man to her bed. She suspected that would irritate the man almost as much as would her death. His own anger had painted the picture of Lancaster much blacker than it actually was, she assured herself. The man might be a scoundrel, but she doubted he was a murderer. She could not imagine Lancaster would care enough about any female to toss her off a balcony.

When she reached the house her family always hired for the Season, she learned her father and youngest brother were away for the day, exploring museums. Although he had visited all of the sights of London, her father never tired of visiting the museums.

Jane found her mother sitting with Amelia in the drawing room, poring over a book of dress patterns while they waited for tea to be served.

Georgette took one look at her daughter and rose from the sofa. "What has that blackguard done to you? You look worn to the bone."

"Did he hurt you?" Amelia asked, rising from the sofa, a look of concern etched upon her beautiful face.

"No. He didn't hurt me." Jane returned the quick hug her mother gave her. "But it has been a most extraordinary day."

Georgette's light brown brows lifted. "You must tell us everything."

"Yes." Amelia squeezed Jane's hand. "Tell us everything."

She needed to discuss her situation. She needed to feel she was not in this war all alone. Still, she certainly would not discuss the regrettable sensations the man could evoke in her. It was far too embarrassing, definitely much too humiliating, to discuss the way he had manipulated her sensibilities.

Lancaster had taken her completely off guard this morning. Under the circumstances, she supposed this horrible attraction was understandable. It was reasonable to assume the strain of the past few weeks had left her sensibilities vulnerable.

It was understandable that she might find this new incarnation of Lancaster intriguing. Still, he was a scoundrel who would use her attraction against her if she was not careful. She would simply have to remain unmoved by him. Yes, that was all she need do. Each time he provoked her, she would think of the true nature of the beast, the man lurking beneath the facade of Colin MacKenzie. That should be enough to keep her safe from the scoundrel.

Nearly a half hour after she had entered her mother's drawing room, Jane stood near one of the windows in the drawing room, watching a curricle rumble down Curzon Street. The world outside had no idea of her turmoil. Outside of this room the sun shone brightly.

Idly she ran her hand over Arthur's head, her fingers sliding through his thick, soft fur. The dog had not strayed from her side since she had rescued him from the kitchen in Lancaster House a few hours ago. Arthur leaned against her leg as she finished relating to her mother and sister what had happened since her confrontation with Lancaster the previous night. "The surgeon said he might regain his memory at any time."

"So he did suffer something from the blow to his head," Amelia said. "Pity you pushed him out of the way. The blackguard should have been sent straight to his maker."

Jane cringed at the venom in her sister's voice. She glanced at Amelia. Her sister was sitting beside her mother on the green velvet sofa. Sunlight streamed through the window behind Amelia, touching her golden hair. With her delicate features, Amelia looked an angel from heaven, except for the fury in her blue eyes. Jane suspected it would take a very long time for Amelia to recover from the blow of Lancaster's treachery.

Georgette reached over and patted Amelia's hand. If Amelia ever wondered what her mirror might reveal with the passage of years, she need only look at her mother, Jane thought. Although gray streaked her thick golden hair, and a penchant for sweets had thickened her waist, her mother's beauty had not been erased by time.

"Well, one mystery has been solved, at least," Georgette said.

Jane stared at her mother, completely at a loss. "Mystery?"

Chapter Ten

Woe to the youth whom Fancy gains,
Winning from Reason's hand the reins,
Pity and woe! for such a mind
Is soft, contemplative, and kind.
                    —Sir Walter Scott

"Until now, I could not understand why Lancaster would pursue you with such a vengeance." Georgette sipped her tea. "If he had been chasing after Amelia's skirts, I could have understood it. He has a reputation for wanting only the most beautiful females who cross his path."

Jane smiled at her mother's comparison of her beauty to that of her sister. From the time she was a child, Jane had accepted the truth that she was not the prettiest flower in the Eveleigh garden.

Amelia huffed. "I would not have the man if he were the last eligible male in London. I curse the day the scoundrel crossed my path."

Jane refrained from reminding her sister of the days

and nights Amelia had spoken of nothing but Lancaster's charms. Of course, that was before it had become obvious the marquess had set his sights on Jane.

"You know, Jane, if you had made the most of your Season, you would not be in this tangle," Georgette said. "You never did encourage any of the gentlemen who might have offered for you."

Jane thought of the Season she had enjoyed in the glitter of London society. That year she had felt like a princess. Yet it had lasted only a brief time. The financial situation of her family allowed for only one Season for each of the Eveleigh daughters. One Season of new gowns. One Season to attend balls and parties in an attempt to find a suitable husband.

"If only you had been more like Elizabeth and Harriet," Georgette said, her tone as matter-of-fact as always.

Jane had more than once wished she were more like the sisters before and after her in age. Both had taken advantage of their time in London. Elizabeth and Harriet were happily married.

"Of course, we could not have expected you to be the success that your sisters were." Georgette smiled at Amelia before turning her attention back to Jane. "But even though you may not be as pretty as the other girls, that does not mean you could not have found a suitable match. If you had applied yourself, you would not be in this tangle today. And poor Amelia would never have been put through this horrible ordeal. I always said you spent entirely too much time with your nose in a book."

Jane rubbed her arms, feeling chilled in the sunny room. Perhaps she could have avoided this mess if she had not been so determined to find her one and only love. Of course, the mess might also have been avoided if Amelia had not gambled with a known scoundrel. Yet she knew her mother would not see it from that perspective, and she had no desire to hurt her sister's feelings by dredging up what might have been. "I never would have imagined a man would marry a woman simply because she did not like him."

"I suppose Lancaster was simply bored with all the women who were always so anxious to impress him," Georgette said.

Amelia stiffened. "I was never obvious."

"No, of course not, dear. I did not mean you." Georgette lifted the silver tea server from the tea cart beside her and filled a cup as she spoke. "Come have some tea, Jane. You will feel better with a nice hot cup of tea."

Jane crossed the room with Arthur trotting beside her. She sat on an armchair near the sofa, the thickly stuffed cushion hard beneath her. Arthur curled into a big ball at her feet. He hadn't acted this frightened of being abandoned since she had found him three years ago.

Georgette poured cream and sugar into Jane's tea, then stirred the mixture, staring down into the cup for a long while before she spoke. "An annulment will cause a great deal of gossip. And we do have Amelia to consider. And Caroline after her."

Jane glanced to her sister, her chest growing tight. This was Amelia's chance to make a suitable match. Any hint of scandal could chase away her suitors. And what would happen to her youngest sister's chances should Jane cause a scandal? "An annulment is my only chance to be free of him."

Amelia lifted her chin, an uncomfortable blend of embarrassment and guilt filling her eyes. "I did not realize he would do anything so vile."

"I know," Jane said. Still, all of Jane's assurances that she did not blame Amelia had not been enough to mend the damage Lancaster's machinations had caused. Before he had slithered into their lives, Jane and Amelia had shared every confidence, every hope, every dream. Now each time she saw Amelia, Lancaster crept between them like a malevolent phantom.

"It is all that blackguard's fault," Amelia said, her

voice strained with emotion. "He is the cause of all this trouble."

"Yes. He is. You are not to be blamed." Georgette looked at Jane, a hard glint in her eyes. "If you truly are unhappy, then you should be free of him. Even though he is incredibly wealthy."

Jane accepted the cup and saucer from her mother. Fragrant steam brushed her lips as she took a sip of the sweet, creamy tea. "There is a great deal money cannot provide, Mama."

"I suppose. Although it could not be proven by me." Georgette lifted her spoon and idly stirred her tea, then tapped the edge of her cup, silver pinging softly against porcelain. "Do you know, Lady Vivian Rutledge stopped by today. Your marriage to a marquess has elevated the entire family. And one would think it possible for such a connection to benefit not only poor Amelia, who has suffered greatly by this horrible tangle, but also Caroline. I actually thought you might give a ball for Caroline when she was ready to enter society. A ball at Lancaster House would assure her success. I do not suppose you could wait for this annulment until after Caroline is settled?"

"Caroline will not leave the schoolroom for two more years, Mama," Jane said.

Georgette lifted her brows. "I suppose it is too much to ask of you."

Guilt settled upon Jane's shoulders like drops of lead. "Lancaster has given me six months, Mama. I do not believe the offer shall remain open after that time."

"I see." Georgette leaned over and patted Amelia's hand. "Since your sister's Season has been quite torn to bits over all of this, I had hoped you might see fit to sponsor her again next year. But if you are certain this annulment is what you want, then I suppose she shall have to choose from the offers she has received this year."

Amelia lowered her gaze to her tea, the corners of her mouth growing tight. "Yes. I suppose I shall."

Jane felt a few more lead pebbles drop upon her shoulders. Amelia looked as though she were being led to the gallows.

"Amelia was certain Lancaster would offer for her, as was I. And to be humiliated the way she was . . . That man used her dreadfully."

Jane glanced down into her tea. "I am only glad she was not trapped in his net the way I have been."

"Don't be a silly goose. If I had thought for one moment Amelia would not have been happy with Lancaster, I never would have encouraged the match."

Jane looked from her mother to her sister. There was a time when Amelia had imagined she would be happy with Lancaster, but certainly now she must realize she had escaped the gallows. "You must now realize you would not have been happy with him."

"Of course." Amelia kept her gaze directed toward her tea. "It is simply . . . I still cannot imagine why he treated me so cruelly. Did he not see I would have made a marvelous marchioness? What could he have been thinking, to choose you over me?"

"I don't know," Jane said.

Georgette reached over and patted Amelia's hand. "He must be blind, dear."

Amelia glanced up at Jane. "He is a horrible man. I only wish there were something I could do to make things right."

In that instant, as she looked at her young sister, Jane realized Lancaster's assessment of Amelia had been more to the point than she had realized. Amelia would have married him. Even knowing the perfect scoundrel that he was, she would have married him. "You must not blame yourself. You could not have suspected how treacherous he was."

Amelia glanced down at her tightly clenched teacup.

"I did not mean to cause you any pain, Jane."

"I know. I am only glad you were not trapped as I was."

"Jane, you must realize Amelia is not at all like you. She was meant to preside over a great house. If Lancaster had offered for her, I believe they would have made a successful match."

Jane looked at her mother. "But the man is incapable of honest affection."

"For some a great title and a tremendous fortune can go a long way in fostering affection, dear. I realize you may be having trouble seeing the advantages, but they do exist. Even though you are not happy with him, Lord Lancaster would have been a splendid husband for Amelia. Unlike you, she would have made a marvelous marchioness. And I am afraid the highest she may hope for now is a viscountess, that is if she accepts Breckenridge. And he does have that dreadful lisp. Of course, we do have until the end of the Season. Perhaps she shall make a better connection."

Amelia's lips drew into a tight line. "Everyone assumed I was being pursued by Lancaster. No one would dare cut him out, so most of the eligible peers kept their distance. Now they look at me as someone Lancaster passed over. That blackguard all but ruined my chances for a truly splendid match."

Jane forced a sip of tea past her tight throat.

Georgette cut a slice from the round lemon cake smothered in creamy white frosting that sat on the tea cart and slipped it onto a plate. She looked first at Amelia, then at Jane. "Cake?"

Jane shook her head. "I am not very hungry."

Amelia also refused the cake. "I must think of my figure, Mama."

"Yes, I suppose I should also. Still, Cook did make this because he knew it was one of my favorites. I would hate to disappoint him." Georgette sank her fork into the slice of cake. "Mmm, wonderful. You don't believe Lancaster is really ill, do you, Jane?"

Jane met her mother's steady gaze. "I'm not certain what to believe."

Georgette slipped a forkful of cake into her mouth and slowly chewed it before she responded. "You have always been far too kind and much too trusting for your own good. It is obvious this man is trying to gain your sympathy."

"You would be a fool to believe anything he told you," Amelia said.

Jane looked away from the anger in her sister's eyes. "The surgeon said it was possible he was suffering from some kind of amnesia."

"Amnesia?" Georgette pursed her lips, her blue eyes revealing her skepticism. "I have heard of amnesia, people not remembering who they are. But to imagine you are someone entirely different? I have never before heard of anything so preposterous."

Jane rubbed her thumb over the smooth ivory porcelain of her cup. "It is preposterous, isn't it?"

Georgette nodded. "Ludicrous."

"Another of his tricks," Amelia said.

"How could he possibly hope for anyone to believe him?" Jane sipped her tea, the warm liquid heating her chest. "And that is one of the reasons why I keep wondering if he is truly ill."

"I am not as easily convinced," Georgette said.

"Nor am I," Amelia added.

Jane looked from her sister's narrowed eyes to her mother's calm countenance. "At first I thought it was all part of his strategy."

Georgette nodded. "I am certain it is. That man does not do anything that is not carefully planned."

"I keep wondering, would he actually use a tactic that would make him appear to be so . . . uncivilized? I simply cannot imagine he would pretend to have lost his mind. He has far too much pride."

"Do you honestly believe Dominic Stanbridge some-how imagines himself a Scottish earl from the sixteenth century? Brought here by witchcraft?" Amelia asked.

Jane cringed when presented with the bald facts. "Anderson seemed quite convinced."

"I am certain Lancaster paid him well for his assistance in this game," Georgette said. "No doubt he sent a note to him last night, or early this morning, enlisting his aid."

Had he sent a note to the surgeon, enlisting Anderson's assistance? It would make sense. "He made a spectacle of himself in front of Pembury this afternoon."

Georgette sank her fork into her cake once again. "As I recall, Pembury relies a great deal on Lancaster for funds."

"How do you explain his odd behavior?" Jane asked. "He actually walked down the street in his dressing gown."

"It is a trick," Amelia said. "A ploy to gain your sym-pathy. He made a bargain with you and he intends to win."

Jane nodded. "It could be. It would suit him. It is just . . . he is so sincere. I am not certain Lancaster could lie without betraying himself."

"Scoundrels often have that ability, dear." Georgette scooped a dollop of frosting off her plate with the tip of her fork. "It is what makes them successful scoundrels."

"I know." Jane looked down at Arthur, reviewing all the reasons she should not believe Lancaster. "Still, if he is actually ill, it is my duty to tend to him."

Georgette pointed her fork at her. "That is what he wants you to think."

"It is his way of trapping you." Amelia leaned forward in her chair. "You must not allow him to manipulate you."

"I suppose it is possible that he is playing a game with me, but—"

"Jane, you haven't much experience with men, and Lancaster is hardly an ordinary man." Georgette swirled her fork through the icing. "For an intelligent girl, you are certainly acting terribly foolish."

Jane knew far too well how vulnerable she was where this man was concerned. He was beyond her experience in every way.

"Perhaps you should simply forget all about this silly bargain you have made with him." Georgette dabbed at her lips with a linen napkin. "You are certainly no match for him. Admit defeat."

Jane shivered deep inside when she thought of life with a man who had no capacity for affection. "I cannot imagine a life with him."

"I see." Georgette covered Amelia's hand with her own in a comforting gesture. "I suppose if you must go through with this, you must. Still, I wonder if you can possibly outwit him, when he has already managed to fool you."

"I have no intention of allowing him to manipulate my sensibilities, Mama. Still, I could not live with myself if I were to turn my back on him when he was truly ill."

"And if he pretends to be ill for several years?" Amelia asked. "Then what shall you do?"

Jane felt as though she was wrapped in wool, unable to move, barely capable of drawing a breath. "It is a nightmare."

"It is all in how you look at it." Georgette wagged her fork at Jane. "You could make the most of the situation."

"I am sorry, Mama, but I cannot remain his wife. Not if I have a chance for freedom."

Georgette sighed. "As you wish. There is very little I can do to change your mind. But I do hope you will think on all I have said."

"I will." Jane set her cup and saucer on the table beside

the sofa. She realized she was being terribly selfish, but she could not imagine a life with Lancaster. When she was ready to leave, Amelia accompanied her to the front door. They walked downstairs without a word passing between them.

In the entry hall, Amelia turned to face her sister. "I hope you know it is Mama's wish you stay married to Lancaster, not mine."

Jane would have felt better if Amelia had not looked so unhappy. "I realize Mama expects you to choose a husband by the end of the Season, but if you are not in love with any of your suitors, I think you would be making a mistake to marry one of them."

"And what future would I face if I do not marry?" Amelia glanced away from Jane, focusing her attention on the dog at her feet. "You may have been content to remain a spinster, but it would not suit me. London suits me. I would die if I had to stay in Leicester all of my life. At least Breckenridge will bring me to town each Season."

Jane touched Amelia's arm. "Perhaps you should give yourself more time to find someone you truly care about."

Amelia stiffened. "There is very little time left."

If Jane remained married to Lancaster, her sister need not worry about finding a husband this Season. And Caroline would also be assured of all the time she needed. "Perhaps I am being selfish in wanting this annulment."

Amelia lifted her head, tilting her chin at a proud angle. "Pity Lancaster survived the accident. If he had died, you would have been well situated without being burdened by the blackguard."

Hatred burned in her sister's eyes, so raw it startled Jane. "You're very angry right now. I know you don't mean to wish such a tragedy on anyone."

Amelia lifted one finely arched brow. "A man as cruel as he does not deserve my sympathy."

Jane had never realized how volatile Amelia could be. "Lancaster has given me an enormous amount of pin money. I am certain I can set most or all of it aside for you. In six months, you will have more than enough to have another Season."

Amelia stared at her sister. "What of you? Will you not wish to buy things? New gowns, shoes, hats?"

"I have lived all of my life without that money." Jane grasped Amelia's hand. "I can manage to do without it now. I hadn't planned to use any of his money. But I see no reason why he should not pay to undo the misery he has caused you."

"Oh." Amelia squeezed Jane's hand. "That would be marvelous. Another Season. I am certain I could make a much better match if I only had more time."

Jane brushed her lips against Amelia's soft cheek, the fragrance of rose water flooding her senses. "You shall have your Season."

Amelia hugged Jane tightly, then pulled back and looked at her. "Do be careful with Lancaster."

Jane nodded. "I will not allow him to win."

A breeze brushed her cheeks when Jane left the house, carrying a trace of smoke and dust. Although Jane enjoyed the city when she was here, she preferred the soft, sweet-smelling air and the quiet she could find only in the country. London was forever noisy, with carriage wheels and horses' hooves clattering upon the pavement. Unlike Amelia, Jane could not imagine living in town. Just as she could not imagine living her life with a man she did not love. If she were not careful, that was precisely the disaster that would befall her.

When Jane drew near Lancaster House, someone bumped into her with enough force to make her stumble. She hit a lamppost, ramming her shoulder into the wrought iron. The sudden flare of pain sucked the air from her lungs. She turned and found Penelope Clyde-staff standing a few feet away. She looked too delicate to have delivered the blow that had sent her reeling, but Jane knew that was precisely what she had done. The look of fury in her green eyes startled Jane more than the sudden impact had.

"Oh, my, I am so terribly sorry." Although Penelope smiled, her eyes remained frozen with fury. "I do hope you weren't hurt."

"No. I am fine." Jane could not shake the feeling the collision had not been an accident. Apparently Penelope was once again haunting the street outside of Lancaster House. Had she also taken once more to carrying a pistol? Arthur pressed against Jane's skirt, a low growl emanating from deep in his throat. She rested her hand on his neck.

Penelope looked at the dog, one light brown brow lifting. "A mongrel. I am surprised Dominic would allow the animal into his home. Apparently his tastes have changed dramatically. At one time he wanted only the very best of everything."

Jane could understand why Penelope had caught Lancaster's attention. Penelope was beautiful, with pale yellow hair swept up from her long neck, and features perfect enough to make her appear a porcelain doll. Unfortunately the hard glint in her eyes spoiled her perfection.

Penelope looked Jane over as though she were appraising every detail of her clothes and person. "I can see he is no longer quite so discriminating."

A carriage rumbled by, the clatter of horseshoes and wheels upon pavement pounding with the blood in Jane's ears. "Perhaps he was looking for something that did not bore him."

"You do not have what it takes to keep him satisfied. It is only a matter of time before he sends you away. Perhaps not as far as New York, but to Devonshire at the very least." Penelope twirled her lace-trimmed parasol upon her shoulder. "Enjoy yourself while you may."

Jane watched her walk away, her gown of pale green silk swishing like the tail of an angry cat. Although she did not condone his actions, she could understand why Lancaster had shipped Penelope across the Atlantic. She had the feeling Penelope would be delighted to know of Lancaster's illness. And for some reason, Jane was determined to protect the man from that kind of ridicule.

Jane managed to walk the rest of the way to Lancaster House without incident. Unfortunately the calm did not last. As she stepped through the front door, shutting out the warm afternoon, it was as if she had plunged into a storm.

"Beg pardon, Your Ladyship."

One look at Hedley's expression and Jane felt the urge to run. He was standing a few feet away, his hands clasped in front of him, looking like a man who had just witnessed a murder. "I do not believe I like the expression on your face, Hedley. It bodes ill."

Hedley nodded. "It is His Lordship."

Jane gripped the leather collar around Arthur's neck, holding him when he would explore the house. "Does he have a sword again?"

Hedley's eyes grew wide. "I did not think of that, Your Ladyship. I hope he does not."

"What is it, Hedley? What has happened?"

Hedley cleared his throat. "His Lordship is missing, Your Ladyship."

"Missing?"

Hedley nodded. "I sent a boy with a message to your family's home. He must have missed you."

Jane squeezed Arthur's collar. "What has happened?"

"Millie, that is one of the maids, Your Ladyship, she saw His Lordship leave the house. Walked out the front door, she says. Dressed in a most unusual fashion."

Jane's chest tightened. "I thought he was going to rest. When did he leave?"

"Not more than an hour ago, Your Ladyship. And no

one seems to know where he was going. I thought, given the peculiar way His Lordship has been acting, you should like to know, Your Ladyship."

"Yes." Her mind flooded with all the horrible possibilities of Lancaster prowling the streets of London in his condition. She had to find him before he did something unforgivable.

Chapter Eleven

Star to star vibrates light; may soul to soul
Strike thro' a finer element of her own?
 —Alfred, Lord Tennyson

The scent of burning candles flooded her senses as Jane
entered the small church. She had taken Lancaster's town
coach, intending to search all of London for the missing
marquess. Yet the coach had traveled only a short distance when Jane had seen this church set back from the
street. She wasn't certain what had made her ask Henderson to stop here. It wasn't a place she would expect
to find Dominic Stanbridge. Yet for some reason, upon
seeing the small stone structure, she felt certain she
would find him inside.

She closed the door softly, yet a soft thump echoed
through the church. The noise did not disturb the man
inside. She paused just inside the door, her gaze fixed on
Lancaster, who knelt at the altar at the front of the
church, head bowed, hands clasped in prayer. Sunlight

poured through the stained-glass windows above him, capturing him in its radiance. In that moment everything else in her existence faded into shadow, as if the light were radiating from him, drawing her like a beacon.

The sensation both unsettled and beguiled her. Her skin tingled with the same excitement that assaulted her whenever he was near. She turned, following an instinct that shouted, *Protect yourself!* Yet she froze with her hand on the brass handle. It was her duty to protect him until the time he regained his identity. If he had indeed lost his memory. His own lack of honor did not matter, she assured herself. She would not stoop to his level.

She turned and squared her shoulders. She could and would face this man and the unsettling emotions he evoked within her. Her footsteps tapped on the oak floor, the soft sound warning him of her approach. Yet he did not stir, not even when she paused beside him. Instead he remained in his pious posture, head bowed, eyes closed, earnest in silent prayer. She stood beside him, an intruder into this most private of moments, uncertain of what to say, reluctant to interrupt his prayers.

"I wondered if you might come to me," he said without looking at her, his deep voice a low rumble in the quiet church.

He'd thought she would find him? Here? "I was worried about you."

Lancaster glanced up at her, his expression illuminated by the candles burning on branched candlesticks in front of the altar. In spite of the dark smudges beneath his stunning eyes, he looked so handsome her chest ached. "Because I am a poor man who has lost his mind?"

"If you are truly ill, you should not be wandering about London in your condition. You could get hurt."

He smiled, the grin failing to warm the chill in his eyes. "Your concern is touching, my lady. Particularly when it is for a man you despise."

She held his gaze, bristling at the accusation burning

143

there. He was half out of his mind, she reminded herself, seeking patience. If she were in his situation, who could tell what she might believe? "You are my responsibility. I really wish you would not wander off this way."

He nodded, but his expression told her he was not convinced her motivation was innocent. "Often a walk will help clear my thoughts. When I saw this kirk, I thought I might find some comfort here."

She looked up at the large wooden cross behind the altar, a sense of serenity stealing through her. "This is not a place I would expect to find Lord Lancaster."

"And yet you found me here." He stood and faced her. "I wonder what brought you here, Lady Jane."

"I don't know." She rubbed her arms, feeling chilled in spite of the warmth of the church. "When I saw the church, I simply had a feeling you would be here. It is the strangest thing."

"Is it?"

From his expression, he did not find it at all odd. "How would you explain it? No, wait, let me guess. You would say I used my magical powers to locate you."

He studied her a long moment. "You called me to you over the ages. Now you find me in a place you say yourself is not one where you would find Lancaster. And still you say you are not a witch."

She had no other explanation for the feeling that had gripped her. Still, she sought one far more rational than what he implied. "I suppose I stopped here because the church looked very old and I thought a man who believed he was from the sixteenth century might wander inside." The logical explanation sounded weak even to her own ears. He certainly did not look convinced. "You *are* Dominic Stanbridge."

"I know who I am." A muscle in his cheek bunched with the clenching of his jaw. "I came here to pray for my family. A strange thing, perhaps, since they have all perished long ago."

The anguish in his eyes touched her deep inside. She could only imagine the pain she would feel if she awakened one morning and found that all of her family and friends had perished. "You have five sisters who are all older than you are. But they are very much alive."

He smiled, a hard glint entering his eyes. "I have two sisters, not five. Isabel is two years older than I. She married the Earl of Dunleith five summers past. And Maura, who is five years younger than I. She still lives at Kintair, with my mother, Margaret, and the youngest of my family, Campbell, who is a lad of fourteen summers."

An odd sensation curled in the pit of her stomach as she listened to him. He seemed so certain of himself and the life he had created. It was almost as if she truly were speaking to an entirely different man. "Your mother's name is Vanessa. She married an American after your father died. She lives in Philadelphia. Your father died when you were a boy."

"My father took ill and died just four months past. My mother lives at Kintair. At least she did in my time." His voice deepened as he continued. "Now I shall never again see her face, or the faces of my sisters and my brother. Unless you reverse your spell."

She looked straight into his eyes. "I did not cast a spell on you."

"You look so innocent, lass." He stepped closer, closing the distance between them until he was so close she could feel his warmth slip around her. He touched her, brushing his fingers over her cheek in a slow slide. "Yet if you did not bring me here, who did?"

"No one." Her heart thundered so loudly, she was certain he could hear each quick beat. "There is no such thing as magic."

He shook his head. "I know better."

She had the most uneasy feeling looking into his eyes, as though he knew things that might frighten her. It was all part of his fairy tale, she reminded herself. He was simply drawing her into it. Her own romantic nature worked in his favor. "You are confused."

"The feelings inside of me are confusing." He slid his hands down her arms. Her skin tingled, as though he had slid his palms over her bare skin. "I feel as though you are a part of me, Lady Jane. As though I have been wandering all of my life, not really understanding how lost I was until you came into my life. If not magic, then what has cast this spell upon me?"

Breathe. She really must remember to breathe. Still, the air seemed far too thick to draw into her lungs. "It is the injury. It has done something to your reasoning."

He did not look convinced. Instead he looked even more suspicious. "If you are telling the truth, and you are not a witch, then how did you find me?"

"I told you."

"Aye. You came here because it was an old kirk." He held her gaze, his expression hard and unyielding. "And for all the world, you seem to believe it."

She stepped back from him, hoping the distance might ease the horrible pounding of her heart. It didn't. "And how would you explain it? If you were to accept that I am not a witch."

"It is beyond my ken." He looked away from her, directing his gaze to the stained-glass window above her. "If you be not a witch, was I brought here because this is the path of my destiny?"

Destiny? A man sent across the ages to be with the woman of his destiny. Heaven above, it was so tempting to believe in the fairy tale. "And I found you here because we are linked together in some mystical way? Is that what you are trying to imply?"

He didn't say anything for a long while, simply stood before her, looking at her as if he knew her better than she knew herself. "My duty lies at Kintair. I know not what magic brought me here, but I cannot stay. Not if it means my family will suffer."

She could not afford to believe in this fairy tale, no matter how alluring it might seem. "Your train will be ready by six. If we leave this evening, we will arrive near Kintair early tomorrow morning. Do you feel up to traveling tonight?"

"Aye." He took her arm and ushered her toward the door. "I wish to return to Kintair as soon as possible."

She glanced at him as they left the church. She had reason to doubt him, but when she assessed his costume, she was convinced the always elegant, forever fashionable Marquess of Lancaster was out of his head.

He had tucked his dress shirt inside his riding breeches. The white silk shirt was still unfastened, but the gap in the front would not be noticed so much as his choice of coats. Apparently he had decided one of his sleek black evening coats completed his costume.

A solid parade of elegant carriages crept along the street in front of the church. It was the hour of promenade in London, the time when society headed for the park to see and be seen. As they approached the street, she noticed the looks cast in their direction. "Did anyone happen to stop you on the street to speak with you?"

"No." He frowned down at her, looking uneasy suddenly. "Yet there were more than a few people who stopped and stared, as though I were a Selkie who still wore his sealskin."

She wasn't quite certain what he meant, but she did grasp the gist of his speech. "I am afraid Pierson may decide to jump from the roof when he hears you were seen in public dressed in this manner."

Lancaster's lips tightened, the look of embarrassment that crossed his features unmistakable. "You will show me how to clothe myself so as not to make me appear a fool?"

"I am certain Pierson will set you straight. If we can

147

convince him to come within an arm's length of you."
She glanced down at his side. "At least you left the sword
at home. That is a beginning."

"I have not seen any man carry a sword."

"I am glad to hear it."

She scrambled into the coach, anxious to get Lancaster
out of the way of curious eyes. The coach swayed as he
climbed in behind her. Although he sat on the seat across
from her, he was still too close. In contrast to the up-
heaval he wrought within her, the infuriating creature did
not seem to be the least bit affected by her presence. He
sat staring out the window of the coach, as if the most
marvelous sights in the entire world lay just beyond the
glass.

Could anyone manufacture that look of awe and won-
derment? He was looking at the ordinary streets of London as though each sight were new and special.

"What is a Selkie?" She asked the question partly out
of curiosity and partly because she wanted to see if he
could stick to his role.

He tore his gaze from the town houses they were passing and looked at her. "The Selkie folk are enchanted
beings, akin to fairies. They live in the sea, safe in a
second skin that makes them appear as seals to the eye
of man. Yet Selkies can remove their sealskins like a
cloak. And when they do, a Selkie cannot be told apart
from a human man or lass."

"So they live in the sea and sometimes roam about on
land?"

"Aye. 'Tis said the Selkie folk take great pleasure in
playing tricks on humans."

A glint of mischief filled his eyes, the same look her
older brothers would get when they were ready to play
a joke upon their unsuspecting sisters. Still, she could not
resist her own curiosity. "What type of tricks?"

"Upon each evening's low tide, a Selkie male will hide
his sealskin near the shore and go in search of a comely

human lass, seduction on his mind. So beautiful to behold he is, so powerful, so charming, no maiden is safe. One look in his eyes and she will be his, body and soul. He is an ardent lover, claiming her time and time again while the moon makes its flight across the heavens, taking and giving pleasure until the poor lass collapses in his arms, exhausted, spent."

His words conjured erotic images in her mind, and with the images came a prickling heat, a tightening of her private woman's flesh that made her want to shift on her seat. She squeezed her hands together on her lap. "And after he has had his fill of the poor human lass, then what does he do?"

"He whispers, 'Forget me,' into her ear, then leaves with the first light of dawn. He then dons his sealskin and swims out to sea." Lancaster smoothed his fingertips over his thigh, drawing her attention to the sleek muscles beneath the cloth.

The hot, prickling sensation spread upward and outward from her nether region. For the life of her, Jane could not suppress the insidious excitement simmering through her, just as she could not stop wondering what it might be like to feel his hand upon her skin. "So a Selkie male is a scoundrel who seduces a woman, takes his pleasure, then abandons her."

Lancaster laughed softly, a well-used laugh that had no resemblance at all to the cynical chuckle Lancaster usually employed. "He takes his pleasure, but he gives pleasure in return. And each time a Selkie comes to shore he is taking a great risk. You see, if a human steals his sealskin, he cannot return to the sea. In this way, many a Selkie has been trapped by a lass wanting a bonnie husband."

"And the Selkie females? Do they treat the human male in the same fashion?"

He held her gaze, a challenge in his eyes. "Only if they see one worth the risk."

Jane managed to force her lips into a smile. "In that case, I would guess the Selkies coming to shore are all male."

He winked at her. "You have not been spending your time with the right men."

She eyed him up and down, then met his gaze. "Obviously."

He leaned forward and brushed his fingertips over her knees. Although her gown, petticoats, and drawers protected her, she felt his touch all the same—a tingling sensation, as though his fingers stroked her bare skin. "Is that why you brought me to you?"

She flicked away his hand, as though he were an annoying fly. "Your memories may be buried, but your high opinion of yourself is alive and well."

He leaned back, a slight grin curving his lips. " 'Tis another man you are facing, Lady Jane. One who will not be easily tamed."

"You flatter yourself."

One black brow lifted. "Do I?"

"Yes." Jane held his gaze, even though she wanted to curl up in a corner and hide. "You see, I have no desire to tame you. All I want is for you to regain your memory and leave me in peace."

"Remove your spell, and I will leave you to your Englishman."

She clenched her teeth. "There is no spell."

"So you say." He turned his attention to the window, dismissing her as easily as he might shove aside an empty plate.

She turned her own attention to the window, hoping to appear every bit as nonchalant. Yet as much as she tried to focus on the people or the carriages or the fading day, she could not shove the scoundrel out of her thoughts. *Infuriating brute!* She had thought Lancaster the most odious man she had ever met. But that was before she met Colin MacKenzie. Somehow she would find a way to get rid of the blackguard. She would spark Lancaster's memory, or catch him in this lie. Either way, she would send Colin MacKenzie packing.

Chapter Twelve

While I am I, and you are you,
So long as the world contains us both,
Me the loving and you the loth,
While the one eludes, must the other pursue.
                              —Robert Browning

Colin stared at the small cylinder of light burning behind an etched crystal globe. "Incandescent light," he whispered, repeating the words that Lady Jane had used for the odd candle.

There were many such candles in this chamber, attached to the walls, each encased in fine crystal. All powered by electricity. And Lady Jane claimed she did not believe in magic. How could she not believe in magic when surrounded by such marvels? And how could you not believe in magic if you were a witch who had transported a soul across more than three hundred years?

Why would she lie? He went to the bathtub and stared down into the water. Unless, of course, she needed him to believe he was truly this man Lancaster. For what purpose? All women were mysteries, but Lady Jane was perhaps the most difficult he had ever tried to solve.

He ran his hand through the water tumbling from the gold spout into the large tub. It was warm. He laughed softly, delighted at the silky feel of the water upon his skin. What a marvel, to have warm water tumble from a spout by simply turning a handle.

"Lancaster. Where are you?"

He turned toward the door at the sound of Lady Jane's voice. The irritation in her voice made him wonder what had set her at odds. "I am in the bathing chamber."

A few moments later she breezed into the room, walking in that swift, no-nonsense stride he had come to associate with her. Most women he knew preferred to stroll as though floating across the floor, as though they were ethereal creatures who might take wing at any moment. Not Lady Jane. She always walked as though she had somewhere to be and something to do.

"It seems . . ." She froze, her eyes growing wide as she saw him standing by the tub. "Oh, my good gracious!"

He glanced behind him, searching for the cause of her shock. He saw nothing except a reflection of his image in the mirror. "What is it?"

She pressed her hand to the base of her neck. "Must you always parade about without any clothes?"

His nakedness had shocked her? If he did not know better, he would say the woman had never in her life bedded a man. Yet she was married. It must all be part of her plan, this appearance of innocence where it could not truly exist. "And do men wear clothes to their bath in this time?"

"No. Of course not." A soft blush rose upward along her neck. "I simply do not care to be affronted by such a sight."

"Affronted? The sight of your husband's body offends you?"

"Yes. It most certainly does." She tugged at the white lace collar of her gown. "As it would any respectable lady. It is . . . indecent."

Still, the look in her eyes did not speak of a woman who had taken offense so much as it did a woman confronted with a sight beyond her ken. And in spite of her insistence to the contrary, she was staring at him as though she found the sight fascinating. He felt the brush of her gaze as though her hands slid over him, conjuring heat in her wake. Never in his life had a woman looked at him in this fashion, as though he were the most intriguing man on the face of God's green earth. His blood stirred; his member rose as if answering her siren's call. Her eyes lowered. Her breath escaped in a soft rush.

She turned away from him and grabbed a thick towel from a gold rack on the wall. "Will you please cover yourself," she said, tossing the towel at him.

He caught the towel, the thick white cloth soft upon his skin. He wrapped the big towel around his hips as he said, "You say it is not decent for a wife to see her husband the way God made him?"

"Certainly not." She glanced over her shoulder, then turned, apparently satisfied that he had covered himself. "A lady would not consider anything so vile as to view a man who is not wearing any clothes."

"And what of a husband?" He lowered his eyes, allowing his gaze to travel slowly over her. The gown she wore hugged her breasts. She was not a full-bosomed lass; her curves were slight compared to those of many women he had known. Yet she was sweetly rounded, delicately made. And for some reason he could not shake the feeling she had been fashioned just for him. It was sorcery more powerful than he had ever imagined. "A husband must see his wife's body."

She twisted the white lace at her neck. "He certainly must not."

He stared at her. "If that be true, then how can he make love to her?"

"In the dark." A dusky rose color crept upward, staining her cheeks. "Properly covered. A wife wears her nightgown. A husband does not disturb her more than he must."

"Disturb her?" He shook his head. "And here I was thinking there were so many marvels of your time. I can see there are a few things that have certainly not improved."

She folded her hands at her waist. "We have become more civilized."

"Civilized? Is that what you call it?"

"Yes."

"Cold is what I would say." A lock of hair had tumbled free of the coil she wore high on her head. The shiny brown tresses spilled over her shoulder, drawing his attention down to the curve of her breast. His palms itched to test the weight of those softly rounded mounds. "Now, in my time, as your husband, I would learn every curve of your body with my hands and my lips."

She drew in a sharp breath, as though he had touched her. Her eyes were wide and so filled with innocence he could scarcely believe she was a married woman. Obviously the Englishman she had married had never touched her the way a man should touch the woman he loved.

"I would know the taste of you beneath my tongue. I would breathe your special fragrance deep into my lungs. And each time I made love to you, I would hear your song of pleasure."

She moistened her lips, a quick slide that left an inviting sheen. "We have learned in this time to rise above our more bestial instincts."

"Bestial?" He shook his head. "I am thinking you have yet to taste true passion."

She lifted her chin. "Passion is hardly a proper emotion for a lady."

"And how would you know, if you have never tasted it?"

"You make it sound as though—Oh, my goodness!"

Water splashed his feet as she ran toward him. He turned and saw water spilling over the rim of the big tub. She brushed past him and turned the gold levers that controlled the flow. The water stopped pouring into the tub, but it continued to trickle over the curved rim onto the marble floor.

"Wonderful!" She turned and glared at him. "If you had to choose to assume another identity, I really wish you had chosen someone who did not have a penchant for terrifying the servants."

"I did not choose—"

"Pierson has suddenly taken ill. He will not come within sight of you. Since you have every servant in the house terrified of you, I doubt we shall even coax a maid up here to take care of this mess."

He suspected it was more than the water that had her in a fit of temper. "I could mop the water up with this towel," he said, slipping his thumb between his waist and the towel.

She slapped her hand over his. "Don't you dare."

The dusky blush coloring her cheeks made her eyes seem all the more silvery. He knew he was ensorcelled, because he was certain he had never in his life seen a more beautiful woman. Her fingers had slipped past his hand to burn the skin of his belly. He wanted for all the world to shift her hand to the part of him aching for her touch. "You have a fine, fiery temper, lass."

"I never lose my temper. At least I didn't until I met you." She drew in her breath, then released it. "You have the most annoying way of unsettling my sensibilities."

He slid his hand over hers, holding her fingers splayed against his belly. "And you have the most annoying way of making me ache for wanting you."

"Oh, you really should not say such things."

In her eyes he saw the look of a woman drawn to a man against her will. She burned with a longing that belied all her words of icy decorum. And he could feel the heat of the fire burning within her, the flames licking over his skin.

He glanced down into the water in the tub, an image rising in his mind—of a beautiful gray-eyed witch lying back in that big tub, water lapping at her naked skin, her arms reaching for him. He looked at her, blood pumping slow and hard into his loins. "Join me, lass. Come into the bath."

"I certainly will not." She yanked her hand from beneath his, ripping the towel free with the violent movement. She stepped back, the towel dangling from her fingers. Her gaze lowered to the potent proof of the power she held over him. "Oh, my goodness," she muttered.

He moved to block her way when she would have left him. "Stay, my lady. Join me in the bath."

She swallowed hard. "I told you, it would not be decent, even if we were happily wed. Which we are not."

He stroked his hand down her arm, feeling the fine trembling beneath his palm. She stood so close, he could smell the lemony scent of her skin. "This man Lancaster, he has hurt you?"

"You are ill. I am not at all certain it is a good idea to speak of such unpleasant subjects as our marriage."

"Any man who would harm a woman is not a man at all." He smoothed his hand over the ivory silk of her cheek. "Why have you brought me to you, Lady Jane?"

She shook her head. "I didn't."

"If there is no spell, then why do I want you as I have never wanted a woman before?"

"Want?" The word escaped on a soft stream of breath. She closed her eyes, and when she looked at him, a hard glint filled her silvery gaze. "You want every female who happens into your path."

He shook his head. "I do not allow what is below my waist to rule what is in my head. And yet with you, this need sinks deep into my very bones. I feel I have been searching for you all of my life and beyond. 'Tis magic."

"It is lust. You often suffer from it."

"Lust?" He slipped his hand around her neck and tipped back her head with the tip of his thumb. "And yet it burns hotter than ever before."

She rested her hand on his chest, as if to push him away from her. Yet her fingers curled against his skin, sending heat spiraling through him. She looked up at him, her eyes naked with emotion. He sensed she wanted him with the same powerful need with which he wanted her. Why was she fighting him? If she had called him to her side, why did she resist the attraction that bound them together?

"We must both face the truth. You are Dominic Stanbridge, a man who has lost his memory."

"I know who I am." He paused a long moment and explored her every feature. She looked as innocent as a babe. "And I know what brought me to this time and place. 'Tis you, Lady Jane. You are the reason I am here."

She shook her head. "You hit your head against a stone terrace. That's the reason you are acting this way. And it would be very foolish to imagine you could ever truly feel the things you say you do for me."

She looked so fragile, a delicate flower that could be crushed by a careless hand. And he could see she thought he would crush her if he had the chance. "Are you truly as innocent as you appear?"

She stepped back, dropping her hand from his chest. She glanced away from him, her gaze catching on something on the wall behind him. She blinked as if she were a child coming awake suddenly. "A sea captain."

"A sea captain?" He glanced over his shoulder and found a portrait of Lancaster. This time the man was dressed in dark blue, standing at the helm of a ship.

"Unlike you, I am not in the habit of playing games or deceiving people," she said, her voice growing hard.

"Neither am I."

She shook her head. "You may have lost your memory, but deep down inside, Dominic Stanbridge is lurking. And one day, without warning, he shall surface."

"You are afraid your husband will return?"

She drew in her breath. "It is only a matter of time before you regain your memory."

He held her gaze and shivered. He ran his hand over the bump at the back of his head, doubts whispering over him. Could it be? Was he truly a man who had lost his mind? He thought of his family, lifting their images from his memory, holding fast to the past he knew as Colin MacKenzie. "If you are saying this to make me believe I have lost my mind, it will not succeed. I know who I am."

"So do I." She brushed past him and hurried toward the door.

"Lady Jane."

She halted near the door, her shoulders rising slightly. "What is it?"

"Will you help me with the odd garments of this man Lancaster? Or would you prefer I choose without your assistance?"

Her quick sigh carried across the large room. "I shall be waiting for you in your chamber."

He smiled as he watched her leave. This tale of lost memories and illness could not be true, he assured himself. Though she seemed innocent and honest, she must be the key to his journey across the ages. He could not trust his instincts with this woman. Magic clouded his judgment when it came to Lady Jane.

Still, he knew who he was. Nothing she did would alter his mind. He had to figure out how he had come to this time and place. If the lady thought she could keep her secrets, she would soon find she had met her match. He ran his hand over the surface of the water, smiling down at his image. He would expose her secrets, even if it meant he had to seduce the enchantress. Aye, he just might have to seduce the beautiful witch.

Chapter Thirteen

Love is the tyrant of the heart; it darkens
Reason, confounds discretion; deaf to counsel,
It runs a headlong course to desperate madness.
                              —John Ford

Jane glanced down at the towel she still held clenched in her fist, trying not to think of how he had looked standing before her, naked and aroused. Still, the memories were there, seared across her brain. And with the memories came a lingering restlessness. He was the most infuriating creature on the face of this earth.

She tossed the towel over the arm of a chair on her way to the dressing room. The scent of sandalwood wrapped around her when she entered the large room. Coats, shirts, and trousers hung along one side of the room. It seemed so very intimate, going through his clothes, choosing appropriate attire for the handsome scoundrel. Fortunately Pierson had packed for his master while Lancaster had been gone. Their trunks were already on the way to the train. Still, she could strangle the valet for putting her in this awkward position.

She lifted a pair of drawers from the armoire, the silk cool against her fingers, a sharp contrast to the heat flooding her cheeks. The man had no right to look at her that way, even if he was her husband. It was indecent. No gentleman would ever gaze at a lady in that fashion, as though he wanted to strip away every stitch of her clothes. As though he intended to sweep her up into his arms and make love to her. Which was precisely what he had intended.

Certainly no proper lady would enjoy such a look. A lady certainly would not entertain such a notion as making love in a bathroom. Definitely a proper lady would not be standing here, wondering what it might be like to be swept into those strong arms, to feel the slide of that golden skin against hers, to taste his kisses and more. It was against everything she had learned at Boyington's School for Young Ladies.

Yet deep inside Jane knew propriety was merely a shield for unhappy wives. A means to endure the "marriage act." Both Elizabeth and Harriet had told her enough of married life to allow Jane to know that proper behavior between a man and a woman did not always involve separate beds and darkened rooms and restrictive clothing. Of course they were both happily married. They did not need to worry about tactics and bargains and a scoundrel who had no heart.

Oh, she wanted to scream. No, the truth was she wanted to run far away and hide. Yet she did not have the luxury of retreat. She had a duty to face. Still, even as she forced starch into her spine, doubts crept into her mind. *It is obvious this man is trying to gain your sympathy.* Her mother's words echoed in her memory.

Was this a trap? A way to creep past her defenses? Had he planned it all, every tactic to destroy her?

"No," she whispered. "Even Lancaster would not go to

this length to trap her. He would never allow anyone to imagine he had lost his mind. He would find a different tactic. Wouldn't he?

This was war, she thought, carrying an armful of clothes to the bed. Only the strong would survive. The attraction was startling, considering how she scorned the man. Never would she have imagined his touch could ignite such heat within her. If she was going to overcome this weakness, she must face it. It was lust. An unexpected physical attraction. To a man she despised?

In the past, she had often acknowledged his physical perfection without suffering this horrible debilitating attraction. What was it about this man who called himself Colin MacKenzie? Why did it take every ounce of will to keep from touching him? Yet the answer was clear. She kept seeing another man when she looked at him. In place of Lancaster, she saw a compelling Scotsman.

"He is Lancaster," she whispered. She could defeat Lancaster. All she had to do was think of her sister or any of the other women he had harmed. All she had to do was remember the shameful way he had treated her. Yes, she could and would defy Dominic Stanbridge. With that thought, she left the room. She would help the man regain his memory—under her own terms.

Jane was once again in Lancaster's bedchamber when he left the bathroom. Only she was not alone. She had one ally she could depend upon in the house. One individual sitting by her feet who had no compunction about showing Lancaster just how he felt about him. She stood, appalled at the trembling of her legs. He smiled when he saw her, a warm, embracing smile that added a beat to her already racing heart.

His black hair was swept back from his brow, emphasizing the perfectly carved lines and angles of his face. Water dripped from the black, curling strands, droplets sliding down his chest, catching in the black curls that spread like a hawk's wings upon a shield. His skin glistened in the lamplight, tempting her to test its texture with her fingers. Aside from the white towel cinched around his slim hips, he was bare. Yet she had glimpsed the potent masculinity now hidden by that towel. And a glimpse had only teased her curiosity.

He strolled toward her, each move filled with the peculiar grace that came only with power. She glanced down at the dog who sat by her feet, waiting for him to growl a warning at the man who was swooping down upon them. Arthur would keep Lancaster at bay.

The dog rose. It would come now, the deep growl that had frozen Lancaster upon his prior meeting with Arthur. She stared as her dog trotted forward, tail wagging as though he were greeting his long-lost brother.

Lancaster bent to stroke the dog's head, the towel parting, revealing a long length of finely muscled thigh. He glanced up at her and smiled. "And who is this?"

She had to swallow hard before she could use her voice. "Arthur."

"Arthur." He rubbed the dog's neck with both hands. "Ah, but you are a fine lad. I bet you are good company for your master."

Jane clenched her teeth. "He is my dog. You and Arthur do not get along."

He lifted his brows. "Is that so?"

"Yes. In fact you might say you share a mutual dislike for one another."

"I never would have guessed that."

"I would be careful," she said. "He could attack at any moment."

Arthur chose that moment to lick Lancaster's cheek.

"I can see he is a dangerous beast." Lancaster straightened, one corner of his lips tipping upward in a lopsided smile as he brushed the back of his hand over his wet cheek. "Do you suppose he is intending to drown me?"

She looked down at Arthur, who was sitting at Lancaster's feet, leaning against one long, bare leg. *Traitor!*

"He will probably attack you if you get too close to me. He is very protective of me."

"I see, so you brought him into my chamber to make certain I behaved myself," he said, his dark voice filled with humor.

Jane stiffened as Lancaster closed the distance between them. "I would suggest you keep your distance. Arthur can be a vicious animal."

Arthur tilted his head, his tongue lolling out the side of his mouth.

Lancaster leaned toward her, so close she could see the thick black lashes framing his eyes. "For one of your kisses, I would risk having my throat torn away by this vicious beast."

She stepped back and bumped into the side of one of the wing-back chairs near the hearth. "You and I do not share that kind of marriage."

"Ah, but 'tis a different man you have as your husband now." He nuzzled the skin of her neck. "Perhaps 'tis time you get to know him."

"No, thank you." She pushed against his chest, then slipped away from him. After putting the chair between them, she continued, her voice far less than steady. "I know you as well as I care to."

He idly stroked the fur behind Arthur's ear. The big dog rested his head against Lancaster's thigh. Jane frowned at the traitorous canine. Why in the world had he suddenly decided to take a liking to the scoundrel?

"It must be difficult," he said, his dark voice low and soft.

She glanced up at him. "What?"

"Being married to a man you do not love."

She searched his eyes, looking for a trace of sarcasm, and found none. Instead she saw understanding in his eyes, as well as questions. She supposed he could not help feeling confused. "I had always imagined there was only one honest reason for marriage. A deep, abiding affection."

"Aye." He glanced down at the dog, who looked as though he might fall asleep beneath Lancaster's surprisingly gentle touch. "When I was a lad of eighteen summers, my father came to me one day and suggested I pledge myself to a lass of his choosing. I knew it was expected of me to marry as my father wished. I was the eldest son, the one to carry on the bloodline. Yet I did not wish to do what he asked of me."

It wasn't real, of course. This story was only a creation of his injured mind. This man wasn't real. Yet she could not resist her own foolish curiosity. "What did you do?"

"I asked him to give me time to find a wife of my own choosing. And since he had always been a very generous man, he agreed." He smiled, his gaze still lowered to Arthur. "That was six summers ago."

"Six summers." She stared at him, marveling at the depth of the delusion. "That would mean you are only four and twenty."

He glanced up at her. "Aye. I was born on the seventh day of September, in the year of our Lord fifteen hundred and thirty-eight."

His conviction drew a shiver across her shoulders. Strange, but he looked younger today than he had yesterday. It was in his expression, in the glint of mischief that frequently filled his eyes, and in the smile that sent her heart racing. If she did not know better, she would swear this was another man. And therein lay the problem. "You are actually one and thirty. You were born on the sixteenth day of April, in 1858."

"I know when I was born, lass. But when I first looked in a mirror here, I saw that this man was older than I." He glanced toward the cheval mirror that stood in one corner of the room, studying his reflection a moment before turning his attention back to her. "Still, it appears this Lancaster is fit enough."

He spoke of his looks in a matter-of-fact tone, without a trace of conceit. He spoke of his appearance as though he could look at his reflection and not become enamored of the handsome face looking back at him. "Lancaster takes great pride in his appearance," she said.

He laughed softly. " 'Tis foolish to take great pride in something you had no part in."

Did he really have so little regard for his looks? She had never realized how very attractive the simple lack of conceit could be.

"I am curious." He ran his fingertip over the scar that slashed across the top of his left arm. "It seems a wicked scar. This man Lancaster was not a warrior, was he?"

"In a sense. One of his mistresses tried to murder him."

His black brows lifted. "Murder?"

"Yes. You had her exiled. But she has returned to London."

"And does she still want to murder Lancaster?"

"I would not be surprised."

He released his breath on a long sigh. " 'Twould seem I now have more than one woman whom I can count as an enemy."

Jane shrugged. "I would suppose more than two."

"And out of all of the women he knew, he chose you as his bride." Lancaster studied her a moment. "Apparently he also had an eye for quality."

Jane tried to ignore the fluttery sensation in her stomach. "And what about you? In all of this time, you never found the one woman you wished to marry?"

"No." He looked down at Arthur. "I had almost given up hope of ever finding her. When I went to bed last night, I had thought to pledge myself to the Mac-Donnell's eldest daughter. He had suggested the match. And 'twould help to put my uncle in his place." He looked up at her, all the mischief gone from his eyes and in its place a look that stirred her soul. "I had not planned to meet an angel upon awakening."

Angel. The room wobbled around her. She gripped the chair to steady herself, her fingers sliding against the dark velvet. In spite of her resolve to defend her heart against him, a shaft of longing quivered through her. "And here I was under the impression you thought I was a witch."

His jaw tightened. A glint of steel entered his eyes. "I wish I knew, lass. Angel or witch? Is this a spell that has clouded my mind? Or has some miracle brought me to your side? Have I found the woman of my destiny more than three hundred years in my future? Are you the one woman I was meant to find?"

The soft glow of electric lights embraced him. Yet he seemed a creature from another realm, a place beyond the touch of the modern world—tall, broad-shouldered, so splendid her heart ached to look at him. In place of the bitter sarcasm and icy arrogance she had come to know from this man, there burned hidden fires. The illusion was mystifying.

Colin MacKenzie was more than any dream she had ever dreamed, any fantasy she had ever spun. It was tempting to believe every word he said. So very tempting to lose herself in this fairy tale, to imagine a love so powerful it defied time. Yet she knew the price of believing this particular dream. "If you were well, you would not be speaking this way to me."

"So if I am to believe in this illness, then I must believe I am an English scoundrel."

She nodded, her voice strained as she replied. "Yes. I am afraid you must."

"I also must believe I have imagined the life I have lived as Colin MacKenzie. I must imagine that my family and my friends, all that I hold dear, never existed."

"You are Dominic Stanbridge," she said, reminding herself of the unrelenting truth of her situation. "Marquess of Lancaster. An Englishman without a drop of romance in your veins."

He laughed softly, the deep rumble wrapping around

her like warm velvet. " 'Tis something I cannot accept, my beautiful Lady Jane."

"Perhaps this trip to Scotland will help end the confusion. Once you confront the truth of Colin MacKenzie, you may once again remember your life as Dominic Stanbridge."

He held her gaze while the clock on the mantel behind her marked the passing seconds and her heart seemed to stop beating altogether. "I wonder what you shall say when confronted with the truth.

"More important, what will you think? Anderson said you could regain your memory at any time." She felt a soft tug on her vitals when she thought of losing this man. It was foolish in every regard. She had only known him a brief time, this man who didn't truly exist. Still, in a place locked deep in her soul, she could not dismiss the uncanny feeling that she had been waiting for this man all her life.

Silently she dismissed the notion. She was intoxicated by the romance of his story. The attraction she felt to this man was purely physical, she assured herself. Lust. A simple, all too human reaction to a handsome man who was half out of his mind. Since she had never been afflicted with that particular ailment in the past, it was little wonder she felt so overwhelmed. Now that she realized the cause of her restlessness, she could control it.

"I know who I am, Lady Jane. I will not allow anyone to steal my life from me."

She glanced away from him, trying to shut his compelling image out of her mind. "You will remember who you are. In time, you will remember."

"Is that how 'tis supposed to work?" he asked, moving toward her. "This spell you have cast, will it steal my mind slowly?"

She released her grip on the chair, meeting his gaze as he stalked her. "There is no spell."

"How can I believe you when I am standing here in

this time and place?" He advanced as he spoke, his
strides steady and slow, as if he wanted her to wonder
what would happen when he reached her. It worked.
"How can I believe the innocence in your eyes?"

Chapter Fourteen

Where Desire doth bear the sway,
The heart must rule, the head obey.
—Francis Davison

"I am telling you the truth." Jane bumped into the writing desk that stood against one of the paneled walls.

"Are you telling the truth, my beautiful enchantress?"

When he called her a witch, an enchantress, a sorceress, he actually made her feel as though she could cast spells, the naughty spells of a temptress. With this man she—the terribly ordinary Jane Eveleigh—actually felt like the type of woman who could make a man commit all manner of reckless, passionate acts. "Yes. I am telling you the truth."

"Such innocence." Lancaster moved toward her, more beautiful than the painting of him as a Greek deity that watched from above the mantel. Light from the sconce behind her spilled lovingly over the wide breadth of his shoulders, burnishing his skin. Her gaze dipped, following the play of light upon his damp chest, where thick muscles flexed with each move he made. Excitement coiled deep within her, stirring a restlessness that welled up inside of her, a spring beneath a soft summer rain.

"Don't," she whispered as he drew near.

"What are you so frightened of, enchantress?" He paused before her, so close his bare legs pressed her skirt flat against her legs. "I am your husband."

Her husband. Water dripped from his hair, snagging her attention, drawing her gaze down over the curve of his collarbone and below. She watched a shimmering droplet slide over his skin until it tangled in the soft-looking hair covering his chest. She could touch him; it was her right. She could stroke his skin, learn every curve of his body, all the places he was rough, all the places he was smooth. And be damned in the learning. "No."

"No?" He leaned against her, pressing his bared chest against her breasts. The layers of her gown and corset were not enough to protect her from the sharp stab of sensation he conjured with his touch. "You know I am not your husband?"

She tipped back her head, her breath escaping in a pitiful whimper when she tried to reply. He nuzzled the skin beneath her ear. She felt soft lips, warm breath. Shivers scattered over her shoulder at the slick heat of his tongue against her skin. "You mustn't do this," she said, her voice a harsh whisper.

"No?" He brushed his lips over the curve of her jaw as he spread his hand against her ribs. Heat soaked through her gown, impressing the imprint of each long finger upon her skin. "Tell me, why does this feel so right?"

It did feel right, as though she had been sleeping all of her life, waiting for his touch to awaken her, to bring her to life. Through the haze clouding her mind, a sane voice screamed all the reasons she could not allow this to happen. No matter how it felt, it wasn't right. It could not be right. Not with this man. She had no business being within a mile of this man and his worldly, all too cynical ways. If she were not very careful, he would chop her heart into tiny pieces.

She pressed her hands against the powerful curves of his upper arms, intending to push him away. Her hands slid against warm skin, so smooth and sleek. He spread his fingers, brushing the underside of her breast, ambushing her resolve.

"Why does it feel as though you were fashioned for me?" He slid his hand upward, over the curve of her breast. "Only for me. Is this magic?"

She could not reply, not even if she had the answer. Not with his hand so warm upon her. He found her nipple through the layers of her clothes, rolled the sensitive peak between his long fingers. She gasped at the sudden startling sensation splintering through her. The wall sconces filled the room with a golden light, but for her it seemed the sun had been trapped in the room, heating the air, until it became so thick she could scarcely draw a breath.

"You have bewitched me." He lifted her right hand from his arm and slipped it between them. "Feel what you do to me."

Warm cotton brushed her fingers—the towel cinched around his narrow hips. Slowly he drew her hand lower. She held her breath, knowing she should pull away from him. His hold was firm, yet somehow she knew he would release her should she protest. Still, the temptation of touching him was so great, the allure of the forbidden so near, she could not form the words to end this game.

He slipped her hand past the slit where the edges of the towel met. The heat of his skin trapped beneath the towel washed over her palm. Her fingers brushed skin smooth as velvet. He released her hand, and still she did not pull away. Instead she sought more of the forbidden, closing her fingers around potent masculinity.

He released his breath in a long sigh against her neck,

the damp heat seeping into her pores. He covered her hand with his and slid her fingers up and down the long length of him, moving to a rhythm that echoed deep within her. Without thought she shifted her hips, moving in time with the gentle rocking of her hand upon his flesh. A soft moan slipped past her lips, answering the low growl that escaped him. Suddenly he pulled her hand from his flesh.

"Enchantress," he whispered, sweeping her up into his arms.

Jane caught a glimpse of the hunger in his eyes before he kissed her, his lips sliding upon hers, warm and firm and achingly gentle. A kiss straight out of her dreams. Powerful muscles shifted against her as he carried her to the bed. This had to stop. Of course it had to stop. It was part of her own fairy tale, in which an unexceptional spinster met the love of her life. Yet fairy tales did not come true. Did they?

Silk velvet cradled her as he laid her down upon the bed. He covered her, the weight of his body pressing her into the thick eiderdown mattress. His weight was not oppressive, not frightening as it ought to be. Instead her body reveled in the power of his.

He slid his lips over the curve of her jaw, sprinkled soft kisses down the length of her neck. Shivers skittered over her skin like sparks scattered from a lovely warm fire. "What spell have you cast upon me?"

"There is no such thing as magic." Still, she felt bewitched, as though his touch had transformed her, altered the terribly mundane into something extraordinary.

He flicked his tongue against the sensitive skin beneath her ear. "What do you want from me?"

Everything, she thought. Too much. More than this man could ever give. Yet, lying here in his arms, she could almost believe he loved her. And love was all she wanted, a love that would last a lifetime. The love of a man who would still look at her with warmth in his eyes when they were both old and gray. She wanted all the ordinary things of life—affection, a comfortable home, healthy children. All the ordinary things that made life worth living. "Honesty."

He slipped his hand between their bodies, his deft fingers working the small buttons lining the front of her gown. He spread the garment, pressed his lips into the hollow at the base of her neck, and breathed against her skin. The damp heat sank deep into her pores, an elixir that spread through her, more intoxicating than warm sherry. "Why did you bring me to your side?"

The question sliced through her, like a December wind across a flame. With a harshness she could not ignore, reality pierced the sweet fantasy he had spun around her. How in the world had she been so foolish? She pushed against his shoulders. "That is enough."

He lifted his head and looked down into her eyes. "Is it?"

Damp black strands curled around his face. Lamplight fell softly upon him, highlighting the sheer male beauty of his face. He looked like some dark pagan creature, a Selkie fresh from the sea, a mythical lover who prowled the earth with one goal in mind: seduction. The hard glint in his eyes killed any hope that he'd been swept away by the desire he had tapped deep within her. One look into those incredible blue eyes told her this was nothing but an attempt to seduce some imagined truth out of her. And everything he had said to her, all that nonsense of destiny and love and waiting all of his life for her . . . all of it had been a carefully calculated lie. "Of all the contemptible things to do."

One corner of his lips tipped upward. "Contemptible, am I?"

"And what would you call a man who tried to seduce a woman for his own nefarious purposes?"

He shrugged, apparently completely reconciled to his

own brutish behavior. "A man determined to get to the truth."

"You have the truth. It just isn't what you want to hear."

He held her gaze, looking into her eyes as though he could read all the secrets carved across her soul. "You are trembling. Is it because you want me to leave you, or because you want me to make love to you?"

She pushed against his shoulders, wiggling to free herself from his weight. "Get off of me."

"Careful, lass." He brushed his lips over the tip of her nose. "You just pulled the towel free."

She froze beneath him, certain she could feel the heat of his arousal pressing through her gown. As hard as she tried, she could not extinguish the flames he had ignited deep within her. Her own foolishness angered her. Oh, she wanted to grab those broad shoulders and shake him until his teeth rattled. "Get off of me," she repeated.

He lifted his brows in mock surprise. "And risk injuring your delicate sensibilities?"

"Get off!"

He chuckled, the deep sound vibrating through her before he lifted away from her. When he stood, the towel dropped from his hips. He did not bother to retrieve it, but stood before her, naked, unashamed, and gloriously aroused. He glanced down, then winked at her. "I warned you."

She scrambled from the bed and faced him, refusing to allow him this blatantly male intimidation. Anger thundered through her, pounding to dust all the desire he had awakened within her. "I am not afraid of you, Lancaster. And now I know that no matter who you may think you are, or pretend you are, you are every bit as arrogant and cruel as you have ever been. I should have realized the depths to which you would stoop. Seduction has always been one of your favorite devices."

He held her gaze, the humor in his eyes crumbling

beneath a swift surge of anger. "You set the rules of this contest when you swept me away from my family and home. 'Tis war, my lady. And if you do not feel you can cross swords with me, then perhaps you should admit defeat. If you are wise, you will reverse your spell before you get hurt."

"I did not instigate this war. *You* did." She stared at him, afraid to blink, for tears burned her eyes. And she knew from experience that if she did not blink, they would not fall. "And even though I have never wished to cross swords with you or anyone, I will not allow you to crush me with your treacherous tricks. I may be as green as grass when it comes to men like you, but I learn quickly. And you are an excellent teacher, Lancaster. I now understand I can never trust anything you say or do, no matter what name you may call yourself."

One corner of his mouth tightened. "And so you continue to hide behind this mask of innocence?"

"I did nothing to you." She pivoted and marched toward the door, needing to escape him before she lost control and dissolved into a watering pot.

"Running away like a frightened rabbit? And here I thought you were up to the challenge."

The taunt in his voice dragged her to a halt. She drew in her breath, forced starch into her spine, then turned to face him. "I am not frightened of you."

He glanced at the clothes she had left across the foot of the bed. "Since you are not frightened of me, I think 'tis time you helped me with these clothes. I want to leave for Kintair as soon as possible. I will know what the scoundrel Lancaster has done to my family."

"Fine." She hesitated a moment before she marched to the bed. He could not know her limbs were trembling, she assured herself. If the man wished to cross swords, she would not run like a coward. She snatched the white silk drawers and tossed the garment at him. "You start with these."

He caught the drawers and smiled, mischief in his eyes. "Very smooth. Almost as smooth as your skin."

She clenched her teeth. "The socks go on your feet; the trousers are obvious, as are the shirt and coat. Since you are such a clever man, I'm certain you can manage without any further help from me."

He lifted his brows. "And here I thought you might stay to help make sure I put everything where it belongs."

"You shall have to excuse me. I need to read my book of spells. I seem to have forgotten the right incantation for turning an arrogant scoundrel into a toad." She turned and marched toward the door. "You may meet me in the drawing room when you are dressed."

The sharp clap of the door shutting slammed through him. Colin frowned down at the drawers he held. His actions had been justified, he assured himself. This was war. He was fighting for his life and the lives of his family. Yet he could not shake the feeling that he deserved to be hauled into the street and flogged. There was no need for Jane to explore her book of spells; he already felt like a small brown amphibian.

The woman could not be trusted. Her magic was powerful. Each time he tried to free himself from her spell, her web tightened around him. Even knowing what he must do, it had taken all of his will to resist the temptation of losing himself to her. One kiss and he had been willing to fall to his knees before her.

If he were not careful, he would succumb to this spell she had woven around him. He would forsake his life, his family, his honor for the pleasure of holding her. The witch was definitely dangerous. If she was a witch. Doubts rose from deep within him. What if Jane was every bit as innocent as she appeared? What if she knew nothing of this spell that had been cast over him? It could not be. He had seen her in a dream. He had seen her casting her spell.

He sat on the bed and pulled on the drawers she had tossed at him. White silk slid over skin still hot and aching for the taste of the beautiful sorceress. She had looked so hurt by his attempt to get at the truth. Betrayed. Outraged. Disappointed in him. The woman clutched her innocence to her chest like a shield. Could such innocent outrage be counterfeited?

If she was responsible for this wicked spell, then why had she stopped him from making love to her? He knew enough about women to recognize desire when he saw it, and Lady Jane burned with it. If not to replace the husband she despised, then why had she brought him here? He could understand why she might have called him across the ages to take the place of a man she despised. If he were to believe what she said, her life with Lancaster was far from happy. Yet if she had conjured him to take her husband's place, why pretend he was this man? Unless her magic could not touch his memory. If that were true, then she might wish for him to believe he truly was Lancaster. To what end? What was her plan for him?

He stood and reached for the trousers. Blood surged in his head, pounding in his temples, swimming before his eyes as he lifted the garment. He sank to the edge of the bed and drew a deep breath.

With injuries such as yours, it is not unusual to suffer some confusion.

The surgeon's words swirled in his mind, teasing him. It could not be so. He set his jaw. He knew who he was. And he knew he was not Dominic Stanbridge. This was part of the spell, an intricate piece of the puzzle that was Lady Jane. He supposed he would think more clearly when the pain had faded from his mind. Yet would he have time to recover? What was her plan for him?

Somehow he would force her to remove this spell. Honor and duty bound him to his own place and time.

Chapter Fifteen

On gossamer nights when the moon is low,
And stars in the mist are hiding,
Over the hill where the foxgloves grow
You may see the fairies riding.
                                    —Mary C. G. Byron

"It's a wonder you did not catch your clothes ablaze."
Jane carried a small basin of water across the parlor car,
moving carefully with the sway of the train. She set the
basin on the table beside Lancaster's chair. "Of all the
hen-witted things to do."

Lancaster grinned up at her. " 'Tis but a wee burn."

"A wee burn." She took his left hand and frowned
down at the ugly red welt that had risen just behind the
knuckles. She slipped his hand into the cool water. "What
possessed you to do something so foolish?"

"I wanted to see how this big fine machine worked.
Now how was I to do such a thing if I did not take a
look for myself?"

"Any reasonable man from the sixteenth century would have been frightened at the first sight of a steam engine. It is huge and belches smoke. I would think it would appear like a fire-breathing dragon."

He lifted his brows, a glint of humor filling his eyes. "I believe fire-breathing dragons expired sometime in the twelfth century."

She waved aside his words. "My point is, a reasonable man would not have climbed aboard the engine. You scared the driver half to death. The poor man looked as though Lucifer himself had climbed into the big engine beside him. I can only image what he was thinking when the Marquess of Lancaster grabbed a shovel and began tossing coal into the furnace, laughing as though he were indeed Lucifer adding fuel to the fires of hell."

He shrugged. "I had never seen such a furnace as this."

"A man from 1562 should have been frightened. Yet you went exploring as though you were a child and this a wonderful gift."

"And how can you say 'tis not a gift?" He flexed his fingers under the water. "I may not have wished to come here, and I may need to find my way home, but while I am here I intend to make the most of every moment."

He had managed to dress without her help. Yet he had chosen to omit the cravat, leaving his shirt open at the neck. And as soon as he had entered the parlor, he had tossed aside his coat. He looked like a man very much at home in his surroundings. "Your behavior seems a little strange to me."

He smiled at her, a wide, boyish grin that did something altogether wicked to her insides. With his hair windblown into waves around his face, and that incredibly warm smile lighting the depths of his eyes, he looked like a man who had made his very first trip to London: young, eager, and strangely innocent. He appeared to be a man who had never looked at the world and found it wanting. There was nothing jaded about this man. Nothing worldly or sophisticated or cynical. No, this man looked at every new experience as a delightful mystery to be explored and savored.

Charming. Disarming. Utterly beguiling. And it was all a lie. Still, as much as she wished to ignore it, as dangerous as it might be to lose sight of the truth, she could not crush the all too potent attraction gripping her. She curled her hands into tight balls at her sides to keep from touching his face, from smoothing the thick dark hair from his brow.

"Think of it. I have a chance to glimpse what the world is like more than three hundred years in my future. In a very real sense, 'tis a gift. For this I must thank you."

"You imagine too much. I had nothing to do with this fairy tale you have concocted."

"Fairy tale?" He leaned forward and winked at her. "Is that what you are? A beautiful fairy princess?"

"Of course. That is why I spend my days conversing with infuriating men."

He brushed his fingertips over her arm. "I wish I knew what to believe with you."

And she wished he would regain his memory before she did something unforgivably foolish. "Seeing your train has not sparked your memory at all?"

He glanced around the parlor car as though seeing the emerald velvet–covered sofa and chairs for the first time. "I have never seen a chariot such as this. 'Tis truly a marvel. To think burning coal can be transformed into such incredible power."

"Perhaps the reason you have no fear is because, deep inside, you are familiar with everything. You are a man of the nineteenth century who simply believes he is from 1562."

He held her gaze for a long moment, as though he were evaluating her words and her motives. "I know who I am. 'Tis you I do not know."

The statement took her unaware. "Have you forgotten my name?"

He laughed, a soft rumble that rose from deep in his chest, filling the car with the sound of a man accustomed to laughter. How could that sound emanate from the cold, mocking shell of Dominic Stanbridge? "I know your name. But 'tis the woman behind the beautiful face that I would come to know. Is she an angel or a witch?"

"You can dry off your hand with this," she said, handing him a small white towel.

He took the towel and began drying his injured hand. "Tell me, who are you, Lady Jane?"

She lifted a tin of lard Cook had given her for this task. "I am just an ordinary woman."

"Ordinary?"

"Yes," she said, taking his hand. His fingers curled against the palm of her hand in a soft embrace. She wore no gloves, no protection against the heat of his skin. She frowned down at the blistered skin, determined to ignore the frightening sensations rippling through her. "I wonder if we should have a surgeon examine this."

" 'Tis not a deep wound."

"It could have been very bad." She smoothed lard over the burn, trying her best not to hurt him. Still, his fingers flexed against her skin, a reaction to the pain she knew she was inflicting. "You really should take more care."

"Aye. There is much in this time and place that is beyond my ken. Such as you, my lady." He slipped his fingers under her chin and coaxed her to meet his gaze. A maelstrom of emotion raged in those beautiful eyes, a heated restlessness that was far too similar to the emotions in her own chest. "I have never met anyone like you."

She glanced down as she wrapped a strip of linen around his hand. "I suppose that is because you think I am a witch."

He ran the tip of one long, elegantly tapered finger

along the curve of her jaw, sending a legion of shivers whispering across her skin. "If I did not know better I would say you do not have a treacherous bone in your lovely body."

She glared at him, annoyed by her own wayward reaction to the beguiling scoundrel. "Unlike you."

He tilted his head, his eyes narrowing slightly as he held her gaze. "I would defend my honor to the death, Lady Jane."

He seemed utterly sincere. If she did not know better, she could believe Colin MacKenzie was a man of his word. Handsome. Charming. Romantic. The type of man a woman could depend upon through adversity. A man straight out of her dreams. Unfortunately he could not be trusted. No matter what accent he employed to say such lovely things, he was still speaking lies. She tied the bandage in place, then stepped back from him. "We shall have to keep an eye on the wound for signs of infection. We may need to have a surgeon examine it."

"Such concern. For a man who deserves your contempt."

"You are ill. At least, so it appears. And I am your wife, which means it is my duty to help you recover."

"And you say you are ordinary." He leaned back in the chair, his gaze lowering to the top button of her gown. "Not many women would tend to a man who had mistreated them as Lancaster has you."

She tried to ignore the dark current of admiration in his voice and the odd way that admiration made her chest expand. The praise was not genuine. She pressed her hand to the base of her neck, making certain the buttons were properly fastened. "Duty. Nothing more."

He lifted his eyes, his gaze resting on her lips. "Angel or witch?"

The room was warm, growing warmer. "I am neither."

Slowly he slid his fingertip over his lips, and for some strange reason, she felt a phantom touch of those lips against hers. A magnetic current sizzled through her. It was as if he were the one who could conjure magic—heat and light and excitement—with nothing but a glance. He stood and she jumped.

One black brow lifted while a speculative look entered his eyes. "Frightened of me?"

She lifted her chin, determined to meet his challenge. "I think it is perfectly reasonable to be wary of one's enemy."

"I did not choose to be your enemy, my lady. You set that course for me."

"No. I did not." She turned away from him, appalled by the trembling in her limbs. Her experience in life had not included exposure to scoundrels until Lancaster had slithered into her path. Still, she would meet this challenge. She had no choice. "Anderson said it might help you regain your memory if I could remind you of your past."

"Your fine quack believes a bump on my head has suddenly made me think I am a different man. Do you really imagine I will believe such nonsense?"

"It is difficult to believe." She turned to face him. "Still, if you aren't ill, then you are playing an elaborate game with me. Tell me, what is the truth?"

"The truth. Now, that is what I would like from you." He narrowed his eyes slightly, a lion considering a creature who had invaded his territory. "I wonder why you want me to believe I am Lancaster."

"Because you *are* Lancaster." She lifted a large photo album from the desk that sat against the far wall and brought it to him. "This is one of your photo albums. It was in your dressing room. I thought it might help your memory if you glanced through it."

"My memory is fine." A muscle flickered in his cheek with the clenching of his jaw. "I hold the images of my family etched upon my heart."

His eyes held such anguish. She could not imagine

even Lancaster being able to act with such sincerity. She laid the book on the table beside him. "Your family is alive and well. If you are truly ill, you must try to remember who you are."

"I do remember who I am." He slipped his hand around her arm, holding her when she tried to break away from him. "Tell me the truth, Lady Jane. What part did you play in this sorcery?"

"I have done nothing to you." The heat of his touch radiated through her gown. "Take your hand off of me."

"I know not what to believe with you." He released her arm, but remained close, so close that with every breath she drew his spicy scent into her lungs. "I only know I must return to my home."

His eyes reflected the turmoil of a man who bore great responsibility, a man motivated by loyalty and honor. The story in his head was so intricate, it was hard to imagine it was all a creation of his imagination. "You are home."

Home. Looking into her eyes, Colin had the uncanny sensation that he had at last found his home. What could he believe? He touched her cheek, and she flinched as though he had slapped her. The fear in her eyes pierced him like the sharp blade of a dirk. He regretted that fear, regretted the chasm of lies and treachery between them. In spite of everything, he wanted her as he had never wanted anything in his life. "Lord have mercy upon me, but I want to believe you. Yet each path I take to find the truth brings me back to you. What is the truth?"

"You suffered a bump on the head. It has confused you."

If he believed the look in her eyes, then he had to believe she honestly had no inkling of what had happened to him, or to her husband. What was true? The more he saw of her, the less he believed she was a witch. And as that belief waned, his uneasiness waxed. If she was innocent, if she believed in this story of his illness, then how had he come to be here? A bump on the head had not caused this. Had it?

There existed only one truth he could not deny about this woman—the attraction she held for him. The air crackled between them, as it might before an approaching storm. His skin tingled. His heart pounded. It took all of his will to keep from touching her. "If you did not cast this spell, then explain why I feel bound to you. Why do I feel as though I have known you, wanted you, needed you, all of my life?"

Jane stepped back and bumped into the arm of the sofa. She jumped as though she had been bitten by a serpent. A soft blush rose from the white lace at her neck until it stained the pale satin of her cheeks. "Your tactics will not work. I will not be taken in by your lies. Not again. So you see, it is useless to flirt with me."

"Flirt?" He traced the curve of her lower lip with his gaze. It was plumper than her upper lip, lush, soft. "And what does this mean?"

She folded her hands at her waist in a pose he recognized as one she assumed when she wished to hide the commotion within her. "To flirt is to act as though you have an interest in someone. A loverlike interest. Without truly meaning anything by it."

Colin tilted his head and lifted his gaze to her eyes, those beautiful silvery gray eyes. "A dalliance?"

"Yes." She fidgeted before settling once more into her stiff pose. "There is no need to attempt to dally with me. Your efforts are quite in vain."

He studied her a long moment, reading all she would not say in her eyes. "I have never been a man to dally with a woman's heart."

She laughed softly, the sound filled with bitterness. "You have elevated flirtation to an art."

"I am not Lancaster," he said, keeping his voice low when he wanted to shout.

"So you say." She squeezed her hands together so tightly her knuckles blanched. "Yet a scoundrel by any other name is still a scoundrel. And I can assure you, flirtation and flattery will not move me. Not one bit."

Did she have any idea the challenge she presented him? "If that be true, then you have nothing to worry about should I try to *flirt* with you."

She glanced away from him, her attention drawn to the painting that hung in a heavily carved frame above the desk across from him. It was another of Lancaster; this time he stood by a large black steam engine such as the one pulling this train. "I find it annoying."

"And I find you beguiling."

She fiddled with the top button of her gown, looking for all the world like a child lost in the woods. "Look around. I understand you took many trips on this train. Doesn't anything look familiar?"

Light from the wall sconce behind her fell softly upon her face, touching gold upon ivory silk. He flexed his fingers, quelling the urge to stroke the place where the lamplight touched the crest of her cheek.

"Well?" she asked. "Is anything familiar?"

She stood watching him, waiting for him to respond. He dragged his gaze from her beautiful face and looked once more around the long, narrow parlor car. Artificial candles glowed behind etched crystal, casting a soft glow upon polished wood panels. All of the furniture was covered in a rich emerald velvet. It was the last of six cars attached to the large engine. It was possible for a man to bathe, dine, and sleep while that huge engine pulled him to his destination. "This man Lancaster, he certainly knew how to travel in comfort."

She looked surprised. "Why do you speak of yourself as though you had died?"

He sat on the curved wooden arm of a small sofa across from her. She had changed into a traveling gown of dark burgundy wool. A pale rose ribbon wound in and out of white eyelet that ran down the front of her gown, shaping a vee that dipped between her breasts and dragged his imagination with it. "If what I suspect is true, your husband has been dead for three hundred years."

"You are Lancaster, and you are very much alive." She touched the slim band of lace at the high neckline of the gown as though she knew he was unfastening those small cloth-covered buttons in his mind. "Seeing your train has not sparked your memory at all?"

Never in the past had he allowed lust to rule him. Yet even as his head registered the need to protect himself, his body responded to her silent call. Without a touch, the woman could set his senses reeling. " 'Tis certainly a costly chariot."

"You enjoy spending money almost as much as you enjoy making it."

"I thought this Lancaster was a rich aristocrat who did little but enjoy himself."

She ran her hand over the back of an upholstered armchair. He followed the idle play of her long, slender fingers upon the lush green cloth and tried not to think of her hands upon his skin. Yet the memory lingered, her long, cool fingers stroking his heated flesh. And with the memory came a fresh rush of heat into his loins.

"One of your pleasures is making money."

Golden lamplight slipped into the thick coils of hair piled upon her head. Once free of those pins, would the shiny mass tumble to her waist? He thought of those silky strands sliding upon his bare chest, and the images rising in his mind provoked another part of his anatomy to stir and rise. "I would not have thought this man Lancaster would do anything of any merit."

She smoothed her hand over her hair, as though making certain all the strands were neatly tucked in place. "According to your sister Eugenia, your uncle had control of the family fortune before you came of age. Through poor investments, he lost most of it. When you came of age, your fortune was in tatters and the family on the verge of disaster. You invested in a railroad in America, then in property and mining. It soon became clear you had a talent for making money."

He drew a deep breath, catching a faint scent of burning coal when he craved the clean, lemony scent of her skin. "Apparently this man Lancaster had a few fine qualities."

She gripped the back of the chair. "From what I gather, you are as ruthless in business as you are in everything else."

"And this uncle, he was the man who was annoying you in your husband's house this afternoon?"

"Your father's only brother. Edwin, Viscount Pembury. Does that prod any memories?"

"There are no memories to prod." He rubbed the knee of his trousers, easing the material farther down his leg. The garment had suddenly grown uncomfortably tight. "But 'twould seem this Lancaster also had problems with his father's brother. My uncle and his ambitious ways may cause a war. Or perhaps I should say, he may have already caused it. I will not know until we reach Kintair."

"Yes." She eased the lace away from her neck, as though she were overly warm. "I hope this trip to Kintair will clarify things for you."

"Am I to believe you wish for this Lancaster to regain his memory?"

"Yes, of course."

"If you despise him, why would you want him to return to plague you?"

She drew in a deep breath, the inhalation lifting her breasts beneath the dark cloth of her gown. "And I suppose you do not plague me as you are?"

He caught himself staring at the delicate curves hidden beneath the burgundy cloth and forced his gaze to lift to her beautiful face. "And would you have me accept this sorcery like a lapdog?"

Her lips tightened into a thin line. "Is it not more logical to accept that a bump on the head has caused your memory to become muddled?"

"Only if I am willing to accept that my entire life is no more than an illusion. I am not." He folded his arms over his chest. "If I had not seen you casting your spell beneath the full moon, I might believe in your innocence. Yet each path I take in search of the truth leads me back to you."

She lifted her chin. "You were spying on me last night, and somehow that image has become twisted into this delusion of switched souls. Isn't it far more logical to accept that there is no such thing as magic?"

"But lass, there is." He stood and moved toward her slowly, watching her closely for her every reaction. He saw fear in her face, but not fear of physical violence. No, he saw the fear of a woman attracted to a man against her will. Fear of the desire he sensed simmering beneath the cool surface she presented to the world.

She was like flame behind crystal, contained, controlled, waiting for the right man to free her. She stepped back, then halted, as though loath to betray her fear of him. He paused before her.

"I cannot speak for the people of this time and place, but in my time, we have not closed our eyes to the magic around us. The world is filled with those who can conjure the power that dwells in the earth. My grandmother often told me stories of the Sidhe, the magical people of her home in Ireland."

Her lips parted; a look of surprise crossed her features. "Your grandmother told you stories of the Sidhe?"

"Aye. You seem surprised that I would know of such things." He held her gaze, watching her reaction closely. "Are you one of the Shining Ones? A fairy princess?"

"No. Of course not. They never really existed."

"Yet you know of the Sidhe, or the Tuatha de Daanan."

"My father's mother is Irish. She is fond of such stories. She would talk for hours about the Tuatha De Daanan and their legends. She said they were once thought of as gods but they were not truly divine. People call them the *Sidhe*, or fairies, or sorcerers. And today they live alongside mortals, hiding their magical powers." She moistened her lips. "She said you could meet a Sidhe in a drawing room and never know you were in the company of a sorcerer or sorceress."

"Aye. I have heard the same stories. Your grandmother must believe in magic. I wonder how you can say you do not."

She laughed softly, a sound that was colored with the unease he could see in her eyes. "My grandmother enjoys entertaining her grandchildren. I am certain she doesn't actually believe the stories. At least, I think they are only stories to her. I never imagined she really believed in magic."

"When you heard the stories, you believed in magic."

"When I was a child." She folded her arms at her waist. "Like most sane people, I abandoned my belief in magic when I left the schoolroom."

"Perhaps 'tis true. Perhaps most of the people in your time have abandoned their belief in magic. Yet I know the truth. Magic has existed since time itself. The fairies or sorcerers, whatever you care to call them, have always lived alongside mortals."

"Tara was their kingdom in Erin." Jane smiled, as though recalling a fond memory. "It lay along mortal borders, invisible to mortal eyes. Unless one of the Sidhe invited you to visit."

"In Scotland people may call them brownies, fairies, sorcerers, witches. By any name, those who can wield the power of the earth and the moon do exist."

"You actually believe these things." She glanced away from him, her gaze resting on the painting of Lancaster above the desk. "It is very strange, since you never believed in anything but your own power before the accident."

Angel or witch? His heart told him one thing, his head another. Which was the truth?

He crossed the short distance to the nearest window and looked outside. Beyond the reflection of the room behind him, he could see the moon shining brightly above him. A moon ripe for magic. "There is a ring of ancient stones near my home. Black and shiny they are, with crystals trapped in the stone. Twelve of them stand open to the sky, and each has been carved with symbols whose meaning is unknown by man. It is said that the Celtic fairies still congregate there, on the night of the full moon, to cast their spells upon the mortal world. When I was a lad, I would often leave my bed upon the full moon and go to the rocks that overlooked the ring to watch for them."

"And I suppose you played with these fairies."

"No." He looked at her image reflected in the glass. She was watching him as though she was trying to solve a puzzle. "I would usually fall asleep without catching a glimpse of them. The light of dawn would awaken me and I would hurry back to my bed."

"Perhaps they were casting fairy dust upon you." She smiled as she continued. "My grandmother said they can sprinkle dust upon mortal eyes and blind us to their world."

"Aye. Perhaps that is what happened." He rested his shoulder against the wall and turned to face her. "Except one night something unusual happened to me. To this day I wonder if 'twas a dream, or if it truly happened."

A look of curiosity entered her expression. "What happened?"

"I awakened when the moon was still high in the sky to find a woman sitting on the ground beside me. Beautiful she was, her hair the color of moonbeams, her face so lovely it made me want to weep. I remember she was dressed all in white with tiny gold stars sprinkled over the gown." Colin glanced at the moon beyond the glass, thinking back to that night in the glen. Had he met a fairy princess that night? Or had he only been dreaming of her? "She smiled at me, and said I was a special lad. When I asked her what she meant, she said one day I would know."

Jane was quiet a moment. "I suspect you were dreaming. I have three brothers, so I can say from experience that adolescent boys often dream of beautiful women."

He turned to face her. "Are you truly as innocent as you appear?"

She held his gaze. "Take a look at the photographs. Perhaps they will prod your memory."

A crisp, lemony scent spilled around him as she walked toward him. Her skirts swished, making him wonder what layers were hidden beneath the burgundy wool of her gown. Need pounded through him. He curled his hands into tight fists at his sides in an effort to keep from touching her.

She lifted the brown leather book and handed it to him. "Look at these."

" 'Twill not make me remember people and things I have never known."

"You are a very stubborn man." She released her breath in a long sigh. "It is late. And I am exhausted. Please excuse me; I am going to retire for the evening."

Her scent spilled around him as she marched past him. He wanted to follow her, to take her into his arms, and to seduce her out of all those layers. Yet he was not a stallion crazed by the scent of a mare in season, he reminded himself, fighting the primitive instincts raging within him. He was capable of thought, capable of controlling his desire, even if it felt as though the need for this woman might tear him to shreds. He would not succumb.

The door closed with a soft thump. He released the

breath he had not even known he had been holding.

Too restless to find comfort in sleep, he drifted to the book of photos she had left on the table. He sat on the stiff seat of a velvet-covered chair and opened the book. Slowly he turned the pages. Shades of gray shaped the images of men and women he had never before seen, except for the image of the man he saw in the mirror. Most of the photographs were of this man Lancaster. The Englishman certainly liked his own image. Near the end of the book, a photograph caught his attention.

"By my faith," he whispered, staring down at the photograph of a woman.

The face captured in the photograph mocked him. It was a face he had known since he was a lad. A slender woman with white hair stood beside a plant that sat atop a pedestal. She stared up at him, a slight smile upon her face, as though she found his astonishment amusing.

"It cannot be," Colin whispered. Yet the image was here, captured in shades of gray. As real as the chair that held him. What did it mean?

Slowly he slid his hand over the back of his head, his fingers testing the lump beneath his hair. Was it possible? Had a bump on the head scrambled his mind? Was he truly an English scoundrel named Lancaster?

"No." He clenched his hands into fists on his thighs. He knew who he was. He was Colin MacKenzie. He knew his family. He knew the life he had led. What he did not know was how this photograph had come into existence.

Chapter Sixteen

Love will find its way
Through paths where wolves would fear to prey.
—George Gordon, Lord Byron

Jane sat at the vanity in her sleeping compartment and drew a brush through her unbound hair. Beyond the glass of her window, moonlight skipped over a meadow they were passing. She had often found the gentle rocking of a train relaxing. Yet tonight her insides were clenched so tightly, not even the rhythmic movement could ease her tension.

She rested her brush on the white lace covering the top of the vanity and stared out the window. The moon glowed near the top of the window. A full moon ripe for magic. How had Lancaster known of the Sidhe? It seemed strange for a man like Lancaster to know about Irish legends. Unless he had learned about her grandmother during his investigation into his bride's life. What depths had the scoundrel—

The door to her compartment flew open and slammed against the wall. Lancaster stormed over the threshold like a summer gale. He marched toward her, his eyes narrowed, murder glinting in the blue slits.

Jane scrambled from her chair. "What is it? What is wrong?"

"Witch." He stalked her.

Her heart pounded with an uneasy mix of excitement and fear. She drew back until she bumped into the wall. He closed the distance. She pressed her hands against his chest, determined to keep him at bay. "What do you mean by barging into my compartment this way?"

He was breathing as though he had been running for several minutes alongside the train. He lifted the album of photographs in front of him as though it answered all of her questions. "Your wicked plot."

"My wicked plot?"

" 'Twill not succeed."

She stared up into his eyes, stunned by the honest anger burning in his eyes. "Exactly what plot do you mean? I have so many wicked plots afoot."

He rested his left hand on the wall beside her shoulders and leaned toward her. "The photograph. I know 'twas you who placed it there."

"The photograph?" She searched through the muddle he had made of her brain. He was far too close, and she had far too few barriers to protect her. His legs pressed against the ruffles at the hem of her nightgown. She could scarcely fit together a logical thought. "It might help if you were a little more specific."

He released his breath in a quick exhale. "You placed a photograph in that book you gave me to look through. You wish to twist my mind. But you will not succeed."

"You recognized one of the people in the album?" Her breath stilled in her chest. His memory was returning. With the realization that Lancaster would soon regain his memory came an unexpected stab of emotion, something far too close to regret. "Show me."

"You know which photograph."

"Oh, for heaven's sake." She snatched the album from his hand and pushed it against his chest. "Show me the photograph."

He held her gaze a moment, his eyes wary. Finally he took the album from her hands. He flipped through the thick pages until he found what he was looking for. "Here. This woman."

Jane stared at the photograph, her chest growing tight. "Who do you think the woman in the photograph is?"

"You know very well who she is. The woman is my grandmother."

Jane met his hard glare. "The woman in the photograph is Lady Fiona Stanbridge. She is your father's mother."

"No." He ran his hand over the back of his head. "This cannot be."

"It is a photograph of Lady Fiona. I have met her. I know for certain this is she."

He leaned toward her, his eyes narrowed. "You did this."

"No. And if you were not such a stubborn oaf, you would realize I had nothing at all to do with your illness."

He cupped her face in his big hands, his long fingers plunging into her hair. "I could snap your neck with one twist."

She stared into his eyes, seeing the fear beneath his anger. Would he do it? She clamped down hard on her rising panic. Panic and fear would not win this battle. "If you wish to murder me, I cannot prevent it. You are far larger and much stronger than I. Still, it will not alter the truth."

He flexed his long fingers against her scalp. "I am not this Lancaster. Nothing will convince me that I am he. I will have the truth from you."

She held his gaze, refusing to buckle beneath the weight of his anger. "You fell and struck your head on the terrace. The next day you awakened believing you were a Scottish earl by the name of Colin MacKenzie. That is the truth. You are Dominic Stanbridge, ninth Marquess of Lancaster."

"No." He pulled away from her. An odd expression crossed his features, a look of sudden surprise. He lowered his head and lifted his hand to his brow.

Jane grabbed his arm. "You'd better sit before you swoon and do more damage."

He sank into the chair at the vanity, propped his elbows on his thighs, and dropped his face into his hands. "My head. I feel as though I have been kicked in the head."

"Yesterday you had a very nasty fall." She knelt beside his chair. Although he showed the outward signs of illness, she, too, was devastated by his discovery. She felt as though she had been kicked in the chest. It was inevitable, she reminded herself. He was Lancaster and he would remember.

Yet she hadn't expected to regret losing Colin. He was infuriating, but she had never felt truly alive until he had careened into her life. "Today you have been running about like a hen-wit when you should have been resting. You shall have yourself dreadfully ill if you continue in this way."

His breath came short and hard, as though it took great effort. "I need answers. I will not find them lying in bed."

"I would say you found answers in this book."

"No." He drew in his breath, then lifted his head and blinked, as though trying to clear his vision. "I found only more questions."

"In time it will all become clear. I realize it must be a shock. But in time your memory will return and the confusion will fade."

He looked at her, the determination in his eyes glittering like steel in the lamplight. "I know who I am."

She held his gaze, regretting the words she must speak. "Colin MacKenzie is not real."

"I am real." He gripped her arms and drew her close, as though clutching a lifeline. "And if you are telling the truth, and everything deep within me wants to believe you, then somehow, someone has cast a spell upon me."

She shook her head. "It is the illness."

He considered this a moment while he searched her features, as if he could find the truth hidden within her. "A part of me wants to believe you are truly as innocent as you appear. Yet if you are, then who did this?"

"No one."

"What were you doing last night, lass?" He pulled her closer, until his lips were no more than a whisper away from hers, far too close to allow for rational thought. The powerful muscles of his thighs pressed against her hips. The heat of his chest soaked through the thin barrier of her nightgown, spreading across her skin. "When you were standing beneath the stars, whispering to the moon? If you were not casting a spell, then what were you doing?"

How she wished she could believe in him and this wondrous feeling he evoked within her. Yet the truth could not be banished forever. "It doesn't matter."

"Aye, it does. I need to know the truth about you." He brushed his lips against her brow. Heat slid across her skin as he released his breath in a long sigh. "I know what I feel inside, but can I trust these feelings? Are they real or is this a spell you have cast upon me?"

She pushed against his chest, desperate to quell her rising need. If she were not very careful, she would drown in the desire he conjured within her. "I am not a witch. I have not cast any spells upon anyone. Now let go of me and leave my compartment."

He pulled her off the floor and dragged her across his lap. "I will have the truth from you."

She clutched his shirt, afraid she might slide headfirst off the side of his lap. He cinched one powerful arm around her, anchoring her against him. She wished for all the world she had not discarded her chemise, petticoat, and drawers. One thin layer of cambric was the only protection she had against his blatant masculinity. "You have no right to treat me in this manner."

Lamplight fell golden upon her face, exposing the perfection of her features. The small mole just above one corner of her lips drew his attention, as though tempting him to test its texture with his tongue. Was this the face of an angel or a witch? He had to know what was real and what was merely an illusion. Could he trust the feelings she had awakened within him? Or was it all a lie? "Tell me the truth."

"You are a stubborn brute. That is the truth." She pushed against his shoulder. "Now let go. . . ."

He clamped his mouth over hers, intent on teaching her a lesson. He would not be manipulated by her. No matter her game, he would not play. Not one moment longer. If she thought she could defeat him with her tricks, she would soon discover she had trapped a lion in her snare.

She struggled, pressing one slender hand upon his shoulder, the other against his chest, squirming on his lap. The lush curves of her bottom rubbed against him. His blood surged, sending a river of liquid fire into his loins. He was achingly aware of the thin barriers between them—wool and silk and the softest cotton he had ever felt. Thin layers easily banished. And he would strip away the barriers. He would take her, here and now. Unless she saved herself with the truth.

He slanted his lips over hers and opened his mouth upon her in a blatant assault. This was what happened when beautiful witches cast their spells upon poor unsuspecting mortals. He would force her hand. If the witch wanted to end this, let her tell him the truth. Or use her magic. Now. If she turned him into a toad, so be it. He would have his answer. He would know the truth.

Without warning, a soft sigh quivered upward from her chest. It escaped against his lips, sliding warmly upon his skin. He felt the moment she stopped fighting, the instant she surrendered to him. She slid her arms around his neck, parted her tightly clenched lips, and kissed him. If he had not been sitting, the impact would have sent him reeling.

Her lips moved upon his, soft and eager and incredibly innocent. She kissed him as though she had never truly known the kiss of a man before. It was sweetly searching, the kiss of a maiden. Was this another lie? A married woman who kissed as though she had never bedded a man before. How could this be?

In all of his life he had never tasted a kiss more stirring than this. Although he had not led the life of a monk, he had never been careless in his liaisons. He was his father's heir. He had responsibilities. He was expected to marry appropriately, and he would. It was not his intent to leave a litter of bastards scattered across the countryside.

At sixteen he had learned his first lessons in pleasuring a woman. His teacher had been a lovely widow five years his senior. He and Lady Larena had remained lovers for three years, until she married again. Even then she had tried to coax him back to her bed. But Colin believed in the vows spoken between man and wife. He would not bed another man's wife. And here he was, holding the wife of a man named Lancaster. But he knew that if Lancaster were here, he would fight for this woman, so powerful was her hold on him.

She slipped her hand inside his shirt, sliding her fingertips over his chest as though she loved the feel of his skin. With shy ardor, she explored him, teasing his hair, sliding her hand across his skin, until her exploring fingers bumped into his nipple. There she lingered, rolling the hard nub between her fingertips, sending sensation shooting through his body like sparks shot from a fire.

In the part of his brain still functioning he realized this was not proceeding as he had planned. Instead of her crumbling beneath his assault, her power was growing. He felt her strength in his own weakness. If he did not stop now, he would be lost.

He dragged his lips from hers. She lay across his lap, her neck against his arm, her hair tumbling in wild disarray. Her cheeks were pink, her lips red and wet from his kisses. He flexed his fingers against her waist and arm in an effort to keep from kissing her again. It took a moment for her to open her eyes, and when she did she looked as though she were coming awake from a lovely dream. She stared up at him as though he were the one who could command the power of the moon and stars. She looked at him as though he could slay dragons in her name. And heaven help him, he wanted to fall to his knees and beg her to command him.

"Tell me the truth." He slid his fingers through the thick hair that tumbled over his arm and pooled upon his thigh. Cool strands of silk caressed his skin. "Why have you cast this spell upon me?"

She flinched as though he had slapped her. He watched the swift flood of realization enter her face. The corners of her soft mouth tightened. "I must be insane."

"Tell me your purpose in bringing me here."

She scrambled off his lap so quickly she lost her balance. She smacked into the vanity, then turned to face him, rubbing her hip. "If I were a witch, you would be sitting in the nearest swamp, croaking your troubles to the moon."

If he believed in her innocence, he must believe in the truth of these feelings she had evoked within him. It was far easier to believe in her treachery. "If you were not casting a spell last night under the moon, then what were you doing?"

She glanced away from him, as though she were afraid he might read some secret in her eyes. "It is none of your concern what I was doing."

Light from the lamp shone upon her thick lashes, casting lacy shadows upon her cheeks. "Then I must believe 'twas a spell."

"It was not a spell. I am not a witch." She glared at him. "And if you must know, I was indulging in a moment of self-pity."

"Self-pity?"

"Yes. I was wishing for my life to be different. Is it a crime in 1562 to make a wish?"

"No." He held her angry gaze, understanding washing through him. Suddenly his disbelief shattered and fell into shards around him. This woman had such expressive eyes, a face that could never support a lie. As difficult as it might be to face the truth, he could no longer evade it. "I believe you."

She glared at him, her eyes narrowing. "Is this another of your tactics?"

"No." Heat prickled his neck when he thought of the way he had treated this woman. "I realize now I was wrong to treat you as an enemy."

"We are enemies. But not for the reason you believe."

"Your husband is your enemy, not I."

"You are Lancaster," she said, as though she needed to remember who he was as much as he did.

He saw now what he had seen before: the pain in her eyes. Only now he believed the emotion he saw in the silvery depths. "That night, under the moon, what were you wishing for?"

Her lips tightened. "I would rather not say."

He held her gaze, certain of what she had wished without understanding how he could know. Yet he accepted the knowledge as he accepted the sun would rise in the morn. "Was it for someone to take Lancaster's place? Your true love?"

Her eyes widened. "You were listening."

"No." He rubbed his temples, feeling the blood pound beneath his fingertips. "Yet I feel the truth of it deep within me. I cannot explain it."

"I did not wish for you to come into my life."

Light from the lamp rippled through her unbound hair, finding gold amid shades of brown. His fingers twitched, anxious to explore the thick, shiny silk, to feel the strands slide against his chest. "What did you wish for?"

She looked away from him, directing her gaze to the window. "Even if I did wish for my own special someone to come into my life, it certainly is not you. Because you do not exist. You may imagine you are another man right now, but you are Lancaster. And soon your memory will return."

"I am not Lancaster." He stood and she took a step back. The fear in her eyes stabbed him far too close to his heart. "There is no need to fear me. I will not harm you."

She moistened her lips. "I am not frightened of you."

"If you did not cast the spell that brought me to you, then I am at a loss to understand how I came to be here. 'Twas for that reason I was so desperate to believe you were a witch. If your witchcraft had summoned me across the ages, then I had a chance to make you reverse your spell."

"I understand." She fiddled with the lace at the high collar of her nightgown. "It is all due to the illness."

"Lancaster was hit over the head, not I." He smoothed his hand over the lump at the back of his head. "There must be a reason I saw you in my dream. You are the key. Could a wish have brought me to you?"

"No. A wish did not bring you to me. You saw me from your balcony last night. And now it is all tangled in the confusion of your mind."

"Somehow I must get to the truth of how I came to be here. 'Tis my only chance of finding a way back to my family." With those words came a constriction in his chest, a pain at the thought of leaving her. Had she truly come to mean so much to him? In a day? Yet the answer was there, deep within him. It might not be witchcraft, but it was magic, the way he felt when she was near.

"Didn't the photograph of your grandmother prove anything to you?"

"There must be some reason why the woman in that book looks like my grandmother."

"There is a reason. She *is* your grandmother."

"No, I do not pretend to understand what has happened. I cannot explain the resemblance of my grandmother to this woman. Yet I know in my soul I am not this Lancaster. Just as I know in my soul you are the reason I have been brought here."

She shook her head. "I thought you were beginning to accept the truth."

"I believe you did not cast the spell that brought me to you. But I know you must be the key." The moment he had glimpsed this woman, he had felt as though he had finally found what he had been searching for all his life.

She drew in her breath, then released it on a tired-sounding sigh. "Tomorrow we shall reach Kintair. Perhaps then you shall have some answers."

"You do not actually believe Kintair Castle exists, do you?"

She held his gaze a long moment, as if debating the wisdom of her words. "I am not certain Kintair Castle exists. I am not certain Colin MacKenzie ever existed. I do know you are not he."

"I will prove to you who I am."

"You cannot prove what is not true."

He wanted to grab her shoulders and shake her until she saw the man behind the facade of Lancaster. Until she admitted she felt the same attraction he felt, this need that pounded through his body each time she was near. This hunger that clawed at his vitals. Never in his life had he wanted anything the way he wanted this woman. "Look at me and tell me you see the English scoundrel you married."

"You could awaken tomorrow and remember everything. Colin would be gone," she said, her soft voice barely rising above the clatter of the iron wheels upon the tracks.

He had not thought of that possibility. Would this spell last only a day? What purpose would it serve to bring him across time for one day? "No, it cannot be. There is some purpose behind this magic."

"There is no such thing as magic."

"You believe this. I can see it in your eyes." He touched her arm, wanting to draw her into his arms.

She stepped away from him. "Don't."

He clenched his jaw. "I will not hurt you."

She lifted her chin. "I have no intention of allowing you to seduce me."

The lady was not as immune to him as she would like him to believe. "And here I thought you did not like me."

"I don't. But you have this annoying way of making me want things I should not."

"Do I?"

She fluttered her hands in front of her, as if to disperse the words she had spoken. "You need not be so pleased with yourself. I find my sensibilities overly stimulated, that is all. I am certain it is due to the strain of the past few days."

She looked so flustered and pretty and innocent. Just looking at her made him smile. "Is that what I do, lass? Stimulate your sensibilities?"

"Oh, for pity's sake. I am not good at this. Flirtation is an art I have never accomplished. I really wish you would not tease me so dreadfully." She clasped her hands at her waist. "What I mean to say is that you often in-furiate me."

He pressed his hand to his heart to show how she had wounded him. "And here I thought you were beginning to like me."

"You thought wrong."

"Did I? You did say you prefer me to Lancaster."

She laughed, the brittle sound betraying her anxiety. "Considering what I think of Lancaster, that is hardly flattering."

"Are you going to deny you feel it too?"

She stared at him, her eyes wide and wary. "What?"

"This connection that binds us to each other."

She shook her head. "Your memory will return. And when it does, I do not intend to be left with regrets."

He understood the truth beneath her words. "You are afraid you will come to care for me."

"I am not saying I would become overly fond of you. But I cannot think of anything more foolish than to be-come romantically involved with someone who cannot possibly remain in my life." She looked away from him, but not before he caught a glint of tears shining in her eyes. "I think you should leave."

As much as he wanted to deny her words, he could not. If his family had not survived without him, he would find a way to return to them. The man she knew as her husband had hurt her. Colin would not do the same. Honor bound him to his family. And although he could not explain it, he knew honor bound him to this woman. It was staggering to admit how much she had come to mean to him in such a short span of time. Yet in a very real sense he felt he had known her all his life.

Colin turned and marched from the room. He did not stop until he was behind the closed door of his own com-partment. Yet he still was not safe from her siren call. His blood pounded with need, each surge of his heart screaming for him to take her. He sank to the edge of his bed. If he must leave, he would not leave her weeping for his loss. He prayed his answers lay at Kintair. And he prayed for the strength to resist the temptation of the beautiful Lady Jane.

Chapter Seventeen

Though varying wishes, hopes, and fears
Fever'd the progress of these years,
Yet now, days, weeks, and months but seem
The recollection of a dream.
                                        —Sir Walter Scott

Jane put her cup in the saucer that sat on the table in front of her. She stared at the footman who stood near the table. "What do you mean, His Lordship is missing?"

Dilby's narrow shoulders rose to meet the lobes of his ears. "I went to tell His Lordship that you were awaiting him in the dining car, as you asked, Your Ladyship. But he wasn't in his compartment. And I looked all over, Your Ladyship. Even in the engine. But His Lordship is not on the train."

"Not on the train." A vise closed around her chest. She glanced out the window. The village of Kintair stretched eastward from the shores of the Atlantic, neat rows of stone and wooden buildings lining narrow lanes. And

Lancaster was prowling that village. At least it was a small town. It shouldn't be difficult to find him. And as far as she knew, he had not brought a sword with him. She only hoped he had not gotten himself into some kind of trouble. Jane rose from her seat. "Tell Henderson to have the coach made ready."

"Yes, Your Ladyship."

"I want to leave as soon as His Lordship returns."

"Yes, Your Ladyship." Dilby turned and scurried across the car, heading for the door leading to the servants' quarters.

Jane headed in the opposite direction. Before she reached the door leading to the vestibule and the sleeping compartment beyond, the door swung open. Lancaster strolled into the room as though he had not just shaved ten years off her life.

He looked at her without the grin she had come to expect from him. "I see you are finally up and about."

The brisk, salty scent of the sea clung to him, tempting her to press her lips to the hollow of his neck. She stepped back, afraid she might do something foolish otherwise. His hair was blown into thick waves around his face. His cheeks were red from the wind that whipped off the Atlantic. "Where have you been?"

"I took a stroll about the village."

"You just wandered off? Alone?"

"I am not a stripling lad. I was in no danger of getting lost." He lifted one black brow, a glimmer of irritation entering his expression. "As you see, I even managed to dress myself."

He wore a white shirt, the first few buttons unfastened, allowing the cloth to spill open at his neck. His black wool coat was unbuttoned. At least he had chosen a pair of black riding boots to wear with the form-hugging, buff-colored breeches. He looked like a gentleman who had been out riding. A gentleman who could coax the pulse of any unsuspecting female he met into a headlong gallop. Strange how well the casual attire suited his wild, untamed look. Lancaster had always looked his best in very elegant attire. Still, he did not look the same as he had yesterday.

This morning there was a hard edge to him, like steel that had been honed and polished. And the way he regarded her, it was not with the same compelling heat she had grown accustomed to seeing in his eyes. He looked at her as though he could not stand the sight of her. That icy look pierced her. The sting startled her. She had not realized just how much she had come to rely upon the interest he had shown in her, until this moment. "You should not go wandering about alone."

"Perhaps you were worried about the village folk." His dark voice held a sharp edge. "Did you think they were in danger from the poor madman? As you can see, I did not take a sword."

"You are ill. If you can forget your name, then who is to say what you might do next? What if you had awakened with no recollection of where you were, or who you think you are?" She studied him a moment, searching for some sign of the fiery Scot who had managed to slay her heart in a single day. In his stead stood a stranger. "You are still Colin this morning, aren't you?"

"Aye, my lady. I am still Colin." He held her gaze, his eyes narrowing slightly. "Were you hoping for someone else?"

No. She had been hoping Colin would still be with her this morning. It might be foolish, but she could not deny she wished he could remain Colin for the rest of his life. At least the Colin she had known yesterday. Not this icy stranger who regarded her as though he detested the sight of her. "I was simply wondering if your memory had returned."

"My memory is fine. I remember coming into the village three days ago." He glanced away from her and looked toward the town. "Yet it seems the village I knew no longer exists. I could find nothing here to tell me the fate of my family. And until I know what happened to them, I cannot be content in this time and place."

He looked at her, his eyes filled with turmoil. "Are you ready to leave for Kintair?"

Was she ready for the confrontation that might prod his memory? No. She was not. Yet postponing the inevitable would not make it go away. "Yes."

The road from the village followed the coastline. It rose with the steady upward thrust of the land, the water dropping away until the sea crashed against the rocky shore a hundred feet beneath them. A few trees dotted the land on the edge of the cliffs, twisted by the constant battering of the wind. Jane stared out the window of the coach, watching the countryside slide past her line of sight, trying to ignore the man sitting across from her. It was impossible.

Although the coach was spacious, his presence filled it. Even sitting there in quiet repose, he was like a hungry flame, an irresistible power, consuming the air until she could scarcely breathe. Each time he shifted on the seat, she felt the movement. She felt every breath he drew into his lungs. Yet he seemed to have no trouble at all ignoring her. He sat with his head turned toward the window, his legs stretched at an angle to accommodate their length, his arms crossed upon his chest. A gentleman contemplating the countryside.

The muted light of morning fell softly upon his face, revealing the tight line of his jaw, the sharply chiseled profile that might be at home carved upon a coin. He glanced at her and caught her staring. He held her gaze for a long moment; then his lashes lowered, and he looked at her lips. She felt as if his lips were touching hers and not simply his gaze. He looked into her eyes. One corner of his mouth tipped upward, shaping a crooked smile. The look in his eyes told her he knew exactly how easily he had set her pulse racing, with no more than a look.

Infuriating man. She turned on the seat and fixed her gaze on the rolling waves of the Atlantic. If he could ignore her, she could do the same.

"The cliffs, the sea, they are the same now as they were the last time I saw them. 'Tis a strange sensation to know my family once traveled this road, and now they are no more."

"When you regain your memory, you will regain your family." Although she kept her gaze on the sea, she could see him in the periphery of her vision. He was watching her, as though he found her amusing. "Of course, you do not really get along well with most of your family. You think your sisters are all gossips and bores. You feel your mother is a silly woman who has married beneath her. From what I have seen, your grandmother is the only member of your family for whom you have any true affection."

"Do you mean the woman who resembles my own grandmother?"

"She is your grandmother." The coach swayed, brushing Lancaster's long leg against her skirt. She tingled as though he had stroked her bare skin. She clenched her hands tightly in her lap and kept her gaze fixed on the wide expanse of the Atlantic. "Since you care for her, perhaps that is the reason she was the only relative you recognized from the photographs."

"No." He rubbed the back of his neck. "There is another reason for the resemblance. I am hoping the answers I need will be at Kintair."

"If it truly . . ." She had intended to question the existence of Kintair Castle, but she did not finish her thought, because at that moment a structure came into view. "Is that Kintair?"

He glanced out the window. "Aye. That is my home."

Toward the north, gray stones rose, shaping a sprawling castle that stretched along the cliff's edge. Even at a distance it looked massive.

" 'Tis changed from when I lived here. Still, 'tis good to know it still exists."

She looked at him and found him smiling, a look of triumph in his eyes. "I am certain there is a reason why you knew this castle existed."

"Aye, there is." He leaned forward and winked at her. "I am the MacKenzie."

It could not possibly be as he claimed it was. He could not have come to her from 1562. She had made wishes before, and none had ever come true. He could not possibly be the answer to her wishes, her hopes, her dreams. It just was not possible. No matter how much she wanted to believe in him.

Jane glanced out her window as they drove through an arched stone gate set in a long stone wall. Coach wheels clattered over gravel. Tall trees lined either side of a long, winding drive. Occasionally she caught a glimpse of a large stone structure through the wooded park, teasing her curiosity. Finally, as the coach rounded a bend in the drive, the castle loomed ahead of them. At that moment the sun peeked through the clouds, spilling light over what seemed a hundred towers, turrets, and spires, glittering on hundreds of small diamond-paned windows. The ancient structure sparkled as though it had been sprinkled with fairy dust. Until this morning she had assumed Kintair Castle was part of the fantasy Lancaster had created in his mind.

"It looks like something out of a fairy tale." A place where a princess might wait in a tower for her prince to rescue her. How very easy it would be to believe Colin MacKenzie was a prince from her very own fairy tale. "I wonder how you knew the castle existed?"

"I was born and bred here." He turned his stormy visage toward her. "This is my home. At least it was."

Although he kept his voice low, its harshness revealed

his frustration. He was holding fast to his fairy tale, fighting against the logic she presented him. "You must have visited here at one time. You probably know the present Earl of Kintair."

He glanced away from her and looked out the window. "This was my home. That is how I know of it."

"I realize the life you imagine you lived seems very vivid, but it is only the illness."

His Adam's apple slid up and down beneath the smooth skin of his neck as he swallowed hard. " 'Tis not an illness. I know who I am. And nothing will steal my life from me."

"It may take time, but I am certain you will regain your memory."

"My memory is fine." He looked at her and did something entirely unexpected—he smiled, a wide, boyish grin that lit the depths of his eyes. "I know who I am."

She really wished he would not look at her that way. It made her long for things that could not be. "I wonder if the family is at home."

Lancaster turned his attention back to the house. " 'Tis not the same as when I left it so short a time past."

She looked at the castle. What changes would he imagine had occurred? "I suppose there have been improvements over the last three hundred years. Although the architecture is all in harmony. There are times when castles are altered so severely you can scarcely see anything of the original structure. When I visited Castle Mallory in Hampshire, all I could find of the fourteenth century was one tower."

" 'Tis strange. I feel as though it has been only a day since I have been here." Lancaster rubbed his hands together, as though trying to warm himself. "Yet so much has changed. In my time not a tree stood within an arrow's shot of the castle. Now there is a forest."

"It is very pretty."

217

"And the outer defenses enclosing the grounds, all gone, save the gate we came through."

"I would guess at one time in the past hundred years, perhaps, the grounds were fashioned to suit a mansion rather than a fortress."

"And the castle, 'tis larger. Stretched on either side of the main hall."

A chill gripped her as she listened to him. It was all so clear in his mind, so vivid that at times she caught herself being drawn into this fantasy. The coach halted in front of a large tower and what appeared to be the front entrance. "Shall we see if we can take a tour of the castle?"

"Tour my own home?" He laughed softly, the sound revealing a measure of his uneasiness. "Aye. I would see what changes have taken place. And I hope to see a chronicle of my family."

He climbed from the coach and turned toward her. She expected him to offer his hand, as any gentleman might do. Instead he gripped her waist and lifted her from the coach. She gripped his shoulders, startled by the gesture. Even more startling was the sudden surge of desire inside her, flames ignited by the simple touch of his hands. He held her as though she were as small and delicate as a Dresden china doll.

The warm male scent of him swirled through her senses. He held her at eye level, so close he could have kissed her if he just leaned forward. Would he kiss her?

Her pulse pounded at the base of her throat. She should not allow him to kiss her. No, she definitely should not kiss him. Still, she could not crush the longing swelling within her. She knew the danger. It was foolish even to consider throwing her arms around his neck. Yet it took all of her will to keep from circling her arms around him and kissing him.

Kiss me, she thought. *Please kiss me.*

He held her gaze for what seemed an eternity. And in

that space of time she wondered if he could read her wayward thoughts. A part of her wished he could. Another, the much more sensible part, hoped to heaven he did not know how much she wanted his arms around her, his lips upon hers.

His hands flexed against her waist. Something flickered in his eyes, as if he were waging an inner battle. His lashes lowered, his gaze resting upon her mouth. The corners of his mouth tightened. Then he set her on her feet and turned away from her, as though completely immune to the attraction between them. "I want to see those chronicles."

She watched him march toward the large double front doors, trying desperately to ignore the injury he had inflicted upon her poor abused heart. It was obvious she meant nothing at all to him. And it was every bit as obvious that she was a very foolish woman.

How had he come to mean so much to her in so short a time? The answer was there, lurking in a shadowy place deep within her. For some reason she could not even begin to explain, she felt she had known him all her life. A man who did not exist. A man who could ignore her as easily as he could believe in his own fairy tale. She squared her shoulders, gathered her tattered pride, and followed him to the entrance.

A tall, thin man opened the door. Jane's first impression was that the man's neck looked far too thin to support his head, which was covered with thick white hair. The old gentleman looked from Jane to Lancaster without so much as a whisper of a smile crossing his thin lips. She was just about to explain their appearance at the front door of the castle when the old man spoke.

"We were not expecting you, my lord."

Jane glanced up at Lancaster. "Expecting you?"

Lancaster's eyes narrowed, his gaze fixed on the butler. "You know this man Lancaster?"

The butler lifted his white brows. "Aye, my lord."

"In that case, Lancaster must know your master." Lancaster did not wait for an invitation to enter the house. He strolled past the butler as though he owned the place.

Jane followed him, trying not to dwell on all the rules of etiquette they were breaking. She only hoped Lancaster and Kintair were good friends.

The thump of the front door closing rumbled through the huge entrance hall, echoing softly on the dark, polished wainscoting. The scent of beeswax and lemon oil lingered in the large room. "Will the usual staff be joining us from London, Your Lordship?"

The usual staff? Did Lancaster have a habit of bringing his own staff with him when he visited? Of course, it would be like him. Jane could imagine him taking command of any house in which he stayed, imposing his will over the staff, disrupting the order of life for everyone in his path.

"We had not planned on staying," Lancaster said, with all the authority of a man who had not lost his memory.

"We were simply wondering if Lord Kintair might be in residence," Jane said.

The butler's thick white brows lifted, the only change in his otherwise stony expression. He looked past Jane to Lancaster, then back to her. "Aye. He is."

"I would see the *Chronicles of Kintair*." Lancaster looked around the large entry hall. "They were always kept in the great hall, but 'twould seem the great hall is no longer."

"The *Chronicles of Kintair*, my lord?"

Jane handed the butler one of Lancaster's cards, as well as her own. "We would like very much to have a few moments of Lord Kintair's time. Lord Lancaster is very interested in learning more of the history of the castle."

The butler looked down at the card. "You wish to have a few moments with Lord Kintair?"

"Yes." Why did the old man look so confused? Jane wondered. "You did say he was in."

"Aye. He is." The butler looked up from the card to Lancaster. "You would like to speak to him?"

"Aye. I would meet this man who bears my title." Lancaster planted his hands on his hips. "And I would see the chronicles."

"I see." The butler smiled. "Aye, Your Lordship. I understand. Please follow me."

Jane could not shake the odd prickling sensation at the back of her neck. Something was not right here. She couldn't quite put her finger on it. They followed the servant across the hall, down a connecting passageway, and into a large library. There had been something in the butler's eyes when he had looked at Lancaster, something that was far too . . . conspiratorial. That was it. The butler had looked at Lancaster as though he had access to a secret. She didn't like that look. She didn't like the suspicion gripping her.

"By my faith." Lancaster paused in the center of the room, then turned around in a small circle, staring at the books like a boy who had been set loose in a sweetshop. "A library. Here at Kintair."

"Aye, Your Lordship," said the butler. "And a very fine library it is."

Jane glanced at the oak bookcases that lined the first floor and the gallery above. The room easily housed ten thousand books. It was obviously the library of a collector, a person who loved books. The room itself was beautiful. Three separate scenes depicting life on Mount Olympus were painted in roundels amid elaborate gilt and scrollwork on the ceiling high above them. The carpet repeated the same roundels, only this time in a floral pattern of dark blue, burgundy, ivory, and gold. Cut velvet drapes of the same floral pattern hung at the long windows.

Lancaster paused before one of the many bookcases

that lined the walls. He rested his fingertips on the edge of a shelf. "This was once part of the great hall. The walls were stone, not plaster and wood as they are now. And in all of Kintair, there were only one hundred and forty books."

It was strange the way he could imagine what the castle had looked like over three hundred years ago. Jane glanced around, trying to visualize this elegant room as he had described it. How could it all be so clear to him? Her gaze snagged upon a portrait hanging above a large claw-footed desk. Her breath caught in her throat. For a moment all she could do was stare, her mind too shocked to form a logical thought.

As Jane recovered from the shock, the full import of her discovery struck her like a clenched fist in the belly. "Lancaster!"

A shape moved in her periphery. Distantly she recognized the tall form as Lancaster. Yet she could not drag her gaze from the portrait above the desk.

"What the devil is that doing here?"

Lancaster's low voice ripped through her, still colored with a Scottish burr. Yet she now knew the truth. It stared at her from the confines of an ornately carved mahogany frame, as clear as the inscription on the brass plate below the portrait—*Dominic, Ninth Earl of Kintair*. A chill whispered over her skin as she looked up into the handsome face of Dominic Stanbridge.

"I do not understand," he said.

Jane turned to look at the scoundrel standing beside her. He was frowning at the portrait. "What game is this?" she demanded.

He looked at her, his expression filled with surprise. "What do you mean?"

"Explain this," she said, gesturing to the portrait.

He shook his head. "I cannot explain it."

"Unfortunately, I can." She turned and marched toward the door. Oh, she was a fool. An idiot. A mutton-headed dolt. Because she had believed his act of illness and confusion. She glared at the butler as she passed him.

The butler lowered his eyes, avoiding her direct look. "Beg pardon, Your Ladyship."

Lancaster grabbed her arm when she reached the door. "What are you doing?"

She pulled away from him so violently she stumbled into a cabinet near the door, whacking her elbow against the carved wood. She sucked air between her teeth and silently cursed the man standing before her. "I'm leaving."

"I do not understand."

She left the room, not wanting to provide a show for the butler. She rubbed her sore elbow as she hurried back down the hall that led to the entrance.

Lancaster followed her, matching her quick strides. "Why are you leaving now? When there are so many questions left to be answered?"

"I know everything I need to know. I know you are a scoundrel. I know you believe I am naive enough to swallow this nonsense about losing your memory."

Temper flared in his eyes. "I never said I had lost my memory. You and your quack did."

She glared at him. "You obviously paid Anderson to back up your lies."

One corner of his mouth tightened. "I never saw your quack before you sent him to prod and poke and bother me."

"So you say."

"What do you imagine seeing that portrait proves?"

She glanced at him. "What did you think? If you brought me here to this beautiful, oh so romantic castle, you could manage to seduce me?"

"Seduce you?" He grabbed her arm and spun her around to face him. "Do you truly believe I would need to drag you all the way here to have my way with you?"

No, she did not. The horrible, humiliating truth lurked

deep inside her. "You are playing on my sense of romance."

A low huff issued from his lips. "I would not need a castle if I took it into my mind to bed you. And you know 'tis true."

His words struck her with the force of an open palm. "I see. So you have no desire for me, is that it?"

"No desire for you?" He drew in his breath, a slow, steady inhalation that lifted the fine black wool covering his broad shoulders. "From the first moment I saw you, I have wanted you in my arms. Last night it took all my will to leave you."

Blue flames flickered in his eyes, a desire for her that burned intensely. Yet the hunger in his eyes did not shock her as much as the response from deep within her, the sudden stirring in that part of her he had awakened. She felt a need so raw, she ached to touch him. Was this all a game to him?

"I stayed away last night because I did not want to hurt you."

"Hurt me? As I recall, I told you to leave."

"You wanted me to stay; I could see it in your eyes. You wanted me in your bed."

The truth slapped her. "You imagine a great deal."

He shook his head. "I could not stay. Not last night. Perhaps never. I would not leave you weeping for the loss of me."

The soft Scottish burr rippled through her, ambushing her defenses. Dear heaven, the man knew precisely how to manipulate her. She pulled free of his grasp. "You are the most arrogant, detestable man I have ever met. To imagine I would weep over you is . . . contemptible."

"What do you think you are doing?" he demanded as he followed her down the hall.

She did not so much as glance at him. "I am going home."

"By my faith, woman, I am not this Lancaster. I do

not know why a portrait of an English scoundrel is hanging in my house."

"You said yourself it was ludicrous to believe a bump on the head could have altered you so drastically." She shook her head, angry at her own foolishness. She turned at the front door and glared at him. "Well, you may have fooled me once, Lancaster, but you shall never do it again."

"Fine." His eyes narrowed into glittering blue slits. "Run like a frightened rabbit. I will not beg you to stay."

"Fine." Still, she hesitated, her wounded pride warring with a nagging sense of doubt. "You might as well end the game now. You have lost."

He gripped the brass handle and yanked open the wide oak door. "Go. I will not suffer your insults another moment."

Why didn't he just admit the masquerade? "All right. I will go."

He nodded. "Farewell."

"Farewell." She pivoted and marched from the castle. He was not a man in need of her help, she assured herself. He was a scoundrel who wanted only to trap her. There certainly was no reason why she should feel as though she were deserting him. Yet she could not quell the guilt rising inside her. She was doing the right thing, she assured herself. Let the scoundrel plot another way to defeat her. This ploy of illness and switched souls would not succeed.

Chapter Eighteen

Remembrance wakes with all her busy train,
Swells at my breast, and turns the past to pain.
                              —Oliver Goldsmith

Colin hit the door with his open hand, slamming the oak against the doorjamb. The loud crash vibrated through the huge hall, as though screaming out his own foolishness. If the woman was so stubborn she could not see the truth when it stood before her, then he was better rid of her. He certainly would not chase after her. No, he would not beg her to stay with him. It was better to do without her than to endure her accusations. He was a man of his word. He did not need her. He would find the truth on his own. And if he kept repeating that to himself, perhaps this ache in his gut would stop churning.

Someone cleared his throat behind him. Colin turned to find Lancaster's butler standing a few feet away. "Is there anything you require, Your Lordship?"

Colin glared at the man. "Why is it you did not say anything about my being Earl of Kintair?"

The old man did not so much as blink as he replied. "I thought Your Lordship had his reasons for not wanting the lady to know you were the earl."

How had a jackanapes like Lancaster come to inherit Kintair? Questions swirled in his brain along with the doubts he could not completely banish. He needed answers. "What is your name?"

The butler stared for an instant before he responded. "Doyle, Your Lordship?"

"You do not seem certain of that."

Doyle shrugged his narrow shoulders. "I was thinking perhaps His Lordship had another name in mind for me. Something that might better suit the particular role you wish me to play. It might help if I knew precisely what role you wish me to play, Your Lordship."

"I do not wish for you to play any role."

"Pardon me, Your Lordship. I thought with the lady, you might wish for me to assume a role that might better suit your own."

Colin speared the man with his gaze. "I am not playing a role, you foolish jackanapes."

Doyle lifted his chin. "I beg your pardon, Your Lordship. I cannot imagine what may have given me that impression."

Colin dragged air into his tight lungs. He had never felt this way before, as though he had been tossed into a deep lake, with his hands and feet tied. He had to find his way to the truth. "Where are the *Chronicles of Kintair* kept these days?"

Doyle pondered this a moment. "The *Chronicles of Kintair*?"

"Aye. The history of Castle Kintair and the family MacKenzie."

"In the library?"

Colin glared at the man. "Do you know that for a certainty?"

"Aye, Your Lordship. Since the history of Kintair has

always been of particular interest to you, your question simply took me by surprise."

"Lancaster was interested in the history of Kintair?"

Doyle's brows lifted over the look of surprise entering his dark eyes. "Aye, Your Lordship. You always have been, since you came here as a boy. I mean Lord Lancaster has always shown an interest. Are you not Lord Lancaster today?"

The muscles in Colin's neck ached with the tension twisting his muscles. "Apparently I am."

Doyle looked lost. "Apparently, Your Lordship?"

"If I am to believe what they tell me." Colin rubbed the back of his neck, ignoring the look of puzzlement in the butler's eyes. "There was an accident. They tell me I have lost my memory."

Doyle's lips formed an *O*. "Your memory."

"Aye. 'Twould be best if you were to think of me as a man you have never met."

"Never met." Doyle nodded, a look of understanding filling his eyes. "You wish for people to believe you have lost your memory. I see, Your Lordship."

Colin could see as well. Doyle believed this was part of Lancaster's game. Was there any wonder Lady Jane had gone running from him? A sharp pain stabbed his chest when he thought of her, a need he quickly crushed. "Show me to the books."

Doyle smiled. "Of course, Your Lordship."

Colin glanced down at the stone slabs beneath his feet as he followed Doyle back into the library. These stones were the same as they had been in his time. Worn now by footsteps through the ages. Yet here he knew his mother's feet had trod, as had his sisters' and his brother's. A horrible sense of loss welled inside him as he glanced around the hall, where polished wooden panels had replaced tapestries upon stone. So little of Kintair remained as it had in his day. Even the wide staircase winding upward in one corner had been altered. So little remained of his home. And nothing remained of his family.

He forced air past the growing tightness in his throat. Although he wanted to fall to his knees and weep for the family he had lost, he knew there was nothing to be gained in self-pity. For now he must discover what had happened to his family. And if that English scoundrel had somehow destroyed his loved ones, he would search the rest of his life for a way back to them. An image of Lady Jane rose in his mind, and with the image came a searing need. He would set things right, no matter what the cost to his own soul.

Doyle led Colin to a bookcase near the large claw-footed desk in the library. "The history has been documented in these volumes," he said, indicating two shelves filled with leather-clad books.

Colin drew one of the books from the shelves. He recognized the words *Kintair Castle* above a date tooled in gold upon brown leather. An odd print filled the pages of this book, along with drawings and paintings. The drawings and paintings were clear enough, but the letters and the words were difficult to decipher. "Where are the *Chronicles of Kintair*?"

"I beg pardon, Your Lordship?"

He met Doyle's confused gaze. "There should be books that have been kept by each Kintair laird."

"Your father commissioned Sir Henry Filmore to compile the history of Kintair Castle. I have no knowledge of any documented history aside from these books, Your Lordship." Doyle smiled, a conspiratorial glint in his eyes. "Of course, since you have lost your memory, you would not be expected to know this."

Colin clenched his jaw. "Lancaster's father commissioned an Englishman to document the history of Kintair?"

Doyle nodded. "From Oxford."

Colin glanced through the thick books on the shelf,

until he came to the one with the years 1500 to 1600 tooled on the cover. Slowly he explored the pages. Although he could make out a few words, it was like reading a foreign language. "Is there anyone in the house who might know what has become of the *Chronicles*?"

"No, Your Lordship."

What had become of them? He could not imagine one of his descendants abandoning the tradition his grandfather had commenced. He glanced up at the portrait over the desk. How had an English scoundrel come to inherit Kintair? He must be connected to Lancaster in some way. Did his connection to this man have anything at all to do with his flight through time? He looked at Doyle. As much as he regretted it, he would need the butler's help in deciphering this mystery.

The quick tap of footsteps on stone made Colin turn. His heart thudded when he saw Jane enter the room. She paused near the door and fixed him with a steady stare. She looked like an angel, a beautiful avenging angel, angry enough to send him straight to hell. Still, the anger did not prevent the sudden rush of excitement sprinting through him. His chest expanded with the simple pleasure of seeing her again. "That will be all, Doyle."

"Aye, Your Lordship."

Jane glared at the butler when he approached her. "Apparently your memory has returned."

"Aye, Your Ladyship. Beg pardon, Your Ladyship." Doyle bowed his head as he scurried past her.

At the departure of the butler, Jane once again turned her fierce gaze upon Colin.

Colin did not flinch. "I am glad you came back."

"Give me one good reason why I should stay."

"I need your help."

She wagged her finger at him. "I am warning you, Lancaster. If I discover you are playing some vile game with me, I shall make certain you regret it."

In spite of her stern tone, he smiled. She had come

back to him; that was all that mattered. "I am not playing a game. And if you truly thought I was, you would never have come back to me."

She shrugged and directed her gaze to the tip of her shoe. "I have been thinking. . . . Perhaps the portrait answers a great many questions. Instead of pronouncing you guilty, it may actually help prove you are ill."

"And how might it do that?"

"You are the Earl of Kintair. It explains how you knew about the castle and Colin." She slid her fingers back and forth against each other. "Perhaps your knowledge of Kintair has somehow become twisted in your mind."

The history of Kintair has always been of particular interest to you. He resisted the urge to smooth his hand over the lump at the back of his head, just as he resisted the doubts clamoring within him. "I need to discover what has happened to my family. The answers should be in this book. But I have a wee bit of a problem with it."

She moved to his side, her gown swishing softly against the layers beneath. "A problem?"

The crisp scent of lemons drifted to his senses, tugging on him deep inside. He held her gaze, setting aside the pride that might keep the truth of his weakness from her. He needed her help and he would not allow pride to keep him from it. "I cannot read them."

She glanced from the book he held to the other volumes on the shelf beside him. "Is there something wrong with them?"

"Not exactly."

"Not exactly?" She withdrew one of the large leather-bound books and started leafing through the pages.

Sunlight slanted through the windows behind him, falling with a soft golden hand upon her face. He lowered his gaze to the wispy curls lying upon her neck. Need pumped more potent than brandy through his veins. He wanted to touch her, to test the softness of those curls beneath his fingertips. She had such soft-looking hair, strands of brown and gold all piled high upon her head. All except for these wispy, wayward curls.

In spite of her attempts to appear harsh and distant, he knew there existed another side of her locked deep within. He had tasted her passion. He had felt only a glimmer of the fires burning deep within her. Yet she had seared her essence into his soul.

"I really . . ." She glanced up at him, her words halting on a sharp intake of breath as she met his gaze.

He saw recognition in her eyes, a woman's knowledge of a man's hunger. With the recognition came her own soft rush of desire, revealed in the widening of her silvery eyes, betrayed in the soft exhalation of her breath. She wanted him. He could feel it. "You really what?"

"I, ah . . ." She glanced down to the open book she held. "I really don't see what the problem is. The print seems clear enough."

As clear as the soft quaver in her voice. "Aye, but the words are not."

"The words?"

"The books might as well be written in a different language, for all I can decipher this English of your time."

She stared at him. "You don't remember how to read?"

"Of course I can read. But I cannot read this language of your century. At least not without a great deal of trouble." He glanced back at the bookcase. "I was hoping to find the chronicles that had commenced with my grandfather. My mother would have documented all I need to know."

A chill gripped Jane as she listened to him. Lancaster spoke with such conviction of something that could not possibly be true. He stood close without touching her. Still, her body could not extinguish the heat simmering through her veins, just as she could not crush the tingling excitement that had commenced coursing through her limbs the moment he had looked at her. "I should think everything you need to know would be documented in these books."

"I hope 'tis true. I need to know what happened to my family the year I left. 'Twould be in this book." He handed her the book he was holding, the brown leather cover warm from his touch. "Will you read it for me?"

"You look exhausted. You should rest before you collapse."

"Not until I know what happened to my family. If your scoundrel could not save them . . ." He hesitated, his lips flattening into a tight line. "Then I will find a way back to them."

She glanced down at the book she held. What was hidden between these pages? More important, what would Lancaster do when he learned the truth? Had Colin MacKenzie ever existed? "It shouldn't take long to learn if there was a clan war in 1562."

He clenched his jaw. "Lord in heaven, I pray your scoundrel was able to save my uncle from his madness."

And she hoped she could save Lancaster from his madness. For in his salvation she would find her own.

"Come, lass," he said, taking her arm. He ushered her to the nearest sofa, then sat beside her.

Her fingers trembled as she opened the book. Did he have any idea how difficult it was to concentrate on anything else when he was sitting so near? She tried not to think of how cozy it felt sitting with him this way. She could imagine spending lazy days here with this man, simply enjoying his company. Yet it wasn't to be.

She focused her attention on the book in her lap and tried to ignore the foolish yearning for a man who did not truly exist. Each chapter documented ten years of life at Kintair Castle. She skipped through the book until she found the chapter that began with the year 1560. As she read, an uneasy feeling coiled in the pit of her stomach. They were all here, documented in this book. Colin

MacKenzie had inherited the title when he was four and twenty, after his father's death in the winter of 1562.

Colin MacKenzie had existed. He had lived in this castle with his mother, his sisters Isabel and Maura, and their young brother, Campbell. It was all as Lancaster had imagined. There was a logical explanation, she assured herself. Lancaster must have read the history. Of course he would have read the history.

"What happened to them, lass?" He leaned over her shoulder, staring down at the book. "Did my uncle march against the MacDonnells?"

The subtle spicy scent of his skin spilled around her, adding a beat to her already racing heart. "No, he didn't."

"Praise to the Almighty," he whispered. "What happened?"

"According to this, Colin MacKenzie, third Earl of Kintair, married Adaira MacDonnell on May 15, 1562. It says: 'From all accounts it was a shrewd alliance. With one stroke, Colin ensured the loyalty of his clan, cutting off the threat Malcolm MacKenzie had presented with his plot to gain power.' It goes on to say Colin remained in control of the clan until his death in 1612. At which time his eldest son inherited."

Lancaster was quiet for a moment. When he spoke there was a touch of humor in his voice. "So Lancaster married the ice maiden."

She glanced up from the book to give him a stern glance. "Colin MacKenzie married her."

"It appeared as though I did. But if I am here, Lancaster went there. And a better fate I could not imagine for him." He wiggled his eyebrows at her. "Adaira was known as the Ice Maiden. Beautiful, heartless, cold as a December wind. She could freeze a man with a glance."

"I thought you had planned to marry her?"

He shivered. "I would have married her as a last desperate attempt to prevent war. Not for any other reason."

She glanced down at the book, trying not to allow the

intriguing possibility to take hold of her. "According to this, Colin and Adaira had seven children. She was obviously not quite as icy as people thought."

Lancaster whistled softly. " 'Twould appear your scoundrel met his match. At least he found a way to thaw the ice."

It was a compelling thought to imagine Lancaster cast back more than three hundred years, into the arms of a woman every bit as cold as he was. "It certainly would be justice."

He leaned closer, his arm brushing hers as he tapped the book with one long finger. "Tell me about my family. My mother and sisters, Campbell. How did they fare?"

She kept her gaze focused on the page before her, forcing her mind to concentrate. The next few pages provided a sketch of the rest of the MacKenzie family. "Apparently they did just fine without you. Your mother lived to see her grandchildren grown. And it appears she had quite a few grandchildren to see. Isabel and Earl Dunleith had seven children. Your sister Maura married the Earl of Banburgh, an Englishman. They had six children. Your brother married another of the MacDonnell girls. Since it states he had five children, I think we can assume it was a love match. It appears as though they all lived long and prosperous lives."

"Maura married an Englishman?"

"Perhaps Lancaster had some influence over her."

He laughed, a soft rumble that curled around her. "You still do not believe me. Do you, lass?"

She closed the book and rested it on her thighs. "There is nothing in here to make me believe in your fairy tale of switched souls."

"I am here, and since my life continued after I was brought to you, then 'tis logical to suppose Lancaster has taken my place."

"I would think if Lancaster had awakened in your body, he might have reacted the same way you did. Yet there is no mention of Colin MacKenzie's sudden plunge into insanity."

"If your husband was as shrewd as you say he was, he would have realized he must adapt if he were to survive. He would gain nothing by insisting he was not the MacKenzie. He would gain much by assuming my life."

Jane could see the logic in that. Still, she could not accept his story. "Lancaster would have left some message for his family. If for no other reason than to shock them."

Lancaster studied her a long moment. "What will it take to convince you?"

"How can you convince me something impossible is possible?" She glanced down at her tightly clasped hands and acknowledged her wish that he could prove to her magic did exist in the world. "I suppose if you knew something about Colin or the castle that no one else could know."

"I know all there is to know about me. I can show you where I tumbled from a tree and sliced open my brow. That is how I got this scar." He smoothed his finger over his right brow. "Only 'tis not there. Because this is not my face."

"Yes, it is."

He released his breath on a long sigh. "If I am not Colin MacKenzie, how do you suppose I knew so much about his life?"

"You apparently have read the history of the castle."

"What can I do to prove to you I am Colin?"

"I wish I knew." She wanted him to prove the impossible. "Even if you could tell me something that no one else could know about Colin's life, how would you prove it? If it were some piece of history, the only way you could prove it to me would be to show it to me in a book such as this one. And if it is documented, then it is hardly something only you could know. Do you see my logic?"

"I see my problem." He rose and looked around the

room. "I lived here. This was my home. A tapestry hung upon that wall, a scene of Vulcan in his fall from Olympus. And a bench sat in that first window alcove, with pillows my mother and sisters made. If I close my eyes I can see the delicate needlework of flowers and leaves."

How could it all seem so real to him? At times she could not separate reality from fantasy. In a strange way Colin was more real to her than Lancaster. "I cannot explain why it all seems so clear to you. I don't understand why the illness has caused you to believe you are Colin MacKenzie. Yet I know it must be the illness. And I know one day you will regain your memory. You've already remembered your grandmother."

He turned to face her, the strength of his will etched upon his features. "Ever since I have grown into a man, people have told me I am the image of my mother's father. Yet that does not make me James Campbell. Only his grandson."

She considered this a moment. "And since Lancaster inherited the title, it would make sense that you and he are related. Somewhat distantly."

"Although I do not care to imagine this man a descendant of mine, 'tis likely. My face is not so very different from that of this man." He wiggled his eyebrow. "Of course, I am much better-looking than this English scoundrel."

"Better-looking?" Good heavens, if he were any better-looking, he would have to be kept under lock and key to save unsuspecting women from fits of rapture. "I see where Lancaster inherited his conceit."

He grimaced. "You are a stubborn lass."

"Practical." And it was hardly practical to fall in love with a man who had died three hundred years before she was born. "You should rest now. The remainder of the history can wait."

"I am fine." He paced to the windows, stared into the gardens for a moment, then turned and walked back to her. "Suppose what you say is true, and I am truly ill from a bump on the head."

"It is easy to suppose," she said, "since it is the truth."

"Is it?"

"Yes." A loud thump made her jump. She turned and found a large red leather book on the floor near the sofa.

Lancaster retrieved the book and slipped it back onto the shelf. He turned and looked straight into her eyes in that way he had of making her feel he knew her better than she knew herself. "If you could be certain I would remain as I am, if you knew I would always think of myself as Colin MacKenzie, would you want me to regain my memory?"

In his eyes she saw a longing he did not try to hide. A longing that mirrored the need lingering deep within her. "If I could be certain you would remain as you are?"

"Aye. Would you want Lancaster to regain his memory?"

She hesitated, aware of how much she would reveal with her answer. Yet looking into those clear eyes, she could not evade the truth. "No."

He closed his eyes as if in silent prayer. When he looked at her, she saw something new in his eyes: hope. "I want to stay with you, lass. Now and always."

Need twisted around her heart, a sharp reminder of a truth she could not ignore. She wanted to believe in him. She wanted to believe in the magic of her one and only love. She glanced down at the book upon her lap. "There is no good hoping for things that cannot be."

"It can be." He knelt before her and took her hand. "My family thrived without me. And although I shall miss them dearly, I understand the reason I was brought to this time and place. 'Tis you, my lady. I was meant to be with you, and you with me. 'Tis destiny."

His words wrapped around her, as warm and beguiling as a gentle embrace. Her hand looked so pale against his skin, small and delicate in his grasp. She eased her hand from his and stood. She walked to the bookcase and slipped the history of Kintair back onto the shelf. "You don't really mean these things."

"Aye, lass, I do." He went to her and rested his hands upon her arms. He drew her back against him until her back nestled against the hard plane of his chest. "It seems I have been looking for you all my life. And through some twist of magic I have finally found you."

Lord help her, but she wanted to believe in this miracle. She wanted to lean back against him, to feel his arms close around her. Still, she could not afford the luxury of such lovely dreams. She eased free of his gentle touch and stepped away from him, breaking the physical contact. Yet the distance did not sever the connection she felt to this man. As much as she would like to dismiss it as simple physical attraction, it was far more dangerous than lust. When she looked at this man she could not dismiss the feeling that she had been waiting for him all of her life. It could not be. It was all an illusion. "There is no such thing as magic."

Again, a book fell from the shelf beside her. It whacked the carpet, making her jump. She glanced down at the large red leather volume. The title was tooled in gold upon red leather: *Scottish Myths and Legends*. It looked like the same book that had fallen before. "That's odd."

"It must have been too close to the edge." Colin bent, retrieved the book, and slipped it back onto the shelf. He turned to face her, a slight smile curving his lips. "Since you do not believe in magic, you do not believe in me. Is that the way of it?"

"You shall have to pardon me if I prefer to believe in the logical explanation rather than a fairy tale."

"And the logical explanation is that I fell and hit my head one day and the next morning I awakened believing I was an entirely different man. With no memories of

Dominic Stanbridge and all of the memories of Colin MacKenzie."

Somehow it didn't sound quite so logical when he said it in that tone of voice. "Yes."

"And this bump on the head is what has made me fall in love with you."

"In love with . . ." She gripped the edge of a bookshelf, her legs suddenly weak. "You are not in love with me."

"Aye, lass, I am." He leaned toward her. "I have been in love with you since the first moment I saw you in my dreams."

She shook her head. "It is the illness speaking."

He kissed the tip of her nose. " 'Tis magic."

Another book tumbled from the bookshelf. It plopped onto the floor, landing on its spine, the white pages spilling open at her feet. It was a large book with a red cover. Could it possibly be the same book? "How strange."

Lancaster bent to retrieve the book. Yet this time he did not slip it back onto the shelf. Instead he studied the page before him. "By my faith."

"What is it?"

"This woman." He tapped the page. "I have seen her before."

Jane moved to his side and glanced at the page. An illustration in color filled the entire page. The painting was of a woman, one of the most beautiful women she had ever seen. Hair as pale as cornsilk fell to her knees, brushing her flowing white gown. Tiny gold stars glittered in the gauzy fabric. The slant of her golden brows accentuated the large almond-shaped eyes beneath. Those silvery blue eyes seemed to look straight at Jane, as though she had a secret she wished to share. "You have seen this woman?"

"Aye. I am certain of it." He drew in his breath slowly, as though it were difficult to pull the air into his lungs. " 'Tis the woman I saw beneath the light of a full moon, near the ancient stones. When I was a lad."

Jane looked at the inscription under the painting and shivered. " 'The Matchmaker of Tara.' "

He handed her the book. "I must know what is written about this woman."

Chapter Nineteen

No one can be more wise than destiny.
—Alfred, Lord Tennyson

Colin paced the length of the library, trying to quell the impatience swelling like a tide within him. He paused in front of the sofa and gazed down at Jane. "What does it say about this woman?"

Jane glanced up from the large book resting on her lap. "If you give me a few moments, I will be able to tell you."

" 'Tis important."

She lifted her brows. "Then perhaps you should give me a chance to read about her, rather than interrupting me every minute."

He sank to the edge of the sofa beside her. "One of the first things I will do in this new life is to learn how to decipher your letters."

"I will be happy to teach you." She slanted him a look. "Later. I am also rather curious about this woman."

He clasped his hands between his knees in an effort to control his impatience. From the time he was a lad he had wondered about the woman he had met on that long-ago night. As he had grown, he had accepted the fact that it was probably all a dream. Yet deep within him, he had always hoped she was real.

He watched Jane's face as she read the pages before her. Her expression revealed her thoughts: curiosity, surprise, and finally a frown, as though she did not like what she had read. "What is it?"

Jane stared at the painting in the book. "You could not have met this woman."

"And why is that?"

"It says her name is Aisling." She looked at him. "And she is a sorceress, one of the Sidhe."

Colin released the breath he had not even realized he had been holding. "She was a fairy princess."

"It is a legend. Aisling does not exist."

"Just as I do not exist?"

She moistened her lips, a quick slide of the tip of her tongue that made him think of how soft and warm those lips had felt beneath his. "You are ill. She is a myth."

"This is the woman I described to you the other night. Even her gown is the same. How could I have known of her if I had never met her?"

Jane frowned, an uneasy expression crossing her features. "I suppose you must have heard the legend at one time. You probably read this book. That must be it. You must have read about her and it stayed in your memory."

"Stubborn lass." He tapped the page with his finger. "What does it say about her? Why do they call her the Matchmaker of Tara?"

She hesitated a moment. "According to the legend, she goes about meddling in the lives of mortals, bringing together men and women she feels are destined for one another."

"Destined for one another?"

"Yes. It says neither time nor distance shall dissuade her from her purpose. Upon the full moon she will bring together those souls destined to love. And only upon the full moon can her spell be removed."

His breath stilled. "The spell can be removed?"

"Yes." Jane kept her gaze focused on the painting of Aisling. "It says Aisling will entertain the pleas of any lover who does not wish to follow the path she has set. One need only speak to her on the first night of the full moon."

He stared at the wispy curls beneath Jane's ear. He could leave this place. He could return to his family, his home, all he held dear, if he was willing to leave Jane behind.

"Some say that Aisling lost her true love and now gains satisfaction by bringing lovers together. Other people feel she is doing it for an entirely different reason."

"What is that?"

"It doesn't say much. Only that it may have something to do with the bloodlines of the Sidhe and her attempt to save her people."

"I have heard the legends of the Sidhe. It is said they have taken refuge in faraway places to keep their heritage alive. But some of them prefer to live in the mortal world, to practice their magic in secret." Colin slid his palms together. "I wonder if that is true about her."

Jane closed the book. "The truth is, she does not exist."

"She does exist. I met her. I know now 'twas her voice speaking to me the night before I came to you. 'Time to meet your destiny.' I did not know what she meant, at least not then."

"It is impossible."

He lifted his brows. "You are speaking to a man who has traveled three hundred years to meet his destiny. I can tell you, nothing is impossible."

"I never suspected you had such a wonderful imagination." Jane glanced away from him as though she wanted to hide her emotions from him. "Still, it is important to remember this is all part of your illness."

"No, lass." Colin turned on the sofa, his knee brushing her gown. Although he could not feel her form through the layers of her clothes, she reacted as if he had touched her bare leg with his skin. Her soft intake of breath, the widening of her beautiful eyes, betrayed the attraction she would deny. "Aisling is the one who cast this spell. She brought me to your side. 'Tis destiny."

"No. It is not." She clasped her hands on top of the book. "It is a rather nasty bump on the head."

She was frightened of him. Frightened he would go to bed one night and awaken a different man, the man she despised. *With injuries such as yours, it is not unusual to suffer some confusion.* He clamped down hard on the doubts stirring deep within him. "I am Colin MacKenzie."

She put the book aside and stood. She crossed the room and stared out at the gardens beyond the terrace for a long moment. Then she turned to face him. When she looked at him he could see she had pulled her defenses close around her. "You are Dominic Stanbridge. And one day you will remember who and what you are. In time it will all become clear once more."

It was clear to him. This woman was the key to his flight across the ages. He had been brought here to be with her. He had left behind his family, his friends, his life, to be with her. Yet the spell could be reversed. He could return to his own life. He thought of his family, his chest constricting with the pain of loss. Yet in spite of all he had lost, he knew in his heart that he would choose to stay in this place and time. "I know who I am. And I know you are the woman destiny meant for me to find."

It was so beguiling, his notion of a love that could span the ages. Yet Jane knew destiny had not played a hand in her union to this man. A scoundrel had manipulated her life. He is Lancaster, she reminded herself, the man who could send her pulse racing with a glance, the beguiling Scot who could conjure sweet poetry within her. If she continued to go about thinking of him as another man, and admitting her own foolish infatuation with that man, she might as well walk straight off the cliffs that stood just beyond the gardens. "Destiny has nothing to do with you and me."

"Are you going to tell me you do not feel it too?"

He had discarded his coat. She tried not to notice the way his shirt fell open at his neck, revealing a wedge of warm-looking skin and soft-looking curls. "What?"

"This attraction that draws me to you." He stood and moved toward her. "This need that pounds through my body each time you are near. This hunger that claws at my vitals. Never in my life have I wanted a woman as I want you."

It wasn't real. No matter how alluring Colin MacKenzie might be, he was not real. Unfortunately, the pain twisting like a steel band around her heart was real. "Whatever it is you feel, it is not real."

He paused before her, emotion naked in his eyes. "Is that what you truly believe?"

Her chest felt as if a thick slab of marble were pressing upon her. No matter how much she wanted to deny the truth, it was there, like a crouched lion between them, waiting to devour her should she forget its presence. She stepped away from him, hoping distance would bolster her weakening resolve.

She paused beside a round pedestal table standing near the window. Dried rosebuds and sprigs of dried heather filled a porcelain bowl, lending a sweet fragrance to the air. The feelings he evoked within her could not be trusted. If she surrendered to these feelings, she might go to bed with Colin and awaken beside Lancaster. "The feeling you have cannot be real because you are not real."

He moved toward her, tall and broad-shouldered. She had often imagined what he would be like, the one man destined for her. He would be honest, gentle, and compassionate. The type of man who would enjoy sitting with her in the evening, content with her company. He would love her with all of his heart and soul, love her in a way that allowed her to give all of the love she held safely hidden deep inside her. Colin MacKenzie might be that man—if he were more than a figment of Lancaster's imagination. What twist of fate had brought this man into her life? What terrible thing had she done to be presented with everything she had ever wanted, when it could never truly be?

He rested his hand on her arm. "Look at me and tell me you do not want me."

The soft Scottish burr rippled across the pool of longing deep within her. "I do not want Lancaster in my life," she said, keeping her gaze fixed on the dried flowers.

"I did not ask you about that scoundrel." He slipped his fingers under her chin and tipped back her head. "Look at me, Jane."

She resisted, fearing what might happen if she should look into his eyes. Instead she stared at his chin. "I will not be bullied by you."

"Bullied?"

She glanced up at him then, meeting his gaze. Somewhere in the back of her mind it occurred to her how easily a woman could get lost in the clear blue depths of those eyes. And she wondered if she had already stepped too far. "Intimidated. Coerced."

He cupped her face in his large, warm hands. "I am not the scoundrel you married. I would never do anything to hurt you."

She wanted to moisten her lips, but her mouth had dried to parchment. "Yes, you are. And I am afraid you will."

One corner of his mouth tightened. "I shall have to prove you wrong."

Challenge glinted in his eyes. She didn't like that look. Not one little bit. It made her feel too much like an antelope facing a hungry lion. "There is nothing you can do to make me change my mind."

He slid his fingers down her neck. "Does your pulse race this way when Lancaster touches you?"

She pressed her hands against his chest, intending to push him away. Her fingertips sank into the soft white silk of his shirt. "My pulse is racing simply because I find this disturbing."

"Disturbing?" Lancaster held her captive with his look. "You are trembling, lass."

She stepped away and bumped into the back of one of the velvet-clad sofas. "You are one of the most infuriating men I have ever met."

"And you are one of the most vexing women I have ever met." Lancaster closed the distance between them. She sidestepped, intent on escape. He whipped his arm around her waist and hauled her against him. "Vexing and beguiling."

She pushed against his shoulders. "Take your hands off me," she said, appalled at the breathless sound of her voice.

One corner of his lips tipped upward, and a fierce look entered his eyes. "Prove to me you do not want me, and I will never touch you again. Prove to me you do not want me, and I will leave you upon the next full moon."

A horrible feeling gripped her when she thought of losing this man, pain and despair so potent it slid through her like jagged glass. It took all of her effort to suppress the need within her. "I do not want you."

He slid one hand upwards along her back, his fingers conforming to her ribs, inching upward until his fingertips brushed the side of her breast. "Prove your words."

Jane stared up into his eyes, searching through the rubble he had made of her mind for any weapon to use against him. "What proof do you need? I have already told you I cannot abide your touch."

"Show me," he whispered, lowering his head.

"I really must—"

He slid his lips over hers, stopping her protest. Need rose and quivered inside of her at the slow slide of his lips over hers. A voice screamed in her brain—*He is Lancaster.* Yet that declaration had little impact on her. She no longer saw the icy arrogance of Lancaster when she looked at her husband. Instead she saw the fiery passion of Colin. And therein lay the danger.

He slid his other arm around her and drew her closer. Her breasts pressed against the hard plane of his chest. Powerful muscles shifted against her, arousing sensation after sensation.

He lifted his head just enough to whisper, "Tell me you do not want me, my bonnie Jane."

She was on the edge of a cliff, and the stones were crumbling beneath her. "I don't want you," she said, sliding her hands upward along his chest.

"Aye, I can feel how much you do not want me." He opened his mouth over hers, kissing her as though he had been waiting three hundred years to kiss her like this, a hundred lifetimes to hold her like this.

She fought the crumbling of her reserve. Her freedom was at stake here. Her chance to find the man she was meant to love. Yet a part of her, somewhere deep within her soul, spoke a truth she did not wish to acknowledge: This was the man she was meant to love. She felt the stones tumble out from beneath her. If she did not stop him now, all would be lost. Yet in this war she was fighting more than one enemy. Her own need had risen to fight against her.

He touched the seam of her lips with the tip of his tongue, silently demanding entry. She opened to him, while the last stones fell away from beneath her. She gripped his shoulders, holding him as though he were the only solid thing in her entire world. Slowly he plucked the combs from her hair, tossing them to the floor. They fell noiselessly to the carpet.

He slid his hands through her hair, smoothing the long mane from her shoulders to her waist. "You make me burn, my bonnie lass," he whispered against her lips.

She moved as though in a dream, sliding her hands along his shoulders, absorbing the heat of him, the hard breadth of him through soft white silk. He gripped her hips and pulled her up against him, a low growl escaping his lips. Through the layers of her petticoats she could feel no more than a hint of the blatant masculinity pressed against her. Yet she knew the shape and texture of him, the hard length of velvet over steel. And the memory served only as fuel to the fires burning within her.

"Jane." He brushed his lips over her cheek, nipped her chin, then slid the tip of his tongue down her neck while he slipped his hand between their bodies.

Dimly she was aware of his deft fingers upon the buttons lining the front of her gown. Distantly she thought of bridges that were about to go up in flame. Yet she could not dredge up a protest within her. It felt too right, this slow seduction of her senses, as though she had been waiting for this moment all her life.

One button after another fell open beneath his touch. Little by little he peeled away the prim green wool, revealing more and more of her skin to the soft touch of his lips, the warm brush of his breath. If her pulse had been racing before, now it surged so quickly she could scarcely differentiate one beat from the next.

He peeled back the cloth, exposing her prim white chemise. Yet he did not stop kissing her. He pressed his lips to the soft cambric between her breasts and released his breath. The slow, steady stream of damp heat seeped through the white cotton, spreading like warm brandy over her skin. When the last button was released he slipped the gown off her shoulders. Soft wool tumbled with a sigh to the floor around her feet.

"So many layers." He brushed his fingertip down the front of her, from the blue ribbon at the top of her chemise to the waist of her petticoat. "I have never seen such garments before."

He was wearing far too many layers as well. She fumbled with the buttons lining his shirt, wanting to feel the heat of his skin. Soft silk tore beneath her impatient hand, buttons tumbling from her trembling fingers. She plunged her hands inside his shirt, then slid her palms over silky black curls. A soft sound rose from deep in his chest, a sound that made her wonder if lions could purr.

He rained kisses upon her lips, her cheeks, her brows while he plucked open the pale blue ribbon at the top of her chemise and unfastened the tiny pearl buttons exposed above the edge of her corset. Jane gasped against his cheek when he pulled the chemise from her shoulders, baring her breasts.

"Look at you," he whispered.

She followed the direction of his gaze. The tight corset lifted her breasts, as though they were an offering presented to a pagan god. Her nipples were puckered into tiny pink buds where her pulse throbbed with each beat of her heart. She had seen the sight of her naked breasts before. Yet somehow seeing them now, knowing he was looking at her, made the pale globes seem exotic, forbidden fruit. Standing half-naked before him, she did not feel like the ordinary woman she was. She felt powerful, an enchantress with the magic to bring this man to his knees.

He cupped her breasts in his hands and slowly slid his thumbs over the tips. She sucked in her breath. He lowered his head, flicked his tongue over the crest of one breast, then slowly drew the nipple into his mouth. She gripped his shoulders, hoping she would not collapse at his feet. She had never imagined anything so wanton before, anything so deliciously naughty as the feel of his mouth upon her breasts, his lips, his tongue, his teeth performing wicked magic. When he untied her petticoat and pushed the soft cotton from her hips, she realized this was but a glimmer of what would come.

"Layers upon layers," he whispered, pulling the pale blue ribbon at the top of her drawers. He flicked open the three pearl buttons just below her waist. "Your garments are like you, layers waiting to be explored."

The air felt cool upon her damp nipples. He slid his hands over her hips, peeling away her drawers, exposing her to the sunlight slanting through the window behind him. Yet the golden light paled beside the heat of his gaze. He followed the slow slide of her drawers, brushing kisses upon her belly, her hip, her thigh.

"More beautiful than my dreams," he whispered, sinking to one knee before her.

Dreams. Yes, that was where she had known this man. Yet her dreams had never been filled with anything as intimate as this—his lips upon the sensitive skin of her inner thigh, the brush of his hair upon her skin, his hands sliding upon her naked bottom, his breath warm upon her most private region. She gripped the sofa, watching him move upward. He couldn't mean to . . .

Her heart stopped at the first touch of his lips upon her, a kiss too intimate to imagine. "Oh, that is wicked. You shouldn't."

He brushed his lips against her belly. "Aye, lass, I should."

She tipped back her head, caught unaware, trapped by the sweet waves of desire lapping over her. Even as the pleasure swelled within her, she realized it might all be as fleeting as mist in sunlight. His memory could return and with it the icy shell that was Dominic. Fear clenched her stomach, dread fighting the heat he conjured within her. "Colin, I . . ."

He stood and urged her down onto the sofa. The soft cushions gave beneath her, silky velvet cradling her back.

He covered her, his weight pressing her back into the cushions. Soft wool brushed her inner thighs. She drew in her breath, absorbing the fragrance of sandalwood and a spice that was his alone. The scent swirled through her, sidetracking her attempts to examine the consequences of what she was about to do.

"My angel," he whispered. He brushed his lips against hers, a touch barely felt. Yet she shivered with the sweetness in that kiss. He opened his mouth over hers, deepening the kiss, dipping his tongue into her mouth, withdrawing until she followed his lead, teasing him with the same plunge and retreat.

His fingers grazed her belly as he unfastened his trouser buttons. The heat of him pulsed through the soft white silk of his drawers. She felt as though everything inside her had grown tight in expectation of what would come. She felt a deep, abiding need for this man, only this man.

She imagined each button falling free as he unfastened his drawers. Still, she was not prepared for the first touch of his hardened flesh upon her. He rocked his hips, sliding against her nether lips. She felt moisture, warm and abundant, a purely feminine response to blatant masculinity.

"I have waited all my life for you," he whispered, lifting his head to look down into her eyes.

So had she. She felt the truth of that deep in her soul; a truth she could not explain with logic or reason. She felt as though she had been half-asleep all her life. Until this man careened into her life. This wonderful man.

He shifted his hips, pressing the velvet hardness of his aroused flesh against her most private threshold. The pressure startled her, the slow slide brought both fear and an overwhelming need to succumb to this temptation.

"Tell me you want me, Jane."

She could not deny the truth; it burned like flame

within her. She wanted this man with all her heart and soul. Wanted this man all the days of her life. Yet Colin would not be here all the days of her life. He could vanish as quickly as he had come to her. And when he left she would face the icy arrogance of Lancaster. A lifetime with a man she despised. The realization hit her like a clenched fist plowing into her belly. "I can't," she whispered, pushing against his shoulders.

His lips parted; a look of disbelief crossed his features. "You can't?"

"No." She pushed against his shoulders. "Please don't force me to do this."

"Force you?" A grimace crossed his features. "You think I would force you?"

"Please let me up."

He lifted away from her. She scrambled from beneath him, too quickly to gain her balance. She hit the floor on her knees, then stood, all the while aware of his gaze upon her. Still, she could not face him. Humiliated, she stood in nothing more than her corset, chemise, stockings, and shoes in the middle of a library, with an aroused male who believed he had come to her from 1562. She suddenly had the horrible feeling she was the one who was insane.

She snatched her gown from the pile of discarded clothes on the floor nearby. Before she could step into the gown, Colin grabbed her arm. He pulled her around, forcing her to look at him. The raw anger in his eyes made her cringe.

"What was this? Did you mean to punish me?"

She blinked. "Punish you?"

"Aye." He grabbed her other arm and hauled her against him, flattening her bare breasts against his chest. "You meant to punish me for the crimes another man committed."

"No. I would never—"

"Or is it me you meant to punish?"

"You?"

"Is it me you despise?" He dragged her upward until her toes brushed the floor and her face was just below his. "What did you mean to do, Jane? Tease me with a glimpse of heaven, only to shove me into hell?"

Her temper flared. That dark, wounded look in his eyes was not at all fair. "I was not the one who started this. You were."

"Aye, I was." He released her and stepped back, looking at her as though she had just slithered out from beneath a rock. "Well, never fear, my lady. I shall not make the same mistake twice."

"Neither shall I." She clutched her gown to her breasts, watching him march from the library. The loud crash of the door slamming behind him made her flinch. "Arrogant, infuriating oaf!"

If he never touched her again, it would suit her just fine. Still, she could not banish the memories of his hands and his lips and his tongue upon her. She could not crush the excitement that still coursed through her veins. For the first time in her life she had truly felt the full extent of her own femininity. And it was wonderful. She closed her eyes and tried to calm the rush of her pulse. She could not fall in love with a man who did not exist.

A loud thud made her jump. She turned and found a book lying on the floor near the bookcase across from her. A large book encased in dark red leather. A prickling sensation brushed the nape of her neck. She glanced around. Yet there was no one in sight. She was alone. She stepped into her gown and fastened the buttons before she crossed the room and looked down at the book. It had opened to the legend of the Matchmaker of Tara. Shivers whispered along her back.

She lifted the book and looked into the face of a fairy princess. Aisling seemed to be smiling right at her, as if she had a secret she wanted to share. "It cannot be," she whispered, closing the book. "There is no such thing as magic."

Chapter Twenty

White shall not neutralize the black, nor good
Compensate bad in man, absolve him so:
Life's business being just the terrible choice.
                                    —Robert Browning

Colin had postponed the inevitable for three days. He could delay no longer. The oak door swung on well-oiled hinges, spilling a stale scent into the air. Sunlight slanted into the stone building from narrow windows near the ceiling, the light falling upon the tombs of his family. He went to his mother's tomb. She was lying beside his father, as he'd known she would be.

Colin brushed his fingertips over the likeness of his mother carved in the marble slab above her earthly remains. He had mourned his father. The passing of time had eased that wound. Yet until now, until he felt the cold marble beneath his fingers, he had not truly accepted his mother's passing. It was hard to believe she was gone, that beneath this marble little remained of her but dust.

He thought of the last day he had spent with her. If he had only known it would be the last time he would look upon her face, the last time he would touch her hand, he would have treasured each minute. He would have told her how much she had meant to him. He pressed his lips to her cheek, touching cold marble instead of warm skin. Grief raked his throat; the heat of tears stung his eyes. "Farewell," he whispered.

He lingered a moment longer, then searched for his brother. A narrow marble slab upon the wall marked the place where he was interred. The likeness carved upon the marble was not of the lad he had known. Here was a man who had lived a full life. Campbell had always worshiped his older brother. Colin wondered if the man who had taken his place had grown fond of Campbell. The lad had followed Colin about like a happy puppy. What had Lancaster done when he had found himself with a young, adoring brother?

His sisters were not here. He supposed each of them had been buried with her husband. Finally he found the tomb of Colin MacKenzie. How strange it was to gaze upon the sculpted likeness of the man lying here.

It was his face, only different. This was what he would have looked like if he had lived to the age of one and seventy. Lancaster had lived a long life. He had married. Seven children had called him father. Without knowing the reason, he was certain Lancaster had been happy in the life he had found. Colin's life. How long had it taken him to find his way?

Colin rested his hand on the carved marble hands that lay crossed upon the sculpted chest. "What did you do to my bonnie Jane? Did you slay her heart with your wickedness? Did you destroy any chance I might have had at finding my own happiness here in your life?"

He bowed his head and closed his eyes and prayed for the strength he would need. "Is it right for me to stay? Am I a fool to imagine I can make a life here, with a woman who wants nothing I have to give her? Perhaps I should return to my own home, return to my family. Help me find my way."

The tightness grew in his chest, as though a thick band of steel were closing ever tighter around him. May his family forgive him, he did not wish to return to the life he had led. Not if it meant leaving behind the infuriating woman who had captured his heart. Still, he had never before felt so alone.

It was better this way, Jane assured herself. She stood by a window in the center tower, watching Colin walk along the cliff path. He had spoken no more than a handful of words to her since their encounter in the library three days ago. He had taken to riding the cliffs each morning. The rest of each day he prowled the castle and grounds, as if searching for something, perhaps a past he imagined he had lived. She wasn't certain what he was looking for; she did know he was content to avoid her.

Unfortunately, no matter how hard she tried, she could not force him from her thoughts. By day he haunted her. Each moment she wondered where he was, what he was doing, how he was feeling. By night he invaded her dreams, holding her, kissing her, loving her. She had awakened the past few mornings clutching her pillow, a horrible feeling of emptiness clawing at her heart.

She had never in her entire life been more fascinated by a man. Mesmerized. Beguiled. Enchanted. All the words she could summon failed to describe this feeling. If she believed in magic, she could almost imagine he had somehow bewitched her.

It must fade. This horrible need, this humiliating longing . . . it must be an infatuation. It could not possibly be love. No, she had not made the unforgivable mistake of falling in love with a man who did not exist. She was much too practical to do anything so reckless. All of her life she had known she was the sensible sister. Her mother was fond of recounting her strengths. Practical. Sensible. Steady and sure. That was Jane.

Yet Colin had discovered another woman hidden beneath the sensible veneer Jane saw in her mirror. A terribly vulnerable female who wanted with all her soul to live her life with a man who could make her blood stir and her heart sing. No matter how much she tried she could not crush the feelings within her. Was it truly better to keep her distance, never to know his love? Or was it better to grab happiness while she could? He could be taken away from her at any moment. Perhaps it was best to live her entire life in a few days.

She felt as though something precious had been broken and there was nothing she could do to put the pieces together. Not unless she was willing to sacrifice her future freedom for a few moments of love. Oh, she was being foolish even to imagine living a fairy tale. She knew very well she could not alter what had happened, or—more precisely—what had not happened between them. It was as it must be. This separation, this anger he had in his eyes each time he looked at her, it was for the best. Still, it hurt. My goodness, it hurt to know how very much he disliked her.

She rubbed her arms, feeling chilled as she watched him. He looked so lonely, a solitary figure walking along the cliffs. It was better this way. Far safer to keep her distance. Yet even as she acknowledged the danger in what she was doing, she was running across the hall toward the stairs. She could not continue this way. She could not allow him to believe she did not care what happened to him. The truth might be dangerous, but she could not live with a lie.

She left the house without taking time to grab a hat or coat. She could not explain the urgency within her. She only knew she felt as though she had already wasted too much time. Colin could be lost to her tomorrow, which made today all the more precious.

A cool breeze swept off the Atlantic, catching her skirt, tossing it about her like a wayward sail. The wind tugged at her hair, dragging several strands free of their mooring pins. The wayward strands whipped against her cheek while she made her way along the cliff path.

She found Colin standing near a single oak tree that grew near the edge of the cliff. He stood with his face to the sea and the wind. He looked wild, untamed, a mythical creature of the sea, trapped here in a world he did not know. Lost, alone, and so terribly sad.

Jane paused on the path a few feet from him, her heart pounding, her throat tight around the words she needed to speak. She wanted with all her heart to slip her arms around him, to hold him close and reassure him all would be well. Yet dare she bare her heart to this man? To do so, to confess all that she felt, would mean to risk her freedom. How could she hold him at a distance once he understood how very much he had come to mean to her?

"How did you know where I would be?" he said without looking at her.

"I saw you come this way."

He stared at the restless churning of the sea. "Why did you follow me?"

"You looked sad. I thought you might want to speak with someone."

"I went to my mother's tomb today." He focused on a place in the distance. "I feel as though her passing was yesterday and I never had a chance to say good-bye."

She stared at his profile and sought for something comforting to say. Reminding him that he was not truly Colin MacKenzie and that his family was still very much alive would not do. He was far too immersed in the life he had created. And somehow his creation had become part of her own reality.

"All my life I have had the warmth of family around me. And now . . ." He closed his eyes and lifted his face to the dying rays of the sun. "They are gone. Everything that mattered to me has turned to dust. And I am left to wonder why."

"I realize we have not always been friendly." She took a step toward him. "But I want you to know you can rely upon me to be here should you need me. I hope we can be . . . friends."

His gaze plunged a hundred feet to the rocky shore. "Friends?"

Friends. It was such an insignificant-sounding word when compared to the feelings he stirred within her. Friendship was such a small part of what she wanted from this man, what she wanted to give this man. But she was afraid to say more. "Yes."

"You are here because of duty to a man you despise." He laughed, the sound harsh and brittle. "I was ripped from my family, tossed three hundred years into the future, to find a woman who wants to be my friend. Apparently even a fairy princess can make a mistake."

She touched his arm. His muscles tightened beneath her touch. "I want to try to explain about the other day."

"There is no need to explain." He turned to face her, the sheen of tears in his eyes. "You cannot see beyond this mask I wear. You see only the man you knew, not the man before you. And you do not want that man. You do not want me."

"It isn't true." Jane touched his face, brushing her fingertips over the tight line of his lips. "I want Colin more than anything in this world."

He gripped her arms and dragged her close against him. "Your words say one thing, your deeds another."

The tangy salt of the sea clung to him, melding with a scent all his own. The wind whipped his hair into thick waves around his face. He looked fierce and forbidding and at the same time incredibly vulnerable. She should not be here with him. She should never have left the house. For she could not resist touching him, and touching him would be her undoing. She pressed her hand against his cheek. "All my life I believed there was one special man in the world for me. I never dreamed he would come to me this way."

Something fierce flickered in his eyes. "And friendship is what you want from me?"

"Yes. Friendship. And more. More than I should want."

He opened his hands on her arms. "Do not pretend with me. Do not say words you think I need to hear because you pity me."

"I pity myself. For I have fallen in love with a man who does not truly exist. A man who will disappear with the awakening of another man's memory."

"Fear." He slid his hands down her arms and wrapped his fingers around her wrists. A look of understanding replaced the anger in his eyes. "It is fear that keeps you from me."

"Yes." Fear closed her throat until the word was no more than a whisper.

"I cannot make you believe in me. I have no proof to offer." He lifted her hands and pressed his lips first to one wrist, then the other. "I ask only that you listen to what is in your heart."

Her heart would lead her to disaster.

"I would never harm you." He brushed his fingers over her cheek. "I would give my life to protect you."

He looked so unhappy, filled with the same longing that clawed at her vitals. She had to swallow hard before she could use her voice. "You should not say such things to me."

"Because I am not real to you?"

"You aren't real. When your memory returns, Colin will cease to exist."

"Look at me and tell me I am not real."

She closed her eyes, shutting out the compelling image of his face. "You are ill."

"Will you ever accept me for who I am, my bonnie

Jane? Or will you hold me at a distance until everything between us has withered and died?"

How much time would she have with this man? Days, months, years? The future was so uncertain. Still, one thing she could not deny: She loved him. Staying away from him, keeping herself safe, did not make sense to her. She would wither and die inside. She lifted on her toes and brushed her lips over his. The soft touch, barely more than breath upon breath, shivered through her. "I have been waiting for you all my life."

He squeezed her arms. "Yet you turn me away from you."

She drew her fingertips over his cheek; his skin was rough from the dark stubble of his beard and cool from the sea breeze. "I wish I could believe you would stay."

"Aisling can reverse this spell. I feel the truth of it deep within me. Would you have me call to her upon the next full moon? Would you have me return to my life and leave you in peace?"

The thought of losing him pierced her heart. She rested her hand upon his chest and felt his heart pumping hard and fast, echoing her own racing pulse.

"What do you want from me?" he whispered, his voice harsh with emotion.

The truth was something she had always admired. She could not escape it now, no matter how frightening it might be. She rose upward on her toes and kissed him, allowing him to taste the desire for him she could no longer deny. She opened her lips upon his, kissing him with all the passion she had kept hidden.

She felt the moment he surrendered his anger, the instant desire broke through his defenses. His breath streamed upon her cheek. He plunged his fingers into the chignon at the base of her neck and worked his fingers through the heavy coil. Pins scattered beneath his marauding fingers. She sighed with pleasure when the heavy mass tumbled down her back, releasing the pressure against her scalp. He slid his fingers through her hair, touching her back.

"You are my destiny," he whispered against her lips.

Destiny. Yes, she felt the truth of it deep within her. He was her destiny. And this moment was as inevitable as the sun succumbing to an evening sky.

He kissed her as though he had dreamed of this ultimate surrender. He kissed her lips, her cheeks, her neck, while he caressed her with his hands, cupping her breasts, sliding his thumbs over her nipples. She regretted the layers of clothing that kept his hands from her skin. As though he could read her thoughts, he unfastened the buttons lining the front of her gown. And then he was lifting her, cradling her against his chest for one brief moment before he laid her down upon the thick grass growing beside the path.

He covered her, pressing her down into the grass while he slid his hand into her chemise. She gasped at the sharp stab of pleasure when his fingers first touched her breast. He lowered his head and dragged his open mouth down her neck. He pushed her skirts around her waist and touched her through the slit in her drawers. She arched against his hand, anxious for a taste of the pleasure she had once experienced in his arms.

He closed his mouth over her breast while he stroked her most private flesh. She rolled her head back and forth, grasping his shoulders, while he suckled her and stroked her, his fingers dancing upon her and inside of her. Once again she knew the magic of this man, the desire and passion that bubbled up inside her like a spring emerging. She dragged her hands down his back, felt his muscles tense and quiver beneath the white silk of his shirt.

He covered her lips, kissed her long and slow while he unfastened the front of his trousers. The solid heat of his arousal pressed upon her belly. Fear and pleasure mingled within her at the acceptance of bridges about to be burned. He shifted his hips and pressed against her.

She opened to him, arching her hips in silent invitation.

She had waited all her life for this man. Even if he disappeared with the morning light, she wanted this moment with him, this connection, this consummation. Pain pierced her with the first thrust of his body into hers. She grabbed his shoulders as if he could keep her from tumbling down the black hole that had opened within her.

"By my faith." He lifted above her, far enough to look into her eyes. She saw confusion in his eyes, need and hunger and uncertainty. "I have hurt you."

The pain had already receded into a dull ache. And somewhere beneath the ache dwelled the pleasure he had conjured within her. She brushed her fingers over his damp cheek. "Make love to me, Colin."

Although his features revealed his confusion and anguish, he smiled. "You called me Colin."

"If you imagine for one moment I would be lying here with anyone else, think again." She slid her arms around his neck. "I know there is more to this than what has passed, and I would experience it all. If only this once."

"Once?" He shifted his hips and moved within her. " 'Tis just the beginning, my bonnie lass."

He slid his hands beneath her hips and lifted her, supporting her weight while he moved inside her, long, slick strokes, gliding in and out. He kissed her, dipping his tongue into her mouth to the same intoxicating rhythm. The dull ache of his first penetration narrowed and faded as the pleasure expanded within her.

She hugged him close, lifting to meet his every thrust. She did not know what magic had brought him to her. Logic and consequences had no place in this moment. She wanted only to love him as she had longed to love him from the first moment Colin had held her in his arms. She wanted only to live the dream she had cherished since she was a young girl, to love and be loved. Yet soon she realized this was more than any dream she had ever imagined.

Pleasure surged with each furious beat of her racing heart. It did not matter how this man had come into her life. It mattered only that he was here, holding her, loving her. Soon all thoughts vanished, washed away by the waves of pleasure breaking over her. She heard her name on his lips, a low growl that shivered through her while her body arched and shuddered as she experienced the ultimate pleasure.

He eased against her, resting his brow against her shoulder, his hands still on her hips, holding her tight against his loins. She smoothed her hand over his shoulder, then toyed with a curl above his ear. When she found enough air to use her voice, she said, "That was the most extraordinary experience of my entire life."

He lifted himself away from her. "On the cliffs. By my faith, you must think me an animal."

She smoothed her hands over his shoulders. "I think you are the most marvelous man I have ever met."

"I had no idea 'twas your first time." He shook his head.

He looked so beautiful. Flustered and sweet in his concern for her. "It's all right. I thought it was all rather exciting."

A soft moan slipped from her lips as he slipped from her body. Dimly she was aware of the tall grass swaying around her. In all her dreams of what it might be like to make love to her one and only love, she had never once imagined lying on a carpet of grass beneath the last rosy rays of the sun, her breasts naked to the breeze, her skirts bunched around her waist. Even more shocking than the circumstances was the fact she was not the least bit ashamed. She stretched, lifting her arms above her, offering her breasts to the salty breeze. It had all seemed so natural with Colin. As though she had been wandering though the world with her eyes closed until this moment.

Still, he didn't look happy. He was staring at her upper thighs, frowning. He gently pulled her skirts down around her, then glanced down at his member. Quickly he adjusted his garments, sheathing himself inside his trousers.

"I have hurt you." He pulled the front of her gown closed and started fastening the buttons. "You were a maiden."

"Of course." She brushed her fingertips over the back of his hand. "I have been waiting for you all my life."

"How can this be?" He paused, his fingers upon the last button at her waist. "You are Lancaster's wife."

A chill whispered through her blood at the mention of her husband. With an act of will, she shut out all the reasons she should not have given herself to this man. Colin could disappear at any moment. She had paid a great price for this happiness. She intended to make the most of each and every moment in Colin's company. "It is a bit complicated. And I would rather not discuss it. Not now."

He lifted her into his arms and stood. "After you have bathed and rested we shall talk."

Jane glanced to the east, where the spires and towers of Kintair rose from the cliff's edge. "You can't mean to carry me all the way back to the castle."

He looked pained suddenly. "You are bleeding."

She brushed her fingers over his cheek. "You didn't break me, Colin. It is only natural the first time. I'm fine."

He did not look convinced. "You need to rest. And then we shall talk."

Since he seemed quite determined, she decided not to argue. It was far too lovely being held this way, cradled against his chest. She looped her arms around his neck and snuggled against his big body. Thick muscles flexed against her side with each movement he made. He carried her along the cliff path, back to the castle, up the stairs and down miles of corridors until he reached her chamber. He did not even seem to be breathing hard when he laid her upon the rose silk counterpane.

He smoothed the hair back from her brow and stood looking at her a long moment. The look of concern in his eyes wrapped around her, as warm and comforting as an embrace. "I will send a maid. And tea. You would like some tea, would you not?"

She smiled up at him, hoping he could see her contentment. "Yes. Tea would be lovely. But there is no need to send for Lillian. I would prefer to take care of my bath without any help."

He swept her with his gaze, as though looking for signs of injury. "Are you certain?"

"Yes. I am fine." She squeezed his hand. "You know, my bathtub is large enough for two. If you would like, you could stay and—"

"No." He stepped back from the bed. "That would not be a good idea."

"It wouldn't?"

"By my faith, woman." He plowed his fingers through his hair. "How can you imagine I could bathe with you and not want to take you again?"

She shrugged. "I suppose I was hoping you might want to take me again. The first time was lovely."

"I will not be hurting you again." He backed away from the bed. "You have to heal. Now, do not be tempting the beast in me."

She felt like a temptress, wild and wanton. And the feeling was deliciously free. Still, beneath the joy lurked the reality she would have to face one day.

She resisted the urge to run after him when Colin left the room. She wanted to hold him close against her, keep him locked away in this room. Yet she knew deep inside nothing would stay the hand of destiny. If Lancaster's memory returned, her world would come to an end.

Still, she did not regret what had happened with Colin. He was her one and only love. She knew it, felt it deep in her soul. If she were to live until she was a hundred, she would never care for another man the way she did for Colin. And if the price of this bliss meant she would live the rest of her life in a cold travesty of marriage to Lancaster, it was a price she would pay. At least she would have a few precious memories to keep her warm.

She crossed the room, intending to draw her bath, when someone knocked on the door. It was too soon for tea, she thought. Colin must have changed his mind about the bath. She hurried across the room and pulled open the door. Only it wasn't Colin standing in the hall. She stared at the small, white-haired woman at her door, stunned to see her here.

Chapter Twenty-one

He loved the twilight that surrounds
The border-land of old romance;
Where glitter hauberk, helm, and lance,
And banner waves, and trumpet sounds,
And ladies ride with hawk on wrist,
And mighty warriors sweep along,
Magnified by purple mist,
The dusk of centuries and of song.
   —Henry Wadsworth Longfellow

"You look as though you have taken a tumble down a hill." Fiona Stanbridge tilted her head, a glint of humor entering her blue eyes. "It makes me wonder what you and my grandson have been doing."

Jane knew she was blushing. "We just came in from taking a walk."

"I see I have surprised you. I had not planned to join you on your wedding trip. But then I had expected my grandson to travel to Italy, not Scotland." Fiona did not wait for Jane to invite her into her chamber. She swept past Jane in a swirl of lavender scent. She walked to one of the windows that overlooked the Atlantic, her dark blue gown rustling softly.

Though she must be close to seventy years old, Fiona had not relinquished the vitality that glowed in her face, the regal tilt of her head, her proud carriage, her quick stride. She could send debutantes screaming in terror with one lift of an eyebrow, but Jane had always found the countess surprisingly amiable. Jane closed the door and joined Fiona at the window.

"I have always loved this place." Although she looked out at the ocean, Fiona seemed to be looking beyond the water to a distant place only she could see. "I raised my family here."

"It is a beautiful place."

"A fine and wondrous place to live. A place filled with so many memories." Fiona pursed her lips. She remained quiet a moment, and in that space of time Jane sensed she was looking back upon her life at Kintair. "Dominic's father died when he was four. His mother married an American two years later. My husband insisted Dominic remain with us. He could be very influential. Since Vanessa had her girls, she thought it wise to allow Charles to have his way. When she left for Philadelphia, in a very real sense I became Dominic's mother. Looking back, I acknowledge it may not have been the best decision for him."

Jane wondered if his mother's decision had colored Dominic's attitude toward his mother and women in general. Strange, she had never truly wanted to understand the scoundrel. Until now.

Fiona stared out at the ocean, where the last rays of the sun skipped over the rolling waves. "Dominic once told me he felt more at home here than he did anywhere."

"He did?"

"Yes. As a lad, he would often run through the castle

carrying a wooden sword, pretending he was Colin MacKenzie defending the castle against a wicked foe. Usually it was Colin's uncle, Malcolm, who was the enemy. The Marauding Malcolm, he would call him."

A chill gripped Jane. "He would pretend he was Colin?"

"Quite often. He was fascinated with everything about Kintair."

Colin's fondness for the castle, his infatuation with a distant ancestor, could be the key to his illness. Yet Jane could not explain her own reaction to the truth, this horrible tightening around her heart that came with . . . disappointment? It could not be. It wasn't as if she had come to believe Lancaster was truly Colin. Had she? Still, the man had a way of making her want to believe in magic. "His interest in Colin explains a great deal."

Fiona turned to face her. "Does it?"

"Did you not receive my note about his illness? I thought that was the reason you came."

"I did read your note. Unfortunately I was out of town, and did not read it until yesterday afternoon. By then I had already heard the gossip about my grandson."

Jane's stomach clenched. "The rumors must be spreading as quickly as the plague."

"I am afraid they are." Fiona released her breath in a tired-sounding sigh. "Yesterday morning, Harriet Gladthorne and Sylvia Wadswyck paid me a call. I am certain they had been haunting the street outside my house, waiting for my return from Kent. After they left, I paid a call at Lancaster House. Hedley informed me of what had happened. Anderson supplied the rest of the information I required. He told me my grandson believes he is Colin MacKenzie, brought here by magic. Is it true?"

"Yes. He believes he is Colin. He thinks his soul was switched, that Lancaster has been cast back three hundred years to live his life."

"Are you certain Dominic is not playing a game with you?"

"I thought he might be at first. But I have come to believe he is truly ill." If Lancaster were playing a game, he would have declared victory this afternoon on the cliffs. Yet he still believed he was Colin. May heaven help her, but she hoped he never regained his memory.

Fiona pursed her lips. "Are you aware of the plot my son Edwin has been hatching?"

"Plot?" Jane pressed her hand to her racing heart. "We left for Kintair the night after the accident. I have heard nothing of what Pembury might be plotting."

Fiona studied her a moment, her blue eyes narrowed slightly, as if she was trying to evaluate Jane's honesty. "Has Dominic regained any of his memory?"

"I thought he might be remembering something of his life when he recognized a photograph of you. But he is convinced you only look like his own grandmother."

"This is not good." Fiona stared out the window for a long while before she finally looked at Jane. "When my grandson told me he intended to marry you, I was surprised. For more than one reason. I had almost given up hope that Dominic would ever marry. I thought if he did, he would choose an opera dancer, simply to shock the rest of his family."

Jane managed a smile, even though her chest was so tight with anxiety it felt as though a mastiff were sitting on her. "I am afraid several members of your family feel he did not do much better."

Fiona dismissed her words with a wave of her hand. "Your father is a gentleman. Your family respectable. And from all I have seen, you have a great deal of sense. I am certain Edwin's objections are due more to his own hopes being dashed than to any concern he might have for your suitability as Dominic's wife."

"His own hopes?"

"My son does not want Dominic to leave behind an

heir. He has always hoped one of his own brood would inherit the title." Fiona executed a delicate shiver. "For once, my grandson chose wisely. Although I do not condone his methods."

Jane held Fiona's gaze. "His methods?"

"I know about your sister and Dominic's tactics. I learned of them shortly before your wedding." Fiona pursed her lips. "I hope you shall forgive me for not coming to your aid. But I do not care to see my husband's title inherited by Edwin's insipid eldest son. Or, for that matter, by any of Edwin's brood. It was selfish, I admit. But I assumed you would come to see the advantages to marrying my grandson. Wealth and title and all that comes with it."

"I am afraid I have never sought a title or wealth."

"I know you are not fond of my grandson." Fiona wagged her finger at Jane. "You are, however, his wife. And as such, I have faith that you will stand by him in this crisis."

"I may not have chosen to marry him, but I do respect the vows I made." And she would protect Colin at any cost.

Fiona held her gaze a long moment, as if taking Jane's measure. "We must prevent Edwin from succeeding. I have tried, but he will not listen to me. He is far too ambitious to give up his plan. Somehow we must find a way to protect Dominic until he is capable of taking care of himself."

"What does Pembury intend to do?"

Fiona took Jane's arm. "Sit with me. There is a great deal we must discuss."

Colin dragged a brush through his damp hair. He had managed to dress for dinner, except for the neckcloth. That stiff piece of linen felt too much like a noose about his neck. He saw no reason to abuse himself while he was here at Kintair. He stared at the reflection in his mirror. What kind of man married a woman as beautiful and desirable as Jane and did not consummate the wedding?

There was a great deal he needed to know about the woman who had captured his heart. She had touched his soul with her sweetly innocent response to him this afternoon. But even though he had claimed her body, the woman remained a mystery. One thing he knew: she still did not believe he had been brought to this place and time to be with her. She still imagined he was Lancaster.

At a soft rap on his door he crossed the room and opened it. Jane was standing in the hall. His heart kicked into a gallop just looking at her. She had not changed since their encounter on the bluffs, but there was a troubled look about her expression.

"What is it? Are you all right?"

"I'm fine."

"You do not look fine." He took her arm and ushered her to the nearest chair. "Sit, and tell me what has stolen the color from your cheeks."

"It isn't what you think." She sat on the edge of one of the large blue velvet chairs near the hearth. "Your grandmother is here."

"My grandmother?"

"Lady Fiona." She laced her fingers together. "Lancaster's grandmother."

"And what would she be doing here?"

"She came to warn you." She glanced down at her hands, then up at him. "Your uncle is plotting against you."

"Aye, I know my uncle is plotting against me. Or was. Three hundred years ago."

"Lancaster's uncle, Edwin Stanbridge, Lord Pembury. The man you met in the hall at Lancaster House the day after the accident. He is plotting against you."

" 'Twould seem I am to be plagued by my father's brother in both lifetimes." He rubbed the taut muscles in his neck. "What is it this man has planned against me?"

She moistened her lips. "He intends to have you declared incompetent due to insanity. He intends to be appointed your guardian, and when he is, he will have you committed to an asylum."

"He can do this? Even though I am married to you? Are you not the guardian of your husband?"

"Apparently he has some very influential friends. As a wife, I will have no say in what they decide. In fact, although insanity is not necessarily a cause for annulment, he hopes to have our marriage dissolved. Lady Fiona suspects he will be successful."

"I see." The danger in her words trickled over him, burning like a steady stream of acid. He marched toward the door. "I will not allow anyone to put me in a cage. I will fight this man."

She hurried after him. "What do you think you are going to do?"

He paused with his hand on the brass handle. "I intend to teach this man he should not go about plotting against me."

"If you go storming back to London, you will only serve to help him in his vicious plot."

"I will not sit idly by and allow this jackanapes to take control of my life. I cannot imagine you would want me to."

"Of course not. You must fight him. But not with a sword." She tilted her head and frowned up at him. "You are planning to use a sword, aren't you?"

"I will fight the man to the death. I will fight anyone who tries to put me in a cage. No one will take you away from me."

She rested her hand on his arm. "Lady Fiona has a plan."

"A plan, does she? And what plan is this?"

"She is waiting in the crimson drawing room. I think it would be best if you hear what she has to say."

Jane looked tired and frightened. He rested his hands on her slender shoulders. "You have not had your bath."

"There wasn't any time. Fiona arrived soon after you left me."

He rubbed his fingers against the taut muscles in her shoulders. "You should rest."

She shook her head. "We have a great deal to do if we are to defeat Pembury."

"There is a great deal I wish to know, my lady. When you said you did not have an affectionate marriage, I did not realize your husband had never consummated your marriage vows."

"We can discuss it later." She rested her hand on his chest. "Right now the most important thing is to keep you out of danger."

He brushed his lips over hers. She sighed against his cheek. He pulled away from her, stunned by the heat she could conjure with a simple kiss. She opened her eyes and gazed up at him with a look of wonder. "We'd better leave before you awaken the beast in me."

She patted his chest. "I rather like the beast."

He kissed the tip of her nose. "Later, my love."

Jane's stomach clenched when she thought of the danger Colin faced. She sat on one of the sofas in the crimson drawing room, watching him. He stood near a window, staring out at the gardens. Although he stood as still as a sculpture, she could see the tension in his posture, the slight lift of his shoulders, the tight fist he held against his hip. If their plan did not succeed, the only chance he would have to keep his freedom would be to escape, to live his life in some distant outpost. And she would have a choice. She could go with him, or remain in England with her family. Yet she knew what the answer would be. As much as she would miss her family, she would travel anywhere she must to be with this man.

"Edwin is clever and ruthless." Fiona drummed her

fingertips on the carved wooden arm of her chair. "He certainly will not listen to me. He never did. If you do not change, Edwin will succeed in taking everything from you. Including your freedom."

"I will not be caged," Colin said, his deep voice a rumble in the large room.

Fiona's eyes narrowed. "If you are playing a game, my lad, it is time to end it."

Colin turned and faced her. Moonlight streamed through the panes behind him, limning him. Yet that light seemed to radiate from him, as though the raw power of the man could not be contained. He held Fiona's gaze for a long moment before he spoke. "I am not playing a game. I am Colin MacKenzie. I was brought to this time and place by Aisling of Tara."

"You swear to me you honestly believe this?" Fiona demanded.

"I know this to be true."

Fiona stared at him a long while, looking at him as though she meant to intimidate him into the truth. "It cannot be true, young man. You must remember who you are."

"I know who I am. What I do not know is how this man Lancaster came to inherit my title."

Fiona looked surprised. "I bestowed the title upon your grandfather when we married. I was a MacKenzie before I married Charles Stanbridge. I am a direct descendant of the first Kintair earl."

How strange it must seem to him, Jane thought. To face an old woman and think he was her ancestor.

Colin's brows lifted. "You married an Englishman."

Fiona sat up in her chair, prepared to fight. "I married a good man who just happened to be English."

A grin curved one corner of his lips. "Tell me what became of the *Chronicles of Kintair*."

A look of puzzlement crossed her features. "The *Chronicles of Kintair*?"

"Aye. The history of Kintair, kept by each Kintair laird."

Fiona considered his words a moment. "I have never heard of these chronicles."

"I was hoping to read what my mother might have written about the time after I left." Colin turned back to the window. "It would seem little has survived from my time."

Fiona glanced at Jane, then turned her attention back to Colin, a strange mix of curiosity and doubt in her eyes. "When you were a lad, you would often pretend you were Colin. Apparently that bump on the head has cast you back to your childhood."

Colin curled his hands into tight balls at his sides. "Lancaster pretended he was me?"

"You pretended you were Colin." Fiona rolled her eyes. "I find this all rather disturbing, speaking to you in this manner. I think it is time you accept the fact you are Dominic and try to remember something of your past."

"You were born and bred in the Highlands?" Colin asked.

Fiona frowned. "What are you getting at, young man?"

"If you are a Highlander, you must know there is magic in this world. 'Tis all around us."

Fiona clasped her hands in her lap. "And I suppose I am to believe that magic is the reason you believe you are one of your ancestors?"

"Aye. It was the magic of Aisling. The Matchmaker of Tara." Colin looked at Jane. The sheer intensity of the need in those stunning eyes wrapped around her. All the air in her lungs evaporated beneath that look. It took all of her will to keep from running to him and throwing her arms around him. "She brought me here to meet my destiny."

Jane fiddled with the lace beneath her chin. Her pulse was racing so hard her collar seemed overly tight. Was it possible? Could a love exist that was so powerful it could travel across the ages? Until she had met Colin, she had not believed in magic. Yet she had no idea what had wrought such a change in the man she had married. The only thing she could be sure of was the way he made her feel. She wanted to believe in him. As insane as it was, she wanted to believe in magic.

"And this Aisling is a fairy?" Fiona asked.

"She is one of the Sidhe," Colin replied.

"Her story is in a book of Scottish legends we found in the library," Jane said.

"A book of Scottish legends?" Fiona smoothed her fingertips over the arm of the chair. "Of course. Aisling. Now I recall. The legend of the Matchmaker of Tara. She would go about meddling in the lives of mortals for some mysterious reason. I used to read that book to you when you were a lad. The legends were wonderful fairy tales."

"Aisling is not a legend. She is real. And she is the one who sent me here." Although Colin kept his voice low and calm, Jane had the feeling it took all of his will to maintain his composure.

"This fascination you had with Colin when you were a lad, and now a story I read to you." Fiona glanced at Jane, then back at Colin. "The illness has obviously dredged the legend from a distant part of your memory. For some reason you are reliving part of your childhood, only it all seems real to you now."

It was obvious, Jane thought. Somehow a distant part of his memory had come to life. And one day the memories that had transformed him into Colin would once again slip into the shadows in his mind. That day she would lose him. Jane clasped her hands tightly together, hoping to contain all the emotion swelling within her.

Colin crossed the room and rested his hand on Jane's shoulder, as if he knew how very much she needed to feel his warmth. "I realize 'tis difficult to accept what has happened. But I am Colin MacKenzie."

Jane swallowed hard, pushing back tears. Lord in heaven, she wished he were Colin.

"You obviously believe you are Colin. You must also believe that if you continue to go about telling people you have been brought here by a sorceress, there will be nothing I can do to keep Edwin from tossing you into an asylum. He can be very influential. You do have enemies. They will enjoy destroying you."

Colin's lips curved into a smile, his eyes glittering with rage. "I will put the ruffian in his place."

Fiona drew in a deep breath, her narrow shoulders lifting the cloth of her dark blue gown. "If you mean you intend to threaten him with bodily harm, you will only succeed in hastening your own defeat."

"And what is it you intend to do?" Colin asked.

Fiona pursed her lips. "Jane told me you recognized me from a photograph."

"You resemble my grandmother. But after seeing you, I can see the differences. My grandmother had gray eyes. Your eyes are as blue as mine." He tilted his head. "And there are other differences in your face. She was also a wee bit taller than you are. The resemblance is strong. But I can clearly see you are not the same."

"Strange how it can all be so clear to you. I had hoped you would remember." Fiona glanced down at her hands. "Still, if you cannot remember who you are, then we shall simply have to make people believe you can remember. You shall learn once again to be Dominic. Jane shall help me mold you back into the man you were."

Colin looked at Jane. "Is that what you want, lass? Do you want me to become the man I was?"

Jane squeezed her hands together in her lap. No, she wanted to scream. She did not want him to change. She wanted Colin to stay, now and forever. Yet that kind of thinking would only lead to his ruin. "It is the only way to protect you from Pembury."

Colin held her captive with his gaze for a moment

281

longer before he turned away from her. He crossed the room and looked out the window. "So I am to become this English jackanapes."

"English jackanapes." Fiona shook her head. "If we are to prevent my son from succeeding, we must strike before he does, take the venom out of his bite. We must present you to society, show everyone your little lapse was no more than a game you were playing with your new bride. I would say we have no more than three weeks before we must strike."

"Three weeks?" Jane stared at Fiona. "Do you plan to take him back to London in three weeks?"

"It is possible he will regain his memory in that time."

Colin shot her a glance. "My memory is fine."

Fiona dismissed his words with a delicate wave of her slender hand. "We cannot delay. I cannot say how long it will take for Edwin to realize where we are. Three weeks may be more time than we have. We must return to London and show everyone that Dominic is well, before Edwin can strike. A ball at Lancaster House should serve our purpose."

"A ball. There is a great deal he must learn. He doesn't even use a fork." Jane shuddered when she thought of the humiliation he would suffer should he be released upon society too soon. "I cannot imagine that he could prepare for a ball in three weeks."

"We must present Dominic on our terms. We shall cut Edwin at the knees." Fiona rose and walked toward Colin. "Are you up to the challenge, Dominic?"

Although he smiled, Jane sensed the anxiety churning within him. "If I must learn to be your grandson to win this war, then I shall do it."

Fiona tapped his chest. "From this moment on, you are Dominic Nathaniel Stanbridge. Remember it. Because if you cannot learn to present the face of Dominic to the world, there will be nothing I can do to save you from the fate Edwin has in mind for you."

Colin looked at Jane. "I will do what I must."

Anderson's words echoed in Jane's memory. *The more you remind him of his life, the more he may remember.* If they were to mold Colin back into Lancaster, they would spend days pounding all the details of Lancaster's life into his head. Could it spark his memory? Still, what choice did they have? As much as she would like to take Colin and run, she could not. It would not be fair to him. All she could do was help him in this battle against Pembury, and pray Lancaster would not remember who and what he was. She might have only days with Colin, days to live a lifetime.

Chapter Twenty-two

One hour of right-down love
Is worth an age of dully living on.
                    —Aphra Behn

"I was hoping you would come to me tonight."

Colin paused near her bed. Jane stood near the windows of her bedchamber. Moonlight poured through the diamond-shaped panes, embracing her. She seemed an angel descended from heaven, delivered to him in a column of silvery light. He had come only for the discussion that she had avoided all evening. He had made up his mind not to bed her again. Not so soon after the careless coupling he had committed on the bluffs. She would be sore, and he had no intention of hurting her again. Still, watching her move toward him, the soft white cloth of her gown rippling around her long legs, made his skin tingle. "There is much I would know, my lady Jane. How does a married woman remain a maiden?"

"With Lancaster, it was quite easy. I actually imagined

I could make it through the next six months unscathed."
She rested her hands upon his chest. "And then you came
into my life, speaking of magic and destiny. Now look
at me."

He could not help looking at her. Her hair fell in unbound waves around her shoulders. White lace brushed
her chin and hid her wrists. The gown of white cotton
covered her from her neck to her toes, hiding all but a
suggestion of the womanly curves beneath. Yet he knew
what lay beneath that chaste white cloth. In spite of his
best intentions, the blood stirred in his loins. The woman
could don chain mail and he would still find her one of
the most alluring females he had ever seen.

He clenched his teeth and sought to crush his desire.
If he weren't careful, he would lose control. If he did not
tether his lust for her, he would find himself in her large
bed, pounding into her like a great, rutting stag. He was
not a mindless beast. He could and would control his lust.
"Why is it Lancaster never bedded you?"

"You want to talk." She ran her fingers down the front
of his shirt. "Do you know what I want to do?"

Moonlight spilled across her face. Her lips were parted,
her eyes drowsy-looking. She had the appearance of a
woman intoxicated by lust. "You get those thoughts out
of your mind, my darling Jane. I will not be causing you
any more pain. There will be no bedding. Not this night."

"I have never felt more alive in my entire life." She
slipped her fingers into the waistband of his trousers.
"Make love to me."

He curled his hands into fists at his sides to keep from
touching her. If he touched her he would be lost. "I did
not come here to be seduced."

"I will have you know I am a very proper lady. And
a proper lady would never imagine seducing a man." She
nuzzled the hollow of his neck, then flicked her tongue
against his skin.

He gripped her shoulders, intending to hold her at bay.

The woman did not know what was best for her. Still, he could not find the will to push her away from him. "And what would you be calling this behavior?"

She looked up at him, her eyes wide with mock surprise. "Do you mean I might actually seduce you by something so innocent as a kiss? And I didn't even kiss your lips. What would happen if I kissed you?"

"We will not be finding out. What happened this morning—" He sucked in his breath when she brushed her fingers over the front of his trousers. "Now, you must not do that. I did not come here to—"

"I know. You came here to talk."

He swallowed hard. "Aye. And I will have my answers."

"Of course you will." She dragged her nails over the wool covering his swelling shaft. He could not prevent a groan of pleasure. A grin curved her lips.

"Jane, my love, you must take care." He gently put her away from him, then stepped back until three feet of moonlight separated them. "I was a great, rutting beast this afternoon."

She held his gaze, her eyes narrowing slightly. "I can see you are very determined to resist me."

And he could see she was very determined to undermine his good intentions. Need pumped through his vessels with each squeeze of his heart. "Perhaps we should talk tomorrow."

She flicked open the small pearl button at the top of her gown. "Tomorrow is such a long way away."

"You will feel better tomorrow." He turned away from her and marched toward the door. Tomorrow she would not be as tender as tonight. The last thing she needed tonight was a great hulk of a man making love to her. The images his thoughts conjured stabbed him low in his belly. Lord in heaven, he had to get away from here. Now.

"All my life I have felt as though I have been moving about in shackles. Until I met you."

Her soft voice coiled around him, a silken ribbon binding him there. He halted a few feet from the door, fighting his base instincts, the need that demanded he turn and take her. "Shackles?"

"Yes. All tied up by other peoples' expectations. I was always the practical daughter, the sensible sister. Dependable. Sensible. Logical. Ordinary Jane. Until you."

A voice screamed in his head: *Do not face her.* Because if he faced her, if he saw desire burn in her eyes, he would be lost to his lust. "And I have altered that?"

"You make me feel all manner of things. Wild and wicked and wanton. I feel like a temptress when you are near. I actually feel beautiful. More than ordinary. Special. Because of the way you look at me and touch me. Before you came into my life, I never would have imagined standing here like this and slipping off my nightgown. Like this."

The soft rustle of cloth tempted him to turn toward her. He tipped back his head and closed his eyes. *Lord Almighty, give me strength.* "You must be bruised in a hundred places from the way I touched you this afternoon."

"If you can find any bruises, I shall let you kiss each and every one. Oh, now that I think of it, I did find a little bruise on my inner thigh. Right at the top, near my—"

"You do not truly want this tonight."

"You have a gentle touch, Colin. I love the feel of your hands upon me, your lips. I love all of you. I want you tonight. I want you always."

His heart was beating so loudly, he felt certain she must hear it. The room had grown warm. It was growing warmer. He sensed her move toward him, felt the air move over his skin.

"And I would very much like to feel your body against mine."

Desire coiled within him. Blood pumped hard and fast into his loins. If he did not leave now, he would . . .

She touched his back. "I want to feel your skin slide against mine."

He should not look at her. Yet he could not resist. He turned as though she had taken hold of him and physically forced him to look at her. Instantly he knew he was lost. Moonlight slid over her, stroking the firm, high peaks of her breasts, streaming over her smooth belly, tangling in the curls at the joining of her pale thighs. "Tell me to leave."

"You must face the truth, Colin. You have made a wanton of me." She gripped the edges of his shirt and tugged, sending studs popping from the silk. She slid her hands inside his shirt, smoothed her fingertips over his skin. "Now you really must make love to me, or I shall die from this need you have awakened."

He tried to swallow, but the heat she conjured within him had burned all the moisture to dust. She slid her hands upward, over his chest, his shoulders, stripping the silk away, baring him to the heat of her gaze. His member pushed against the barriers of his clothes, hungry and eager to taste her once more.

She leaned toward him, brushing her breasts against his chest. "Take me, Colin."

All of his good intentions crumbled beneath her innocent seduction. He wrapped his arms around her, drew her close, and kissed her. She returned his kiss, parting in welcome at the first touch of his tongue upon her lips. He plunged past her silken lips and tasted a trace of the chocolate they had enjoyed in the drawing room before retiring. The sweet, creamy drink was only one of the things he enjoyed about this century.

He lifted her and carried her to the bed. She sighed when he laid her down upon the soft silk sheets. Her gaze never left him while he stripped away the rest of his clothes. When he was bare, she reached for him. He wrapped his arms around her and turned, pulling her across him. Her hair glided over his skin, brushing his thighs, and teasing the flesh made hungry and greedy by her touch.

"You control the joining, my love. You take me as you want me," he said, sliding his hands down her sleek back. He gripped her hips and lifted her until her belly brushed his aroused flesh. The contact sizzled through him, snatching the air from his lungs.

She smiled down at him, a look of wonder in her eyes. "You want me to take control?"

"Aye." He smoothed the backs of his fingers over her cheek. "And if it hurts, you should end it."

She smoothed her hand over his shoulder. "Wouldn't that leave you in a particularly uncomfortable state?"

"I would find it more uncomfortable to hurt you."

"We shall see, my darling." She pressed her lips to his neck and nuzzled his skin. "We shall see."

She stretched her body atop him and kissed his lips. Sensation unfurled within him like a silken scarf cast to a warm summer wind. Her legs brushed his, smooth against rough. She moved against him, wiggling as though she wanted to wrap herself in his skin. He stroked the warm satin of her back, her sides, her shoulders. He slipped his hands between them, cupped her breasts, and drank soft sighs from her sweet lips.

He thought he might shatter from the need pounding inside him, the driving hunger that made him want to plunge deep inside her. With great force of will he reined in his desire, allowing her to feel her way. At the first brush of damp feminine curls upon the heated length of his aroused sex, he nearly came apart. She slipped her cool fingers around him and slowly led him to her entrance, where sweet femininity wept for completion.

He could not control his moan of sheer pleasure as she

sank slowly upon him, taking him into the haven of her body. Ample moisture oiled their joining, easing the slide of his swollen flesh into her tight passage. She paused above him as though adjusting to the sensation of having him deep within her. He lay still beneath her, holding his breath, waiting for a decision that would leave him in agony or lift him to heaven. And then she began to move, tentatively at first, a maiden learning the intricate steps of this ancient dance, a woman bewitching her man.

He slid his hands upward over her back, easing her toward him until he could pay homage to the beauty of her breasts. He licked the valley between them, slid his tongue upward along the soft slope. Moonlight spilled upon her skin, beckoning him. He drank the silvery light from one taut pink nipple, then drew the peak into his mouth and suckled her. Soft sounds of pleasure escaped her lips. He had traveled what seemed a hundred lifetimes to find this woman. She was his destiny, and he wanted to show her just how much she meant to him.

His control threatened to unravel when the first delicate contractions of feminine release tugged on his flesh. Still, he bowed to her command of him. She grasped his shoulders, riding him, meeting his every upward thrust while the pleasure rose and expanded. Tiny spasms, quick and hard, grasped his aroused flesh, dragging him with her. A low growl shuddered from his chest as he followed her, surrendering to the pleasure, joining her in a realm beyond the touch of logic and mortal cares.

Jane sagged against him, her quick breaths matching his. Her breasts were soft against his damp chest. She sank one hand into his hair and pressed her cheek to his. The clean fragrance of lemons mingled with the musky scent of their lovemaking. He held her close, all the doubts of his existence melting in the warmth of her body. All he had lost was found again, in this woman. His one and only love.

"You smell like lemons," he said, stroking his hand over her hair.

"It's soap. There is something about lavender or rose water, really just about any kind of floral scent, that makes my skin itch." She folded her arms, upon his chest, rested her chin on her arms, and smiled at him. In that moment he knew he had never seen anything more beautiful than Jane in the moonlight. "Mrs. Crawley, my mother's housekeeper, makes a big batch of lemon-scented soap for me each summer."

"I like it." He lifted a handful of her hair and rubbed the silky strands against his cheek. "The scent of you, 'tis light and fresh, and makes me think of summer."

"I always wanted to wear a scent that smelled like flowers. My sisters all wear rose water. I am the only one who cannot go about smelling like a pretty blossom." She touched his chin with her fingertips. "Yet tonight, for the first time, I feel as though my lemon soap is something special."

"You are special, my love. My own rare flower." He smoothed his fingertips over the curve of her smile. "You were untouched until I came to you. 'Tis a wondrous gift. One I should not question."

She kissed the tips of his fingers. "Still, you should know the reasons. I do not like to think of them, because it makes me face reality. And reality is something I would like to avoid."

"The reality of you and me?"

"Yes." She closed her eyes. "The reality that I will lose you one day."

"Lose me?" He cupped her cheek in his hand. "I have traveled three hundred years to find you. I will never leave you."

"My darling Colin." She rubbed her cheek against his palm. "As much as I want to believe in your fairy tale, I know it cannot be. One day Lancaster's memories will return, and you will disappear."

"You still cannot believe in magic?"

She pressed her lips to his palm. "As long as you believe in magic, as long as you continue to be you, then it doesn't matter what I believe."

"My beautiful Lady Jane." He tugged gently on a lock of her soft hair. "One day you shall believe in magic and in me."

A sad, wistful quality entered her smile. "That would be wonderful."

She was so dear to him, more important than his own life. His chest ached at the sadness in her smile. Still, he knew there was little he could do to chase away the darkness behind her smile. Only when she believed in him would she truly accept the special gift they had been given. "How is it the man you married never touched you, when you are the most alluring woman on the face of the earth?"

"Alluring?" She laughed softly, a delicate sound he had seldom heard from her. "I married Lancaster the day of the accident."

"You were married the day of the accident. And this blow to the head kept him from consummating your vows?"

"No. He was anxious to consummate our vows." She stiffened against him. "The thought of his touching me made me ill."

"How did you escape the monster?"

"His pride. He thought I had actually wanted to marry him, that I was pretending to dislike him as a ploy."

Colin thought about this for a moment. "I suppose a man such as he could not accept the idea that any woman would not want him."

"Exactly. The night of our wedding, when he realized I did not want him, Lancaster made a bargain with me." With her fingertip, she traced a wavy pattern upon his shoulder. "If I could remain untouched for six months, he would give me an annulment. I would have my freedom."

Colin's breath stilled in his chest when he realized the full cost of the gift she had given him this day. "You gave up your chance for freedom from this man by lying with me?"

"Yes."

"When you still believe I am he?"

She rested her palm against his shoulder. She stared at her hand for a long moment before she looked into his eyes, the wealth of her love revealed for him in her silvery gaze. "I realized I might not have forever to love you, but I would not waste the chance I had been given to be with you."

He realized then that he was not the only one who had sacrificed so they could be together. "There is no reason to be so frightened, my love. I will never leave you."

"Lancaster's memories." She gripped his shoulder. "If they return, I will lose you. Anderson said the more you were reminded of your past, the more chance you had to remember."

He saw the anguish in her eyes and realized the full extent of her generous spirit. "Yet you plan to mold me back into Lancaster. To save me?"

"There is no other choice. Except to run away. And that would not be fair to you, or your family. Or my family." She flexed her fingers upon his shoulder. "I am hoping desperately you will remain Colin inside. You must try to remain Colin. Please do not alter the man inside."

"I am Colin." He cradled her cheek in his palm and slid his thumb over the curve of her lips. "Believe in me, my love. Believe I will never leave you."

She closed her eyes. "I want to believe in you. More than anything in life, I want to believe you will stay."

"My poor, beautiful Lady Jane. You cannot bring yourself to believe in magic."

A single tear slipped from beneath the dark fringe of her lashes. "I want to believe. I really do."

"You will, my love." He swept the tear away with his fingertips. "In time you will believe."

"I believe we have a lifetime of memories to make in the time we have together." She looked at him, a sad little smile curving her lips. "You know, I thought I heard you say you intended to kiss all of my bruises. Perhaps if I pointed them out to you, it would make it easier."

He laughed, a sound that held more happiness than he had known in a long time. Still, his happiness was tempered by the sadness he sensed within her and the specter of his own doubt. If it took him another three hundred years, he would make this woman believe in him. For now, all he could do was love her. "Where would you like me to begin?"

Chapter Twenty-three

The intelligible forms of ancient poets,
The fair humanities of old religion,
The power, the beauty, and the majesty
That had their haunts in dale or piny moun-
    tain,
Or forest by slow stream, or pebbly spring,
Or chasms and watery depths,—all these have
    vanished;
They live no longer in the faith of reason.
    —Johann Christoph Friedrich von Schiller

Jane stood at a window in the gold drawing room, watching Colin ride across the lawn toward the stables. Her
brothers were wonderful riders, as was Lancaster. Still,
she had never in her life seen a man who looked more
commanding in the saddle. Colin rode as though he could
communicate with the large black gelding beneath him.
In a very real sense they moved as one, the man leaning
low in the saddle, his black hair whipped by the wind,

295

thick muscles in his thighs flexing with the movement of the horse.

"I think we need to do more work with the way he moves," Fiona said, behind her. "He has a certain grace about him, but he is far less contained than Dominic."

"Yes. There is a difference." A marvelous difference, Jane thought. For the past eight days, she had been living a fairy tale. Each day with Colin was a gift. Each night she slept in his warm embrace. Each morning she awakened praying he would still be the man who had stolen her heart. Each time he swept away her fears by making love to her, every morning, every night.

Fiona joined her at the window. She stood watching for a moment before she continued. "My goodness. I have never seen him ride like that. Such a wild and untamed style."

Jane could not prevent a feeling of awe each time she watched him atop a horse. "He rides as if he could communicate with the animal."

"It is odd he would ride so differently. But then I find so many things odd about this illness of his." Fiona turned away from the window when Colin disappeared around the corner of the house. "The illness has brought about some startling changes in him. At times it is difficult to remember he is Dominic."

"Yes, it is." Jane only hoped and prayed and wished the differences would remain.

"I am concerned about his handwriting." Fiona handed Jane a sheet of white parchment. "I cannot understand how it could have changed so dramatically."

Jane stared down at the elegant script upon the paper. It was no more than a copy of a few of Shakespeare's verses, but it was a major triumph for a man who could not read or write two weeks ago. Once he had learned how to read, Colin had commenced to devour the books in the library. He was like a boy turned loose in a sweetshop. "It must be something about the illness. The same reason he could not read until we taught him."

"The illness." Fiona pursed her lips. "It is the strangest illness I have ever heard of. Amnesia I can understand. But to think you are an entirely different person. It is almost beyond belief. I suppose the changes in him must have something to do with the fascination Dominic had for Colin when he was a lad."

Jane didn't know the reasons, but she was grateful for the changes. "It would make sense."

"I find little makes sense. But I am glad to discover my grandson is more remarkable than I ever imagined." Fiona took the paper and stared down at the writing. "To learn so much in such a short time."

"Do you think he will be ready for London?"

"We have a great deal more to do. If it were left to me, he would not have gone riding this morning. But I suppose he needed a little exercise." Fiona frowned down at the sheet of paper she held. "I am surprised that all of the information we have been pumping into his head has not triggered his memory. I had thought it might."

Jane's chest constricted at the reminder of the danger lurking in the shadows of Colin's mind. "Yes. I thought as much also."

"Anderson said Dominic would remember. Yet I have not seen a glimmer of my grandson behind that handsome face."

"Perhaps he is more ill than Anderson imagined." Perhaps he would never remember. If prayers and wishes and hopes came true, Lancaster would never revert back to the horrible man she had married.

Fiona glanced up at Jane, a frown digging lines into her brow. "You have grown quite fond of Colin."

"Yes. I have."

"I understand. I should not admit it, I certainly should not feel it, but I find him much more approachable, much more . . ." Fiona waved her hands, pausing as if to find the proper word. "Charming. He is much more likable than he was before the accident. I almost regret that we must pound him back into the man he was before."

Jane smoothed her fingers over one of the gold velvet drapes. "Perhaps we will succeed in altering only the outer man."

"Perhaps." Fiona glanced down at the paper she held. "I found my father's journal this morning. I wasn't even looking for it. I simply came across it in the back of my armoire. I was leafing through it when I noticed an entry about the *Chronicles of Kintair*. It said he had given up hope of finding where his father had hidden them. My grandfather was killed in a carriage accident when my father was a young boy. Apparently he never got around to telling my father where the *Chronicles* were kept."

Beneath the rose-colored wool of her gown, chills scattered across Jane's arms. "The *Chronicles of Kintair* existed?"

"Yes." Fiona tugged the lobe of her right ear. "But I wonder how Dominic knew of them."

"He must have read about them. In the journal."

"No. I am quite certain he has never read my father's journal. I tucked it away long ago, before Dominic was born."

"Perhaps they were mentioned in the history of Kintair."

"No. I worked with Henry Filmore when he was documenting the history of the castle and my family. We never came across anything that mentioned the *Chronicles*."

"There must be a logical explanation." It seemed Jane was forever trying to find logical explanations for things these days. Even though she wanted very much to turn her back on logic. "Perhaps you mentioned it to him."

"Perhaps." Fiona drifted to the sofa. She sat on the edge of the gold velvet cushion and lifted her cup and saucer from the tea cart. "But I doubt it."

"How do you imagine he did know of them?"

Fiona sipped her tea. "That, my dear, remains a mystery."

Jane sank into a chair across from Fiona. "There is something about this place, I think. Something that makes one want to believe in magic."

"The Highlands are filled with mystery. Enshrouded in mists of magic." Fiona settled her cup against her saucer. "I read once again that book of Scottish legends you mentioned finding in the library. I had heard many of the stories as a child. And I have to confess, I wonder at times if perhaps we are not surrounded by magic every day. Only we are too blind to notice."

Jane clasped her hands tightly in her lap. She wanted to believe. If Colin could just remain with her, she would believe in magic.

"Now, I was thinking we really should work on his accent. He still sounds far too Scottish."

Jane refrained from saying how much she enjoyed the soft burr in his dark voice. Fiona was right. They needed to teach him to sound much more English. Still, she could not prevent a pang at the thought of how much of Colin they had already altered. If things were different, she would not change a thing about him.

"When you walk into a room, glance around as though you have a secret that no one else knows," Jane said.

Colin watched Jane walk across the room, her head tilted at an odd angle, her chin high, her eyes half-closed. He sat on a large chair in the room Doyle had called the crimson drawing room. It was only one of three drawing rooms he had discovered in this new Kintair. Although the walls were paneled in white with gold trim, he supposed the room had taken its name from the burgundy silk that covered all the sofas and chairs. He might not care for Lancaster, but he had to admit the man had managed to amass a great deal of wealth. "You look like you are half-asleep."

Jane bumped into the side of a sofa. She started, then looked at him, a sheepish grin on her face. "I suppose it does take some getting used to."

For days upon days Jane and Fiona had been pounding him with all the details of how to become a proper Englishman. And not just any Englishman, but an arrogant jackanapes. Each morning, Jane looked at him as though she were afraid he had turned into a monster during the night. Although she still refused to believe in him, at least he had the satisfaction of knowing she loved him. Dearly. Unfortunately their joy was always shadowed by her anxiety. Somehow he had to find a way to ease her fears.

"When you pass a mirror, always look into it and admire your own reflection." She glanced toward him and smiled, a haughty expression on her face. "Remember you believe you are the most perfect creation ever fashioned by the hand of the Almighty."

Colin laughed. "I see little to admire in this man. I am thinking perhaps 'tis time this Dominic Stanbridge made some changes in his life."

"It is time."

"Aye, that is what I said."

"Yes. Not aye. And it is, not 'tis." She moved toward him and paused before his chair. "It is very important for everyone to believe you are the same as you were before the accident."

"I am a different man." He winked at her. "I thought you might have noticed."

"I notice daily." She leaned down and kissed his brow, spilling the scent of lemons around him. "But we need to be careful, my love. You must try to remember to speak as an Englishman speaks."

Colin rested his chin on the steeple of his fingers. "Even when we are alone? Do you want me to be English in our bedchamber?"

She fiddled with the cameo pinned to the high neck of her dark green gown, and regarded him from beneath half-lowered lashes. "If you change anything about your behavior in our bedchamber, I will hit you over the head."

He lifted his brows in mock shock. "Such violent thoughts."

"If you awaken as Lancaster one day, I will feel obligated to hit you over the head. You would not expect me simply to allow you to slip away from me."

Colin saw the fear that lingered beneath her teasing. When would she look at him and feel confident he was who and what he said he was? He stood and offered her his hand. "Come with me."

She rested her hand on his open palm. "Where?"

He closed his fingers around her slender hand. "For a walk."

"But there is so much more we need to cover today."

He squeezed her hand. "If you want to continue the lesson, you can tutor me while we walk."

She glanced toward the windows. "It looks as though it could rain."

"It is a fine, soft day. Are you going to allow a few clouds to keep you locked away?"

She smiled. "I suppose it wouldn't hurt to take a short walk."

He lifted her hand and pressed his lips to the inside of her wrist. "Come along, then. The day is half gone. And I have something I want you to see."

Jane knew she should continue with the lesson, but walking hand in hand with Colin, she could not bring herself to think of the odious marquess. When Colin led the way to the path that wended along the edge of the cliffs, her curiosity got the better of her. "What is it you want me to see?"

He looked at her, a slight grin curving his lips. "It is a surprise."

"A surprise."

He winked at her. "It is not far from here."

They walked a grass- and stone-strewn path that hugged the edge of the cliffs. A breeze heavy with the scent of the sea whipped the hem of her coat and flicked the dark blue ribbons of her hat against her cheek. The soft swish of waves crashing against the rocky shore below, the occasioned cry of a gull, were the only sounds that pierced the companionable silence between them. At times like this they felt no need for words. It was enough simply to be near him, to feel the warmth of his bare hand wrapped around hers.

Up ahead, the path turned away from the sea, blocked by an outcropping of tall rocks. The ground sloped down from the edge of the cliff to a wide expanse of open field. Yet instead of turning toward the field, Colin looked as though he intended to try skirting the rocks on the cliff side of the path.

Jane halted on the path. "What are you doing?"

"There is something beyond the rocks. Something I want you to see." He stepped off the edge of the path onto a ledge, then turned and tugged on her hand. "Come with me."

Jane glanced over the edge of the cliff. Waves crashed against the rocks below, casting plumes of water and foam upward toward the sky. It looked like a very long way down. "I am not certain this is safe."

"There is a path here, if you know where to look."

She clutched the neck of her coat. "And you know where to look?"

"Aye, lass. I will keep you safe." He squeezed her hand. "Come with me."

This was foolish. To even imagine stepping off of the cliff with a man who was half out of his mind was nothing short of insanity. She looked into his eyes, saw the fierce look in the blue depths, and realized the importance he placed upon this act of trust. She stepped off the path and onto a narrow ledge.

She followed close behind him, keeping her gaze on his back, one hand in his, the other against the rocky side of the cliff while he led the way to . . . where? Good gracious, she didn't even know where he was leading her. Perhaps she was the one who had lost her mind. She wasn't certain how far they walked—it seemed a lifetime of clinging to the edge of the cliff—until they reached their destination.

Colin turned and smiled at her. "Here it is."

"Here" was a large shelf carved out of the rocky cliff. It was the size of the ballroom at Lancaster House, with three walls of rock, the fourth open to the sea, and a ceiling of sky. Gray clouds swirled above her. Jagged peaks of rocks surrounded the opening above, shielding this place from prying eyes. Grass grew here in tall, waving clumps. Yet the stones that seemed to rise from the floor of this secluded shelf caught and held her attention. They looked sculpted, as though each had been carefully carved into the shape of a pyramid. Twelve stones formed a circle open to the sky.

She turned and found Colin standing behind her, resting his shoulder against the rocky wall. He was watching her, a look of expectation in his eyes. "This is the ring of stones you told me about."

"Yes." He glanced up at the rocks above them. "I would climb atop the stones overhead and wait to see the fairies work their magic. It was there I met Aisling."

She bent to examine one of the stones. Even though the sun hid behind a cloud, the crystals embedded in the stone glittered as if reflecting some inner light. Symbols and figures had been carved into the shiny black stone. They looked Celtic in origin, ancient, as though carved at the beginning of time itself. She ran her fingertips over the carved figure of a bird. A strange, tingling warmth rippled along her arm. She pulled back her hand, then touched it again, certain the sensation would not repeat itself. The same tingling warmth coursed through her arm.

"You can feel it. The power that vibrates through this place."

Jane looked at him and found him smiling. "The stones must capture the heat of the sun. That is why it feels warmer here."

Colin glanced up at the gray clouds swirling overhead. "Not today."

The sun had not peeked out from behind the clouds all day. As she recalled, yesterday had also been a cool, cloudy day. Yet the air felt warm here, so warm she unfastened her coat. There was something odd about this place. Although the wind was blowing inland, she could not feel a whisper of it in this alcove. It was as if time itself stood still here.

"Can you look around you and still deny there is magic in this world?"

Standing here, she could almost believe fairies and sorcerers came to this place to cast their spells upon the world. It had that quality about it, as though it stood apart from the mortal realm. She stared out at the sea, imagining what it might be like to stand here beneath a full moon. "It must be an ancient worship site. Like Stonehenge. The Druids probably created it."

"The Druids worshiped the ones who truly created this place."

She turned to look at Colin, an uneasy sensation coiling low in her stomach. It wasn't logical to accept the things he said. Yet she could not completely banish the possibility from her thoughts. If she was willing to accept the possibility that magic existed, then she must accept the possibility that Colin was everything he said he was. Could it be?

"Believe in me, my lady," he said, his soft voice wrapping around her like a warm embrace.

"I want to believe in all you have said, Colin. But I

am afraid of what might become of me if it is not real."
She looked away from his beautiful eyes. "At least now
I can prepare myself for what might come to pass."

"Ah, lass." He closed the distance between them and
took her into his arms. "I cannot stand to see you so sad.
I see the fear in your eyes every morning when you look
at me and wonder if I am still Colin."

She slid her arms around his waist and hugged him
close. Yet she knew no matter how tightly she might hold
him, she could not prevent the memories from returning.
"I cannot help it. I love you so much. The thought of
losing you makes me want to die."

"There is no need to fear, my love." He pressed his
lips against her hair. "I shall never leave you. Not until
the hand of the Almighty reaches for me."

She tipped back her head and looked up at him.
Strange, but she loved every aspect of his face. The faint
lines that creased the corners of his eyes when he smiled.
The way one corner of his lips tipped higher than the
other when he grinned at her. The glint of mischief in
his incredible eyes. Strange because this same face had
never been dear to her when Lancaster's soul lurked behind these handsome features. She lifted on her toes and
pressed her lips to his. "I want to believe you."

A look of resignation crossed his features. Still, he
smiled down at her. "In time, you will."

A fat raindrop plopped upon her cheek. There were
lessons that should be taught. As much as she dreaded
any reminder of Lancaster, she knew she must do her
best to mold this wonderful man into the image of a
scoundrel. "I suppose we should be heading back."

Colin glanced up at the sky, then back at her, a glint
of mischief entering his eyes. He lifted one of the ribbons
of her bonnet and tugged, slowly unraveling the bow beneath her chin. "Have you ever felt the rain upon your
bare skin?"

Chapter Twenty-four

There was the Door to which I found no Key;
There was the Veil through which I might not see.
                                        —Omar Khayyám

Colin's words conjured a naughty image in her brain.
Jane could not prevent the tingles scattering across her
skin. "Do you mean on something other than my face
and hands?"

Colin pulled the bonnet from her hair and tossed it to
the ground. "I want to lick the raindrops from your
breasts and your toes, and everywhere in between."

Heat flickered in that secret place that only he had ever
claimed, a sweet, simmering heat. It was wicked. Certainly wanton. Still, she was a woman who had allowed
this man to make love to her on the bluffs. Modesty did
not have any place between them. She slipped her hands
inside his black coat and peeled the garment from his
shoulders. It fell with a whisper to the ground at their
feet. "I suppose we might linger here a little while
longer."

"That is my bonnie Jane."

Slowly, as if they had all their lives ahead of them, they stripped away each other's clothes until they stood naked amid the ancient stones. Rain drizzled over Jane's skin, warm and soft, like silken ribbons gliding upon her, awakening every nerve to the glory of pure sensation. She felt in that moment as if they were the only people in existence, man and woman, destined for what would come.

She spread her arms toward the gray clouds above, her breasts lifting to the kiss of the raindrops. The freedom of this act, of simply standing here naked to the rain, of knowing she owed nothing to propriety, to rules, to constrictions, proved far more intoxicating than wine. Colin's eyes lowered, his gaze touching her with an intensity that spread heat across her skin. Excitement sizzled through her, tingling along her limbs, gathering in her belly like a slow drizzle of hot oil.

Colin stood before her, stripped bare of social trappings, as wild and untamed as the cliffs and the ocean beyond. So beautiful. So splendid. His black hair was slicked back from his face, curling in wet tendrils behind his ears. With her gaze, she traced the slow slide of a drop of rain down his neck. When it tangled in the hair below the hollow of his neck, she captured the droplet on her tongue, tasting the faint salt of the sea and of his skin. He drew in his breath on a slow inhalation.

"Looking at you, I can believe the tales of mythical creatures who leave the sea to wander the earth in search of mortal females." She slid her hand down his chest, her fingertips brushing silky damp hair, powerful muscles quivering beneath her touch. "It makes me want to hunt for your sealskin, to hide it so you may never leave me."

He laughed softly, a deep rumble that curled warmly around her. "You have, lass. You have hidden it away in so secret a place, I could never find it. Even if I were to look for it. Yet why would I want it? I am where I want most to be."

Dear Lord in heaven, let it be true. She prayed this man would never leave her. Yet the fear would not go away. No matter how much she tried to ignore reality, it was always there in the shadows, lurking to snatch away her happiness.

He touched her breast, rubbing the backs of his fingers over the tip. Sensation shot through her at his touch, as though he were a spark touched to brandy. She watched him lower his head, her breath trapped in her throat with the anticipation of what was to come.

He brushed his lips against her neck, his wet hair brushing her chin. She stood like a canvas before him, her body coming to life beneath his hands and lips, like a painting taking shape beneath the skillful brushstrokes of a master. He slid down her body, drinking the rain from her skin, his mouth hot upon her, his hands gentle, warm, and sure. The rain seemed to turn to steam at his touch, and inside she turned to melted butter, all hot and liquid. He did as he promised, sliding and gliding upon her skin, kissing and touching her everywhere, until she was trembling, until he summoned the pleasure to rise within her, until it expanded and filled her and escaped in a soft cry from her lips. Only then did he surge upward along her body. He slipped his arms around her and lifted her. She slipped her legs around his waist, her arms around his shoulders, heated and desperate for the plunge of his body into hers. He thrust into her and she cried with the sheer joy of their joining.

She tossed back her head, lifting her face to the sky. Rain streamed over her cheeks, washing clean the tears she could not withhold. Joy and fear, pleasure and pain. If she lost this man, she would lose her world. *Please, let him stay.*

* * *

The storm followed them back to Kintair. By the time they reached the castle, water ran in rivulets from their sodden clothes. The echo of the front door closing had not faded in the hall before Fiona emerged from one of the adjoining corridors, and she was not alone. Jane's heart stumbled when she saw Pembury beside Fiona. It was far too soon to face him. Colin was not ready for battle. They would need a miracle to get through this.

"It would seem we have a guest."

Chills scattered across Jane's skin at the sound of Colin's voice. It had been such a long time since she had heard Lancaster's voice. The sound of it—low, leisurely, each word colored with a trace of contempt—brought a deluge of memories. She glanced up at Colin. He was staring at Pembury, one corner of his lips lifted, his eyes slightly narrowed, his head at an angle.

Dimly, she was aware of Pembury and Fiona halting before them. Still, she could not drag her gaze from the man standing beside her. The transformation was startling. All trace of the beguiling Scot had vanished. It was as if Colin had never existed.

"I see you have taken to wandering about in the rain." Pembury lowered his gaze to Colin's side. "Although it would seem you have decided to leave your sword behind today."

"I shall wander about when and where I please, Edwin." Colin rubbed the tip of his forefinger over the arch of one black brow. "As for the sword, I am certain we can find a pair of swords. If you would like to try your hand at crossing blades with me? Or is that far too direct to suit you? From what I have heard, you much prefer to approach from the rear."

Jane tried to swallow. Yet there was no moisture in her mouth. Deep inside, doubts shifted in the shadows. She glanced away from Colin, frightened by what she saw in his face. Pembury stood staring at Colin as well, his expression revealing his own doubt. Could seeing

Pembury have been the spark that had ignited Lancaster's memories? Had she lost Colin? An even more sinister thought crept through her mind—what if it had all been a game?

Pembury cleared his throat. "It would seem you are feeling much more yourself this afternoon."

Jane looked up at the man standing beside her, searching for some trace of Colin. Yet all she saw was the icy shell of Lancaster.

"It would seem you have a talent for poor judgment." Colin crossed one arm over his chest, rested his elbow against his wrist, and propped his chin in his hand. "Never underestimate me, Edwin. You could end up in very deep water."

Pembury's nostrils flared. "I have no idea what you might mean."

Colin's lips curved into a cold imitation of a smile. "I suppose the rumors of your sudden wish to become my guardian again have been dramatically misunderstood."

Pembury's shoulders lifted. "I was only thinking of your welfare."

Colin held his gaze a long moment before he spoke. "Of course you were. Now, will you excuse us? My wife and I need to bathe and change before dinner. Will you be staying for dinner before you leave?"

Pembury cleared his throat. "I had thought I might stay a few days."

Colin lifted one black brow. "I am certain you have no intention of intruding upon my wedding trip. It would put me in such bad humor."

Pembury glanced at Fiona. "But Mama is here."

"Fortunately I have always enjoyed her company. I shall see you at dinner."

Jane allowed Colin to take her arm and usher her toward the staircase. Although her legs felt like wood, her heart felt like porcelain, fragile, so easy to break. She did not glance at Colin as they climbed the stairs. She could not bring herself to look at him as they walked the corridors leading to her chamber. What if she had lost him?

Finally at the door to her chamber, he slipped his fingers under her chin and coaxed her to look at him. When she did, he winked at her. "Colin?"

He laughed softly. "I thought I saw a glint of terror in your eyes."

She pressed her hands against his chest. "It is still you, isn't it?"

He kissed the tip of her nose. "Not to worry, my heart. You cannot be rid of me that easily."

A sweet tide of relief rushed through her, washing away her anxiety. "You were amazing down there. You looked just like him. You sounded just like him."

"For a few minutes." Colin released his breath in a low hiss. "I cannot say I am looking forward to dinner."

Jane turned at the soft footsteps upon the oak planks in the hallway. Fiona was hurrying toward them, her expression revealing her anxiety. "What the devil were the two of you doing out in this? The last thing we need is to give Edwin any more reason to think you are insane."

"I needed to stretch my legs." Colin chucked Fiona under the chin and gave her a smile designed to melt the ice in her tone. "And I wanted to show Jane the fairy ring."

Fiona's eyes widened. "Fairy ring? What fairy ring?"

"The ring of stones on the cliffs," Jane said.

"A ring of stones on the cliffs?" Fiona shook her head. "I have never heard of such a thing."

Jane untied the wet ribbons beneath her chin. "You have never heard of them?"

"No. I have seen such rings before, but never here at Kintair."

Colin smoothed the wet hair back from his brow. A drop of water slid down his cheek and caught at the corner of his smile. Jane looked away from him, but she could not stop the memories from creeping out, memories of his finely molded lips brushing her skin.

"It was ancient in my time," Colin said. "Hidden. Secret. You can reach it only by a narrow path that hugs the face of the cliffs."

Fiona looked horrified. "You walked the cliff path?"

"Actually you must walk along a ledge that runs below the cliff path." Jane swept the wet hat from her head. "Getting there is a bit frightening, but the stone ring is fascinating. The stones have crystals embedded in them, and are carved with symbols and figures."

Fiona stared at Colin, her lips parted, her eyes wide. "You actually took Jane to this place on the side of a cliff?"

"It is a very special place." Colin winked at Fiona. "If you like, I will take you there tomorrow."

Fiona licked her lips. "You actually walked a narrow path that hugged the face of the cliffs?"

"It is safe," Colin said. "As long as you mind your step. Which is what I must do with Edwin."

"I wondered how long we would have before Edwin learned we were here." Fiona studied Colin a moment. "You did well, my lad. But I am afraid he will not give up so easily. Be prepared for a battle at dinner. And make certain you allow Pierson to attend you. Heed his every word. No more of this neglecting your neckcloth. I did not coax Pierson back into your employ for you to have him sit about on his thumbs."

Colin nodded, a glint of steel entering his eyes. "I will do what needs to be done, even allow that little man to fuss over me."

Fiona squeezed Colin's arm. "Off with you now. Get out of those wet clothes before you catch lung fever."

Colin smiled at Jane. "And you do the same, my lady."

Contentment filled her when she saw the warmth of affection in his blue eyes. "I will."

Colin turned and left the women alone while he walked to the adjoining chamber. When he entered his room,

Fiona took Jane's arm and ushered her into Jane's bedchamber. She closed the door, then turned to face Jane. "Did you actually find a fairy ring today?"

"Yes."

"On the cliffs?"

"It was as he described it to you." The stark look of astonishment in Fiona's blue eyes surprised Jane. It was a look that spoke of surprise and apprehension. "Is something wrong?"

"I do not know what to make of this." Fiona turned away from Jane. She paced a few steps, then pivoted and faced her. "Ever since Dominic was a small boy, he has been terrified of heights. Until today, I have never known him to have walked the cliff path."

Jane's breath caught in her lungs. It could not be possible, she assured herself, fighting to crush the hope rising within her. Hope was far too dangerous an emotion; it stripped one bare, allowing no defense against heartache. He could not possibly be Colin MacKenzie. "Lancaster is frightened of heights?"

Fiona pressed her hand to the base of her neck. "Yes."

"But I have stood with him on one of the balconies of Lancaster House. Perhaps he has outgrown the fear."

"No. He manages well enough if there is a sturdy railing about him. Although he still does not care to venture near the edge of a balcony. Did he do so when you were with him?"

Jane tried to remember that evening he had taken her out onto the balcony of the music room to show her the extent of the gardens. She had been so heartsick that evening, she could not remember much of anything. "I don't believe he did."

"No. I should not think he would." Fiona pressed her palms together and rested the tips of her fingers beneath her chin. "He would never dream of walking the cliff path. And a narrow ledge below the cliff path would freeze him in his boots. He simply could not do it."

Chills gripped Jane's shoulders. "How could he have known about the stone ring?"

"I cannot imagine." Fiona spread her hands, then pressed the palms together once more. "I lived here most of my life, and I have never heard a whisper about a fairy ring before today."

"There has to be a logical explanation." Jane snatched at the possibilities. If something looked impossible, it usually was. "He must have heard of the stones . . . at some time in his life."

"And the bump on the head gave him the courage to explore the cliffs until he found them?"

Jane nodded, trying not to think of how weak the explanation sounded. "He did a great deal of exploring before you arrived."

Fiona drew in her breath. "I suppose it is possible."

"Still, I wonder how he could describe the fairy ring to me before we arrived at Kintair."

Fiona tapped her fingertips against her chin. "I suppose he might have found them on an earlier trip. And never told anyone. But then he would have faced the cliffs without the benefit of a bump on the head."

Jane clasped her hands at her waist, her wrists pressed against her damp coat. "There must be a logical explanation."

"It is strange," Fiona said, her voice little more than a whisper. "But at times I find myself thinking he truly is Colin. And as much as I hate to admit this, I think I shall miss him when he goes away. I suppose it is inevitable, though. He could not truly be Colin."

"No." Nonetheless, the possibility swirled through her, beguiling and frightening. "Of course he could not."

Fiona looked back to the stairs. "Still, I wonder."

"What do you wonder?"

"It is merely a bit of fancy." Fiona shook her head as though dismissing a thought. "I was born and bred in the Highlands. From the time I was a wee lass, my mother would tell me stories of fairies and magic. I wonder if it is possible. Has my grandson been whisked away and another man left in his place?"

The possibilities crowded Jane's chest until it hurt to draw a breath. "Do you really believe it is possible?"

"I'm not certain what is possible and what is not. Did a bump on the head truly alter him so thoroughly? What of you? After spending time with him, can you honestly say you look at him and think of Dominic?"

"No. I cannot. But to accept that he has been brought here from another time . . . is far too fantastic." No matter how much she wanted to believe, she could not. She did not want to think of what might happen should she release her hold on reality. Could a fairy tale come true?

"Well, no matter what is the truth, he must convince Edwin and everyone else that he is Dominic." Fiona rested her hand on Jane's arm. "You'd better change, dear. I have kept you standing in these wet clothes long enough."

A single lamp burned on the table beside the bed in Colin's bedchamber. The flickering light glowed softly in the shadows, reaching for the woman who moved toward the bed. Colin's heart quickened each time he saw her. Even dressed in one of her modest white gowns, as she was this evening, he thought her more alluring than any woman on the face of the good green Earth. "I was beginning to wonder if you were coming to bed. I was about to go looking for you."

"Fiona came to my room when I was getting ready for bed. She wanted to talk a bit."

He pulled back the covers in silent invitation. The mattress dipped as she climbed into bed beside him. Her cold feet brushed his warm leg, sending a chill shooting along his nerves. "Your feet are like ice."

"I suppose I should have put on a dressing gown and

slippers," she said, pulling back from him. "It's chilly tonight."

"Stay close to me, lass." He hooked his arm around her and pulled her against him. The crisp scent of lemons curled around him. "I will have you warm in no time at all."

"I know you will." She rested her head against his shoulder and snuggled against him. "You always make me feel warm inside."

He smoothed his hand over her arm. "What is it, my heart? Why are you so sad tonight? I thought I did a fair job of putting Uncle Edwin in his place."

"You did." She smoothed her fingertip over his bare chest, tracing a serpentine pattern through the black hair. "Fiona seems to think you convinced him your lapse of sanity was merely a game you were playing with me."

He brushed his palm down her arm. Beneath the soft cotton of her sleeve, he felt the tightness in her muscles. "You do not seem happy about this little victory."

"I am. Of course I am." She rubbed her fingertip against his chest. "It is just unsettling seeing you don the mask of Lancaster. I find myself looking for you under all that icy arrogance."

He pressed his lips against her hair. "I am here, my heart. And here by your side I will stay."

She released her breath, the soft inhalation warming his skin. "How did you know about the fairy ring?"

"I found it when I was a lad exploring the cliffs."

She turned her head and looked up at him. "Fiona said you could not possibly have found the fairy ring by exploring the cliffs. She said that ever since you were a boy, you were terrified of heights."

He would be the happiest man in the world except for the fear and desperation he often saw in Jane's beautiful eyes. "Perhaps Lancaster is afraid of heights. I am not."

She held his gaze a long moment.

He flicked open the pearl button at the top of her gown.

316

"Tomorrow I wonder if you would do something with me."

She laughed, the soft sound curling warmly around his heart. "It would seem I will do almost anything with you."

He rolled the second button between his thumb and forefinger. "Marry me."

She looked as though he had just asked her to take a trip back to 1562 with him. "Marry you?"

"Aye. Come to the chapel with me. Allow me to speak my vows and hear you pledge yourself to me."

"But we are married."

"No, lass." He opened the second button. "You married Lancaster. I am asking you to marry me, Colin."

"But it would raise questions if we were to send for a minister and—"

"Just you and me in the chapel." He ran his fingertip down her neck, feeling the quick throb of her pulse beneath his touch. "Marry me."

A smile slid over her lips, a warm smile that filled her eyes with light. "Yes. I would love to speak my vows to you, my darling."

Emotion uncoiled within him. "Tomorrow, my heart."

"Would you mind if Fiona attended? I think she would like to be there."

"I would like her to be there. She has come to mean a great deal to me. I think of her as my own grand-mother." He slipped the small loop fastening the third button free. "I hope you do not mind if I make love to my future bride tonight."

She glanced down to where his large hand rested against her gown, his skin dark upon the white cloth. "I would mind very much if you didn't."

Chapter Twenty-five

For now I see the true old times are dead,
When every morning brought a noble chance,
And every chance brought out a noble knight.
                              —Alfred, Lord Tennyson

"Eugenia has four children. Freddie, the eldest, followed
by Harry, Oliver, and Fanny. You will see Freddie in the
reception line. The others are still in the schoolroom. And
you need not worry about knowing them. You think of
them as 'the brood.' As a matter of fact, you think of all
of your nieces and nephews in terms of a nameless pack."

Fiona's voice buzzed in Colin's ears. For the past three
hours she had been pounding the details of Lancaster's
family into him. Again. At the moment she was sitting
beside him on one of the sofas, pointing out photographs
of the various family members.

Colin had looked at photographs and listened to de-
scriptions until he felt he could pick Lancaster's family
members out in a crowd. He had not expected that the

intense discussion of family would dredge up memories of his own. Yet it had, and with the memories came the painful reminder that he would never again see their faces, hear their laughter.

He glanced to where Jane sat at the desk, reading the history of Kintair. Since she knew little about Lancaster, these last few days Fiona had been his teacher. His wife could only sit near and lend quiet support.

My wife. He concentrated on Jane and tried not to linger on the bittersweet memories of loved ones he would never again see. Yet as much as he tried, he could not sit here, in this elegant library, and not think of times he had spent with his family in what was once the great hall. It was difficult to believe this was the same house he had known. Still, he knew that behind the bookcases and the polished wooden panels stood the stone walls of what had been the great hall. Was it still the same as he had known? "I wonder."

Fiona looked up from the book of photographs she held open on her lap. "What do you wonder?"

If he could find the *Chronicles*, he would at least be able to read what his mother had written of those years he had not been able to share with them. "Fiona, did you say your grandfather was the one who created the library as it is now?"

"Yes. He made several improvements to Kintair. The library was a favorite of his." Fiona closed the book. "Why do you ask?"

"According to what was in your father's journal, your grandfather was the last to have possession of the *Chronicles of Kintair*." Colin rested his chin on the steeple of his fingers. "I am thinking I may know where they are."

"How could you possibly know where they are?" Jane asked.

"I knew where they were kept in my day. And I am thinking there was no need to find another place to keep them."

"If you knew where they were in your day, then why haven't you retrieved them?" Fiona sat back against the sofa as if she was startled by her own words. "I cannot believe I am having this conversation with you. Your day is this day."

"No. It is not. And I am thinking you know the truth deep in your heart." Colin glanced at Jane, speaking as much to her as he was to Fiona. Jane frowned, an uneasy look entering her eyes.

"I may have moments of doubt, but to believe your story would be far too fantastic," Fiona said. "I am certain one day, perhaps soon, you will regain your memory."

Colin patted her hand. "My memory is fine."

"For the sake of argument, let us say you truly are Colin." Jane smoothed her thumb over the cover of the book she held in her lap. "Then where would you find the *Chronicles*?"

"In my day, the *Chronicles* were kept in a vault that was hidden behind a stone in the great hall. That part of the hall is now this library." He stood and crossed the room. "The stone that hides the vault is now buried behind this bookcase."

"If my grandfather covered over the hiding place, then it would cease to be a hiding place." Fiona drummed her fingers on the arm of the sofa. "If what you say is true, then my grandfather must have moved the *Chronicles* before he had the library built."

"Perhaps not." Colin slipped two books from the top shelf and laid them on the floor nearby. "Perhaps he just altered the way to get to them."

"Altered the way to get to them?" Fiona set the album aside and joined Colin. She studied the bookcase a moment before she spoke. "Do you mean there would be a way to get behind the bookcase?"

"That is exactly what I am thinking." Colin pulled several more books from the top shelf and rested them on the books he had already placed on the floor.

Jane moved to stand beside Colin. "What do you have in mind?"

"I am going to empty this bookcase and see if there is any mechanism that might cause it to swing away from the wall."

Although he sensed that both ladies thought him insane, he also knew both Jane and Fiona had enough doubts about his identity to want to get to the truth. No matter how fantastic. He knew that was the reason both of them helped him empty the bookcase. When the shelves were empty and the books piled in six neat stacks on the floor, Colin began searching for any means to get to the wall behind the bookcase. After a careful search, he found . . .

"Nothing." Fiona clasped her hands at her waist. "I am not certain why you may have taken this notion into your head, but it is obvious there is no way behind this bookcase."

"There has to be a way to get to the wall behind here." Colin gripped the edge of a shelf. "I know the vault would still be there."

The long case clock that stood in one corner of the room struck the hour, chiming midnight.

"Dominic, dear, it is getting late. I suggest we all get some sleep. I think tomorrow we must work once more on your handwriting. It is still so very different from what it was. It is puzzling how it could change so dramatically," Fiona said, crossing the room. "Good night, children. I shall see you both early in the morning."

Although Colin bade her good evening, he did not turn away from the bookcase. If he could just get past this wall, he knew he could find the vault.

Jane touched his arm. "Are you coming to bed?"

She looked exhausted. He knew the thought of returning to London in a few days weighed heavily on her mind. He also knew her fear was more than facing a pack of gossip-mad idiots. She was afraid of losing him. Every day she sat listening while Fiona poured facts about Lancaster's life into him. Every day she was afraid one of those facts would spark memories he had never made. And nothing he did or said could alter her thinking. His beautiful wife was steadfastly certain her husband would one day turn once more into a monster. He had to find a way to prove himself to her. A way to slay his own doubts.

"I want to look at a few things down here." He smoothed his fingertips over her brow. "I will be up later."

Jane rested her hands on his chest and lifted to meet his kiss. "Good night, my darling."

"Good night, my heart."

He watched her leave, noting the way her shoulders sagged beneath the weight of her worries. When he was alone he turned once more to face the wall of bookcases. If he were Fiona's grandfather and he knew of the vault—which the man must have—he would certainly not choose another hiding place for the *Chronicles*. It was tradition, for one thing. The *Chronicles* had been kept there since the first word had been written in them. Still, if he wanted to create this fine library, he would not leave one stone wall exposed. No, it made sense to conceal that wall, but leave a way to get to it.

He walked to the center of the room, then turned and looked at the bookcases. It was disorienting, looking at the rows of bookcases. Difficult to get his bearing. He closed his eyes and conjured the memory of this room as it had been in his day. Then he opened his eyes and saw his mistake.

Jane awakened the next morning to find herself alone in bed. *Odd.* Since she had first welcomed him into her arms, Colin had slept each night beside her. She could not imagine what had kept him from coming to her, unless . . . The thoughts flitting through her brain caused her heart to beat faster and harder until she could scarcely breathe. She threw off her bedclothes, then ran across her room and the adjoining withdrawing room that led to his chamber. She did not knock upon his door. Instead she threw it open and hurried inside. His bed had been turned down. Yet no one had slept there.

Where was he?

He could not still be in the library. Could he? After donning a dressing gown and shoving her feet into a pair of black mules, she hurried to the library. She nearly collapsed with relief when she found Colin sitting in a chair near the windows, his feet propped up on a footstool, a pile of leather-bound books stacked neatly on the floor beside his chair. He glanced up from the book he was reading when she entered.

The smile he gave her eased the constriction around her chest. That smile belonged only to Colin. "Good morning, sweetheart."

"Good morning." Jane crossed the library and dropped a kiss upon his lips. "Were you here all night?"

"I have been reading." He set the book he had been reading on the stack by his chair.

His eyes held a spark of mischief and more. He looked like a man who had just found a leprechaun's pot of gold. "It must have been fascinating reading."

"It was." He gripped her waist and pulled her down upon his lap.

The scent of sandalwood and man registered in her senses, tugging at her vitals. She wanted to know what had made him so pleased with himself. But then he kissed her, long and deep, sliding his lips upon hers until he wiped away every thought, leaving only pleasure and heat in their wake. All too soon he lifted away from her. When she opened her eyes he was grinning at her.

"I found them, my love."

Jane frowned while she tried to make sense of his words. She brushed her fingers over his cheek, enjoying the rasp of his beard. "What have you found?"

"The *Chronicles*."

His words ripped through her. She sat up on his lap and gripped his shoulders. "The *Chronicles of Kintair*?"

"Every book that was kept."

It was impossible. He could not possibly have known where to find them. "Where were they?"

He looked toward the wall across from him. "Behind a bookcase."

Jane followed the direction of his gaze. Beside the bookcase they had emptied last night stood a square gap where a bookcase had been swung away from the wall, revealing the stone wall behind it.

"I had the wrong bookcase last night. After you went to bed I found the right one. There is a small latch on the top shelf. It opens the lock that holds the bookcase in place. It swings open like a door."

"Oh, my good gracious." Jane slid off his lap and walked toward the wall. Her legs felt like wood, and her heart was beating rapidly. There was a hole in the stone wall, a place where two stones had been removed. Only on closer inspection did she notice the stones were merely a veneer covering a thick slab of wood that had been drawn back on a set of hinges. "There is a vault here."

"There has been for a very long time." He moved behind her and rested his hands on her shoulders. "I am hoping this is the proof you need."

Proof. Dear heaven, how else would he have known of the vault? Yet how could this be true?

"What in the world?"

Jane turned at the sound of Fiona's voice. "Colin found the *Chronicles*."

Fiona crossed the room in a soft swish of petticoats. She halted beside Colin and cast a critical look at the stone wall and the vault. "I see it was behind a different bookcase."

"The room had changed so much. It misled me for a while." Colin winked at Jane. "Still, the chronicles were here. I spent last night reading. It was good to read my mother's words and know for certain my family fared well without me."

It was real. Colin was real. All the possibilities raged through Jane. Magic. Colin had been brought to her across the ages. Hope fluttered within her like rose petals swirling in a spring breeze.

Fiona pursed her lips. "I wonder when you found this?"

"Last night. After you and Jane went to bed."

"No." Fiona looked up at him. "I mean I wonder when Dominic found the vault."

Jane's breath halted in her throat. "What do you mean?"

Fiona looked at her. "It is obvious. Dominic must have found the vault during one of his explorations. He was forever searching the castle. He was the one who found the underground passageway that runs from the east wing to the cliffs."

All the hope within Jane stilled. She stared at Fiona. "Dominic had a fascination with Kintair. He was always exploring the castle," she said, remembering Fiona's words.

"Yes. From the time he was a young boy he would search out 'secrets,' as he liked to call them." Fiona clasped her hands at her waist and gave Colin a stern look. "I wonder when you were planning to tell me about this little discovery."

"By my faith." Colin plowed his hand through his hair. "Tell me how it is that I can read my mother's hand when it was written in sixteenth-century script?"

"You have been reading medieval manuscripts since you were twelve years old," Fiona said. "Tell me, did you find anything in the *Chronicles* that said Colin suddenly took the rather odd notion that he was from 1889?"

Jane held her breath, still hoping for the impossible.

Colin glanced from Fiona to Jane, then back again, a look of frustration filling his expression. "No."

Jane silently acknowledged her own foolishness. She had known better than to believe in fairy tales. It was far too dangerous. Hope was a horrible thing.

"I doubt my mother would have wanted all the world to know of her son's bout of insanity. That would explain why there is nothing in the *Chronicles*. Would you document this lapse that you believe Dominic has had?"

Fiona considered this a moment. "No. I do not believe I would."

"And neither would my mother have done such a thing. So the fact that there is nothing in the *Chronicles* about Lancaster believing he was from another time is inconclusive."

"So we're back where we started." Fiona said.

Colin released his breath in a tired-sounding sigh. "Is there nothing that will make you believe in me?"

How could one prove the impossible? Jane only wished he could.

"I am certain it is only a matter of time, my boy." Fiona patted Colin's arm. "One of these days you are certain to remember just who you truly are."

Jane turned away from him, miserable at the thought of the day Lancaster would regain his memory.

Colin rested his hand on her shoulder. "I am Colin."

Jane could not face him, not now. Not when her hopes lay broken within her. "I'd better get dressed."

Somehow Jane managed to find her way back to her chamber. She bathed and dressed and got through the rest of the morning as though she had not taken a blow to the heart. Later, she sat in the library reading the *Chronicles of Kintair*—at least the volumes that were not written in ancient script—while Fiona pounded more of Lancaster's past into Colin's head. And while she tried to concentrate on the words written by MacKenzies who had long ago turned to dust, she tried not to think of the fate of a man who believed he was a MacKenzie from the distant past. When would it happen? When would Lancaster remember and Colin disappear?

Jane had not expected to find the answer to a mystery hidden in the book Fiona's grandfather had written. Yet it was here. She glanced at Colin. He was sitting beside Fiona on a nearby sofa, listening as she told him precisely how he must behave at the ball. Jane had to swallow hard before she could use her voice. "Fiona's grandfather knew of the fairy ring."

Both Fiona and Colin turned to look at her. Colin's expression revealed first surprise and then an impatience that Jane knew came from frustration.

"My grandfather knew of the fairy ring?" Fiona asked.

"Yes. He describes it in detail in his volume of the *Chronicles*. He said it was a secret that had been passed down to each generation of the family. He intended to tell your father about it when Neill reached the age of sixteen. He didn't want him crawling about on the cliffs before that."

"He died before he could pass on the legacy." Fiona glanced at the vault, then turned her gaze upon Colin. "That is how you knew of the fairy ring. You read about it in the *Chronicles*."

"Yes. It makes sense," Jane said, her voice little more than a whisper as it escaped her tight throat. Lord in heaven, she never should have accepted this fairy tale, not for an instant.

Colin released his breath in a long sigh. "I am Colin MacKenzie."

Fiona wagged her finger at him. "I really do wish you had told me about the *Chronicles*. It was not at all fair to keep them to yourself."

Colin shook his head. "If Lancaster had discovered the *Chronicles*, I believe he would have told you about them.

If nothing else, just to show you how clever he was in finding them."

Fiona lifted her brows. "I am rather surprised you did not."

Colin looked at Jane, a fierce look in his eyes. "It does not make sense. Lancaster would have told someone of his discovery."

It didn't make sense. But believing that Colin had traveled over three hundred years to be with her made far less sense.

"Now that I think of it, I was away when you returned to London from Kintair in March." Fiona tapped her forefinger against her chin. "And when I first saw you, you had other matters on your mind. As I recall you were on the hunt for Jane."

Colin released a low groan. "It would seem there is no means to prove I am truly Colin."

One could not prove what was not true. Jane glanced away from him, afraid Colin would see the horrible disappointment in her eyes.

"In time, I hope both you and Jane will come to accept me for who I am. Because I am not going away."

Jane knew his words were spoken for her benefit. She could only hope and pray that was true. She had no idea how much time they might have with one another. She did not intend to waste any of it wallowing in self-pity or regrets or any such misery. Each day with Colin was a gift. And she intended to celebrate each moment she had with him.

Chapter Twenty-six

He who can simulate sanity will be sane.
              —Ovid, Publius Ovidius Naso

Jane had attended twenty-two balls during her Season. At
most of them she had spent her time standing on the
fringe of the gaiety, watching other girls dance and flirt
and enjoy the evening. This ball was different. This night
she and Colin were the center of attention of each and
every person who walked through the large front doors
of Lancaster House.

The soft strains of a waltz provided a background for
the laughter and conversation in the room. The scent of
spring flowers wafted from vials of perfume hung in each
chandelier. The room glowed and shimmered like something straight out of the pages of a fairy tale. Although
Jane had never before attended a ball at Lancaster House,
she knew the ballroom was one of the finest in all of
England.

Fiona had arranged everything while they were in

Scotland. At the moment, Her Ladyship was sitting on a gilt-trimmed Grecian longue near Jane, holding court like a queen. Jane doubted Fiona's knees had been shaking as she welcomed their guests earlier this evening. Jane had trembled so badly, she was certain she would have bruises from her knees knocking together.

If it were simply a ball, Jane's nerves would not have been so tightly wound. But she knew that most of the people crowded into the huge, gilt-trimmed ballroom were expecting—in fact hoping—to see the mad marquess perform some trick for them. So far Colin had managed to act his part to perfection. At the moment he was waltzing with Sylvia Wadswyck. From the smile on the dragon's face, Jane surmised—and hoped—Colin's charm had extinguished the woman's fiery tongue.

"I see Lancaster is back to his old arrogant self." Amelia fanned herself languidly, fluttering the tiny gold curls framing her flawless face. "I knew it would happen."

Jane had not disclosed everything to her mother and sister. Upon their return to London three days ago, she had paid a call upon her mother, only to find Georgette and Amelia too involved with several other callers to allow private discourse. When she had tried to see them the next day at the time she had mentioned she would return, she had found they had gone shopping. Apparently they had been too busy to visit her at Lancaster House as she had requested. Now she wondered if perhaps it was unwise to confide the truth about Lancaster's illness. "I find he is not quite so arrogant as he was before the accident."

"You could not prove that by me. He appears unchanged."

Jane could not agree. To her eyes it was obvious another man's spirit had possessed the body of Dominic Stanbridge. Lancaster had never danced the way this man danced, each fluid movement rippling with power and grace. Had it been only a week ago that Jane had taught him the steps of the waltz? Looking at him, she could believe he had been waltzing since he'd left the schoolroom.

"You are looking at him as though you actually have some affection for the man." Amelia closed her fan with a snap. "Has the scoundrel managed to slither his way into your far too tender heart? Or are you simply growing accustomed to being Lady Jane, Marchioness of Lancaster?"

The venom in her voice startled Jane. "Amelia, you know I never sought a title."

"No, of course not." Amelia tapped her fan against her open palm. "I did not mean to imply you did. I just do not wish to see you taken in by that blackguard."

"There is no need to worry. I have no intention of losing my grasp on reality." Still, even as she spoke the words, Jane acknowledged the doubts within her. She knew there must be logical reasons for what seemed impossible. Even though she could not for the life of her discern what they might be.

Jane glanced at Colin, watching him lead his plump little partner through a series of sweeping turns. In his arms, following his lead, even Sylvia looked graceful. Light spilled from the five crystal chandeliers high above. The golden glow slipped into his thick black hair and lovingly highlighted the angles and planes of his handsome face. Tonight his hair was swept back from his face in carefully disciplined waves. His clothes were perfectly chosen and arranged, his manner graceful and scrupulously contained. Still, when she looked at him, she saw Colin. In spite of the elegant black evening clothes and all the rest of the social trappings, Jane could see the untamed Highlander beneath the dreadfully civilized mask.

Colin glanced in her direction, as though he sensed her gaze upon him. Their gazes met and locked. Jane's world narrowed until there existed only one man and one woman. Everything around her dissolved into a blur of color, like a chalk painting in the rain. Colin was her every dream. *Stay with me, Colin, for all the days to come.*

Colin winked at her. Even though she stood half a room away, her heart still kicked into a gallop. She wondered what their guests would think if they knew Colin had only to glance at her and she—the terribly ordinary, frightfully practical Jane Eveleigh Stanbridge—was ready to drag her husband off to his bedchamber.

"Do you see the man standing over there by the potted palm, speaking to Lord Hartleigh?" Amelia asked.

Jane dragged her attention from Colin and looked in the direction Amelia indicated. "The tall, dark-haired man?"

"Yes. He is the Earl of Woodbridge." Amelia flicked open her fan. "He has only just returned from a trip to New York. Mama said he is worth ten thousand a year. And look at him; he is really quite handsome."

Jane could not help wondering if it was the title and ten thousand a year that Amelia found attractive. "Yes. He is."

"I bumped into him a few moments ago." Amelia swished her fan back and forth beneath her chin. "He asked for the next dance. I believe he was truly quite taken with me."

"I hope he is as nice as he looks."

Amelia smiled. "Did I mention he has a town house on Berkeley Square?"

"No. You did not."

"And his country estate is in Hampshire. I have heard Woodbridge hall has twenty-three bedchambers."

"It sounds quite impressive."

Amelia laughed softly. "Yes. I think the Earl of Woodbridge has a great deal of potential."

Jane only hoped her sister looked beyond all of his possessions to the man beneath the title. "Remember, there is no need to rush into anything. I will make certain you shall have another Season, should you want it."

"I know." Amelia eased her fan closed. She glanced down at the floor a moment, then looked up at Jane. "You are very good, Jane. Better than I deserve for all the pain I have caused you."

Jane squeezed Amelia's arm. "You are not to think again of that unpleasantness."

Amelia looked toward the dance floor as the last strains of the waltz floated across the crowded room. Jane looked in the same direction and saw Colin escorting Sylvia from the dance floor. "If I could, I would make amends for everything that has happened."

"It is all right. Truly."

"You are far too kind." Amelia smoothed her fingers over the strand of pearls she wore. "Is Woodbridge coming this way?"

Jane glanced behind Amelia, then met her sister's excited expression. "Yes. And you look delightful."

Amelia lifted her chin. "We shall see, dear sister. I may not need that second Season."

Woodbridge claimed Amelia for the dance and led her toward the crowd gathering on the dance floor. Although Jane had not promised this dance to anyone, she knew Colin would not be allowed to claim it. Fiona had made them both promise to share only three dances this night. It was important for Colin to dance with as many influential women as possible. Yet the woman approaching Colin was not even on the guest list. The woman who had just taken hold of his arm was a disaster about to explode in their faces. Jane started for him, intending to rescue Colin from a confrontation that would catch him completely unaware. She made it ten feet before Sylvia Wadswyck stepped in front of her, blocking her way.

"My dear, I never would have suspected it of you." Sylvia rested her hand on Jane's arm. "You were such a quiet little mouse when you made your debut."

Jane's heart hammered against her ribs. She had to reach Colin before Penelope Clydestaff had a chance to expose him as a fraud. "I really must—"

"Who could have guessed there was a lion tamer behind that pretty face of yours."

Jane glanced around the room in time to see Penelope and Colin leave the ballroom. "Lion tamer?"

Sylvia laughed, a sound akin to the shrill whinny of a horse in pain. "Lancaster told me all about the little wager you made."

"The wager?"

"Yes. Although he refused to divulge exactly what he would win from you should he actually parade about the street in his dressing gown carrying a sword." Sylvia leaned closer. "I do not suppose you would care to divulge the secret, would you?"

Jane managed to force her lips into a smile. "I think certain things are best left to one's imagination."

"Well done, my girl." Sylvia patted her arm. "Well done. Oh, I really must find Harriet. She will simply die when I tell her what Lancaster confided in me."

Jane cringed when she thought of the rumors that would be flying around London tomorrow. She did not even want to imagine what people would assume had been the stakes of the "wager" she had made with Lancaster. Still, it was far better than the rumors of the *Mad Marquess*. The plan to restore Lancaster's name was going well. At least it had been before Penelope had decided to barge into the party.

Jane hurried after Colin and Penelope. What in the world was Penelope Clydestaff doing here? The woman had once shot Lancaster. Certainly she would not do anything so rash again. Would she?

Colin had long thought any man who considered himself an expert on the subject of women was a fool. Although he certainly did not claim to be a fool, he did know enough about women to recognize trouble when he saw it. And the beautiful blonde walking beside him looked like an entire wagonload of trouble. Who the devil was she?

From her familiar attitude, he surmised she knew Lancaster well. He suspected she was one of his former mistresses, one who had not parted with him on good terms. Unfortunately that did not narrow down the list of possibilities. Fiona had filled his head with as many details as she knew of Lancaster's private life, including his mistresses. Still, dredging through that information did not enlighten him. Apparently Lancaster had a history of selecting beautiful women to share his bed. Women who were every bit as cold and calculating as he was. Of his most recent mistresses, one had shot him; another had leaped from a balcony. He did not have a good feeling about the confrontation that would follow.

He ushered her into Lancaster's study. If the woman intended to attack him, she could do it in private. He would not allow her to ruin the evening for Jane and Fiona. He leaned back against the door until it closed with a soft thud. The woman sauntered to the desk. She lifted something from the desk and turned to face him. "I see you still have this."

He looked at the paperweight she held. It was brass sculpted into the shape of a galloping horse. And apparently it held some significance. He tilted his head and regarded her with one of his Lancaster looks. Colin had discovered that imitating the man was not difficult. All he need do was appear bored and disdainful of everything and everyone. "And you still have a talent for stating the obvious."

Her delicate nostrils flared. She threw the paperweight at his head. He dodged the missile. The door behind him was not so fortunate. The paperweight crashed into the solid oak, then thumped against the floor at his feet. He frowned at the scar in the polished wood. Apparently

Lancaster appreciated volatile females. "I always did admire your composure."

"My composure is not what you admired in bed." She strolled toward him, the emerald silk of her gown switching like the tail of an angry cat. She drew her fingernails down the front of his chest. "As I recall, you always liked the feel of my nails upon your skin. On your back, your chest." She slid her fingers lower, over the waistband of his trousers. "Your great, throbbing—"

He grabbed her wrist and pulled her hand away before she could grasp him through his trousers. "Is there a point to all of this reminiscing?"

"You have not forgotten." She tipped back her head and stared into his eyes. "I can see it in your eyes. You remember what it was like to feel my flesh close around your rod."

Since assuming the identity of Lancaster, Colin had learned that people often saw what they wanted to see. He released her.

"Since I am now a married man, I see no point in this discussion."

Her eyes narrowed. "I must say I was surprised to hear of your marriage. And even more surprised by your choice of bride."

He strolled to a large leather chair near the hearth and sat on the arm. "And so you came here to tell me of your surprise?"

"I came to tell you I have returned to London." She lifted her chin and glared at him down the length of her slim nose. "If you thought I would remain in exile forever, you were mistaken."

Exile. Now, that narrowed the possibilities. As far as he knew, Lancaster had sent only one mistress into exile. At least, Penelope Clydestaff was the only one he knew about. Still, Colin would not assume she was the only mistress the jackanapes had sent into exile. "And you suppose your return to London should have some significance to me?"

Her lips twitched. "I had heard you were insane. Yet it would seem you are the same as ever."

He shrugged. "People do tend to exaggerate."

She glanced at the paperweight on the floor near her feet. "Tell me, what was it about her? What made you marry her?"

Although he suspected Lancaster might return a cutting reply, Colin could not. There might not have been love between this woman and Lancaster, but she had been hurt all the same. "Who is to say what draws a man to a particular woman? All I can say is that I took one look at Jane and knew I wanted her for my wife. It does not take anything from your beauty or your appeal."

She looked up, anger flaring in her green eyes. "I did not come here for your pity."

His attempt to cushion the blow had only insulted her. "I did not intend to—"

"One day you shall get precisely what you deserve, Dominic." She turned and pulled open the door. The door hit the paperweight. She bent, retrieved the brass horse, then threw it at Colin's head again. The brass horse whizzed past him. It smashed into the andirons on the hearth.

"I despise you." Her skirts flared as she stormed from the room.

Colin flinched at the crash of the door slamming behind her. He released his breath. How many other women were out there, waiting to pounce on him? The door handle dipped. He tensed, his muscles preparing for battle. Apparently the woman had not finished with him. Yet instead of a furious former mistress, his wife entered the room.

"Are you all right?" Jane asked, hurrying toward him, the icy blue silk of her gown swishing softly against her petticoats.

337

"Fine." He glanced at the paperweight, which lay on its side on the hearth.

"Do you think you convinced her you were Lancaster?"

"I think she was definitely convinced." He slipped his arms around her waist and drew her between his knees. The layers of her clothes provided him only a glimmer of the woman hidden beneath. Still, heat flickered low in his belly. "She tried to take off my head with a paperweight. Fortunately she does not have great aim."

She looped her arms around his neck. "Fortunately she did not bring her pistol."

"I take it that was Lady Penelope Clydestaff. The woman responsible for the scar across Lancaster's arm."

"Yes." She drew her fingertip over his sleeve, above the smooth white scar carved into his skin. "How did you manage to deal with her without even knowing her name?"

"It did not take much to realize she was a former mistress. I simply acted arrogant and bored. It worked." He smoothed his fingertips over the silk-covered buttons lining the back of her gown. A few hours ago he had surprised her in her bath. Although he had made love to her twice before the ball, he was hungry for her again. "How much longer do you suppose we need to stay at the party?"

"I am afraid we really must stay until the last guest has departed." A smile curved her lips. "Still, I think we may not be missed for a short while."

"Are you suggesting what I think you are suggesting?"

She leaned into him, brushing her breasts against his chest. "There is a lock on that door."

The undiluted pleasure of holding her near, of knowing she wanted him as much as he wanted her rose within him. "Shall we lock it, my lady?"

She laughed, the soft sound reminding him of the bubbles that had brushed his nose with his first taste of champagne this evening. "Wait right here."

He slipped off his coat as he watched her hurry to the door. Was there any wonder he had thought this woman a witch? She had bewitched him the first moment he had looked at her. She turned and smiled at him, and his world tipped. "Come to me, my gorgeous witch."

"At your command, my wicked Highlander."

Chapter Twenty-seven

> The sense of the world is short,—
> Long and various the report,—
> To love and be beloved;
> Men and gods have not outlearned it;
> And, how oft soe'er they've turned it,
> 'Tis not to be improved.
>
> —Ralph Waldo Emerson

"From what I can tell, the rumors of Dominic's insanity have been choked from a river to a trickle." Fiona sliced a plump sausage. "However, there are a few other rumors circulating about the two of you."

Jane paused, her teacup halfway to her mouth. Fiona had arrived at Lancaster House this morning to join them for breakfast and to inform them of what she perceived as their progress in restoring Dominic's reputation. In the past eleven days Jane and Colin had attended three dinner parties, a ball, a matinee, three tea parties, and a perfectly dreadful amateur theatrical. All of this as well as the theater and the opera. They had spent as much time as possible in public, doing the best that they could to appear very normal. At least as normal as Lancaster might appear to anyone. "What rumors?"

Fiona's lips tipped into a grin. "Apparently people are calling you Lady Jane, the lion tamer."

Jane cringed. "I was afraid of that."

A soft chuckle from the opposite end of the table brought her gaze to her husband. He was slathering butter across a piece of warm scone he held, apparently content to leave the discussion to the ladies. The hazy light of a foggy morning poured through the window, illuminating his smile. "It isn't amusing," Jane told him.

Colin looked up from the scone and winked at her. "But it is true."

"And it is far better than all of London running about calling Colin—I mean Dominic—the Mad Marquess." Fiona pressed her napkin to her lips. "I believe Edwin has abandoned his attempt to take charge of the family and the Lancaster fortune. At least for now. Although I must say he still has not reconciled himself to the possibility of your heir. I daresay he is hoping you and Jane never meet in a bedchamber."

Colin looked at Jane with such intensity, she felt as though he were sliding his arms around her. "I will do my best to disappoint Edwin."

Jane sipped her tea, the steamy liquid warming her throat and chest. Yet the heat coiling through her had nothing at all to do with the beverage and everything to do with the memories Colin had given her. If she could only be certain Lancaster would never return, she would be the happiest woman under heaven.

"I have been thinking that Lancaster is getting a bit bored with London." Colin spooned a generous mound of strawberry preserves onto his scone. "I think he is going to retire to Scotland early this year. That is if the beautiful lion tamer is ready to leave."

Jane looked at Colin, her heart expanding with the affection she saw burning in his eyes. She had never been overly fond of London. The air was always filled with a trace of burning coal and horse droppings. It was crowded with people who wanted nothing more than to find fault with everyone they met. And every day was another opportunity for Colin to see something or hear something that might spark his memory. "When would you like to leave, my darling?"

"After dinner." He popped the scone into his mouth. "I am thinking I would like to spend the night traveling."

Jane sipped her tea and thought of the trip back to Kintair. There was something soothing about the gentle rocking of a train upon the tracks. And from the glint of mischief she saw in Colin's eyes, she had the feeling this trip would be one she could press between the pages of her memory. Still, in spite of her happiness, she could never completely keep the demons at bay. Each day she wondered if this would be the day something sparked Lancaster's memory.

"I would prefer if you stayed a few more weeks," Fiona said. "And you certainly cannot leave tonight. You are attending the opera with me, in case you have forgotten."

"I apologize. I had forgotten." Colin inclined his head to Fiona. "Then we shall leave tomorrow night."

Fiona shook her head. "It would not be a good idea."

"Do you think it would cause too much of a stir if we left London so soon after our return?" Jane asked.

"It might. Since things are going so well, I would rather not risk it."

Colin groaned. "I *will* be insane if I am forced to attend many more of these crowded parties. A man scarcely has room to breathe."

Fiona sighed. "Very well. Stay only another week."

"For you, my dear Fiona." Colin raised his cup in a

salute. "But after a week, I am taking my bride back to Kintair."

Jane made her discovery five days after they returned to Kintair. There were two large chambers on the uppermost floor of the west tower. Apparently both of the huge rooms had been collecting items discarded by the residents of Kintair for many years. Things that for one reason or another had come into disfavor with a member of the family, but were considered too valuable to completely exile from the castle.

In the largest of the rooms, beneath dusty covers, Jane discovered delicate gilt-trimmed chairs that might have graced Versailles during the rein of Louis XVI. Inside a tightly wrapped length of canvas, she discovered a tapestry that she suspected hailed from the sixteenth century. Perhaps it had hung in the castle during Colin's time. Of course, her Colin would not truly know, but she thought he might like to see it. With that in mind, she went searching for him. She found her husband sitting at his desk in the library, making additions to his volume of the *Chronicles of Kintair*.

She crept up behind him, slipped her arms around his neck, and whispered, "I have a surprise for you."

He brushed his lips over her hand, sending tingles through her. "What kind of surprise?"

She kissed his temple, his soft hair brushing her cheek. The scent of sandalwood slid through her senses. "You shall have to come with me to find out."

He turned and winked at her. "I am at your service, my heart."

When he looked at her that way, it took all her will to keep her mind focused on anything other than dragging him back to her bedchamber. Instead she contented herself with a quick kiss, then took his hand and led him to the treasures she had uncovered. The scent of dust swirled around them as they entered the huge tower room.

Jane glanced at the stacks of canvas-covered mysteries crowding the room as she led Colin to her discovery. Although she was anxious to rip off each cover and discover the treasure beneath, for now she concentrated on the tapestry. It lay unrolled, the top draped across an eighteenth-century settee, the bottom half spilled across the old needlepoint carpet that covered the floor. "I found this wrapped in canvas."

"By my faith." Colin knelt on one knee at the foot of the tapestry. Brilliant colors shaped a scene depicting the fall of Vulcan from Olympus. "This hung in the great hall. It is faded a bit, but otherwise it is the same."

Each time he spoke this way, it made her wonder if magic had truly touched their lives. "Both of the chambers on this floor are filled with treasures. It shall take days to uncover everything."

Colin rose and glanced around the huge room. Sunlight streamed through the long windows that were not blocked by crates or stacks of furniture. Dust motes drifted through the sunlight, making it seem as though time had slowed to a lazy rhythm in this place of forgotten treasures. "This could be interesting."

Jane hadn't realized how interesting the search would prove to be until nearly two hours later, when she found a stack of portraits in a corner of the room. There were seven portraits, all tightly wrapped in canvas, all of the same subject. A small brass plate had been nailed to the bottom of each ornately carved frame. On each plate, the words *Colin, third Earl of Kintair* had been inscribed, along with a date. When placed in a row, as she and Colin arranged them, the portraits revealed the gradual aging of the laird, from a young man in his twenties to a grandfatherly figure with white streaks in his black hair.

"I wonder why they are in here, instead of hanging with the other portraits of Colin and his family that are in the portrait gallery. I wonder if they were stored here during one of the improvements that were made to the castle, then simply forgotten." Jane stood and brushed the dust from the dark green wool of her gown. She glanced at Colin when he did not reply. He was staring at the portraits as though he were looking at a ghost. "What is it?"

"I posed for this portrait." He indicated the first one they had uncovered.

A young man gazed up at her from the confines of the ornately carved wooden frame. The man had posed on the cliffs with Kintair in the background behind him. Thick black lashes framed a pair of startling blue eyes. Eyes that held a glint of mischief, as if he knew the secret of enjoying life. A scar slashed a narrow white line through the outer edge of his right eyebrow. Although a neatly trimmed beard covered his chin and curved along his jaw, the hair did not disguise the resemblance of this man to Dominic Stanbridge. "He looks enough like you to be your brother."

"Aye. There is a great resemblance between us." Colin's accent had slipped as it often did when they were alone. "I did not pose for the other portraits. Lancaster must have commissioned them after our souls were switched."

A shiver rippled through Jane at his words. He still believed in the fairy tale. And she still gave thanks every day that he did. "We must have them cleaned and hung with the other portraits of the family."

"It is very odd." Colin closed his eyes as he released a slow breath. "I feel as though I could close my eyes and this man would be here."

"Beg pardon, Your Ladyship. But a letter just arrived for you."

Jane started at the intrusion. She turned and found one of the footmen standing near the entrance to the room. "And you thought I should have it immediately?"

"It is a letter from Lady Fiona." He moved toward her, slowly making his way through a narrow corridor between the crates and covered pieces of furniture. "And it is marked urgent."

"Urgent?" Jane's heart plunged into a gallop. What disaster had befallen them now?

She walked toward the slow-moving footman, anxious to see what message Fiona had sent. Odd, she thought she was aware of all the servants at Kintair, but she could not recall seeing this footman before. There was something familiar about him and at the same time something that seemed strange.

When the footman stepped into a column of sunlight that slanted through one of the long windows, she recognized the features of . . . "Viscount Newbridge?"

He paused before her, a smile curving his lips. "I am surprised you recognized me."

Newbridge had either darkened his hair or he was wearing a wig. Still, the question of his hair was only one of many that flickered in her mind.

"What are you doing here?" Colin asked, his dark voice once more potraying the icy, bored tones of Lancaster.

"I have come to settle a debt." Newbridge lifted his right hand. Sunlight glinted on the barrel of the pistol he held. Before she could draw a breath, Newbridge grabbed her arm and swung her around to face Colin. Her breath jolted from her lungs as he shoved the pistol against her ribs. "If you move, I will shoot her."

Colin clenched his hands at his sides. He looked at Jane, then lifted his gaze to Newbridge's face. "Let her go."

"If you think you can reach me before I can pull the trigger, I believe you are mistaken."

Colin's shoulders lifted the white silk of his shirt as he drew in his breath. Although his voice was low, it was honed like a steel blade when he spoke. "If you hurt her, I will tear you apart with my bare hands."

Colin stood just beyond the reach of the column of sunlight. Still, she could feel the power radiating from him. Power and fury, so intense she could feel it brush against her like a hot summer wind. Newbridge must have felt it as well. She could sense his fear, feel it in the shudder that gripped him.

"I intend to make you pay for what you did." Newbridge dragged Jane backward, past the crates and the shrouded lumps of furniture. Colin followed them, stalking every step Newbridge took.

Chapter Twenty-eight

Unless you can think, when the song is done,
No other is soft in the rhythm;
Unless you can feel, when left by One,
That all men else go with him;
Unless you can know, when unpraised by his
    breath,
That your beauty itself wants proving;
Unless you can swear "For life, for death!"—
Oh fear to call it loving!
                    —Elizabeth Barrett Browning

"He didn't murder your wife." Jane forced the words past the tightness gripping her throat. "Lancaster is afraid of heights. He could not have pushed her from the balcony."

Pain splintered along her nerves as Newbridge squeezed his fingers around her arm. "I know bloody well he didn't push her," he said, dragging her into the hall. "Still, it might as well have been his hand upon her."

Jane blinked against the bright sunlight that streamed

through the windows high above in the domed ceiling. Sunlight poured over him as Colin entered the circular hall. He looked like a warrior poised for battle. She only prayed he would not do anything rash. If he lunged for Newbridge, someone would die. She sought some means to avert disaster. "If you know he didn't murder her, why are you doing this?"

"I want him to pay for what he did to me." Newbridge pushed her against the wooden and brass balustrade that ran in a semicircle around the hall before plunging down the winding staircase. "It was your fault, Lancaster. You ruined her. If not for you, I never would have lost my temper that night. It was your fault."

Colin's eyes narrowed. "You murdered your wife?"

"I did not murder her. I loved her. I love her still." Newbridge groaned like an animal in pain. "Our marriage would have been as it should, if not for you."

Colin opened his hands at his sides. "Your wife chose to bed another man."

"Damn you. I would have forgiven her. I would have forgiven her anything. I went to her that night. I wanted to make amends. I told her I forgave her. And you know what she did? She laughed at me. She said I could never please her the way you did."

Jane searched through the fear cluttering her mind, seeking some means of escape. Yet the pistol pressed hard against her side. If she moved, he would kill her.

"It was your fault." Newbridge squeezed her arm, dragging a groan of pain from her lips. "I didn't mean to push her. Oh, God, I shall never forget the look on her face as she fell."

"It was an accident." Colin took a step toward them. "There is no need to continue with this. You can walk away from this without anyone else getting hurt."

"You must pay for what you did. Damn you, if you hadn't moved that morning at your house, I would have ended it there. I thought it was fitting. You would have

died from a flowerpot that had fallen from a balcony."
Newbridge waved the pistol. "And now it has become
much messier."

"You dropped that pot from the balcony?" Jane asked.

"And you saved his blasted life." Newbridge slipped
his arm around Jane's waist and hoisted her onto the
narrow balustrade. She gripped the balustrade, her damp
palm slipping upon the smooth wooden rail.

"Let her go." Colin stepped toward them. "Your quarrel is with me."

Newbridge laughed, the sound shrill against Jane's
ears. "Tomorrow they will say the Mad Marquess tossed
his wife down the stairwell, then shot himself."

Jane's world slowed until each beat of her heart
seemed to stretch into an eternity. She felt Newbridge
push against her. In the same instant she saw Colin lunge.
Yet it all seemed to happen in a slow-moving dream.
Through her panic she realized the pistol was pointed
straight at Colin's chest.

She rammed her elbow into Newbridge's side, trying
desperately to spoil his aim. Newbridge grunted at the
impact. Her weight shifted. She felt the downward plunge
as the explosion of the gunshot shattered the sunlight.

"Colin!" His name tore from her lips. She threw out
her hands, seeking purchase, while the earth fell away
from her. Her fingers struck the cold brass of a baluster.
She grabbed it. Her body jerked with the sudden halt of
her fall. Pain wrenched through her shoulders. Yet she
managed to hold tight to her only chance at life.

Above her, she could see the two men fighting on the
landing. Grunts and curses flew. Jane struggled to pull
herself back toward the landing. Yet she was unable to
drag herself to safety.

Newbridge still held the pistol. Colin struggled to pry
it from his fingers. The metal captured the sunlight, glinting red and gold as it swung back and forth between
them. Jane's fingers were slipping. She struggled to hold

on to the three slender rods of brass that shaped the baluster. Her palms were slick. Her weight was tugging her fingers from the brass. A low moan slipped past her lips. She could not hold on any longer.

Colin slammed his fist into Newbridge's chin. Newbridge groaned and stumbled out of Jane's line of sight. Colin bent and grabbed her wrists. He hauled her upward as though she were a trout he was pulling from a stream. He whipped his arm around her and dragged her over the baluster. When her feet touched the floor, her legs gave out beneath her. She crumpled against Colin. He held her tight against him for one brief moment, and then he was shoving her away from him.

Jane stumbled a step and hit the wall. Through the pounding of blood in her ears she heard Newbridge.

"Damn you, Lancaster. I will send you straight to hell."

Jane turned in time to see Newbridge raise the pistol and aim straight at Colin's chest.

"No!" She staggered toward Colin, intending to push him out of the way. Still, she knew she would not make it to him in time. Her nerves tensed with the expectation of the shot that would end her husband's life. Yet instead of a gunshot, she heard Newbridge scream, a look of horror etched upon his features. He was staring above Colin as though something were hanging there over her husband's head. In the next instant Colin plowed into him.

Colin gripped Newbridge's wrist and wrenched it above his head. Yet the viscount clenched the handle of the pistol, refusing to yield. The men struggled, their feet shuffling along the floor, bringing them close to the top of the stairs.

Jane looked around for something to use as a weapon. There was nothing in the hall.

Colin slammed Newbridge's hand against the wall, trying to dislodge the pistol. And still Newbridge held fast.

Jane ran into the huge storage room. Frantically she tore at covers, throwing the canvas cover off a sofa, a chair, searching for something to use against Newbridge. Finally she grabbed one of the portraits of Colin. Nothing else was portable. She ran into the hall. The men were struggling far too close to the stairs. Before she could reach them, Newbridge stepped back, off the top stair. He fell, taking Colin with him.

Jane's heart turned over in her chest. Her scream rose as the men plummeted. Deep masculine groans pierced the air, ripping through her. She dropped the portrait and ran for the stairs. Yet each step seemed to take an eternity. She grabbed the newel and stared down the long length of winding stairs. Colin was there, caught on the landing of the next floor. He wasn't moving. Newbridge lay partially beneath him. He was also as still as death.

"No!" Colin could not be dead. Jane lifted her gown and hurried down the stairs, a prayer silently repeating over and over in her brain: *Please, God, please let him live.*

Jane sank to her knees beside the two men, fear closing like a hawk's talon around her throat. Gently she turned Colin, cradling his head and shoulders in her lap. Thick black lashes rested against the crests of his cheeks. He didn't seem to be breathing.

"Colin," she whispered, smoothing the hair back from his brow. The silky strands curled around her fingers. "Colin, please."

A soft groan filtered into the air. For a moment she wasn't certain if the sound had come from Colin or the man lying beside him. She nearly collapsed with relief when Colin opened his eyes. "Thank God."

He sat up and ran his hand over the back of his head. A grimace twisted his features. "My head."

A faint sense of unease settled over her, like mist. "You hit your head."

He slipped his hand from the back of his hair and

frowned down at the blood on his fingertips. "Apparently I cracked it open."

A hard hand clutched Jane's heart. A bump on the head had brought Colin to her. Would a bump on the head take him away? "How do you feel?"

"All things considered, I am all right."

Jane could not breathe. "Do you know who you are?"

He looked at her, a frown cutting deep creases between his black brows. He glanced at the man lying beside him, then at Jane. "I know who I am."

His accent. It was pure English. His expression pure Lancaster. Jane felt the blood draining from her limbs. If she had been standing she would have crumpled beneath the weight of dread pressing against her.

"An angel," Newbridge whispered. He struggled into a sitting position. "She was behind you on the landing, floating above you. Did you see her?"

"The only angel I saw was the one you tried to murder." He stood and retrieved the pistol that lay a short distance away.

Newbridge turned to Jane. "Did you see her?"

Jane could scarcely form a steady thought. "You saw an angel?"

"Her hair was like moonbeams. She was dressed all in white and she was so beautiful. She distracted me. If she hadn't, I would have shot you." Newbridge rubbed his temples, his gaze fixed on the man standing nearby. "I cannot imagine what an angel was doing looking after a devil like you."

Jane watched her husband smile at Newbridge, a cold twisting of finely molded lips. "You will have plenty of time to contemplate your angels, Newbridge. In prison."

Two hours later, Jane sat on a sofa in the library, waiting for her husband to return from town. Lancaster had taken Newbridge to the constable in the village. She could only hope Colin was the man who would return to her. Idly she ran her fingertips over the smooth brass handle of the poker that rested against her leg, while she contemplated the seven portraits of Colin MacKenzie lined up against the bookcases across from her.

There was something strange about the portraits. Something that had nagged her since the footmen had propped them up for her inspection twenty minutes ago. They were placed in a row in accordance with the dates on the brass plates. She stood and walked toward the portraits, carrying the poker with her. An odd sensation gripped her as she drew near the paintings. The men in the portraits looked different. Although the features were the same, the expressions they wore altered their appearance in some subtle way.

She knelt, resting the poker on the carpet beside her. She looked at the brass plates of the first two portraits. They had been painted within a year of each other. Yet in the second portrait Colin looked years older, more worldly. Instead of choosing the cliffs as a setting for the portrait, he had been painted in the great hall. The tapestry they had found in the storage room hung behind him. He sat in a large wooden chair, looking regal. And then she realized what had bothered her about the portrait. The man in that portrait wore the same haughty expression as Lancaster. Her breath halted in her throat. It was as if Lancaster were looking straight at her from the canvas.

"I see you had the portraits brought down from storage."

Jane started at the sound of that deep masculine voice. It still held the icy ring of Lancaster. She stood and faced the man who was strolling toward her, while she clutched the poker in her hand. "Did everything go well?"

"Newbridge is behind bars, where he will stay until someone from Scotland Yard arrives to take him to London." He glanced down at the poker she held. "Still a little nervous?"

"A little." Jane was nervous, but not about any intruder. "How are you feeling?"

"Well enough." He ran his hand over the back of his head. "Fortunately I have a hard head."

She rubbed her thumb back and forth against the brass handle of the poker. "I was wondering just whose head it is that was cracked."

He lifted his brows, a puzzled look entering his expression. "Whose head?"

She squeezed the handle of the poker. "Yes. Just exactly who do you think you are?"

He held her stare a long moment, understanding dawning in his eyes. "Not to worry, my heart. I am Colin."

Jane frowned as she looked him over from his wild, windblown hair to his boots. "Are you certain?"

He laughed, a soft sound that wrapped around her like a warm embrace. "Aye, lass. I am certain."

She dropped the poker and ran to him. He opened his arms and she threw herself against him with enough enthusiasm to knock him back a step. He lifted her in his arms and spun her around, his laughter mingling with hers in perfect harmony.

"Colin," she whispered, sliding her hands through his hair. She kissed him long and hard, allowing him to taste all of her fear and relief and joy. "I was so worried that you had left me."

He set her on her feet but did not release her. A glint of mischief filled his eyes. "And if I had not answered properly, were you going to hit me with that poker?"

She shrugged. "I wasn't going to let you go without a fight."

He kissed the tip of her nose. "I am glad you decided to ask questions first."

A muted thump behind her made her jump. She glanced to where the portraits were standing, and found the last one in the line, the one of Colin when he was an old man, lying facedown upon the carpet. "That's odd. I thought they were fairly steady against the bookcases."

Colin crossed to the painting and went down on one knee beside it. "It looks as though they may need a few repairs before they are hung in the gallery. This backing has come loose."

She knelt beside him to examine the leather stretched across the back of the frame. A darker piece of brown leather was sticking out from beneath the buff-colored backing. "What's this?"

Colin pried the leather backing further away from the frame. A thin book slipped from between the painting and the backing. It fell facedown upon the carpet.

Although she could not say why, her heart raced and her fingers trembled as she lifted the thin book. The cover was blank. Inside, the pages were yellow. Yet the words written upon the pages were clear and distinct, written in a hand she recognized from the days upon days of trying to teach Colin to shape his letters in precisely this manner. "My goodness."

"What is it?" Colin took the book from her trembling fingers. He read the first page, then glanced through the rest of the book before looking at Jane. "I had wondered if Lancaster might find some way to leave a message for those he left behind."

Jane snatched the book from his hands and read the first page once again. In a bold script were the words: *I, Dominic Stanbridge, Marquess of Lancaster, Earl of Kintair, have found myself lost in a seemingly mad adventure. But I assure you, dear reader, I am not mad. And after having accepted my journey to this place and time, I realize I have found my destiny.* Proof. Was she truly holding proof of a fairy tale? "It was written by Dominic. After he awakened in the body of Colin MacKenzie."

"I suppose there could be a logical explanation for the journal being there."

Jane looked at the man kneeling beside her on the carpet. "Logical?"

"Let's see." He rubbed his fingertip over his chin. "Perhaps I wrote the journal when I was twelve, and I slipped it behind the portrait."

"Why would you do that?"

"Hmmm. Why would I do that? Perhaps I simply thought it was a wonderful game at the time. And perhaps it is somehow all tangled up with all the other logical reasons why a man would suddenly think he has traveled over three hundred years to meet the woman of his destiny."

Jane didn't want to think of logic, not now. "Colin."

"The logical thing would be to believe I am simply wandering about like a man in a dream."

She slipped her arms around his neck. "Colin."

"I am certain if you think about it long and hard, you can find a sane, logical reason for that very ancient-looking journal to have been hidden—"

She pressed her lips against his, cutting off his words. She hugged him close until the heat stirred deep within her, the delicious warmth and light chasing away every last icy fear that lay hidden in the shadows of her soul. She kissed him until he was holding her as though he would never let her go, until she felt a quiver rippling through the powerful muscles of his chest. Only then did she lift away from him, only far enough to look into his beautiful eyes. "Colin, my love. Sometimes you really do talk too much."

He grinned at her. "I have one more thing to say."

She pushed against his shoulders. He fell back upon the carpet, taking her with him. The scent of his skin swirled through her senses, tugging softly on her vitals. She slipped her legs along the hard length of his and folded her arms upon his chest. She smiled into his incredible eyes. "What is that, my wicked Highlander?"

"I love you. Now and always." He smoothed his fingers over her cheek. "I will never leave you, my beautiful witch. This is my promise to you."

"I love you, Colin MacKenzie." Jane had wanted to find proof that he would remain with her all of her days. And it was here, shining up at her from the most beautiful eyes she had ever seen. "And should you ever think of leaving me, remember, I shall always have a poker nearby."

Colin laughed softly, the rich sound of a man who loved life. "Kiss me, my heart."

Epilogue

My soul is an enchanted Boat,
Which, like a sleeping swan, doth float
Upon the silver waves of thy sweet singing;
And thine doth like an Angel sit
Beside the helm conducting it,
Whilst all the winds with melody are ringing.
                        —Perchy Bysshe Shelley

Colin sat near the bed in Jane's bedchamber. The lamp
on the bed table was the only one burning in the room.
It cast a golden light upon the woman who lay sleeping
there. Her glorious hair was spread in golden brown
waves across her pillow. The ordeal was finally over.
After seven hours of struggle, his wife had delivered into
this world their fifth child. Jane had come through strong
and hearty. She had even managed to eat dinner before
falling asleep. As with their other children, Colin had not
known relief until he knew his wife would be well again.

He looked down into the face of the daughter he held

in his arms. Aisling stirred in his arms, snuggling against his chest. Although the family had thought the name an odd choice, Jane and Colin knew the secret behind their choice of names for their youngest daughter. He rested his head against the back of the chair and closed his eyes, content with the world.

You have found your destiny.

The soft voice rippled through him. He opened his eyes. A shaft of moonlight slanted through the windows, capturing the woman standing beside his chair. The moonlight seemed to radiate from her. She was tall and slender, her pale blond hair tumbling over the white silk of her gown, flowing in a silken cascade to her knees. The tiny gold stars embroidered in the gauzy overskirt of her gown glittered in the moonlight.

It was the same woman he had seen when he was a lad. The same woman who graced a painting in a book of Scottish legends. She smiled down at him, then turned toward the window. The moonlight shimmered around her, growing brighter until woman and moonlight seemed to dissolve one into the other.

He rose from his chair and stood beside the bed, looking at Jane's face. He smoothed the soft hair back from her cheek. Her lashes fluttered and lifted. She smiled up at him.

He pressed his lips against her brow while he cradled Aisling against his chest. "I didn't mean to awaken you."

She pulled the covers back from the bed beside her. "I always sleep better in your arms."

He rested Aisling in her mother's arms, then slipped into bed beside his wife and daughter. In time Jane's breathing eased into the deep, even rhythm of sleep. Yet Colin did not surrender to the pull of slumber. Instead he lay watching his wife sleep, thinking of the words spoken by a fairy princess. Had she come to him in a dream? Deep in his heart he knew the truth. He had traveled more than three hundred years to meet this woman, to love her, to share his life with her. Jane was his destiny.

Author Note

Was Colin transported three hundred years to meet his destiny, or did a bump on the head alter Dominic for the better? I will let you be the final judge.

Although there is a Lancaster House in London, I have taken artistic license and altered both the house and the family so that neither bears a resemblance to reality. Kintair is also a creation of my imagination. Since I truly believe a trip through the imagination can be one of the most rewarding we take, I hope the time you spent with Jane and Colin was enjoyable. I hope *MacKenzie's Magic* left you wanting to believe in magic.

For excerpts from my books, a glimpse at my current project, and a little about me, visit my website at:

www.tlt.com/authors/ddier.htm.

I love to hear from readers. Please enclose a self-addressed, stamped envelope with your letter. You can reach me at:

P.O. Box 4147
Hazelwood, Missouri 63042-0747

BEYOND *Forever* DEBRA DIER

1999. He appears to her out of the swirling fog on the cliff's edge, a ghostly figure who seems somehow larger than life. Dark, handsome, blatantly male, he radiates the kind of confidence that leads men into battle and women into reckless choices. But independent-minded Julia Fairfield isn't about to be coerced into anything, especially not a jaunt across the centuries in search of a miracle.

1818. Abducted from her own time, Julia finds herself face-to-face with this flesh and blood incarnation. Gavin MacKinnon is as confounded as Julia about her place in his life, but after a night of passion, they learn that their destinies are inextricably bound together, no matter what the time or place.

___4623-7 $5.50 US/$6.50 CAN

Dorchester Publishing Co., Inc.
P.O. Box 6640
Wayne, PA 19087-8640

Please add $1.75 for shipping and handling for the first book and $.50 for each book thereafter. NY, NYC, and PA residents, please add appropriate sales tax. No cash, stamps, or C.O.D.s. All orders shipped within 6 weeks via postal service book rate. Canadian orders require $2.00 extra postage and must be paid in U.S. dollars through a U.S. banking facility.

Name_____
Address_____
City_____State_____Zip_____
I have enclosed $_____ in payment for the checked book(s).
Payment <u>must</u> accompany all orders. ❑ Please send a free catalog.
        CHECK OUT OUR WEBSITE! www.dorchesterpub.com

DECEPTIONS & DREAMS

DEBRA DIER

Sarah Van Horne can outwit any scoundrel who tries to cheat her in business. But she is no match for the dangerously handsome burglar she catches in her New York City town house. Although she knows she ought to send the suave rogue to the rock pile for life, she can't help being disappointed that his is after a golden trinket—and not her virtue. Confident, crafty, and devilishly charming, Lord Austin Sinclair always gets what he wants. He won't let a locked door prevent him from obtaining the medallion he has long sought, nor the pistol Sarah aims at his head. But the master seducer never expects to be tempted by an untouched beauty. If he isn't careful, he'll lose a lot more than his heart before Sarah is done with him.

_____4582-6 $5.99 US/$6.99 CAN

Dorchester Publishing Co., Inc.
P.O. Box 6640
Wayne, PA 19087-8640

Please add $1.75 for shipping and handling for the first book and $.50 for each book thereafter. NY, NYC, and PA residents, please add appropriate sales tax. No cash, stamps, or C.O.D.s. All orders shipped within 6 weeks via postal service book rate. Canadian orders require $2.00 extra postage and must be paid in U.S. dollars through a U.S. banking facility.

Name_____
Address_____
City_____State_____Zip_____
I have enclosed $_____ in payment for the checked book(s).
Payment <u>must</u> accompany all orders. ❑ Please send a free catalog.
  CHECK OUT OUR WEBSITE! www.dorchesterpub.com

The Sorcerer's Lady

DEBRA DIER

Victorian debutante Laura Sullivan can't believe her eyes. Aunt Sophie's ancient spell has conjured up the man of Laura's dreams—and deposited a half-naked barbarian in the library of her Boston home. With his bare chest and sheathed broadsword, the golden giant is a tempting study in Viking maleness, but hardly the proper blue blood Laura is supposed to marry. An accomplished sorcerer, Connor has traveled through the ages to reach his soul mate, the bewitching woman who captured his heart. But Beacon Hill isn't ninth-century Ireland, and Connor's powers are useless if he can't convince Laura that love is stronger than magic and that she is destined to become the sorcerer's lady.

___52305-1 $5.50 US/$6.50 CAN

Dorchester Publishing Co., Inc.
P.O. Box 6640
Wayne, PA 19087-8640

SAINT'S Temptation

DEBRA DIER

Seven years after breaking off her engagement to Clayton Trevelyan, Marisa Grantham overhears two men plotting to murder her still-beloved Earl of Huntingdon. No longer the naive young woman who had allowed her one and only love to walk away, Marisa will do anything to keep from losing him a second time.

___4459-5 $5.99 US/$6.99 CAN

Dorchester Publishing Co., Inc.
P.O. Box 6640
Wayne, PA 19087-8640

Please add $1.75 for shipping and handling for the first book and $.50 for each book thereafter. NY, NYC, and PA residents, please add appropriate sales tax. No cash, stamps, or C.O.D.s. All orders shipped within 6 weeks via postal service book rate. Canadian orders require $2.00 extra postage and must be paid in U.S. dollars through a U.S. banking facility.

Name_____
Address_____
City_____ State_____ Zip_____
I have enclosed $_____ in payment for the checked book(s).
Payment <u>must</u> accompany all orders. ❑ Please send a free catalog.

DEBRA DIER

SHADOW of THE STORM

He is her dashing childhood hero, the man to whom she will willingly surrender her innocence in a night of blazing ecstasy. But when Ian Tremayne cruelly abandons her after a bitter misunderstanding, Sabrina O'Neill vows to have revenge on the handsome Yankee. But the virile Tremayne is more than ready for the challenge. Together, they will enter a high-stakes game of deadly illusion and sizzling desire that will shatter Sabrina's well-crafted facade.

___4397-1 $5.99 US/$6.99 CAN

Dorchester Publishing Co., Inc.
P.O. Box 6640
Wayne, PA 19087-8640

Please add $1.75 for shipping and handling for the first book and $.50 for each book thereafter. NY, NYC, and PA residents, please add appropriate sales tax. No cash, stamps, or C.O.D.s. All orders shipped within 6 weeks via postal service book rate. Canadian orders require $2.00 extra postage and must be paid in U.S. dollars through a U.S. banking facility.

Name_____
Address_____
City_____State_____Zip_____
I have enclosed $_____ in payment for the checked book(s).
Payment <u>must</u> accompany all orders. ☐ Please send a free catalog.
    CHECK OUT OUR WEBSITE! www.dorchesterpub.com

OFFICIAL ENTRY FORM

Win a $1,000 U.S. Savings Bond!

To be eligible to win, contestants must correctly answer the following questions based on *MacKenzie's Magic,* by Debra Dier.

Be sure to give us your complete and correct address so we may notify you if you are a winner.

(Please type or legibly print).

1. Who is the Matchmaker of Tara?_____

2. What is the mission of the Matchmaker of Tara?_____
   _____

3. Where are the Chronicles of Kintair discovered?_____
   _____

NAME: _____

ADDRESS: _____
_____

PHONE: _____

E-MAIL ADDRESS: _____

MAILING ADDRESS FOR ENTRIES:
Dorchester Publishing Co., Inc.
Department DD
276 Fifth Avenue, Suite 1008
New York, NY 10001